PRAISE FOR THE CHLOE EI

"Chloe is an appealing character, and Ernst's depiction of work at a living museum ler___ involving plot."—*St. P*___

"Greed, passion, skill, ___ outing."—*Publishers W*___

"Interesting, well-draw___ this a very satisfying re___

"Entertainment and edification."—*Mystery Scene*

"A wonderfully woven tale that winds in and out of modern and historical Wisconsin with plenty of mysteries. Enchanting!"— Sandi Ault, author of the WILD Mystery Series and recipient of the Mary Higgins Clark Award

"Clever plot twists and credible characters make this a far-from-humdrum cozy."—*Publishers Weekly*

"Propulsive and superbly written, this first entry in a dynamite new series from accomplished author Kathleen Ernst seamlessly melds the 1980s and the 19th century. Character-driven, with mystery aplenty, *Old World Murder* is a sensational read. Think Sue Grafton meets Earlene Fowler, with a dash of Elizabeth Peters."—Julia Spencer-Fleming, Anthony and Agatha Award-winning author of *I Shall Not Want* and *One Was A Soldier*

"*Old World Murder* is strongest in its charming local color and genuine love for Wisconsin's rolling hills, pastures, and woodlands … a delightful distraction for an evening or two."—NY-JournalOfBooks.com

"This series debut by an author of children's mysteries rolls out nicely for readers who like a cozy with a dab of antique lore. Jeanne M. Dams fans will like the ethnic background."—*Library Journal*

"Information on how to conduct historical research, background on Norwegian culture, and details about running an outdoor museum frame the engaging story of a woman devastated by a failed romantic relationship whose sleuthing helps her heal."—*Booklist*

"[A] museum masterpiece."—RosebudBookReviews.com

"A real find … 5 stars."—OnceUponARomance.net

"Engaging characters, a fascinating (real-life) setting, a gripping and believable plot—this is the traditional mystery at its best."—Jeanne M. Dams, Agatha Award-winning author of the Dorothy Martin and Hilda Johansson Mysteries

The
Light
Keeper's
Legacy

-A CHLOE ELLEFSON MYSTERY-

The Light Keeper's Legacy

KATHLEEN ERNST

MIDNIGHT INK
WOODBURY, MINNESOTA

MIDNIGHT INK

First Edition
First Printing, 2012

Book design and format by Donna Burch
Cover design by Kevin R. Brown
Cover illustration © Charlie Griak
Editing by Connie Hill
Interior map by Llewellyn Art Department, based on Map of Rock Island State Park, Wisconsin Department of Natural Resources, Bureau of Parks

Midnight Ink, an imprint of Llewellyn Worldwide Ltd.

Library of Congress Cataloging-in-Publication Data

Ernst, Kathleen, 1959-
  The light keeper's legacy : a Chloe Ellefson mystery / by Kathleen Ernst. — 1st ed.
    p.   cm.
  ISBN 978-0-7387-3307-4
  1. Women museum curators—Fiction. 2. Murder—Investigation—Fiction.
  3. Rock Island (Wis.)—Fiction. I. Title.
  PS3605.R77L54   2012
  813'.6—dc23   2012 017514

Midnight Ink
Llewellyn Worldwide Ltd.
2143 Wooddale Drive
Woodbury, MN 55125-2989
www.midnightinkbooks.com

Printed in the United States of America

DEDICATION

For the Friends of Rock Island, and for park staff,
past and present, with admiration and gratitude.

AUTHOR'S NOTE

Rock Island State Park is a real place. I've tried to describe the island, Pottawatomie Lighthouse, the Viking Hall and Boathouse, and the site of the former fishing village accurately. The lighthouse has been magnificently restored by the Friends of Rock Island State Park, working with the Wisconsin Department of Natural Resources. My husband and I have had the pleasure and privilege of serving as live-in docents at the lighthouse for several week-long stints. Since this is a work of fiction, however, I fabricated events to suit the story—including moving the restoration process back in time by a decade. Chloe's experiences as guest curator are completely imaginary.

Most of the places mentioned on Washington Island are also real: The Jackson Harbor Maritime Museum, The Washington Island Farm Museum, The Washington Island Historical Archives, the Jacobsen Museum, and Nelsen's Hall.

You can learn more, and plan your own trip, by visiting these websites:

Rock Island State Park:

http://dnr.wi.gov/topic/parks/name/rockisland/

Friends of Rock Island State Park:

http://uniontel.net/~cmarlspc/

Washington Island Visitors' Guide:

http://www.washingtonisland.com/visitors-guide/

You can also find photos, a tour guide, and maps of relevant places on my website: www.kathleenernst.com

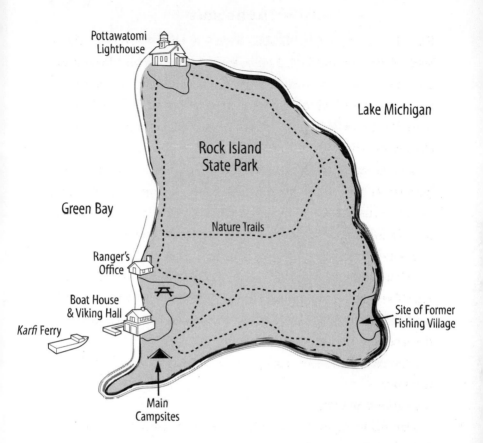

Pottawatomi
Lighthouse

Lake Michigan

Rock Island
State Park

Green Bay

Nature Trails

Ranger's
Office

Boat House
& Viking Hall

Karfi Ferry

Site of Former
Fishing Village

Main
Campsites

CAST OF CHARACTERS

Contemporary Timeline (1982)

Chloe Ellefson—curator of collections, Old World Wisconsin

Roelke McKenna—officer, Village of Eagle Police Department

Ralph Petty—director, Old World Wisconsin

Nika Austin—intern, Old World Wisconsin

Skeet Deardorff—part-time officer, Village of Eagle Police Department

Mrs. Saddler, Penny Sloan—Eagle residents

Denise Miller—EMT, Village of Eagle Fire Department

*Jack Cornell and Jeff Cornell—captain and son of the passenger ferry *Karfi*

Garrett Smith—manager, Rock Island State Park

Stig Fjelstul – deputy sheriff, Door County; former game warden, WI Department of Natural Resources

Brenda Noakes—archaeologist from Michigan; former Washington Island resident

Melvin Jenks—maintenance man at Rock Island State Park; semi-retired fisherman

Herb and Lorna Whitby—members of the Rock Island Support Circle

Sylvie Torgrimsson—member of the Rock Island Support Circle; part-time commercial fisherwoman

Ruth Gunderson—potential artifact donor, Washington Island

Natalie and Tim Ridgeway—kayakers who camp on Rock Island

Spencer Brant—photographer who visits Rock Island

Richard Dix—lighthouse enthusiast who visits Rock Island

* real people

Historical Timeline (1869–1906)

*Emily Rohn Betts and William Betts—assistant keeper and keeper, Pottawatomie Lighthouse

Ragna and Anders Anderson—Danish immigrants, Rock Island fishing village

Paul and Christina Anderson—Ragna and Anders' children

Evert Anderson—Paul Anderson's son

Carl and Jens—Ragna's brothers

Carrick Dugan—Irish immigrant

Mette Friis—Danish immigrant

Berglind Fridliefsdottir—Icelandic immigrant

*Anton Jacobson—last fisherman to leave Rock Island fishing village

*James McNeil—murder victim

Jeanette Gunderson—friend of Emily Betts; Ruth's grandmother

*Chester and Juliana Thordarson—last private owners of Rock Island

*real people

ONE: 1982

"THIS TRIP OF YOURS is a *very* bad idea," Roelke said soberly.

Chloe Ellefson sighed. "You sound as if I'm disappearing into some trackless wilderness. Rock Island is a state park, for God's sake." They stood in her driveway. She'd already locked the old farmhouse she rented.

"An island with no roads. No houses. With Labor Day past, there might not be anyone in the campground."

"That seems unlikely," Chloe said, with sincere regret. She picked up her backpack and stowed it in her Pinto. "Now that school's started, I imagine that lots of people who like peace and quiet are heading out for excursions."

"Weather on Lake Michigan can turn nasty with very little warning."

Chloe removed the tent pole she used to hold the Pinto's hatch open. It slammed closed. "I know that. Remember, I've got a nice old lighthouse to sleep in."

1

He leaned against her car and folded his arms. "A lighthouse without electricity or heat or running water—"

"Geez Louise, Roelke, I'm not a child!" Chloe frowned at him, trying to stifle her exasperation. Roelke McKenna was a cop. She knew he had good reason to anticipate trouble anytime, anywhere. Still. "Look, you've only known me for a few months, but I've done a lot of camping. In all kinds of weather, and in places a lot more remote than Rock Island. I'll be fine. *Please* don't go all Neanderthal about this."

"Are you sure this isn't going to get you in trouble at work?"

A sensitive question. Chloe busied herself by re-tying the ribbon on the end of her long blonde braid. She'd only been collections curator at Old World Wisconsin, the state's largest historic site, since June. Her relationship with site director Ralph Petty might euphemistically be called "strained." "I am still on probation," she acknowledged. "But the request for research assistance came from another state agency, so I'm officially on loan. I get to be guest curator at a lighthouse! It's a real honor."

"What about Olympia?"

An even more sensitive question. Chloe kept her back to the house, afraid she'd see her kitten at the window with a frantic *Please don't leave me!* expression. "Dellyn is looking after her." Dellyn, a good friend, had jumped at the chance.

"Well, I got you something." Roelke fetched a book from his truck. "This one just came out. It is sort of a cop book, but the main character is a woman."

Chloe accepted the gift: *A Is For Alibi*, by Sue Grafton. "Thank you, Roelke. That was thoughtful. Just the thing for quiet evenings."

"Anyway." He looked away. "I wish I could go with you. I wouldn't mind a little R and R. There's no way I can ask for vacation, though." After four years of part-time status, Roelke had only recently been awarded a permanent position with the Village of Eagle Police Department.

"I'll only be gone for a week, Roelke."

Roelke tapped the heel of one hiking boot against the toe of the other. "Here's the thing. I feel like we're treading water. We can try being friends, or we can try going out. But I need to know which it's going to be."

It's a reasonable request, Chloe thought, even as she struggled with a flash of panic. "We'll talk when I get back, OK? I promise." She slapped her palms against her jeans. Time to get moving.

Roelke straightened and stepped behind her. Chloe hesitated before letting him pull her against his chest. They were about the same height, but somehow her head nestled perfectly against his shoulder. She had no idea if she and Roelke had any kind of future. But she had to admit, they fit well together.

Before she could get too comfortable, she pulled from his arms. "I've got two ferries to catch," she reminded him.

"Call me when you get home?"

"I will." She watched as he walked back to his pickup truck. He was off-duty today, wearing faded jeans and a snug blue T-shirt.

In his own uptight way, Roelke McKenna was a good-looking guy.

Chloe turned away and got into her car. Thoughts like that were exactly why she needed to get on the road.

TWO: 1869

RAGNA ANDERSON HAD NOT expected to quickly become one of the best net makers on Rock Island, but to her surprise, she had. Everyone said so. She needed only three days to make a gillnet, five feet by one hundred twenty. She charged a dollar each and no one complained.

"A thing of beauty," Anders declared each time she handed him a new net, whole and perfect. She learned how to pack a net too, floats on one side and weights on the other so they'd flow smoothly from their wooden boxes when he set them. The nets came back torn and fouled with lake weeds, algae, bark from the lumber drives, clinkers tossed from passing steamships. She found blood spots on the mesh as well—perhaps from struggling whitefish, perhaps from Anders' wet and cold-cracked hands.

Back in Denmark, Anders had grown wheat and potatoes, and she had excelled at *hedebosøm*—needle lace. When Anders took cartloads of produce to sell in the busy market near Copenhagen's harbor, she brought table linens and handkerchiefs, folded into muslin to keep them clean. Her lace sometimes graced wedding dresses and baptismal gowns. Her handiwork had made people happy.

Anders had not expected to be happy in their new home, but to *his* surprise, he was. He took joy from being on the water and satisfaction from each lift. Ragna took pleasure in knowing that she and Anders had survived the journey and settled here in Wisconsin. They would work hard here, put down new roots. Their children would never go hungry or whimper from want of a warm blanket. Usually such thoughts were enough.

Sometimes, though, as twine unspooled from her netting needle and her fingers danced among the mesh, all she saw was inevitable death.

THREE

Chloe reached Door County—Wisconsin's geographical thumb extending into Lake Michigan—in under four hours. She passed more hotels and shops than she remembered from childhood, but the magic was still there: fields that overlooked the great lake, huge brick farmhouses in the old Belgian settlements, cherry orchards and second-growth forests.

As she drove north, Chloe felt a physical sense of lightening. She loved Old World Wisconsin, but her first few months on the job had been challenging. She cared about Roelke McKenna, but getting to know him had also been challenging. The unexpected arrival of her Swiss ex last summer hadn't helped. The ex was gone now, back to Switzerland, but Chloe was emotionally exhausted. She needed time away from her job, and from Roelke. She craved solitude. When the request for curatorial assistance came from the manager of Rock Island State Park she'd pounced.

Besides... Old World Wisconsin was a magnificent site, but Petty's constant criticism and make-work projects and micromanagement were wearing her down. Chloe was committed to honoring the often nameless and forgotten people she studied. Researching and interpreting their lives was fascinating; it also brought a responsibility. A consultant gig like the one waiting on Rock Island—one free of her megalomaniac boss's scrutiny—would be joyful.

Chloe arrived at the tip of the peninsula just in time to see a car ferry heading away from the mainland toward Washington Island. "Are you off schedule?" she asked the woman in the ticket booth, handing her a twenty. "I thought I'd make the two o'clock."

The woman counted change. "We had to make an emergency medical transport from Washington this morning," she said. "That threw things off. We've had severe winds today, too."

"Think I can still make it to Rock Island this afternoon?"

"Could be," the woman replied cheerfully.

"Well, I'll see how it goes," Chloe said, with equal cheer. She liked places where nature was in charge.

Chloe pocketed her ticket, parked in the designated line, pulled on a sweatshirt, and walked down to the dock. A pay phone stood nearby, and she paused. She could call Ethan. During their college days, each got in the habit of calling the other before venturing out alone to go hiking or paddling or caving.

But I just don't want to talk to anybody, she thought. Not Roelke, not her mom, not even her best buddy Ethan.

She shoved her hands in her pockets and looked toward Washington Island. The six-mile-wide channel provided the shortest navigational passage from Lake Michigan into Green Bay, but sailors had to navigate among rocky-shored islands, hidden shoals, and dangerous currents. *Porte des Morts,* early French travelers called the channel. Death's Door.

Chloe winced as she imagined birchbark canoes and wooden schooners pummeled to splinters in sudden squalls. Still, her spirits rose as she faced the passage. She was heading beyond Death's Door. Perverse it might be, but in her present mood, that sounded appealing.

———

Chloe managed to drive into her designated matchbox-sized spot on the ferry without embarrassing herself. The trip to Washington Island was uneventful. She drove eight miles across the island and parked in the small lot near Jackson Harbor. A much smaller, passengers-only ferry named *Karfi* waited by the dock. Rock Island was visible a mile away.

As Chloe approached the *Karfi*, a man and boy emerged from the pilothouse. "Are you making another trip today?" Chloe called.

"Are you the curator?" the man asked. He was dark haired, well-muscled.

"That's me."

He offered a firm handshake. "I'm Jack Cornell, and this is my son, Jeff. We've been waiting for you." He reached over the railing, grabbed Chloe's heavy backpack, and swung it aboard with ease. "Don't sit near the front unless you want to get wet."

This trip was shorter and wilder. The *Karfi* bucked and slapped over the waves, tossing fans of cold water back over empty benches. Chloe zipped a jacket over her sweatshirt and hung on, grinning.

One of Rock Island State Park's best-known features, a great Viking Hall, was visible across the water. The island's last private owner had designed the red-roofed structure to honor his Icelandic heritage. The massive building marked the Rock Island landing, but Captain Cornell aimed well upwind of the dock. He gauged wind and currents perfectly, and coasted to a smooth halt beside the long pier.

"Nicely done!" Chloe exclaimed. Jeff jumped to the dock and moored the boat.

A sixty-ish man wearing the Department of Natural Resources' tan and green hurried down the dock. "Chloe? I'm Garrett. Thanks for coming."

"Thanks for inviting me."

Garrett Smith, park manager, was a trim man with the deeply tanned skin of an outdoorsman. His face was relaxed and friendly, his eyes watchful—a combination she'd seen before among park personnel who had to be both welcoming and vigilant, every moment. Same thing was true about staff at historic sites, come to think of it.

"We've got a lot of Ellefsons in the area," Garrett said. "Any relation?"

"Nope," Chloe said. Her mother, genealogist extraordinaire, had given her the name of someone who was Chloe's father's second cousin's aunt. Or something like that. "In case you have time to connect," Mom had said. Chloe didn't plan on making contact.

"We're excited about the lighthouse project," Garrett told her. "Now that RISC is up and going—"

"RISC…? Oh, right—the Rock Island Support Circle."

"They're taking the lead on getting the lighthouse restored and interpreted." Garrett thrust his hands in his pockets and jingled keys. "And God bless 'em for that. Damn budget cuts have my hands tied. Have you visited Rock before?"

"No," Chloe confessed, making a mental note to refer to the island simply as "Rock" so she'd sound like someone in the know. "I'm eager to see Pottawatomie." Pottawatomie Lighthouse, the oldest light station in Wisconsin. And she, Chloe Ellefson, had been asked to prepare a furnishing plan for it. How cool was that?

Garrett cleared his throat. "Just a couple little wrinkles."

Chloe almost heard Roelke muttering *I told you so.* "Yes?"

"We tested water from the old pump last week, and it didn't pass state standards. I asked Mel Jenks, our maintenance man, to leave you jugs of drinking water. You'll have to haul water for dishes and cleaning up from the lake in buckets."

OK, that qualified as little. "No problem."

Garrett jingled his keys again. "One more thing. We've had some wicked storms this year. Erosion causes rockslides from the cliffs, and wind and waves work the rocks down the beach. Can't have them crashing into the pier, so periodically we dredge."

"OK," Chloe said cautiously, waiting for the bad news.

"The dredger cut the phone cable yesterday. I'm not sure how quickly we'll be able to get it spliced. That means no pay phone, no 9-1-1 callbox."

"Ah." This time Chloe could almost hear Roelke frantically shouting *Abort! Abort!*

"Still game?" Garrett asked.

"Absolutely."

His smile reached his eyes this time. "Good." He handed her a key and pointed north. "Just head up the trail there. It's about a mile." He glanced at the *Karfi*. "I wish I could show you around, but the park boat is out of service, and my ride's waiting. A few RISC people will be over on the one o'clock ferry tomorrow to meet you."

"Sounds good."

"There are several lanterns in the lighthouse, a bed in the keeper's room on the first floor, and a couple of extra sleeping bags in case it gets cold. Outhouse is stocked."

"Is the campground empty?" Chloe asked hopefully.

"Not quite. There's an older couple in the main campground and a young couple in one of the remote sites on the southeast shore. Kayakers."

Chloe tried to hide her disappointment. She'd never been alone on an island before. Well, she'd be here for a week. Maybe she'd still get her chance.

"The kayakers were set to head out today, but decided to wait. In good weather, it's an easy paddle back to Jackson Harbor. When you mix this wind with the currents, though…" Garrett shook his head. "It can be too much for even experienced paddlers, although most of 'em don't want to hear me say so."

Chloe smiled. "Historic site visitors don't want to hear me caution them against posing their toddlers beside oxen or tasting week-old stew, either."

"It should be a quiet week," Garrett said. "Labor Day weekend was busy, and things will ramp up again with the fall color crowd, so my ranger and naturalist are using vacation time." He began backing toward the *Karfi*. "Have a peaceful evening."

Chloe picked up her pack and shrugged into the shoulder straps. "Thanks."

As the *Karfi* began bouncing back to Jackson Harbor, Chloe walked away from the dock. The main compound included several cobblestone buildings built by the last private owner, now used by park employees. Once beyond them she hiked uphill through beech and maple trees. Late afternoon sunlight slanted down as if through cathedral windows, illuminating lush stands of ferns. Two cedar waxwings flitted ahead of her. The air smelled ripe and loamy.

Chloe grinned. Life on Rock Island was going to be very good.

Finally the trail crested a rise and descended into a clearing. And there it was: Pottawatomie Lighthouse, standing on a cliff, silhouetted against the sky.

"O-oh," she breathed, coming to a halt. The lighthouse was a massive cut-stone structure with a wooden lantern room, and a small frame summer kitchen attached at the south end. This was the building she was going to live in, learn about, *think* about, for the next week.

A skeletal metal tower rose from the woods to the west—the modern tower, fitted with a battery-powered light maintained by the U.S. Coast Guard. Even that modern intrusion seemed OK, though. It's all part of the continuum, Chloe thought, as she walked across the clearing and hitched out of her pack. Pottawatomie people had built signal bonfires on the precipice. A century-plus of lightkeepers had tended lamps. Today, despite all the modern marvels of 1982 technology, ship captains still relied on the Rock Island light.

Chloe regarded the small Igloo cooler—her ration of drinking water—sitting on the steps beside two gleaming buckets. It would be a good idea to fetch wash water right away. Then she could truly settle in.

The beach trail led past a crumbling stone foundation—from an old barn, maybe?—and descended into the woods. Chloe hadn't gone far before she noticed a small cave in a limestone outcrop off to her left. She hesitated, then kept going. Chores first.

Ancient stone steps led to the edge of the cliff, where a long wooden staircase dropped more steeply down to the lake. She counted: one hundred and fifty-four steps, all told. She'd have to be prudent with water. But she'd done that before, on countless dry-season camping trips in the Appalachians, and in northern Wisconsin too.

Chloe put the buckets down. Lake Michigan rippled restlessly north in front of her. The water was clear and looked green in the shallows near shore, darker blue farther out. Two merganser ducks bobbed nearby, but otherwise she was *alone*. Chloe spread her arms and tipped her face to the sky. This island was a perfect place to just *be* for a while.

After a moment she began picking her way along a narrow beach of cobbles and rubble stones, admiring stunted cedar trees and moist gardens of moss and ferns growing on the cliff's jagged limestone walls. Just ahead, a tumble of sharp-edged boulders, gray with lichen, testified to Garrett's comment about erosion and rockslides. A second slide was visible a short distance beyond the first. This one was more recent, the exposed planes of stone gleaming raw and white. One small uprooted cedar tree lay among them, forlornly pointing north.

Something lay between the two rockslides, right at water's edge. Chloe frowned, trying to identify a strange... *thing*, long and pale, rocking back and forth as waves lapped at the shore. A dead fish? If so, it was one whopper. Sturgeon, maybe?

"Oh, geez." Chloe sighed, some of her ebullience fading away. Death was a part of nature, but she didn't really like to stare at it.

She started to turn back, then hesitated. Something didn't quite make sense. She climbed over the first rock slide, then crossed her arms over her chest, squinting. The thing wasn't a sturgeon. Not a fish at all. It was a dirty beige, and an odd texture.

Three more steps. Ah—she was seeing a fishnet. Layers and layers of fishnet, tangled around something. A log? But that seemed wrong, too.

One more step, and Chloe's knees went mushy. Her stomach clenched. Something hot and bitter rose in her throat.

No. It couldn't be.

Another wave shoved the bundle with more force. Chloe stared at the fingers poking through the netting. Slender human fingers, white as a fish belly, curled as if imploring someone, anyone, for help.

FOUR: SEPTEMBER, 1869

WHEN THE RYE BREAD was set to cooling, Ragna knotted her shawl around her shoulders and stepped outside. Anders might be home any time now, with fish and nets to unload and clean.

We did right to come here, she thought, although she hadn't always been sure. She'd pushed Anders to leave Denmark, and his doubts had followed him onto the ship. He was not a handsome man until he smiled—and oh, how she had missed that smile during their long voyage! She'd longed to see his ready grin, so broad and infectious that people who saw it laughed without even knowing why, just for the joy of it.

But since settling on Rock Island, his smile had returned. When the Andersons had arrived in the little fishing village last spring they picked a roofless cottage (any structure with no roof, they were told, was considered abandoned) to make their own. In the space of a single summer they'd added neat rows of cedar shakes overhead, and a border of daisies planted with seed carried across the Atlantic. It was becoming a *hygge* home—warm and welcoming.

Their homesite was on the far northern edge of the village, and that pleased them both. The Danes and Norwegians on the island had welcomed them; the Yankees and Irish too, mostly. Still, sometimes Ragna liked hearing birdsongs through the window instead of a babble of foreign voices.

Now Denmark seemed as far away as the moon. She'd written to her brothers, urging them to come. Carl and Jens had no more opportunities in the old country than Anders did. They will like it here, Ragna thought as she strolled south, passing cabins and cottages. Several children darted past, shrieking with laughter, and the rhythmic thumps of mallet and froe rang from one of the cooperages. The air smelled of whitefish and smoke.

A path led down to the beach, lined with Mackinaw boats pulled onto the cobbles. Fishermen were emptying their boats and women taking nets to dry. A boy was stacking cordwood on the dock for the next steamer. The lake rippled gently beneath a soft pink sky. Ragna smiled, well pleased.

Then an angry voice knifed through the evening. The boy was being berated by a stocky man. One of the Irishmen… Carrick Dugan, wasn't it?

Carrick Dugan whipped the hat from his head and slapped the boy with it. The boy cowered, hands raised. Dugan smacked the child with his hat again.

Ragna snatched up her skirt and pounded down the dock. "Here, now!" she said, in Danish because she had little English yet. "There is no cause to beat the boy."

Dugan glared at Ragna, pushing his chest out like a riled rooster. His red hair reminded her of a rooster, too.

Two men stacking kegs of salt on the beach paused in their work. "Let it go, Dugan," one of them called.

Dugan kicked the child.

"*Stop!*" Ragna grabbed Dugan's arm. She meant only to pull him away, but Dugan stumbled against the firewood. Windmilling his arms, he fell backward from the dock, landing in waist-deep water with a splash that dampened Ragna's skirt. The men on the beach whooped with laughter.

The sputtering Irishman scrambled to his feet. Water streamed from his clothes, his hat. Dugan looked at Ragna with such rage that something beneath her sternum went cold. Then he floundered ashore and stalked away.

Mette Friis, one of the other Danish fishwives, paused to scold the laughing men before hurrying down the dock. She spoke softly to the boy. Then Mette put an arm over Ragna's shoulders and led her to shore. "You must stay clear of Dugan," she advised in a low voice. "You shouldn't have intervened."

"He was hitting a child!"

"Dugan is a bad one," Mette said, her tone hushed. "He has always been quick to anger, but after his wife ran away—"

"His wife ran away?"

"She did. I helped her hide away on a passing sloop." Mette lifted her chin. "You must *never* repeat that. I hope she is far away, living a happier life."

Ragna didn't know what to say. What kind of life could a runaway wife hope to find?

"She was *Danish*," Mette added. "She humiliated Dugan by running away. You must stay away from the man."

That night, when the fish had been gutted and cleaned and packed, Ragna told Anders what had happened. "I think I made an enemy."

"It will blow over." Anders pulled his pipe from his jacket pocket. "Dugan started the trouble."

"But Dugan was the one who ended up in the water!"

"We've come to a good new place." Anders began tamping tobacco into the pipe. "I will always thank you for insisting that we come here."

"But—"

"Don't dwell on one sorry incident. The man is a bully, and got no more than he deserved."

The man *is* a bully, Ragna thought. And whether in a school-yard or on a village dock, bullies didn't like being shamed.

FIVE

CHLOE'S BREATH WAS RAGGED by the time she climbed back to the top of the cliff. She walked a few paces, trying to catch her wind, but the urge to run was too strong. Heart hammering, she jogged past the lighthouse and back toward the boat landing.

She was gasping long before she reached the main compound. She stared at the channel. What the hell should she do now? She'd watched the last employee of the day leave on the *Karfi*. Then she remembered: two kayakers were on the island. The passage back to Washington Island might still be too rough to paddle, but she wouldn't know until she asked.

Forty secluded campsites were sprinkled across the southern end of the 900-acre island. The young couple was in one of the remote sites, but where were *those*? She set off in what she hoped was the right direction.

Chloe searched for what seemed forever before hearing voices. A tent was pitched in a small clearing at the edge of the trees. The campers were on the beach just beyond. A blonde guy was sharpening a long stick with an army knife while a dark-haired young woman laid out the makings for s'mores: marshmallows, graham crackers, Hershey Bars.

Both of them scrambled to their feet as Chloe burst from the trees. "Um, what's up?" the guy said.

Chloe leaned over, hands on knees, feeling lightheaded. She took a deep breath before straightening and introducing herself. "I came to spend a week at the lighthouse, doing research."

"I'm Tim Brown," the guy said. "That's Natalie."

They were… what, twenty? Maybe twenty-two? Tim was a good-looking kid in a low-key kind of way, short but powerfully built through the upper body. Natalie seemed a less-likely paddle rat, with hair that probably—when clean—fluffed in floppy layers.

"I was down at the beach below the lighthouse a little while ago," Chloe began, "and I found a… a body."

"A *body*?" Tim took a step backward.

Natalie's eyes went wide. "Oh my God! Who is it?"

"I have no idea. A woman's body is sort of tangled up in a fish net."

Tim's mouth twisted. "Grody."

"Yeah," Chloe agreed, "but here's the thing. There aren't any park employees on the island tonight, and the phone isn't working. So I'm really not sure what—"

Natalie gestured toward the kayaks pulled up on the beach nearby. "We can go for help."

"Really?" Chloe asked. "Garrett told me conditions weren't good for paddling the channel."

"That was this morning," Natalie scoffed. "The wind's been dropping all day."

"Are you sure?" Chloe asked, thinking, Please be sure. Please be sure.

"No problem," Natalie said.

Tim shrugged. "Yeah, I suppose so."

Natalie and Tim packed away the food and fetched paddles, a compass, and flashlights from their tent. They donned dry suits and life preservers, and shoved the two kayaks into the shallows. Chloe splashed in, the water biting like ice at her ankles, and helped push them off. "Be safe," she called.

Natalie took the lead, angling her kayak to loop around Rock Island's east shore before cutting south and west toward Washington Island's Jackson Harbor. Soon they had disappeared from sight.

Chloe returned to the trail, hiked back across the island, and down to the dock. She could see the kayaks in the distance. Natalie's was green and easy to miss, but Tim's bright yellow boat shone like a beacon. The two paddlers appeared to be crossing without difficulty. Chloe found a picnic table where she could see the channel, and settled down to wait.

————

Sometime later Chloe watched as a rescue squad wrestled the body up the last of the steps from the beach. The men lowered the stretcher to the ground, no doubt relieved to have managed the climb. The sun hadn't set, but it was gloomy beneath the cedar trees. As Chloe tugged her jacket's zipper closer to her chin, she recognized one of the two men bringing up the tail of the procession. "Garrett!" she called softly.

The park manager was now dressed in civvies. "Sorry business," he muttered.

The second man looked at Garrett expectantly, waited a beat, then introduced himself. "Stig Fjelstul, Door County Deputy Sheriff." He pronounced his name the Scandinavian way: *Steeg Fyellstewl*. Fjelstul was solid and square-shouldered, at least six-four, with a piercing gaze behind horn-rimmed glasses.

"Chloe Ellefson. I'm here doing research."

"I'm sorry your stay on Rock Island began with … with this," he said.

"Do you know who the woman is?"

Garrett answered. "No."

"No," the deputy echoed, as if Garrett hadn't spoken. "She's definitely not a local."

The park manager blew out a long sigh. "So, Chloe, do you still want to stay?"

It hadn't occurred to her to consider anything else. "Well, yeah. Of course."

The deputy frowned. "Perhaps you should—"

"I believe Miss Ellefson has made a decision," Garrett said pointedly.

Chloe looked from one man to the other. What was up with these two? "Don't worry," she told the deputy. "I do want to stay."

The stretcher-bearers picked up their load again. When they reached the clearing Garrett cocked his head toward the DNR truck parked nearby. "I need to drive the body and the crew down to the landing. I'll see you tomorrow, Chloe. If Mel can get the *Ranger* running I'll be here by nine."

Mel... right, the maintenance guy. And the *Ranger* must be the park boat. "Sounds good. Oh—just one more thing." Chloe hunched her shoulders. "When you talk to reporters, could you leave my name out? I don't want my family to worry." And—geez Louise, Roelke. Roelke would *not* be happy to know she'd found a body on the beach.

"I'll try."

When Garrett and the rescue team disappeared down the trail, Deputy Fjelstul stayed where he was. Chloe gave the man a sideways glance and noticed the emblem on his jacket. "You're DNR? I thought you said—"

"Used to be a game warden. Now I'm with the county sheriff's office, out of Sturgeon Bay down the peninsula. I took the call because I live on Washington Island."

Which was fortunate, Chloe thought. Otherwise it would have taken much longer to get a deputy to Rock. "Have any boats been lost lately?"

"Not that we're aware of. I'll see what I can ascertain."

Ascertain? Who said "ascertain"? Chloe rubbed her arms, trying to banish gooseflesh. "It's horrible."

"Lake Michigan often doesn't forgive mistakes, especially when squalls blow up." Fjelstul removed his Brewers cap, ran a hand over his hair, and slapped the hat back in place.

"Um... it seemed to me that the woman was not wearing clothes."

"She was not. She appeared to be college-age, nineteen or twenty. Probably a couple out for a romantic sail went skinny-dipping and something went wrong. Even at this time of year, hypothermia's a real risk. Especially if alcohol is involved."

"But… how would she end up tangled in the fishing net?"

The deputy waved a dismissive hand. "There are probably thousands of lost gillnets moldering away in Lake Michigan."

"Really?" Chloe knew little about commercial fishing—OK, nothing at all—but it had never occurred to her that all the nets taken out to open water didn't return. "Don't they pose a threat to fish?"

"They can." He rubbed the back of his neck. "It's a problem, especially with fishermen and the DNR clashing over quotas and regulations. Did anyone take a statement from you?"

"No," Chloe said. "I just pointed the rescue team down the beach when they got here." A handful of men had zipped over the channel in motorboats. Chloe, a confirmed silent sports enthusiast, had never been so glad to hear the roar of engines. She couldn't remember if Stig Fjelstul had been with that first contingent or not.

"Washington Island doesn't have its own police force," he explained. "Anyway, just tell me what happened. I don't see any reason to suspect foul play, but our office routinely investigates any accidental death."

Foul play. Two little words, melodramatic and chilling at the same time. "There's not much to tell," Chloe said. "I came over on the *Karfi* this afternoon, talked with Garrett for a few minutes down at the landing, then walked up to the lighthouse." She described going down to the beach and spotting the body.

"Did you touch anything?"

Chloe shuddered. "It—the body—was face-down in the water, so I was pretty sure the person was dead, but I… you know. Figured I had to check. I rolled the body over. The net was dirty but I could see it was a young woman tangled up in all the layers. I saw long black hair clinging to her skin. Once I got a good look through the netting, I was absolutely certain she was beyond help."

"Yeah." To Chloe's immense relief, Deputy Fjelstul let it go at that. "Well, I hope the rest of your stay is more convivial."

Who said "convivial"? "Thanks."

Two minutes later, Chloe was alone again. Twilight's shadows stretched long. The clearing, so tranquil in daylight, now felt a bit spooky.

Defying the impulse to hide indoors, Chloe set up her back-packing stove on a picnic table outside. After a cup of hot tea, some peanut butter on crackers, and a handful of trail mix, she felt a bit more settled. Confronted with dirty dishes, though, she realized that she'd left both buckets on the beach below. Well, washing could wait until tomorrow. No way was she going back to the beach in the dark. Exploring the lighthouse would have to wait for tomorrow, too. She wasn't in the mood to traipse through shadowed rooms with a lantern.

She hit the outhouse, took her dishes inside, and locked the door behind her. Then she unstrapped her sleeping bag and carried it into the keeper's bedroom on the first floor, which held the promised bed. It was an antique, but the RISC folks had thoughtfully provided a modern mattress. Chloe felt a little better once she'd slid into the sleeping bag, which held memories of many wonderful camping trips.

I want to be here, she thought. No ... I *need* to be here. She'd made a commitment, and she intended to honor it. She owed the lightkeepers that, and the RISC people and park visitors too.

Besides, she needed time to sort out her feelings about Roelke McKenna. She had a bad track record with men, and she was terrified of making another mistake, but she owed Roelke an answer.

For a while Chloe read *A Is For Alibi* by flashlight, trying to stave off dreams of vacant eyes and fish-nibbled skin. Then she settled down, promising herself that dawn would bring a fresh start.

But long before dawn an unexpected sound penetrated her sleep. She opened her eyes groggily and found only the velvet black of deep night. The sound came again. Nothing ominous, nothing scary... just a child's happy laugh.

Chloe blinked. Was she actually awake? Her eyes felt sandy, the lids too heavy to hold open. There was nothing to see, anyway. The room was cloaked in darkness. And although she listened hard... well, she tried to... there was nothing to hear.

SIX: JUNE, 1871

EMILY ROHN BETTS SIGHED happily. "Oh, William. Pottawatomie is such a *fine* lighthouse." She walked slowly through the first floor, circling from the parlor to the keeper's bedroom to the kitchen. She'd visited the lighthouse before, of course. William was a good friend of her father's. And now he is my husband, she thought. And Pottawatomie is mine to help tend.

William stood back, watching her delight with quiet pleasure. Emily knew that some people questioned his choice of bride. William was twenty-two years older than she was, a veteran of the Civil War, widely respected.

Well, she thought, I shall prove the naysayers wrong. She might be only sixteen, but she was daughter of the Pilot Island Lighthouse Keeper and Assistant Keeper. She'd been helping to run a lighthouse for far longer than William had.

Emily put her hands on her hips, surveying the kitchen. I shall rearrange a bit, she thought. The official lighthouse service china should be on display, and the iron cookware tucked away in the closed cupboard. But so much room to work in! And oh, the *sink.* Rainwater collected in underground cisterns could be pumped directly up pipes into the kitchen. How wonderfully handy!

William smiled. "Soon, I know, this kitchen will be filled with delightful aromas to tempt me down from the watchroom."

"It will indeed." Emily joined her husband, stood on tiptoe, and kissed him lightly. She would enjoy cooking for William. He'd been a bachelor for far too long.

Her plans included more than food, however. Emily intended to apply for the vacant assistant keeper position. The money she earned would come in handy when she and William had children. Emily came from a family of seventeen, and the only fault she could find with this light station was its empty silence. Pottawatomie Lighthouse would not become a home until it rang with their children's laughter.

SEVEN

CHLOE WOKE TO THE sound of a lot of birds singing a lot of songs. The shadows had paled to a pearly gray. As she sat taking in the morning, the memory of the body on the beach returned. She acknowledged it, and tried to set it aside.

Then a memory of her dream returned. It had been a dream, right? Odd, though… she couldn't remember anything visual, just the sound of a small child's happy laugh.

"Well, that beats ghosties and ghoulies and things that go bump in the night," Chloe muttered, and got up to face the day.

She made a quick trip down to the lake to fetch water. The beach looked serene. A bald eagle, annoyed by her intrusion, launched from a snag and headed south. Two boats that had paused in the channel puttered away in different directions. Life went on.

She was sitting at the picnic table an hour later, adding almonds and dried cherries to her instant oatmeal, when a motorized rumble approached. She stood up as a white-haired man in a

DNR uniform drove the park's ancient pickup truck into the clearing and parked beside the back steps. "Brought you more drinking water," he said. He lifted a full Igloo from the truck bed with ease.

"You must be Mel," Chloe said. "Thanks. I'll grab the one inside." She hadn't quite emptied her supply yet, but she figured she should never turn down a delivery of potable water.

The Igloo swap was quickly made. "You got everything you need?" he asked. He had a rough voice and sun-lined skin.

"I'm good, thanks."

"There's extra toilet paper in the oil house. Basic tools, too." He gestured to a small brick building in the side yard. "I don't keep supplies in the lighthouse basement. Lots of snakes down there."

"OK." Snakes didn't particularly bother her, but there was no reason to impress Maintenance Mel with her cool regarding things reptilian. Niceties complete, Mel drove away.

Chloe lingered over a cup of hot chocolate. A huge flock of migrating blue jays had paused in the clearing, covering the lawn, perching in trees. Today, she told herself firmly, will be good. Once the dishes were washed, she locked the lighthouse and hit the trail.

As she came down the last hill, she could see a motorboat puttering across the channel from Washington Island. Tim and Natalie were sitting on the same picnic bench she'd waited on the evening before. "Good morning," Chloe called.

"Hey." Natalie indicated the bench beside her with a hand: *Want to join us?*

Chloe accepted the invitation. "Listen, I didn't have a chance to thank you last night. Did you have any trouble?"

"Nope," Tim said. "And we came back over on one of the boats with the rescue crew."

"I'm glad you were here." Chloe rubbed her arms.

"Rock Island isn't always as tranquil as visitors expect." Natalie stared over the lake. "Tim and I have paddled around here a lot. On calm days it's very easy to underestimate the danger. I imagine more than a few people have drowned near Rock Island over the centuries."

Chloe tried to think of something uplifting to say. Nothing came. "I'm sorry I had to spoil your last evening on Rock," she said finally.

"Not your fault." Tim shrugged and rummaged in a drybag. "Want a granola bar?"

"Sure," Chloe said instinctively. She wasn't hungry, but she was in backpacker mode: never turn down food. "So, are you guys set to head out?"

Natalie made a visible effort to shake off the willies. "Yeah. We've been out for three weeks, but we took the semester off. We want to visit a few more of the islands around here."

"Three weeks?" Chloe echoed wistfully. Now that she had a real job, three-week excursions were out of the question.

By the time she'd crunched through the granola bar, Garrett Smith had the *Ranger* tied beside the dock. Chloe waved. "Good morning," Garrett said as he approached. "I hope you all managed to get a good night's sleep, with no nightmares."

"No nightmares," Chloe said. "I dreamed about a child laughing, instead. I'm not sure where that came from, but it surely beats the alternative."

"We slept OK too," Natalie reported. "We're about to leave. There's no reason we'd have to hang around, right?"

"I can't imagine why," Garrett said.

31

"Has the body been identified?" Tim asked.

Garrett shook his head. "Not yet."

Chloe felt a little twitch beneath her ribs. Drowning was horrible enough. The fact that this young woman had somehow ended up naked and tangled in a fishnet, to be found by strangers, was even worse.

After Natalie and Tim said their farewells, Garrett gestured toward the *Karfi* heading out from Jackson Harbor. "You'll have guests while you're here, Chloe. People have always hiked up to see the lighthouse, even though it's been locked up tight. The furnishings plan is your first priority, but if you happen to be at the lighthouse when guests arrive, and if you're willing, feel free to show them around and explain the restoration project. Encourage folks to join RISC."

"Glad to, on both counts."

"If you need anything, I'll be in my office for most of the day." He pointed to a small stone building with a spectacular view of the channel. If Ralph Petty does find a way to get rid of me, Chloe thought, perhaps I could work for the DNR.

"Oh—one more thing," Garrett said. "If you wander down the east side of the island, you may run into an archaeologist working at the site of an old fishing village. Brenda Noakes is from Escanaba College, in Michigan's upper peninsula. She's got her own boat, so she comes and goes."

"I'll look for her."

Garrett rubbed the back of his neck. He seemed distracted by the *Karfi*, now arriving at the dock. A few day-hikers disembarked—a young dark-haired guy shouldering a huge camera bag, an overweight man and his overweight wife, two blonde women who

32

looked like sisters. Garret put on a professional smile as he went to greet them. "Welcome! Anyone need a trail map?" The couple and the blondes accepted maps and headed toward the lighthouse.

Garrett rejoined Chloe. "Back to the body," he said. "The story will be in today's papers, but I didn't give your name. With luck, you won't have any ghoul-minded sightseers wandering around."

"Sightseers?" Chloe twisted her mouth with distaste.

"Most of our visitors come because they treasure the island experience—birders or photographers or lighthouse buffs who spend every vacation touring lighthouses—hey there!" Garrett flicked his public smile back on and approached the photographer, who'd ended up standing on the main trail looking bewildered. "Did you decide you need a map?" The visitor accepted a map and wandered off.

Garrett rejoined Chloe again. "Anyway, Door County's got ten lighthouses, so it's a bit of a mecca."

"Ah."

"And I, of course, consider Pottawatomie the crown jewel. Lighthouse people may quiz you on every detail, but they're usually fun to talk with." He sighed. "Anyway, though, every once in awhile we see someone I'd rather stayed home. A salvage diver passing through, or a protester."

Chloe frowned. "Protesting about what?"

"It changes day to day. The park was established just seventeen years ago, in 1965. The purchase was controversial."

"Really? People didn't support the idea?" It seemed incomprehensible. Rock Island was a jewel! Once lost, such places couldn't be reclaimed.

Garrett snorted without amusement. "Stop by my office some time and I'll show you the map of proposed development. It's an artifact now, but I keep it as a reminder that different people had different visions for the island. Even now, some people don't want their taxes supporting the DNR."

"Really?"

"Oh, yes. The park is vulnerable to the whims of urban politicians who don't understand this place. We only use our old truck for emergencies, and for maintenance along the trails. People complain to their legislators that if rangers can drive on Rock Island, they should be able to as well."

The very idea of cars on Rock Island instilled in Chloe a sense of panic.

Garrett worked his jaw. "And a handful of fish tugs still work out of Jackson Harbor. That's bringing us unwanted attention, too. Some fringe environmentalists want the state to outlaw gillnet fishing. Or commercial fishing altogether."

"Outlaw?" Chloe felt her eyebrows rise. "That seems extreme."

"Most of the ruckus comes from people who mean well, but don't understand a damn thing about it." Garrett rubbed his knuckles. "But one of the reasons the zealots cite for wanting to ban gillnets is that they can snare other species, so it's … unfortunate that the woman who drowned got tangled in a gillnet."

"Yeah," Chloe said slowly, finally understanding.

"Nobody wants to see the whitefish thrive more than the commercial fishermen. They're more responsible than the trophy fishermen who—" Garrett stopped abruptly. "Sorry."

"It's OK." Chloe had never understood the lure of killing critters just to hang them on the wall, and she'd stopped eating them too. She considered herself an environmentalist, but bottom line: she didn't know enough about this to take sides.

What she did know was that Garrett didn't need any more headaches. "I'm off," she said. "Here's wishing you an uneventful day."

———

Roelke poured himself a cup of coffee. The chief was at a meeting and the clerk was running an errand, so he was alone in the Eagle Police Department office. He'd come in on his day off to tackle a mountain of paperwork regarding a complicated domestic disturbance call. Instead, he was thinking about Chloe.

He wished he had a clue where he stood with her. They'd gotten off to a rocky start. Just when things were looking good last summer, her stupid Swiss ex had shown up. Alpine Boy had almost won Chloe back.

Roelke tapped his pencil against the desk. In the past few weeks, since Alpine Boy had disappeared again, Chloe had kept things with *him* low-key. "After everything that's happened, I just need some time," Chloe had told him. "Some space."

Roelke had no idea what that meant. What he did know was that he'd met Chloe three months ago and she still couldn't decide if she wanted to go out with him or not. And that, he thought, probably tells you what you need to know.

So maybe he should just face facts and move on. Besides, he really needed to buckle down at work. When the full-time patrolman job had opened up a month ago, Roelke and Skeet Deardorff both applied. Roelke had won the job, with the bump in salary and benefits that came with it. But his promotion had been messy. He needed to prove himself to the chief, to the village board, to Skeet. Getting all hung up on a woman who didn't know her own mind could well be professional suicide.

Roelke set his jaw. All right, that was it. When Chloe got back from this island thing, she needed to fish or cut bait. In the meantime, he wasn't going to brood. He put Ms. Ellefson out of his mind, rolled a piece of paper into the typewriter, and began to peck the keys: September 8, 1982.

So … what was Chloe doing right now? Was she filling a notebook with scrawls about antiques and—and other old stuff? He tried to picture her busy, happy, completing her project more quickly than anticipated, coming home early to surprise him. Instead his mind conjured an image of her alone on a remote island, wandering around some rickety old lighthouse, totally oblivious to all dangers—

"Whatcha doing?"

Roelke jumped. "Jesus!" He hadn't even heard Skeet come in. Not good. Not good at all.

"Sorry." Skeet put a sack lunch in the tiny fridge. His shift was starting.

"No problem," Roelke said. "I was just… um…" The phone rang, for which he was truly grateful.

Skeet grabbed it, scribbled something, said "I'll meet you there," and hung up.

"Trouble?" Roelke asked.

Skeet reached for the car keys. "Sounds like some guy's having a heart attack. One of the new houses on Sunset Way."

The cops routinely accompanied the EMTs on emergency calls. "Want some company?" Roelke asked.

"Suit yourself."

Roelke followed Skeet out the door. He wasn't surprised by the lukewarm response. Since the job got settled, things between the two men were strained. Roelke had tried, really tried, to be supportive. Going out on this call, lending a hand even though he was off the clock, was just one example.

Besides, if he went home, all he'd do was stew about Chloe.

As it turned out, Roelke's presence was pretty much overkill. The victim's wife, Mrs. Saddler, was white-faced but calm as she ushered everyone inside. The bedroom was way too small for the patient, his wife, three EMTs, and two cops. Roelke retreated outside and busied himself by assuring worried neighbors that Mr. Saddler was getting the best possible care.

Ten minutes later the EMTs emerged from the house with their patient. Mrs. Saddler watched bleakly as her husband disappeared into the ambulance. "Thank you," she told Roelke and Skeet. "Thank you very much."

A woman hurried across the lawn and put her arm around Mrs. Saddler's shoulders. "I'm going to drive you to the hospital," the neighbor said. "I don't want you to wait alone."

Denise Miller, one of the EMTs, told the women where to meet them at the Waukesha ER. "And is your husband taking any prescription medications, Mrs. Saddler? It would be best if we take them along for the ER docs to see."

The elderly woman nodded. "Two. Both bottles are on the nightstand."

"I'll grab 'em," Roelke told Denise.

Skeet turned back toward the house. "I got it."

Roelke watched Skeet disappear inside. Great. Ju-u-ust great. Was this how things were going to be?

EIGHT

By the time Chloe got back to the lighthouse the day hikers had already disappeared—perhaps down to the beach, perhaps looping around on the trail that circled the island. Chloe was grateful. She needed to do something important. Finding the body on the beach had overwhelmed her arrival, and she had consciously tried to shut down her inner sensors when she locked herself inside the lighthouse last night. If there were any surprises, she wanted to discover them before the RISC committee arrived.

She started in the kitchen, standing perfectly still, receptive to whatever vibes might be lingering in the lighthouse. Nothing out of the ordinary came to her, nothing surprising—just the typical mild jumble of emotions she usually sensed in old buildings.

Since childhood, Chloe had occasionally perceived the resonance of strong emotions in old places. She never discussed those incidents, and she'd pretty much learned to live with them. Every once in a while an impression became so overwhelming that she couldn't bear to be *in* a building—a potential liability for a curator—but usually the impressions faded into the background like chatter in a coffeehouse…as they did here in Pottawatomie Lighthouse.

"Thank goodness for that," she muttered. She wanted a peaceful week on Rock Island. A chance to work on a project that had nothing to do with Ralph Petty. A chance to discover how she felt about the possibility of a romantic relationship with Roelke McKenna. A chance to collect her thoughts and consider what the heck she truly wanted to do with her life.

She had only five days to accomplish all that, so…time to focus. First up: meeting the RISC committee. She wanted to be ready.

The kitchen held a round table and four chairs. Someone had piled files and notebooks and reference books on the built-in sink's drainboard. Chloe smiled, grabbed some of the files, and settled down at the table. This was the good stuff.

Sometime later, when the sound of raised voices drifted through the summer kitchen's screened door, Chloe got up to greet her guests. No one was in sight, which meant that somebody was talking way too loudly. No tours for you unless you pipe down, she silently told the offenders.

Assuming, of course, that the noisemakers were *not* the RISC committee. RISC members who had invested years of their life into Pottawatomie Lighthouse, raising money and volunteering time and overseeing the restoration, would quite understandably not appreciate any whiff of possessiveness or censure from her.

Three people emerged from the trees. One of the two women walked briskly ahead, hands in the pockets of her jacket, looking down. The man was speaking in strident tones and gesticulating wildly. The second woman walked with arms crossed across her chest—awkward to do, Chloe mused. She must be pretty annoyed.

Chloe stepped outside, letting the screen door bang behind her. "Hello!" she called, with her biggest, brightest, most professional smile.

The woman leading the trio looked up. "Chloe?"

Lovely. This *was* the RISC committee, apparently in high dudgeon before they even sat down with her. "That's me."

"I'm Lorna Whitby," she said, clasping Chloe's outstretched hand in both of her own. Lorna was forty-something. Her expensive pink blouse didn't hide the rigid set of her shoulders. "We're glad you're here," she added. "It's exciting to see the lighthouse project reach this stage."

"I'm delighted to be here," Chloe said honestly.

Lorna turned to her companions. "This is my husband, Herb, and Sylvie Torgrimsson."

Herb still looked miffed, but he made an effort. "Welcome to Pottawatomie Lighthouse, Chloe." He was a soft-looking man wearing a plaid sports jacket and button-down shirt—way too formal for the setting. His gaze was direct and assessing.

The third member of the RISC welcoming committee was perhaps ten or fifteen years older than the Whitbys. She'd captured long gray hair in two careless braids. Her skin was weathered as a piece of driftwood, and she was lean and lithe. "We expect a lot from you," she warned Chloe, but she tempered her words with a genuine smile.

"It's an honor to be involved," Chloe assured her. "The lighthouse is spectacular."

"Many of the old lighthouses around the Great Lakes are past salvation," Lorna told her. "But the DNR stabilized Pottawatomie years ago. It was a safety issue."

41

"The state doesn't have money to pay for internal restoration work, or for guides," Sylvie said. "So that's where RISC comes in. We have big plans."

"Which need to be undertaken one step at a time," Herb said pointedly. Sylvie flapped one hand in a *Go away, you're bothering me* gesture.

O-kay, Chloe thought. "Why don't we start by talking about the scope of my work?" she suggested. "We should all be clear about expectations."

"Sound thinking," Sylvie said approvingly.

Since the afternoon was pleasant they settled at the picnic table outside. "We're in the middle of the restoration," Herb told Chloe. "The first priority was reproducing the lantern room. The iron-work is original, but everything else had to be rebuilt. Exterior tuck-pointing is complete. We also had the lath and plaster within the house repaired, and the paint analysis done."

"Herb took the lead on structural work," Lorna added, patting her husband's hand.

Sylvie shot Herb a dark look before turning to Chloe. "So now we're ready to consider furnishings," she said. "That's where you come in."

"Usually," Chloe began, "the first thing I'd want to do is establish a chronology of use—"

"We know exactly who was here, and when," Herb told her. "From 1836, when the first keeper arrived, to 1946, when the Coast Guard automated the light."

Chloe had been about to make that point, but she smiled and continued. "I read everything I could in advance, and I've started looking through the files inside. Your committee has already done a lot of legwork, which is great. But what about collections? Have you accepted any donations?"

Lorna put her elbows on the table and leaned forward. "Just the bed in the lightkeepers's room, and the kitchen table and chairs. The sink is original—feel free to use the drain, by the way. And weavers on Washington Island made the rugs to protect the floors from workmen."

"I have explained to other committee members, and to potential donors, that we can't accept any other pieces until we have a plan," Herb added loftily.

"Thank goodness we have you to keep us walking in a straight line." Sylvie rolled her eyes. "Chloe, I've put together a list of would-be donors and what they want to give."

Despite the obvious tension bubbling between Herb and Sylvie, Chloe was ready to hug all three of these people. She'd been involved in projects where well-intentioned participants had already made commitments that hindered guest curators instead of helping.

"Fantastic!" she told them. "While I'm here, I'll analyze the raw research and dig deeper in the archives on Washington Island. I'll also visit as many potential donors as I can. When I get home, I'll have access to period catalogs and other periodicals. You can expect my formal report in about a month."

Everyone nodded.

"The plan will include a site description, the chronology, and biographical information about the inhabitants. I'll consider how each room was used, make suggestions for interpreting the lighthouse, and recommend furnishings and other bits of material culture to support the restoration and interpretive themes." She looked around the table. "That all sound good?"

It all sounded good.

"With any luck we'll find primary source material from some of the women and children who lived here," Chloe added. "Sometimes the best clues about furnishings turn up in diaries and letters written by the people who had to clean the pieces."

Herb straightened his shoulders. "I assure you, the light keepers themselves did a great deal of upkeep on a regular basis." He sounded peeved again.

"Yes, of course," she conceded. "And I did read that a couple of women served as assistant keepers here in the nineteenth century." She was delighted about that.

"If you'll study the records," Herb said, "you'll see that my grandfather was a keeper back before World War II. He was a bachelor at the time, but I assure you, he was ready for every inspection!"

Shit, Chloe thought. The first thing she should have done was discover if any of the RISC folks had personal connections to the place. Dumb, dumb, dumb.

Nothing to do now but backpedal. "I'm sure that's true," she said. "If you haven't already written up everything you learned about daily life here from your grandfather, I hope you will. It would be *invaluable*."

Herb looked a little mollified. "I already have. It's in the files inside."

Sylvie got to her feet. "Enough blather. Let's take a tour."

Herb, Lorna, and Sylvie walked Chloe through the lighthouse's first floor: kitchen, keepers' bedroom, parlor. "I can easily imagine lighthouse families eating supper," Chloe said, "and settling down for a game of dominoes in the evening."

"The keepers' attention was always focused out on the channel," Herb said curtly. "In addition to watching for commercial vessels, they kept an eye on local fishing boats. At night the keepers watched to see if the light was shining properly."

Chloe made a mental note: *Keep future flights of fancy unspoken.*

"You know this building isn't the first on this spot, right?" Sylvie asked. "The 1836 cottage and tower failed. Poor mortar. It was a government job, so I expect they took the low bid." She shot Herb another dagger look. "Some things never change."

"I know this structure was built in 1858," Chloe said, as they climbed the stairs to the second story. "There were some fishing families on the island at that time, right? They must have been amazed to watch this huge stone building go up."

Sylvie nodded. "The fisherfolk lived in little cabins, most likely."

Chloe scribbled a note. "I wonder if we could find some written description of the lighthouse from someone in the fishing village. A letter, maybe."

"Observations from some barely literate fisherman would hardly be relevant to this project," Herb said. He pointed to a narrow room, facing north. "This was the assistant keeper's bedroom."

OK, Herb, I get it, Chloe thought. No more references to women, children, or fisherfolk. The Native Americans who fished these waters were presumably off-limits in his mind, too.

"Have you been up to the watchroom and lantern room yet?" Lorna asked. "The original Fresnel lens got stolen at some point, but we had a reproduction made."

Herb glanced at his watch. "We need to cut this short if we're going to catch the last ferry back."

"I'll explore the tower on my own," Chloe assured them, even though they had plenty of time yet. "I don't want to keep you."

They all tramped downstairs again. As they walked back through the main kitchen, Sylvie pointed to a woven rug in one corner. "That rug covers a trap door and stairs leading down to the cellar," she said. "But the steps haven't been rebuilt. If you want to see the cellar, go outside and around. The key you have will open the exterior cellar door."

"There's no reason for Chloe to enter the cellar," Herb retorted. "Nothing down there except snakes."

"So I've heard," Chloe said lightly.

"We have seen snakes in the cellar," Lorna said. Her tone was apologetic—perhaps because of Herb, perhaps because of the reptile contingent. "Mostly little ring-necks, but some fox snakes too."

"If I go down there, I'll keep my eyes open," Chloe promised blandly.

Herb sighed. "There's no reason for—"

"For God's sake, Herb," Sylvie snapped. "Stop being such a pansy ass!"

"Have you seen our outhouse?" Lorna asked Chloe brightly. "Not the modern one, the original. It's the oldest structure in Door County."

Chloe let herself be towed outside and around a lilac hedge, and dutifully admired the oldest structure in Door County. "What a treasure."

"We're lucky the stone walls have held up so well," Lorna said. She raised her voice as angry tones drifted through the hedge. "A man on Washington Island who has a woodlot is going to provide the huge plank we need to restore the door…"

Chloe asked every question she could think of, but an outhouse tour could only last so long. When she and Lorna ambled back around the hedge they found Herb and Sylvie glaring at each other. "Come along, Lorna," Herb said. "There's something I need to check in the Viking Hall before the *Karfi* arrives. Chloe, it was good to meet you."

When Herb and Lorna were gone, Sylvie gave Chloe a wry glance. "Don't mind old Herb."

"With a project this large and complex," Chloe said carefully, "it's inevitable that conflicts arise."

"Herb simply doesn't understand why some of us are interested in the big picture, and not just the lighthouse service itself."

"I do feel strongly about social history," Chloe said. "The lighthouse stories have to be considered within broader contexts or they won't make sense. The fishing village, the region—it's all important."

"Couldn't agree more," Sylvie said cheerfully. "And we've got lots of local sources. In addition to the archives on Washington Island, there's a farm museum, a traditional museum, and the new maritime museum in Jackson Harbor."

Chloe was impressed. A lot of local energy was going into historical preservation and interpretation. That said very good things about the community.

"There's also a small exhibit about Chester Thordarson—the guy who used to own this island—in the Viking Hall," Sylvie added.

Five days here were obviously not going to be enough. "I'll do as much as I can." Chloe promised.

"In a day or so I'll stop back with that potential donations list," Sylvie promised. "And I should warn you, exterior work should have been finished by now, but Herb's numb-nut contractors have put us behind schedule. The guy who did the tuckpointing around the stone did such a poor job that it had to be done over, and we still need to paint."

Chloe tried for diplomacy. "Bringing a building back to its original glory can be … complicated."

"Herb Whitby doesn't know a monkey wrench from a monkey," Sylvie said with a snort. Then her eyes grew serious. "Listen, I understand you found the body on the beach yesterday. Horrid way to start your visit."

"It was," Chloe admitted. "But mostly I'm just sad to think of the poor woman who drowned."

Sylvie looked out over the water. "It's not the first time a body washed up on that beach. Did you know that? There's a little cemetery just up the path there—" she pointed to a trail Chloe hadn't explored yet—"with the remains of a local family that drowned in sight of the island during a big blow back in 1853. And once seven strangers washed up on the shore. Never were identified." She gave a fatalistic shrug. "Bad things can happen out there."

Chloe remembered Natalie's comments: *Rough water around here. Lots of tragedies over the years.* Anyone who spent time on the Great Lakes had to accept their grim legacy of grief. Chloe thought about that, imagining the emotional toll that must have taken on lighthouse families. They tried to keep the passages safe. When disaster struck, they also confronted the wreckage.

"Thanks for letting me know," Chloe said. "I'll pay my respects."

NINE: MAY, 1872

THE AFTERNOON SUNSHINE WAS so inviting that Ragna decided to work outside. Cedar floats and stone weights had to be removed from the nets after each lift, and then reattached once the nets were dry. She had just started tying floats back onto the first net when she heard someone call her name. She smiled as Emily Betts appeared from the north path, swinging a basket.

Ragna waved. "*Velkommen!* I looked for you yesterday."

"The inspector came," Emily explained. She put the basket on the ground, looking pleased. "And hard as he tried, he could find no fault with the station."

Ragna couldn't imagine having a stranger arrive unannounced, set to poke through her cottage and fish shed, ready to criticize any fly speck or tarnished spoon. "I'm glad the visit went well."

"He dropped off a library box, so I have a new book to share," Emily added. She sat on a log near the fire and pulled the treasure from her basket. "*Miriam the Avenger*. I'll read, and you stop me whenever there's a word you don't know."

"That would be happy. Start with 'avenger,' please!"

Emily tipped her head thoughtfully. "Well, an avenger is someone who wreaks vengeance…" She tried again. "Suppose someone killed somebody. If the dead man's brother found the killer and then killed *him*, he would be an avenger. He would get re-venge by a-venging his brother's death."

Ragna reached for her twine. What type of woman was this Miriam? "Very well," she said. Emily settled on a log and began to read.

William Betts had been assigned keeper duty at Pottawatomie Lighthouse soon after Anders and Ragna settled on Rock Island. After Emily married William she visited the fishing village right away, introducing herself and inviting her new neighbors to tour the lighthouse. Ragna had fumbled to make conversation with this confident Yankee girl. "I can help you learn English," Emily had offered.

Now Emily read two chapters before closing the book with a decisive snap. "Very good!" she said. "You knew almost every word."

Not really, but Ragna didn't want to admit that. She wanted to embrace everything about this new place.

"Do you want to practice writing?" Emily pulled a small slate and pencil from her basket. Ragna dropped the net in her lap and carefully wrote her name.

"I always have to remind myself not to say Rag-na," Emily said. "That's what it looks like in English."

Ragna didn't like the harsh sound of that. The Danish pronunciation, *Rhan-ya*, came from the back of the throat, with a much softer and lovelier sound.

"Now the rest of your family," Emily prompted her.

Ragna wrote her husband's name first. Then her brothers, Carl and Jens, who had recently arrived on Rock Island.

"Very good!" Emily beamed at her pupil. Then her smile faded. "The afternoon is almost passed. Anders and your brothers are still out?"

Ragna turned toward the lake. "They are."

"No wind," Emily said sympathetically. "That means a long day."

"They say gillnet fishing is more bad than fifteen years. "

"It would be better to say, 'Gillnet fishing is the worst it's been in fifteen years.'" Emily squeezed her hand gently. "How far out are they?"

"They set nets ten miles out," Ragna said. "Not so difficult yesterday, with a good wind for the sail. Today, they had to row. Once they lift the nets and set new ones, they'll have to row back." Six hours of rowing, perhaps eight. Anders shared his Mackinaw boat with her brothers now, thank heavens. Carl and Jens could take turns at the oars.

"At least they can clean the fish in the boat," Emily said. In rough weather, when pitching waves made knife-work impossible, dressing the fish couldn't begin until the men reached shore.

For a moment both women were silent. Someone was chopping firewood nearby, and one of the Irish women sang a song in her native tongue as she filled net boxes.

"That new law from the State Fish Inspector is a..." Ragna paused, groping for the right English word.

"William said it was a nuisance," Emily supplied. "He said it seemed designed to annoy and hinder fishermen to the fullest extent possible."

Nuisance. Ragna turned the new word over, tucked it away. "Anders wants to obey all laws, but we are so close to Michigan, Illinois…" Her thoughts moved faster than words. Fishermen caught selling fish out of the county would be fined. But if a steamer docked from Chicago with buyers on deck and ice in the hold, did the Wisconsin Fish Inspector expect the men to turn down a sale?

"It's not practical," Emily agreed.

"And with the whitefish becoming more few, the men sometimes argue…" Ragna tied a stone to the bottom of the net. Anders had argued with Dugan, she meant.

"I'm sorry," Emily said softly.

Ragna forced a smile. "No, I am sorry. Anders and I am grateful to be here."

"*Are* grateful," Emily said. "But don't apologize. You're just sharing your thoughts with a friend." Her eyes sparkled. "May I share a secret with you? I have applied to become assistant keeper at the lighthouse."

"They give such jobs to women?"

"My mother was assistant keeper on Pilot Island," Emily said proudly. "I helped my parents tend the light. I'm actually more experienced than William." Emily's hand flew over her mouth. "Don't ever tell him I said so!"

"I would not!" Ragna exclaimed. "I keep your secrets. And—I will give you one of mine?"

"Of course!"

"I will have a child come. Anders wants a son, but I am hopeful for a girl."

Emily clutched Ragna's hands with pleasure. "When the time comes you can send for me, if you like."

"Yes, I would like," Ragna said. She hadn't shared her news with the other women yet. Mette Friis was good and kind, but Emily's good spirits and energy and Yankeeness were most welcome.

Emily gave Ragna a quick hug. "I really *must* go now."

Ragna watched Emily walk away. She hoped that the lighthouse service did indeed appoint her friend as assistant keeper. She couldn't imagine such a thing, but then—many things in America were unimaginable.

When the nets were readied and boxed, Ragna went inside. She ate a piece of bread and put a kettle of pea soup on her tiny stove so a hot meal would be ready for her men. Too restless to settle, she wrapped an extra wool shawl over her shoulders and walked down to the dock. Ice had not long been gone from the shoreline, and the air was cold. She nodded to two men lugging a barrel of salt down the beach, but kept her gaze on the horizon. There was no sign of her men.

And there probably won't be, she reminded herself, for hours yet to come. Still she stood, and watched, and waited. Finally, when the sun was sinking, she turned for home.

A man stood on the beach behind her, hands in pockets. Carrick Dugan. He did this, sometimes… creeping up on her, watching, letting her know he had not forgotten or forgiven.

Ragna stopped, fingers working her skirt like bread dough. Then she steadied her fluttering nerves. Shadows stretched across the beach, but lamps glowed from windows nearby. Two of the

American women were walking along the water's edge farther down the beach. One had a baby on her hip.

Lifting her chin in the air, Ragna walked past Dugan. *No,* she told him silently. *I will not let you frighten me.*

"Men aren't back yet?" Dugan called after her. "Maybe new-come farmers don't belong on the lake. Especially new-come farmers who think they can tell other men their business. Bad things can happen out there, you know. You might want to tell your man so."

Ragna stopped, turned back around, and looked him in the eye. "Mr. Dugan," she said, "you are a nuisance."

TEN

AFTER THE RISC COMMITTEE left, Chloe thought about the people who had washed up below Pottawatomie Lighthouse, past and present. Bad things can happen out there, Sylvie had said. It made Chloe intensely aware of feeling sunshine on her skin, hearing a hawk cry overhead, sucking in air that tasted of Lake Michigan.

All things that the drowned girl would never do again. I wish I had some way to memorialize her, Chloe thought. It was illegal to pick wildflowers within a state park, and they'd be dead themselves within hours anyway. But... she could build a small cairn from beach stones.

Chloe locked the lighthouse and went down to the beach. The more she thought about creating a natural and temporary memorial, the more she liked the idea. But as she approached the first rockslide she spotted a cairn already in place. Someone stole my idea, she thought indignantly.

So, who? She quickly looked around. The beach was deserted.

It is a public beach, Chloe reminded herself. Anyone might have wandered down the steps without her noticing, or arrived by kayak. She walked closer to inspect the cairn. The tower of stones stood about two feet tall. Someone with an artistic eye had placed each piece, sometimes balancing large stones on smaller ones. The effect was striking.

"Mine wouldn't have been as pretty," she admitted to two swans floating offshore.

Then she noticed something else. Someone had arranged tiny pebbles in a zigzag line in front of the cairn.

"Well, hunh," Chloe said, borrowing Roelke's *I'm-processing-new-information* response. The pebbles formed a capital **N**. Had the person who created this memorial known the dead woman's name?

———

Back in the clearing, Chloe fixed generic mac and cheese for supper, made palatable with basil, thyme, and chopped walnuts. A gray-haired couple wandered up from the campground, binoculars in hand, talking of broad-winged hawks and scarlet tanagers. Once the couple left Chloe washed her dishes and hung the dishcloth and towel on the clothesline tucked behind a lilac hedge in the side yard. She spent the rest of the evening sitting on the picnic table, watching birds and thinking.

She didn't know what, if anything, to make of the stone sculpture she'd found on the beach. What would Roelke think? She and Roelke had sometimes talked through problems together. They were such different people that each brought a unique perspective to whatever knot needed untangling.

Well, Chloe thought, Roelke's not here. Which was what she wanted, right? Space and solitude? Exactly.

She just hadn't figured on finding a naked drowned woman on Rock Island.

When it got darker, Chloe moved inside and returned to her research. After Herb's comments, she was perversely eager to discover whatever she could about the women who'd lived at Pottawatomie. The first item she found: in the 1860s, one lighthouse wife taught school for some of the island children in the lighthouse cellar. "With the snakes?" Chloe mused. "Shocking." Another wife, Paulina Capers, served as assistant keeper in the 1860s.

A new keeper arrived in 1870, William Betts. His wife, Emily, had evidently taught lessons for island children as well—and she was officially designated assistant keeper in 1872. "Excellent!" Chloe murmured. Even Herb Whitby couldn't argue with an interpretive plan that included Emily Betts in the narrative.

There were a handful of papers in the Betts file, but Chloe noticed a photograph on the bottom and pulled that out first. It was an eight-by-ten reproduction image showing Pottawatomie Lighthouse from the west. Three figures stood in the side doorway. Penciled on the back was a notation: *Mrs. Betts and two of her nine children.*

Chloe flipped the photo back over and leaned on her forearms, staring at the old image. If only the photographer had been closer! It was impossible to make out any details, much less Emily's face. Still, there was *something* there ... squinting, Chloe held her flashlight inches above the photo. Emily was barely discernable, and yet a message seemed to emanate from her steady gaze.

Tell our story. Get it right.

A fly dove at the flashlight. Chloe blinked and sat up straight. She was used to getting vibes from old houses, but a photo? And a repro at that?

OK. She was tired. Maybe her imagination—and her wish to trump Herb with fun female facts—was getting to her. She'd read more about Emily tomorrow.

She glanced at her watch. Quarter to midnight. Before turning in, it would be fun to climb to the tower.

Two sets of stairs led from the second story to the watchroom and lantern room—one steep, the next steeper. Chloe left her flashlight on the final landing and used both hands to help make the climb, and still managed to konk her head on the hatch leading into the lantern room. How had women done this in long skirts?

The lantern room was nine-sided, with only a narrow walkway surrounding the reproduction Fresnel lens. Chloe made another cerebral jotting: *Study the mechanics of light mechanisms* **before** *any lighthouse junkies show up for a tour.*

She edged around the light so she could stand at the northern-most window. The view was spectacular. A million stars glittered in the sky. The silhouettes of trees showed black against the paler midnight tones of the lake and sky.

The modern Pottawatomie light blinked in the eastern sky, offering automated guidance. And some kind of boat was in the channel. Chloe squinted. Not as big as a freighter, but definitely bigger than your average motorboat. Was it in Wisconsin waters? Across the invisible line into Michigan? She squinted, letting the boat's bright lights blur in her vision, imagining a sloop or steamer instead—as Emily would have seen.

She stood right *here*, Chloe thought. She liked that notion, even though she knew Emily probably didn't have much time to stand idle and appreciate the night.

"Good-night," Chloe said to whomever might be listening. Then she backed carefully down the stairs, and got ready for bed.

She dreamed of laughter again. Children's laughter. More than one child, this time. And this time, she was sure she'd come awake before the laughter faded into the silence of night.

ELEVEN: OCTOBER, 1873

EMILY WOKE AND SAW at once that the light needed tending. The bed she shared with William faced north; she knew what the light should look like, shining on the honeysuckle bushes on the edge of the bluff. She eased from the bed and tiptoed to the cradle. In the moonlight she saw her infant, Jane, sleeping on her back, one thumb in her mouth. Her dream of bringing children and their laughter and games and joy to Pottawatomie was coming true. Emily blew the baby a silent kiss, slipped on her shoes, crept from the room, and lit the lantern kept always ready.

After deeming that whale oil was too expensive for the Great Lakes, the U.S. Lighthouse Service had decreed that tenders use lard instead, hauled smelly and cheap from the Chicago stockyards. She and William always kept a kettle of rendered lard on the back of the second-story stove. I'd like to see one of those officials manage that, Emily thought. Lard congealed quickly. On cold nights she and William made endless trips up the steep stairs to the tower with buckets of hot fat in hand. She'd hemmed her nightdress high so she wouldn't trip while navigating the ladder-like steps with lantern and fuel.

Now she added wood to the stove, filled a pail with liquid fat, and climbed carefully to the tower. The light was burning, but not well. She replaced viscous lard with fresh, and adjusted the vents to improve circulation. There, now. That was better.

I should go down, Emily thought. She'd need to feed Jane before dawn, and she had a full day ahead. Still she paused. The view was spectacular, and she never tired of drinking it in. Above the light's beam, a million stars glittered in the sky. The silhouettes of trees showed black against the paler midnight tones of the lake and sky.

And—thanks to her—the channel was safe for any schooner captain making for Green Bay. It was a privilege to guard the channel, but an enormous responsibility as well.

Emily smiled. Her husband and daughter slept peacefully below, and she had friends nearby. Spending time with Ragna was a special pleasure, but Emily knew all the village women. They called on her when someone was ill or ready to deliver a child. Emily taught school for their children, too. She loved seeing the sons and daughters of fishermen—Yankee, Irish, German, Scandinavian—troop from the woods on schooldays. She had set up a schoolroom in the lighthouse cellar.

Emily took one last look at the night. Sometimes she thought her heart might simply burst with contentment.

TWELVE

I'M LOSING IT, CHLOE thought early the next morning. *Very* early. She sat on the picnic table, drinking bad coffee, listening to the Mormon Tabernacle Choir of avian choruses, trying to figure out what the heck was going on inside her head.

Bottom line: she had no idea.

Her own ideas about having children were tangled, but she surely wasn't conjuring the sound of happy kids out of suppressed maternal instincts. She wasn't sure she was ready for a romance, much less a family. Relationship issues aside, though, she was definitely hearing things at Pottawatomie Lighthouse.

Chloe had never known what to call her mild receptive ability, tuning into the layers of lives come and gone in historic structures. Sometimes those emotions lingered, like perfume that only she could smell. But impressions from photographs? The sound of children's laughter? Those were whole new talents she'd never asked for, never wished for, and she would have to keep hidden.

"Oh, goody," she muttered. Just what she needed. She didn't *want* her powers of perception to grow stronger. She worked in the history field, for God's sake! If her abilities were increasing, would she be able to keep little episodes like this hidden from colleagues?

And… oh geez, what about Roelke? He could sniff out a lie or evasion at fifty paces. But she couldn't imagine confiding in him, either.

OK, she told herself. You don't know how this new little nuisance will develop. It's too soon to panic. For the moment, at least, move on.

She switched over to thinking about the naked young woman she'd found on the beach. A woman whose name evidently began with *N*. Nancy? Nicole? Noreen? Natalie? An image of the young kayaker who'd gone for help, strong and capable and—thank goodness—quite alive, flashed through Chloe's mind. May she always paddle safely on the big lakes, Chloe thought fervently.

Maybe the **N** didn't stand for a name. Chloe tried to think of a religious name or prayer that some curious stranger might have symbolized with the letter N. Something like Jesus or Allah or Mohammed or Buddha. There might be a relevant name in Pottawatomie or Menominee or Ojibwe, and there must be some Catholic saints with N names, but she didn't know.

One word finally popped into her beleaguered brain: *Namaste*. Her college yoga teacher always said that at the end of class. Chloe had never heard a literal translation, but it had to mean good-bye, go in peace—something like that.

"There we go," Chloe told a brown thrasher hopping through the grass. Some grieving yogi had built a cairn on the Pottawatomie beach to say good-bye to a young woman who had gotten drunk on a cruise across Lake Michigan, stripped naked, fallen overboard, and drowned.

Right.

Her mental gymnastics were so absurd that she welcomed the arrival of Maintenance Mel in the truck. After the ritual exchange of empty Igloo for full one, Mel paused. "You doing OK out here?" he asked gruffly.

"Yes, thanks." Except for the naked dead woman and children playing nocturnal games.

"You're pretty isolated out here. Anything could happen, and there's no way to get help quickly if you need it."

Gee, thanks for reminding me, Chloe thought. But he was from another generation, and in his own way, he was probably trying to be nice. "I've done a lot of wilderness camping," she said mildly. "I'll be fine."

Once Mel left, Chloe felt edgy with pent-up energy. She wanted to talk to Garrett, and she had plenty of time before the first ferry arrived this morning anyway. Might as well take the long way down to the dock, circling around Rock Island's east side. Chloe rinsed out her mug, laced on her hiking boots, and headed out.

She came to the cemetery Sylvie had mentioned almost immediately. Chloe bowed her head in respect, then hurried on her way. She wasn't in the mood to contemplate the final moments of anyone drowning in Lake Michigan. It was surely a cold and lonely death.

The trail wound through the woods, offering glorious glimpses of the lake. Chloe descended among stands of birch and beech and juniper. After a mile or so she was ready to unzip her jacket and enjoy the sunshine.

This is why I came here, she thought, drinking in the day like champagne. She'd always relished solitude, always craved being outdoors. During her college days in West Virginia, she'd had plenty of friends to go camping with but still sometimes headed out on solo backpacking trips. Dolly Sods Wilderness Area, Canaan Valley, the Appalachian Trail … the natural beauty, and the absolute freedom to set her own pace, always did her good.

She paused to watch a nuthatch work its way down a tree. And I needed something good, she thought. Even before she found a body tangled in fishnet and started hearing children at night. She remembered how disapproving Roelke had looked as she packed the car. He was so different from any other guy she'd ever dated! She was used to hanging out with history nerds who got passionate about vernacular architecture or colonial foodways, folklorists who wore hand-painted neckties or earrings made from old watch parts, naturalists who didn't blink when a friend headed off for some solitary trek. Roelke was an overprotective, tightly wound, oh-so-German cop.

Who was also smart. Who loved and cared for his cousin's kids. Who had taken her sky-diving when she needed it—even though she hadn't had a *clue* she needed it. Who looked pretty darn fine when he lost the uniform and gun, and went for hiking boots and jeans and a tight T-shirt instead.

My feelings are clear as custard, Chloe thought.

About a mile and a half from the lighthouse, the canopy opened and revealed a meadow. The limbs of several old apple trees were bent with red fruit. The lake rippled in jewel tones of green and blue beneath a sky studded with cumulous clouds.

"*Oh*," Chloe breathed, enchanted. She left the trail as if lured by the Pied Piper.

If Rock Island's green forest still clung to late summer, the meadow had embraced early autumn. Chloe walked through waist-high grasses rippling brown and tan in the breeze. A few clumps of goldenrod and pale purple asters glowed in the sun. With every step a cloud of grasshoppers flew ahead of her. Two crows scolded from a dead birch tree. "Don't mind me," Chloe told them. "I'm just visiting."

The meadow ended at a fringe of shrubby deciduous trees above the cobbled beach. Chloe didn't realize she wasn't alone until she almost stumbled upon another woman. "Oh!" Chloe said again.

"Good morning!" The woman had been crouching beside the trees, winding string between four stakes marking a square of disturbed ground about the size of two shovel widths, but she rose. "I'm Brenda Noakes. Are you Chloe?"

"That's me." Chloe shook the offered hand, trying to think. Ah, yes. Brenda Noakes—the archaeologist.

Brenda was perhaps fifty, deeply tanned, with light brown hair pulled away from her face in a simple ponytail. She wore a blue ball cap monogrammed with **EC**. "Any relation to the local Ellefsons?"

"It's pretty distant. So, you're doing a dig here?"

"I wish."

"Um…" Chloe glanced pointedly at the stakes. It sure looked as if Ms. Noakes was conducting a dig.

"Oh." Brenda gave a wry smile. "I have a permit to define the limits of the fishing village site. Right now I have a little window of time between the summer crowds and the autumn leaf-peepers.

Next week I have to head back to Escanaba. I teach there." She waved her arm in the vague direction of Escanaba, Michigan, which was maybe thirty miles distant across the lake to the northwest.

"Ah!" Chloe nodded. She'd taken one basic archaeology course in grad school, and tried to retrieve some intelligent tidbit from memory's rusty file drawers. "Test pits?"

"Right. I'm excavating a few pits, looking for evidence of buildings."

It was coming back now. Brenda would be making test pits every five meters or so, looking for evidence of human disturbance. "Found anything interesting?"

"Not yet." Brenda pulled a pack of cigarettes and lighter from her pocket. She glanced at Chloe and sighed. "Don't worry, I'm planning to quit."

Chloe shrugged. "No business of mine." Unless Brenda tossed her butt aside.

"Anyway, I've yet to secure funding for a proper dig." Brenda lit up and took a deep drag. "A decade ago, archaeologists found evidence of native peoples occupying Rock going back centuries. Pottawatomie, Huron, Ottawa. But nothing's been done on more recent inhabitants."

"That's too bad." Chloe peered over the steep embankment. "If the fishing village was up here, how did people get down to the water?" The cobbled beach was forty, maybe fifty feet below.

"The slope was more gradual a century ago. Now, there are a couple of footpaths toward the south end." Brenda waved one hand. "White fishermen started arriving in the 1830s. The first were just summer residents, but in 1848, a few families wintered over. In time there were maybe three hundred people living on Rock Island."

Three hundred people, come and gone. "The village didn't last too long though, right?" Chloe asked.

"A lot of men left during the Civil War. In the next decade even more families moved on to Washington or one of the other islands. The harbor here is very shallow. Little Mackinaw boats worked fine, but as boats got bigger, the fishermen needed a deeper harbor."

Chloe considered the crescent-shaped shoreline below. The fishing village wouldn't be a big part of the Pottawatomie Lighthouse story. Still, she needed to understand it. "Is there anything left of the village itself?"

"A couple of stone foundations. A few unnatural depressions. Give me a handful of students and a month, and we'd know a lot more than we do today."

"Funding for this kind of project must be hard to come by," Chloe said sympathetically. She knew what it was like to grovel for dollars.

"And what little funding exists doesn't go to excavating fishing villages." Brenda's tone turned bitter. "Not as sexy as shipwreck diving. And I know of two archaeologists who've gotten money to search for Viking ships and rune stones, for crying out loud."

"Well, I hope the next grant application hits the jackpot."

"Ironically, the fact that Rock is a state park works against me." Brenda exhaled a plume of smoke over her shoulder. "I could drum up more interest if the site was about to be paved for a new strip mall."

Even the mention of Rock Island being paved made Chloe's stomach clench like a fist. "I'm sure there are stories of this place worth preserving in their own right."

"Well, I think so," Brenda agreed. "The community here was as complex as any other. You can't study local history around here without reading about a lot of tragedies. People generally got along, helped each other out, but living in a small isolated community could also magnify problems. There was even a murder on Rock."

"A murder on Rock?" Chloe repeated stupidly.

"It happened back in the 1850s. An islander named James McNeil somehow got his hands on some gold coins. He called them his 'Spanish Ladies,' or his 'Yellow Boys.'" Brenda made air quotes with her fingers. "He talked about them whenever he got drunk. Somebody bashed him in the head."

"Yikes." Chloe made a face. "I assume the gold disappeared?"

"You got it. And from time to time I find new dig-holes on the island."

"You mean people are still searching for the coins?" Chloe asked. "Didn't whoever killed McNeil take the gold?"

Brenda gave a *Who knows?* shrug. "I suppose someone might conclude that McNeil got killed because he wouldn't produce the coins when someone tried to rob him. People have crawled all over Rock looking for the Spanish Ladies." Brenda stubbed her cigarette out on a rock and carefully tucked the butt into an empty plastic prescription medication container. The container went back into her daypack. "Twice Garrett's caught a couple of pirates from out-of-state using a metal detector, which isn't legal in the park. Let me tell you, they'll be sorry if *I* ever catch them messing around with a metal detector."

Chloe understood why an archaeologist would have no tolerance for treasure hunters. Still, she was starting to wish that she hadn't found Brenda Noakes at the enchanted meadow. Brenda Noakes was an enchantment-buster.

Ready to change the subject, Chloe gestured to the gnarled apple trees. "Do those trees date back to the village?"

"Local tradition says they do," Brenda said. "Although Chester Thordarson, the guy who bought most of Rock Island in 1910, did some major landscaping in this area."

"Oh, too bad." Chloe flushed. "I just mean—it would be nice if the village site had been left undisturbed." She tipped her head, considering the peaceful meadow. "How did the locals feel about Thordarson?"

"I suppose feelings were mixed. He was a genius inventor who hired a lot of Washington Islanders—carpenters, masons, landscapers, cooks. He also drank a lot and brought some guests of dubious repute here. Some people grumbled about a wealthy businessman buying so much property and bringing in all his wealthy Chicago friends."

"Some things never change."

"All in all, the Thordarsons were good caretakers. They left most of the island undisturbed, thank God. I've got a pretty good sense of what changes in the landscape came from them."

"That's good to know," Chloe said. "So, do you live on Washington Island?"

Brenda shook her head. "I grew up there, and often visit my dad at the old family farm, but I live in Escanaba now." She jerked her head in the vague direction of Michigan. "I've got my own boat, so it's not too hard to come across."

Not hard, Chloe thought, but a bit of a trip. A beautiful one, though. "Say, I saw a lit-up boat in the Rock passage about midnight. Do you know—"

"*Dammit!*" Brenda's hands clenched convulsively.

"Um … what's the problem?" Chloe asked, wondering if she should back away. Very, very slowly.

Brenda gave a little shake, as if ridding herself of something repugnant. "What did the boat look like?"

"I don't really know. I didn't have binoculars. Definitely not a freighter, though."

Silence.

"So, what might that be?" Chloe asked.

Brenda lifted her chin. "I have no idea."

The lie was so flagrant that Chloe almost laughed. Something told her that might not be a good idea. "Well," she said, "I'll let you get back to work."

Chloe left the archaeologist to her survey. That woman is wound a little too tight, she thought. Fortunately, treasure-hunters and poorly appropriated grants were not her problem.

Learning all she could about the relationship between the village and the lighthouse, however, *was* her problem. And Chloe felt inexplicably disappointed to discover that—aside from a few foundation stones—there was nothing tangible left from the fisherfolk of Rock Island.

THIRTEEN: JULY, 1874

THE FISHERFOLK OF ROCK Island celebrated summer with an annual picnic, and Ragna rose before first light that day. While her young son, Paul, played on the floor, she made *aebleskivers* in the special pan she'd brought from Denmark, and an apple cake too.

By mid-afternoon the plank table set on the beach groaned with stuffed sturgeon, steaming biscuits drenched in maple syrup, potatoes, and beans. Norwegian women brought *krumkakke* filled with fresh-whipped cream. The Irish women brought scones and *barm brack*, a German fishwife came with sugared doughnuts, and Yankee women brought snickerdoodles and gingerbread.

"Such a feast!" Emily marveled. "I must write down your recipes." She'd carried Jane and a blackberry pie from the lighthouse.

"There aren't as many of us on Rock as there once were," Berglind Fridleifsdottir said. She was a heavy-set woman with a broad smile who had immigrated from Iceland.

Mette Friis looked indignant. "But we still set a fine table!"

Ragna let the older women evaluate neighbors—and meals—come and gone. "I'm sorry your husband can't come," she told Emily.

Emily switched Jane, who was fretting, from one shoulder to the other. "Such it is for lighthouse families. Now that I'm officially assistant keeper, William and I can never leave at the same time."

Jane began to whimper. "May I?" Ragna asked.

"Of course." Emily relinquished her daughter.

"There now, little one," Ragna whispered, swaying back and forth. The baby smelled both sweet and a tiny bit sour.

She heard Anders' ringing laugh and glanced toward the men, looking strangely idle as they lounged on logs set near the water. Several were whittling, as if idle hands were too much to bear. Anders, walking after Paul as he chased a butterfly, caught Ragna's eye and grinned. Watching them together made Ragna's heart melt like butter in the sun. "I had not known…"

"Known what?" Emily asked.

Ragna realized with a start that she'd spoken aloud. Berglind and Mette had moved away, and Ragna glanced about to make sure no one else was in earshot. "I love my husband dearly," she said. "But I hadn't known how fierce love can be until—"

"Until you had a child." Emily kissed her daughter. "And the three of you became a family."

"Yes," Ragna agreed. She touched Jane's cheek with a gentle finger. "All I need now is a sweet girl like this one." Although she had weaned Paul long ago, she had not become pregnant again.

But this is a good day, she thought. Not a day for regrets. It was pleasant to see everyone enjoying themselves. And Carrick Dugan had, for his own reasons, stayed away.

His absence was a gift that buoyed her through the feasting, the boat races, the games and singing. When she settled into bed beside Anders that night, she felt a warm sense of contentment.

———

The day after the picnic Ragna cooked pancakes for breakfast, then carried Paul down to the beach to see the men shove off. "We set nets only about five miles out," Anders told her.

"We knew we'd feel lazy after feasting," Jens chimed in, patting his belly. He was the younger brother.

Anders cuffed Jens playfully before turning back to his wife. "The wind is fair. I expect to be home by mid-afternoon."

But Anders wasn't home by mid-afternoon, or late afternoon, or early evening. One by one the other Mackinaws returned. "Have you seen Anders?" Ragna asked. "Have you seen my men?" The fishermen shook their heads, shrugged.

Finally, as the sun was setting, she went to the yellow house at the south end of the village where Anton Jacobson lived. Many of the men worked for Anton, and everyone respected him. "I expected Anders and my brothers home long ago," she told him.

Anton squinted at the sky, sniffed the breeze. "It's fine weather. Your men are good sailors. They can navigate by the stars. I can't imagine what delayed them, but I expect they'll be along any time now."

Ragna put Paul to bed at Mette's house, and then paced the beach with a lantern. She walked in tight circles for what seemed like an eternity. Her husband and her brothers—all out in one boat. Bad things can happen out there, Dugan had said…

Finally she heard the splash of oars. A moment later the Mackinaw came into view, black in the faint glow cast by lantern and moonlight. When Anders stepped out she put the lantern down and ran into the water to meet him, weak-kneed with relief. She tried to help as he stumbled to shore. Carl and Jens hauled the boat onto the beach before sprawling on the ground.

Ragna lifted the lantern. No one looked hurt. The fish boxes were full. They are safe, Ragna told herself. Her men were safe. She filled her lungs with damp air, perfectly aware of the stones beneath her, the soft splash of waves against the shore, the scent of woodsmoke lingering in the night.

Finally she asked, "*Why?* What happened? Why are you so late?"

"Trouble with the buoys," Carl mumbled.

That made no sense. Ragna looked at Anders in confusion.

He crawled to the boat, reached inside, and retrieved... half a buoy. The portion that should have poked from the water was gone. The weighted end of the pole was intact, but the staff had been severed—neatly sawed in two. Someone had done this.

Anders spoke for the first time, and his voice quivered with suppressed fury. "Every buoy was destroyed, right at the waterline. We had no way to find our nets. We couldn't lose them... or the fish... so we just kept searching. Rowing back and forth, back and forth. For hours."

"But—but why?" Ragna whispered. "*Why?*"

"I don't know why," Anders muttered.

Ragna thought of Carrick Dugan and his threats, his eyes narrowing as he watched her from beneath some cedar trees, her relief when he'd stayed away from the picnic. She might not understand why, but she was pretty sure she knew who.

FOURTEEN

AFTER LEAVING THE VILLAGE meadow, Chloe made it around the island in time to watch the *Karfi* arrive. Eight or ten day-visitors disembarked, plus a couple of people with camping gear. Chloe waited while Garrett checked the campers in at the contact station. "Hey," she said when he was free.

"Glad you stopped by," Garret said. "I've given Herb Whitby permission to bring a painter out to the lighthouse this week. I'm sorry it has to happen while you're here, but we're behind schedule."

"No problem," Chloe assured him, remembering Sylvie's irritation about that issue. Herb either had a wish for power or a thick skin to persevere in the face of criticism. "So ... has the young woman who drowned been identified?"

He shook his head. "I'm guessing whoever she was with panicked, and hasn't reported her death. That sometimes happens when drugs or booze are involved. If—can I help you?" He paused to speak to a visitor who'd returned. "Yes, you're welcome to go inside the Viking Hall. Just flip the lights on."

"We tried," the man said. "They're all burned out."

Garret gave Chloe a quick *Why me?* look before turning back to the guest. "I'm sorry. There must be something wrong with a circuit. I'll have my maintenance man take a look."

The joys of being in charge never end, Chloe thought. She waited until the guest left before speaking. "So if the girl's parents or friends didn't know she was going out on the lake, they might eventually report a missing person, but no one would know to check for drowning victims."

"At least not right away," Garrett agreed. He locked the contact booth and they began walking up the hill. "It's always possible that the victim was boating alone."

"Well, I don't know about that." Chloe told him about the cairn and pebble **N** she'd found on the beach.

"I need to document this. I can put out a bulletin, see if any young women with **N** names show up on missing persons lists."

They stopped at the park office so Garrett could leave a note for Mel and grab a camera. Room with a view, Chloe thought enviously, admiring the panorama below as he rummaged for a new roll of film. Then she stepped sideways to study a map—the one he'd mentioned, drawn by a developer who'd fought to keep the state from purchasing the island for a park. The park landing area had been slated for a hotel and condos. The peaceful eastern shore she'd just visited was parceled into lots—some even labeled with presumptive buyers: Stenhoffer, Owings, Kopecky, Brown. Not a Scandinavian name among them. Probably bazillionaires in cahoots with the developer, Chloe thought. "This is chilling."

"Yeah," Garrett said. "There but for the grace of God…" He finished rolling the film into the camera. "Let's go."

They hiked up to the lighthouse together. Chloe was glad she wasn't wearing her backpack. Garrett covered the trail in long loping strides she could barely match, even unburdened. She didn't want to come across as a weenie.

In the clearing, a visitor was taking close-up photographs of one of the lighthouse's downspouts. He looked up and brightened visibly at the sight of Garrett's uniform. "Say!" he said, bounding over to meet them. "These copper downspouts look original! And the lightning cord too!" He gestured to the rope of braided copper that ran from a lightning rod on top of the lantern room to the ground. "These details are important. Any chance I can get inside the lighthouse? I've come all the way from Massachusetts."

"I'd be glad to show you around," Chloe told him. Garrett didn't need her help down on the beach.

"Richard Dix," the man said, offering a firm handshake. Mr. Dix had a flop of brown hair that needed pushing from his face every few moments, and he wore glasses with heavy black plastic rims that needed to be pushed up his nose with equal regularity. The gestures made it hard for him to handle both the camera and a notebook, but he managed.

When Mr. Dix wasn't telling tales of the lighthouses he'd visited from coast to coast, he peppered her with questions. Chloe answered what she could and punted what she couldn't. It was exhausting, but she enjoyed the challenge and admired his ardor. Passionate people like this made preservation projects possible.

"Can we go all the way up?" Mr. Dix asked hopefully, peering up the steps from the third-floor watch room.

"We can," Chloe said. "But please be careful. The hatch is narrow. Don't hit your head." As she had done last night. He scampered up the ladder like a professional.

By the time Mr. Dix was ready to leave, an hour had gone by. He was still asking questions as he walked out, so she felt compelled to follow him into the yard. "Has any archaeological work been done on the site?" he asked, scanning the clearing thoughtfully. "Trash heaps, foundations of earlier buildings, that sort of thing?"

"Not yet," Chloe said. Mr. Dix would have to get in line behind Brenda Noakes on that one.

"May I go into the cellar?"

"I'm afraid not." The RISC committee hadn't forbidden her to take a visitor down there, but they'd discouraged it. Besides, she hadn't gone exploring in there herself yet.

Mr. Dix spent quite some time back on his hands and knees, peering through the cellar windows. "What's the layout down there? A structure so massive must have enormous supports."

"I'm sorry, but I haven't been down there myself yet," she told him. "I'm just not sure."

"Well, thanks for the tour," he said finally, getting to his feet. "It's a wonderful lighthouse."

Chloe grinned. "Isn't it? Come back in a couple of years, when it's furnished and docents are available to give proper tours."

"I will. I most certainly will."

"So, you're traveling through the area? Where to next?"

"I saw Cana and the Eagle Bluff lights on the way up the peninsula," he told her, "and plan to see the rest of Door County's lights before driving down to Green Bay and on around to Michigan's Upper Peninsula."

"Sounds like a fine trip," she said. "Safe travels." She waved as he headed back toward the dock.

Chloe didn't notice the other visitor in the clearing until the young man emerged from behind the oil house in the side yard. "Hi," he said.

She responded in kind, thinking, *Please don't want a tour. Please don't want a tour.* She liked showing off the lighthouse, but at this rate, she wouldn't get any work done. "Would you like a tour?"

"No thanks," he said. "I was just taking some pictures." He gestured toward the camera hanging around his neck.

Something niggled her memory. "Say... weren't you up this way yesterday?" She recognized the camera, which had a lens as long as her forearm, and his longish black hair. She'd seen this guy get off the *Karfi* the morning before.

"Um, yeah. I've been, um, trying different angles. Different lighting. Of the lighthouse. You know."

Chloe's visitor gauge, which had hit one extreme with talky Mr. Massachusetts, swung to the other end of the dial. This guy's demeanor made her want to draw him out. His thin face and long fingers gave him the look of an artist, although instead of romantic pallor he had a sunburn. He looked about seventeen. Probably a few years older, though, she decided. Not many kids in their teens had such expensive gear.

"That looks like a nice camera," she said brightly. "Lots of good subject matter on Rock."

"Yeah." He studied his camera. "I, um, want to do this for real. You know, professionally. Notecards and calendars and stuff."

"The guy who just left here would have been happy to buy a calendar featuring Pottawatomie Lighthouse," Chloe told him. "I'll look for your work in the gift shops one day."

She went back inside and shut the door behind her. With any luck she could get some more reading done before anyone else showed up. She fished a bag of gorp from her pack and settled back at the table with the files she'd abandoned the night before.

Well, she thought as she picked through the trail mix in search of M&Ms, Garrett had predicted that lighthouse guests would include birders and lighthouse people and photographers. She'd already hit the trifecta. She had enjoyed meeting the elderly couple —good birders, quite at home in the outdoors, and affectionate with each other. Mr. Massachusetts had been a trip, but fun in his own way. Camera Guy, though…

She frowned. He'd come to Pottawatomie the day before. He *could* have been the person who built the memorial cairn on the beach.

Chloe swallowed, wiped her mouth with her hand, and wiped her hand on her jeans. Then she went back outside. She had another question or two to ask her young visitor.

Camera Guy, though, was gone.

———

OK, Chloe thought. I need a new plan.

She enjoyed giving tours, but she had a lot of curatorial work to do. From now on she'd spend her days doing research on Washington Island, and save general reading and note-taking for evenings, when the park's day visitors were gone and the campers were tucked in their own cozy campsites two miles away. She checked her watch. If she beat feet, she should be able to catch the 1 PM *Karfi* back to Washington. She could check out the archives, at least get a sense of their collections, and grab the last *Karfi* ride back to Rock.

She was at the dock before it occurred to her that it might be a good idea to let someone know where she was going. She followed the sound of a motor around the Viking Hall. Melvin Jenks was mowing grass. She planted herself in his line of sight, waving. "Excuse me!"

Melvin cut the engine—not off, but at least to idle.

"I decided to jump over to Washington for the afternoon. Will you let Garrett know?"

"Sure thing."

"Great. Thanks." Chloe turned away. This impromptu trip was a good idea. She was like a kid in a frozen custard stand when visiting a new archives, struggling to choose what to sample and knowing that any flavor would be good. She might even find some new bit of information about Emily Betts.

And maybe, she thought, she could find out if anyone had identified the dead girl. Deputy Fjelstul was probably handling the investigation from his home. She felt badly about quizzing Garrett every time she ran into him. The poor man was probably sick of talking about it.

Chloe glanced down at the channel. The *Karfi* was approaching the dock, but she still had a minute. She ran after Maintenance Mel and went through the arm-waving routine again. "Sorry to bother you," she said, after he cut the engine again. "But I was hoping to talk to somebody over on Washington, and I don't know where he lives. Do you know Stig Fjelstul?"

Melvin turned his head and spit in the grass. Then he revved up the mower and marched away.

Chloe stared after him. "Okey-dokey, then," she said at last. "Thanks for the information."

———

Roelke McKenna tried to make eye contact with the young woman hunched in a chair across the desk from him. He'd never met her before, and he was trying hard to put her at ease. "I really appreciate you coming in," he said. "You're doing the right thing."

Penny Sloan might have given him a tiny nod. It was hard to tell. A curtain of brown hair screened her face. The teen was still sniffling too, scrubbing at her eyes every now and again with a wadded tissue.

"We'll take it from here," Roelke added. "Thank you."

He watched Penny leave. She'd shuffled into the EPD looking so traumatized that he'd pegged her as an abuse victim. Once seated it took her another ten minutes to spit the story out. Short version: her boyfriend had offered angel dust to Penny's younger brother. The boyfriend thought it was funny. Penny didn't.

Roelke sighed. He could deal with the boyfriend, but Penny had set herself up for a hard time. High school could be hell. Nancy Reagan wanted to believe that her new "Just Say No" campaign was going to solve the drug problem. Lots of parents wanted to believe that rural villages like Eagle didn't even have a drug problem. "I wish," Roelke muttered.

He was reaching for an incident report form when the door opened again. Mrs. Saddler took one hesitant step inside, scanning the room as if to be sure that Roelke didn't have any hardened criminals shackled to the wall. "Hello?"

"Please, ma'am, come in." Roelke ushered the elderly woman into the chair Penny had vacated moments before. "How is your husband?"

"Much better," Mrs. Saddler said. She looked trim and smart in a navy blue suit with white blouse. "The doctor said we were very lucky. If any more time had elapsed…" She shuddered.

"Good thing you were with your husband when he had the heart attack."

"I wasn't, though." Mrs. Saddler rubbed her wedding ring absently. "I was in the kitchen when it happened. My husband was in the bedroom, and he didn't make a sound. But something made me turn off the coffeepot and go back to check on him. I just knew."

Roelke didn't understand such things, but he didn't doubt her. "I'm glad."

Mrs. Saddler put the paper-wrapped parcel she'd brought on the desk. "I came to thank you and the other officer—what was his name?"

"Officer Deardorff."

"Yes. He was so nice. I wanted to thank you and Officer Deardorff for helping us that day. Is he here?"

"No, ma'am. He called in sick today." That was why Roelke was here, actually. Skeet had called him at home, and Roelke was glad to help out by picking up his shift. The extra money was always welcome, and he was still looking for ways to smooth things over with Skeet.

Besides, working a double shift would keep him from worrying about Chloe.

"I see." Mrs. Saddler sat very erect. "I also wanted to talk with Officer Deardorff about a problem."

"I'd be glad to help you, ma'am."

"Well, it's a problem about the rescue squad that came to the house that day. The EMTs."

The morning went downhill fast. No cop wanted trouble with their local rescue team. If Roelke ever got shot on duty, he really, *really* wanted to be on good terms with the first responders. "The EMTs?" he echoed, hoping he'd misheard.

"Yes. The EMTs."

Roelke began tapping his pencil against the desk again. Thanks, Skeet, he muttered silently. Roelke was pretty sure that Skeet would rather fight the flu than the fire department.

Who'd been on that night? Denise Miller, for starters—one of the best. But the other responders, too ... both of them were good guys, experienced, caring and careful. With his best *I'm here to help you* expression in place, Roelke gave Mrs. Saddler an encouraging nod. "All right, ma'am," he said, reaching for his notebook. "Tell me what happened."

FIFTEEN

THE ARCHIVES ON WASHINGTON Island were extensive and superbly organized. When Chloe explained her project, the elderly volunteer on duty beamed. "You'll find lots of relevant resources," he assured her.

Chloe dug a pencil and notebook from her daypack. "I thought I'd start with the Betts family." She hoped this kind gentleman wouldn't ask why she wasn't starting with Pottawatomie's earliest keepers.

He did not. "We've got a Betts file," he said. "They lived on Washington Island after they left Rock, you know."

"Actually, I didn't."

The man pulled a gray archival file box from a shelf and extracted a file. "Here you go."

Chloe accepted it eagerly. She wanted a portrait of Emily Betts while she lived at Pottawatomie Lighthouse. She wanted Emily Betts' diary.

She didn't get them. The file mostly contained genealogical re-cords and newspaper clippings. The only image was a smudgy photocopy of a snapshot of Emily and William that must have been taken near the end of William's life. Emily had white hair and wire-framed glasses. Chloe stared at the picture, trying to find the whisper of recognition she'd felt when she saw the photo of Emily at the lighthouse.

Zip.

With a sigh Chloe put that page aside. The next item was an obituary from 1950:

PIONEER DIES

Emily Betts, one of Door County's oldest residents and daugh-ter of a pioneer family herself, died of old age. Born on Octo-ber 12, 1854, she came to Washington Island with her parents in 1866. Her father was the lightkeeper at Pilot Island light in Death's Door passage and her mother was assistant lighthouse keeper.

So, Chloe thought. You knew the life well.

On Sept. 29, 1871, she married William C. Betts and the couple became caretakers of the Rock Island light. Their first children were born there, and Mrs. Betts often told stories of the hard-ships endured by early lightkeepers.

Chloe pinched her lips together in frustration. Stories! she thought. I want the stories! The obituary mentioned only one:

On severely bitter winter nights, Mrs. Betts had to carry pans of hot lard to the lamps, which had congealed with the cold. There were ninety steps to the lantern tower, and she made the climb many times a day and throughout the night. This continued for ten years, until the fuel was switched to kerosene.

Chloe sat back. Seriously? *Lard?* Geez Louise.

During their seventeen years at the light, Emily taught their children and some of the island children as well. After moving to Jackson Harbor, on Washington Island, Emily served as a nurse for thirty years.

"Finding what you need?" the archivist asked. "Shall I pull the files on the other lightkeepers?"

"Unfortunately, I'm running out of time," Chloe said regretfully. "I want to make a phone call before catching the last *Karfi* run back to Rock."

"Well, there's a pay phone outside the library," the gentleman said cheerfully. "Come back any time."

The archives and public library shared a roof, so Chloe had no trouble finding the pay phone. Then she hesitated. Hadn't she wanted to be incommunicado this week? And I still mostly do, she told herself. She just wanted to make a quick professional call. That didn't count.

And she got lucky. After dialing Old World Wisconsin's number and getting transferred, her intern picked up the phone.

"Nika? It's me."

"What's up? I thought you were immersed in lighthouse stuff."

"I am. The lighthouse is very cool. Two of the assistant keepers were women."

"Excellent."

"But there was a fishing village on the island as well. My time is tight, and I was wondering if—"

"You want me to do some research?" Nika asked. She was a cut-to-the-chase kind of woman.

"Yeah," Chloe admitted. She watched a middle-aged woman negotiate the library door with an armful of romance novels. "I talked with an archaeologist who's surveying the village site, Brenda Noakes. She knows a lot about Rock Island history, but she got a little… intense when I mentioned a lit-up barge I saw north of the island last night. Her interest seems professional, so I'm wondering if there's something going on I don't know about."

"You think it's relevant to your lighthouse project?"

"I don't know, and Brenda wouldn't say." Chloe nodded politely to an elderly couple as they passed. "But the lighthouse families were members of the island community. I'd like to know as much as I can before I identify interpretive themes for the building."

Chloe could picture her intern on the other end, scribbling notes, eyes narrowed like a cat catching scent of a prey. Nika was a tenacious researcher. Normally Chloe would never ask a colleague to spend time on an extraneous project, but she knew Nika would welcome the challenge.

"I'll see what I can find out," Nika said. "How can I reach you?"

"You can't," Chloe said. "I'll try to catch you. Thanks. Oh, and Nika? Has the auditors' report come in?" Earlier that summer Old

World Wisconsin had been audited, likely prompted by certain politicians' attempts to privatize the state's historic sites.

"Nope."

"Good." When quizzed on curatorial procedures Chloe had done her best, but she wasn't sure how auditors would portray collections care. "Thanks, Nika. Talk to you soon."

As Chloe hung up she smiled automatically at another passing library patron. He walked two more steps before turning around. "Miss Ellefson?"

"Oh—hi!" Chloe blinked at Deputy Stig Fjelstul, standing with an armload of hardcovers. *The Color Purple*, Isabel Allende's *The House of the Spirits, Of Time and Place* by Sigurd Olson… no wonder Fjelstul popped words like "convivial" and "ascertain" into casual conversation.

"I thought you were working at the lighthouse," he said.

"I came over to check out the archives. I was also hoping to run into you, actually. Has the girl who drowned been identified yet?"

He shifted his books from one arm to the other. "No."

"I found a little cairn on the beach where the body was. Somebody made a letter **N** out of pebbles. I told Garrett, and he took pictures."

"Hunh." Fjelstul rubbed his chin.

His expression so reminded Chloe of Roelke that she felt a visceral twinge inside. She hoped Roelke wasn't worrying about her. Maybe I should try to call him tomorrow, she thought. Just to say hi. But… no. Not a good idea. A quick call would seem superficial, and she didn't have time or energy for anything more involved—

"Miss Ellefson?"

Chloe blinked, realizing the deputy had spoken her name more than once. "Sorry."

"Can I offer you dinner?"

Dinner? Chloe felt her eyebrows rise. Was this a friendly offer? A chance to undertake a more detailed interview? A date? "I, um, don't have time," she stammered. "I've got to catch the last *Karfi.*"

"I've got a boat," Fjelstul said. "I'll run you back to Rock later."

Chloe couldn't think of any gracious way to decline. "Well... OK, Deputy. Thanks. I accept."

"Call me Stig," he said. "C'mon. Let's go."

The drive from library to restaurant took Chloe and Stig about ninety seconds. "We're headed for Nelsen's Hall," he said, gesturing as they passed a yellow building with green roof. "I leave the close parking spots to the drunks." He drove for another half mile before parking his pickup in the shade of an old oak.

"Good food?" Chloe asked, as they walked back to the hall.

"Yes, but I thought you'd appreciate the ambiance even more," he said. An actual smile tugged at the corners of his mouth. "An immigrant named Tom Nelsen built the tavern in the nineteenth century."

"My kind of place."

Noise drifted from the building as they approached—raised voices, laughter. Stig held the door, following Chloe inside. Three young women were lounging at the bar, chattering with the bartender who stood beneath a sign which read *Absolutely No Alcoholic Beverages In This Building.*

Half a dozen men in work clothes, beers in hand, were playing pool in the back corner. They were razzing a middle-aged guy's lousy shot as Chloe and Stig approached, but that cheerful din died. The pool players fell silent one by one, treating the newcomers with flat stares or hostile glares.

What the hell? I've only been here for two days, Chloe thought. I can't have pissed anyone off already. Then she flashed on Maintenance Mel spitting on the ground when she mentioned Stig Fjelstul.

Stig muttered, "shall we leave?"

Chloe lifted her chin. "No." These yahoos weren't going to cheat her out of a good meal.

"The dining room's this way." Stig led her past the men and on to a corner table in a spacious dining room, out of sight of the pool table.

A cheerful waitress, her short black hair streaked with light blue, put menus on the table. "Something to drink?" She looked at Stig. "Bitters?"

"Iced tea for me tonight," he said. "But Miss Ellefson may want to join the club."

Chloe wasn't sure she wanted to join any club that had Deputy Stig Fjelstul on the roster. "Well..."

"It's a tradition," he told her. "Old Tom Nelsen lived to be ninety, and he drank a pint of Angostura Bitters every day. The stuff is about ninety proof. During Prohibition, he got a pharmacist's license and sold bitters as a stomach tonic."

"Nelsen's Hall is the longest-running legally operating tavern in Wisconsin," the waitress added. "And we sell more bitters than anyone else in the world."

"Well then, sure," Chloe said with reckless abandon. She wasn't driving, and this was historical tradition, after all. Besides, she *had* found a body two days ago. That was surely worth a shot of something. She opted for supper from the salad bar, and her companion ordered the grilled whitefish special.

"I'll be right back with your drinks," the waitress promised.

Chloe leaned back in her chair, surveying the dining room. A huge cobblestone fireplace filled one corner. The wait station was decorated with smaller kitchen implements, a hutch of antique tobacco tins, and century-old portraits in gorgeous wooden frames displayed below the ceiling. Antique tools hung on walls made from mortar and the butt-ends of logs. "Stovewood construction," she murmured. "Very cool."

"Glad you like it."

"So." Chloe cocked her head in the direction of the pool players. "What was that about?"

"I shouldn't have brought you in through the bar." Stig studied his thumbnail. "Don't worry. Those men won't tar you with my brush."

"And they want to tar you … why, exactly?"

He leaned back in his chair, his face settling into hard lines. "I'll try to make a long story short. I grew up on Washington Island. My ancestors arrived on Rock Island in the 1840s. Those first white settlers learned how to fish from the local Pottawatomie people. They'd been subsistence-fishing for centuries, but our people wanted to fish commercially and make some money."

"And so it ever goes," Chloe sighed.

"My own people have fished these waters commercially for a hundred and thirty years. Protecting the fisheries today presents complex challenges. Fish populations have their own natural cycles. Invasive species have wreaked havoc with the natives. Pollution has been creeping north from Green Bay, changing the lake ecology. And lately, wealthy weekend warriors have pressured the DNR to make regulations that favor sport fishing over commercial fishing."

Chloe was silent. She wasn't eager to plunge into local politics and law enforcement issues, even vicariously.

"In the 1950s, over forty fish tugs worked out of Washington Island," Stig was saying. "Whitefish and herring were still doing pretty good, but trout were almost gone. By the mid-sixties, we were down to about half a dozen fisheries, and the herring had disappeared."

"Sounds like hard times."

"I told you I used to be a game warden." He began making tiny tears along one edge of the white paper placemat positioned over the maroon tablecloth. "All of a sudden I was policing guys I'd known all my life. Friends of my dad's. Guys I grew up playing baseball with. It didn't sit well with some folks."

"Surely people understand that you just had a job to do…?"

"Ain't that simple," he began, stopping when the waitress appeared with a round tray. She put a shot glass of bitters, dark with a reddish tint, in front of Chloe.

Stig gave her a tired smile. "Toss 'er down."

Chloe did. Just as she thought *Not so bad*, she felt a mild burn inside her nose. "It's very… bitter," she said.

The waitress used the bitters dregs to make a thumbprint in the corner of a membership card. "Sign this, and you're officially a member of the Bitters Club," she instructed. That done, she handed Chloe a leather-bound notebook to sign as well. Chloe dutifully added her name to the roster. "Truly wretched stuff," someone had scribbled. The next scrawl said, "I'll party to the bitter end."

Stig picked up a packet of sugar, flapped it twice, and emptied it into his tea. "Two years ago the Michigan DNR banned all gillnet rigs, which made the sport fishermen very happy. People are afraid the same thing will happen here."

"Do you think it will?"

"I hope not, but in addition to the push to eliminate gillnets, new regulations are becoming law all the time." He held up his index finger. "First, limited entry. That's designed to limit the number of commercial licenses and drive out part-timers. You know Mel Jenks, at the park? He fishes part-time and is probably about to get squeezed out. I suspect that's why he took the maintenance job."

And I suspect that's why he spits at the mention of a former warden's name, Chloe thought. She tried not to squirm in her chair. She really did not want to be in the middle of this.

"Two." Stig ticked off another finger. "New geographic restrictions have designated lake zones for commercial fishing, sport fishing, recreational use, and rehabilitation."

That sounded reasonable, but Chloe understood that people would scream about any new exclusion.

"Three. For years men were able to catch chubs with a two and a half-inch mesh, but now…"

Oh my, Chloe thought, as her companion pontificated about nets and "flexible rule measure," etc., etc. She felt her eyes glazing over and tried to tune back in. Deputy Fjelstul clearly needed to talk. The least she could do was listen

"And four. Quotas have been established, and certain fish have been excluded from commercial fishing altogether. In theory, that makes sense. But it's now illegal for a commercial fisherman to take a trout, period. Now, I don't begrudge the sportsmen from having fun on the lake. I enjoy pulling in a trout or salmon as much as the next guy. But that kind of extreme is ridiculous."

Chloe could hear the rising agitation in Stig's voice. Dinner better be good. Stig was an even more effective enchantment-buster than Brenda.

He took off his glasses and rubbed the bridge of his nose. "Almost all of the commercial fishermen I know are good men, honest, just trying to earn a living. Same thing for most of the game wardens I know. But all it takes is a couple of fishermen who think they're above the law…"

"To give everyone a bad name."

"Right. And we've had a couple of embarrassing incidents with over-zealous wardens. One warden set up a sting and actually coerced a fisherman to go find trout. Another time a warden seized some dead trout a fisherman had tagged and was bringing in, as the law requires. Then the warden sold them to a restaurant, even though the fish were over twenty-four inches long!"

"Um…"

"Twenty-four inches is the max for public consumption. Too many PCBs build up in the older fish."

OK, Chloe thought. I'm on the brink of getting profoundly bummed. Fortunately the waitress interrupted, bringing Stig's food. Chloe hit the salad bar. Yahoo! Veggies, fruit, cottage cheese, potato and pasta salads… all much more inviting than her freeze-dried stash at the lighthouse.

When she sat back down, Stig picked up where he'd left off. "This is a way of life that gets handed down, one generation to the next. My older brother fishes with my dad and my eight-year-old nephew. Nobody wants to protect the fish populations more than the men who earn their living with nets."

"But…"

"But laws get made for a reason. And someone needs to monitor the populations."

Chloe was glad she worked with inanimate objects. How did people in law enforcement cope with so many people, so much bad energy, day after day? Roelke loved being a cop. But then again, he was generally tautly wired. How much of that came from genetic roulette, and how much from the job?

Chloe stabbed a cherry tomato with her fork. And how had she ended up having supper with a deputy sheriff, talking about law enforcement, thinking about Roelke McKenna?

Deputy Fjelstul said, "When I started working for the DNR, I thought I had the best job in the world. Once things with the fishing industry got so riled up, though… I was just doing my job, but—hell." He shrugged. "I got tired of hearing people I worked with condemn all commercial fishermen, and tired of hearing friends and family speak of me and my colleagues with loathing."

"Loathing? Is it really that bad?"

"Tempers are flaring. And not too long back a fisherman died of a stroke a few hours after he got arrested for having an illegal trout. Evert was only forty-nine years old." Stig rubbed his temples with his thumbs. "That's when I quit the DNR."

Chloe regarded him. "Do you think someone might get hurt?"

"Get hurt?" Stig blinked, as if surprised to discover an audience. "*No.* And if I seemed to suggest that, I beg your pardon."

"Everything OK?" the waitress asked. She turned to Chloe. "Want another bitters?"

"No thanks. I'll stick with water from here on."

Stig gestured at the empty shot glass. "Now you're a true islander."

No, *you* are a true islander, Chloe thought. She felt sad.

"Listen," Stig said, "I shouldn't have dumped on you like that. All this trouble will settle down again. People have been arguing about fishing regulations for over a century."

"Really? That long?"

"Sure. Same as anywhere else. Wardens are caught between bear hunters and environmentalists in Alaska. Trappers and tree-huggers in the northwest."

"I suppose." Chloe nibbled a slice of cucumber.

"My college roommate works Fish and Game in Louisiana. A gator hunter took a potshot at him one morning last week. The same afternoon he had to arrest this group of crazy kids camping illegally in the swamp, all in the name of protecting the alligators. They were lucky they didn't get eaten." He took a long swig of tea. "Every one of them had a weird name. Lotus, Zilpha, Rainbow—stuff like that."

"Well," Chloe said judiciously, "I'm not sure someone named Stig Fjelstul has much room to criticize in *that* regard." She ate another tomato.

He looked startled. Then he threw his head back and laughed. "You got me there."

"My first name is Ingrid," she told him. "Every Scandinavian name in the book shows up somewhere on my family tree. I'm just sayin.'"

"God, I'm turning into a curmudgeon." He chuckled again, and dug back into his filet.

Chloe was glad she'd been able to make him laugh. She wasn't always good with people. She would count this as a small victory.

SIXTEEN:
SEPTEMBER, 1875

"ANDERS," RAGNA SAID. "DON'T go with the other men tonight."

Anders shaved a curl from the float he was carving. "Of course I'm going! We stand together."

Ragna bit her lip and turned back to the wet net she was over-hauling—pulling it over a pole, spreading the mesh. Anders had caught some trout with the whitefish, and their sharp teeth had torn jagged holes she'd need to repair. The kitchen had a steamy wet weed smell.

"Mama, look!" Paul cried. He'd built a wall from cedar blocks.

Ragna kissed the top of his head. "Well done! Can you add an-other row without them falling?" She waited until the three-year-old had returned to his task before lowering her voice again. "An-ders … we need to talk about leaving Rock Island. More and more of our neighbors are moving over to Washington. We could farm."

"I'm a fisherman."

"You haven't always been a fisherman," she reminded him. "When we came here, our plan was to fish just until we'd earned enough money to buy land."

"It was," Anders admitted. "But after being on the water…" He shook his head. "I can't be tied down by potatoes."

Ragna had known this. She'd seen the change in him, seen his spirit soar. "We can still move to Washington. You can fish from Jackson Harbor. I just…" She picked out a snarl. "This past winter was so difficult." It had been the coldest and longest in anyone's memory, sometimes forty degrees below zero." Worst of all, once the shipping season had ended the Betts family moved to Washington Island for the winter. They'd be gone until the ice left the channel in May.

A small crash interrupted her thoughts. Paul stared at his tumbled blocks with dismay. "Start again," Ragna suggested.

Anders got up and poured himself a cup of coffee. "It is no small thing to move," he said over his shoulder.

Ragna knew that, too. She'd come to love this little cottage surrounded with Danish flowers, the shady woods, the gentle beach.

But Carrick Dugan had become more than a nuisance. Last year, Anders found his nets slashed. A few months ago, the oars left in his Mackinaw disappeared overnight. Dugan never tried the same trick twice, and months might pass without trouble. As more people moved away from Rock, though, the shadow cast by Dugan's temper seemed to darken.

"We once moved from Denmark to the New World," she reminded Anders, "so we can surely manage a move across the channel! There are deeper harbors at Washington. You could get a bigger boat. Or get set with pound nets." Several of their neighbors had switched to pound nets, which corralled fish instead of snaring them, and were set close to shore. No more days spent rowing hour after hour.

"We can't afford a bigger boat." Anders shrugged.

Ragna felt a tiny kick inside, and she placed a palm over her swelling belly. Hush now, little one, she whispered silently to her unborn child. All is well.

Except all *wasn't* well. "I want to get away from Dugan," she admitted at last.

Anders came to her and pulled her into the protective net of his arms. "There is nothing to fear. Dugan struggles through life because he's lazy and ill-tempered."

Ragna pressed her face against her husband's chest. She could hear his heart beating. "They are not always idle threats. Who knows what he'll do next? Perhaps you can ask a sheriff to make Dugan leave."

"I wish I could." Anders sighed. "I want my sons and grandsons to find as many fish as I do, and Dugan is unwilling to fish with an eye to the future. But I can't publicly accuse him of anything without proof." He cupped her face in his rough hands. "All will be well."

Ragna turned away. She hadn't told Anders of the times Dugan had watched her, or made vague but personal threats. She was afraid of what Anders might do.

Her brother Jens opened the door and poked his head inside the cabin. "It's time."

"Anders, please don't do this," Ragna begged.

"It is decided."

Jens added, "Besides, it was your idea!"

103

"It didn't occur to me that you men would actually—"

"Dugan has no concern for anyone but himself." Anders reached for his hat and slapped it on his head. "We need to teach him a lesson."

Jens gave her a little shrug before disappearing. Anders followed, closing the door firmly behind him.

Ragna got back to work on the net—always a net—and tried to think of nothing but tangles and twine. It was no good, though. Finally she grabbed her son's jacket from its peg. "Come along, Paul," she said. "We're going for a walk."

She draped her heavy shawl over her head and shoulders, took Paul's hand, and slipped into a cold, cloudy night. Once her eyes adjusted to the darkness they silently made their way through the village, down to the beach. The men worked silently but she had no trouble spotting them, black shadows against the gray-black sky. If she hadn't seen them, the stench would have given them away.

Ragna looked in the direction of Dugan's cabin, at the village's south end. You brought this on yourself, she told him. Everyone agreed that fish offal must be disposed of well away from the beach. Only Dugan left bloody entrails wherever he wished, ignoring polite requests that he clean up after himself.

Ragna had been walking along the beach with her family two evenings earlier when Paul had slipped on a pile of guts and fallen. "I'd like to fill that man's boat with entrails!" Ragna had snapped, as she tried to comfort her son—and swipe the worst of the mess from his trousers. She'd barely noticed Jens' grin, and the contemplative look that passed between her men.

Tonight Rock Island's fishermen were taking action. When Dugan came to his Mackinaw boat in the morning, he would find it full of rotting, stinking fish guts.

Anders and her brothers seemed to believe that would fix the problem. Ragna was sure that the fouling of Dugan's boat would only make matters worse.

SEVENTEEN

"COME BACK AGAIN," THE waitress told Chloe as she cleared their plates. "As Tom Nelsen used to say, 'You're a stranger here but once.'"

After paying the bill, Stig and Chloe left via the main door and strolled back to his truck. The crack of a bat against baseball and excited cheers drifted from a nearby field. "So," she said, "you commute to Sturgeon Bay every day? That's gotta get old."

"Yeah." He shoved his hands in his pockets. "And giving speeding tickets and negotiating domestic disputes isn't nearly as much fun as working out in the woods and on the lake." His voice was wistful. "Technically I'm on vacation, although that went out the window when that call came in from Rock. I was the closest man available to investigate, so..." He abruptly stopped walking.

"What?" Chloe asked. Then a putrid smell smacked her in the face. They'd almost reached his truck.

"Those sons of bitches," he muttered.

"What *is* that?"

Stig's face settled back into hard planes as he surveyed the bloody, stringy mess on top of the cab and draping the windows. "Fish guts."

———

"Thanks again," Chloe said an hour later, when Stig docked at the pier below the Viking Hall on Rock Island.

"Don't worry," Stig said. "I won't ask you to be seen in public with me again."

She made a point of catching his eye. "I wouldn't hesitate. No more bitters for me, though. I'll leave that pleasure to the next tourist."

His lips twitched in a faint semblance of a smile. As Chloe stepped to the dock she remembered the one genuine laugh she'd wrested from him. That unguarded Stig Fjelstul was gone again.

That is one lonely man, she thought as she watched his boat head back toward Washington Island. At least when she confronted human misery and vice, the people involved were—for the most part—long dead.

Turning, she considered the Viking Hall which loomed above the dock. Sylvie Torgrimsson had mentioned historical exhibits inside. Well, here I am, Chloe thought. She had a couple of hours of daylight left.

In Chester Thordarson's day, boats could putter through two arches made of quarried stone and dock beneath the building, depositing travelers beside an interior staircase. Chloe poked her head into the watery catacombs: dim, dank, and empty. Then she circled outside to enter the building from the east.

Even Chloe, not generally impressed by displays of grandeur, stopped short. Thordarson's great Icelandic Viking Hall was magnificent. High arched windows provided plenty of natural light and views of the channel. Most of the furnishings were original. A runic inscription had been carved into a huge mantel, reminding her of Brenda Noakes' comments about archaeologists' search for evidence of early Viking travel through the Great Lakes.

Thordarson had also commissioned a set of oak furniture intricately carved with scenes from Norse mythology. Chloe knew the story of Odin… and here was Njörd, god of boats and fishermen, relaxing while roasting his catch over an open fire.

The panel on the next chair depicted a man rowing a boat on waves that held within their frothy curls the faces of several young women. Chloe checked a handy guidebook left available for visitors and learned that Aegir and his wife, Ran, ruled the sea. According to legend, Ran pulled drowning men into the depths of the sea with her net. She, Aegir, and their daughters lived in a great hall of their own, illuminated by the gold she stole from sunken ships.

"I really wish I hadn't read that," Chloe muttered, trying to dispel the image of the body she'd found on the beach, wrapped in a net. Enough with the mythical gods.

Chloe found a small corner room which contained exhibits about Thordarson. She admired the man's scientific accomplishments, but skipped over displays about energy transmission grids and volts and transformers. Other stories, while not germane to her project, were more interesting—a sad story about a workman who drowned while rowing from Rock Island back to Washington; a funny one about Thordarson not finding a single deer when he swept the island with a gun crew, determined to kill the animals that habitually nibbled his garden ornamentals. And she lingered beside a female mannequin adorned with the traditional Icelandic dress Thordarson's wife, Juliana, had worn on their wedding day. "I'd like to know more about you," Chloe murmured to the long-dead woman. "Chester seems to get all the attention."

Then she discovered a set of letters Chester and Juliana had exchanged with friends and relatives in Iceland. The originals were framed with typed translations—a clever presentation that allowed visitors to gaze on historical documents and still quickly discover what the Thordarsons had found newsworthy. Chloe waded in eagerly, hoping that Chester and Juliana had taken an interest in the lighthouse on the far end of their island.

Half a dozen pages later, she found a letter of Juliana's that had nothing to do with the lighthouse—but stopped her nonetheless.

The carpenters are finishing updates on another of the fishing cottages, and soon it will be available for guests. One of the men brought his grandchildren to Rock today. "My people lived on Rock," he told me. "It's nice for the little ones to play in the meadow and along the beach while I work." When I stopped by this afternoon to check on the progress, a little girl came skipping to meet me. She clutched my hand and in charming fashion proceeded to give me a tour. After pointing out this and that, she concluded, "And this is the house where the murder was."

Chloe leaned closer. The murder?

As you can imagine, I was taken aback! "You mean the man with the gold coins?" I asked, for we've heard that tale many times. "Oh, no," the waif said solemnly. "The other murder. I heard Mrs. Betts tell Grandmama that—"

Chloe vibrated like a leashed hound. Mrs. Betts! *Emily* Betts? This letter was dated 1921, during the period when Emily was living in Jackson Harbor. It *had* to be Emily.

At that juncture, the child's grandfather hurried forward and hustled her away. When I questioned him, the man politely refused to provide anything further. "Don't listen to a child's fanciful tales," he said. Gudrun, you can likely imagine that I wanted to do just that! The man stood firm, however, so I am forced to let my own imagination conjure what details it may.

The carpenter may not have wanted to upset his employers with unsavory tales, Chloe thought, but still, there was probably at least a kernel of truth in the child's story. The reference to Mrs. Betts conversing with her grandmama was too specific to attribute to a child's whimsy.

That implied that a second murder had taken place on long-ago Rock Island. A murder in the fishing village. A murder Emily Betts had discussed years later. What had *that* been about? A marital affair gone wrong, a theft, some petty squabble that exploded in an alcoholic rage? Chloe agreed with Juliana—it was unfortunate the child's grandfather had intervened when he did.

Odd, Chloe thought, that Brenda hadn't mentioned that tale. The archaeologist had clearly worked through the archival material left by the Thordarsons, but she'd regaled Chloe with the tale of what she called Rock Island's *only* murder victim—the hapless James McNeil, who'd bragged about his gold coins and gotten killed for them.

Chloe stared blindly out a window. Maybe Brenda cared more about finding remnants of everyday life in the fishing village than some sordid tale preserved in oral tradition. Or, maybe she had some hidden agenda. The woman seemed as tightly wound as … well, as Roelke could be when he was focused on solving some crime.

Although Chloe skimmed through the remaining correspondence, she didn't find any other juicy tidbits. As she left the Viking Hall she squinted at the sky. The sun was sinking, but she was pretty sure she had enough time to visit the fishing village site again.

She hit the trail that cut straight across the island at a jog. Her heart was pounding by the time she emerged from the trees. After a short but sharp ascent she felt a sudden lake-scented breeze cool against her skin. The meadow where she'd met Brenda looked deserted.

It is so peaceful here, Chloe thought, as she paused to catch her breath. That whimsical sense of enchantment returned as she wandered toward the beach. When she reached the rise above the shore she sat down by a wild grapevine studded with tiny fruit. Not much to them but she munched some anyway, spitting seeds, soaking in the view. Empty lake, empty beach. It wasn't difficult to imagine this landscape as it had been a century or more before.

Chloe let herself become still, open to a faint sense of busyness that lingered in this now-serene place. She could almost see the cottages built of weathered-silver boards, and cabins with dark logs and stone chimneys; the cooper shops and fish sheds; the dock extending into the lake; Mackinaw boats pulled up on shore, nets drying, barrels of fish and stacks of cordwood waiting for the next trading vessel. It all seemed so real.

EIGHTEEN:
NOVEMBER, 1875

AFTER A WEEK OF gray skies, a feeble sun turned the snow to slush. And after a week of terrible morning sickness, Ragna felt well enough to tackle heavy chores. She hauled enough water to fill her outdoor cauldron, built a fire, and gathered the nets Anders had brought home the day before. She frequently scalded the nets to remove slime. She dyed them with walnut bark, too. Light nets startled the fish. Only the laziest fishermen left their nets pale.

"Always the nets," Ragna muttered. Knitting, dying, mending, boiling, reeling, weighting, packing. She tried to think of every net she handled as getting her one step closer to a *hygge* family farm on Washington Island.

With the nets simmering, Ragna pulled on her thick mittens. Winter was descending fast. Soon Anders would be ice-fishing. She hoped that brought her men better luck, for the autumn lifts had been poor. Their take was down. Everyone's was.

It troubled everyone. "Regulate mesh on the gillnets," Anders said, over and over. "A small change can affect which fish pass through, which get caught." He was relieved when such a new law was finally passed. Changing mesh size meant the making of new nets—no small undertaking. But most of the men had sons to leave their rigs and gear to. No one wanted to see the fish disappear.

Ragna had knit net after net—for her own men, and then for most of the fishermen left on the island. She'd never been busier. Never tucked more coins into the pouch kept beneath the mattress.

And surely soon, she thought, we'll have enough set by to satisfy even Anders. They could buy land on Washington—near the Betts' place, if she was lucky. They'd raise cows and potatoes, and Anders could still slip away to be on the water.

Ragna had just finished feeding the last gillnet into the cauldron of steaming water when she felt Dugan's presence. She went still, leaning over the kettle, sweat beading on her skin. A cloud seemed to sail over the sun. The wren which had been warbling a mighty serenade flitted away.

Before turning around she casually picked up the stout piece of oak she used as a stir-stick. Dugan stood beneath a tree with hands in his pockets. Watching, just watching. He wore filthy trousers and a heavy wool sweater that needed darning. It was difficult to see his eyes beneath the cap he'd pulled down low on his forehead. Little weasel eyes, she thought. He'd be a handsome man if he cleaned up and taught himself to smile.

She loaded her voice with ice. "Yes, Mr. Dugan?"

"I know your man filled my boat."

"No! It was all of them—"

His eyes narrowed. "It was your man at the lead. You both have always wanted to make trouble."

"We *don't*."

"Trouble," Dugan insisted. "It has a way of lying in wait, and creeping up—" He slapped the tree trunk, and Ragna jumped— "just when you least expect it."

Ragna's heart pounded beneath her ribs like a cooper's mallet. "I want you to leave."

"Well, I want a lot of things. A good haul of whitefish. A little company." Dugan let his gaze dip below her face.

As she tightened her grip on the oak stick, a roar came from behind her. Anders flew at Dugan. The two men went down beneath the cedars, tussling, grunting. Anders was bigger than Dugan, and overpowered him quickly with one good punch to the jaw.

Then Anders scrambled to his feet, panting. "We've had enough," he barked. "If you ever threaten my wife again I'll—"

"You'll what?" Dugan sneered. He got up more slowly and stood with feet braced, clearly ready for another round.

Anders' big hands clenched. "Get *out* of here."

Dugan eyed him for a long moment, as if to say *You don't frighten me.* Then he slowly swaggered away. Before disappearing, though, he paused and looked over his shoulder at Ragna. She involuntarily pressed one hand over her pounding heart.

Anders muttered a Danish oath. "I'll let no man live who threatens my wife. And you with child! I'll—"

"Let him go." Ragna laced her fingers through his. "*Please*, Anders. He wants to provoke you by being discourteous to me."

"Discourteous is hardly the right word! I'm going to fetch your brothers."

"Anders!" She tightened her grip, anchoring him. "We need to talk to Anton. Or maybe Mr. Betts." The closest lawman was in Green Bay, but Emily's husband was a government official. Someone needed to intervene before Anders did something that would land *him* in jail.

Anders stood for a long moment. Ragna could feel his quivering rage. Please, please, she asked silently—not sure if she was beseeching her husband, or God. Don't let this get worse.

Finally Anders drew a deep breath. "I'm sorry he spoke to you so, Ragna. You're right. We need to involve the law." He patted her hand. "Don't worry, my love. I was coming to tell you—this morning I found something we can use to send a sheriff after Dugan."

She felt a ray of hope. "What?"

"I don't want you to worry anymore," Anders said. "Your condition is unsettling you. Soon you'll have another baby to tend, and you'll be happier."

Ragna wanted to stamp her foot. Her pregnancy had nothing to do with her feelings about Dugan. "But—"

"I'll take care of Dugan, one way or another."

Ragna's hope disappeared. "One way or another?" she repeated sharply. "What does that mean?"

"Mama?" Paul had appeared in the open cottage door, looking sleepy. He'd been napping.

She sighed, rubbing an ache in the small of her back. "I'm coming," she told her son. She didn't want Paul to hear his parents argue. She'd let Anders' cryptic comment go ... for now.

NINETEEN

"Hey, Chloe!"

Chloe jerked from her reverie. Sometimes her imagination was too vivid. Was that another sign of developing perceptive abilities? Lovely, she thought as she lifted a hand to greet Brenda Noakes, who was walking through the tall grass.

"I didn't mean to startle you," Brenda added. She sat down on the ground beside Chloe.

"I was lost in thought," Chloe admitted. "It's easy to imagine what it might have been like here."

A breeze blew a strand of hair into Brenda's face, and she shoved it behind her ear. "It surely is."

They sat in silence. Chloe thought about asking Brenda about Juliana Thordarson's letter, but decided against it—she wasn't sure how Brenda would respond, and she didn't want to spoil a companionable moment. Instead she said, "Seems like the lighthouse and the Viking Hall get most of the attention. How did you get interested in the fishing village?"

Brenda plucked a piece of grass and idly flicked seeds from the stem with her thumb. "Some of my ancestors lived here. My father's people were Yankees from Illinois, but one of my mom's grandmas, Berglind Fridleifsdottir, came here from Iceland with her husband."

"Cool."

Brenda glanced at her thoughtfully, then looked away. "I don't mention this often, but… want to know what's really cool? When I was seventeen, I was wading off the beach there one day and I found a netting needle."

Chloe's forehead wrinkled. "A netting needle?"

"They're sort of like shuttles, flat, about this long." Brenda held her hands about six inches apart. "Used to make or repair nets. This one was really old, and whoever carved it added some decorative flourishes. One side is incomplete, though. I imagine someone dropped it before finishing the design."

"Oh my gosh!" Chloe exclaimed. "Maybe one of your ancestors made that very piece." Hey, it was possible.

"Could be, I suppose." Brenda shrugged. "I've always been drawn to this place. My grandmother worked for Chester Thordarson, and sometimes my family was invited here for picnics. When I was in high school a few of us used to sneak over sometimes."

"By boat, you mean?"

"No." Brenda looked sheepish. "A reef runs from near Jackson Harbor on Washington Island over to the southeast end of Rock. Most years you get wet maybe to your knees or waist, at the deepest spot. But there are bad currents out there, and waves can form without warning. The passage can be deadly for people trying to walk or even paddle across."

Chloe remembered Garrett complimenting Tim and Natalie for having enough sense to wait out the wind before venturing into the passage. "I heard something about that."

"People don't realize that Lake Michigan is a single ecosystem. A bad thunderstorm in Escanaba affects conditions here. You get current going one way over the reef, and wind going the other—the water just boils. And the reef itself is deceptively serpentine. The rangers tell people not to even consider crossing it. Too damn dangerous. But we were kids, and stupid."

Chloe thought back to a few of her more idiotic adolescent moments. "When I was thirteen, my sister's boyfriend said he'd give me a dollar if I jumped off the roof of a tobacco barn. I might have done it if his mother hadn't seen me start the climb and come running."

"That poor girl who drowned and washed ashore was probably doing something stupid. Drinking tequila and going skinny-dipping, for example."

"Yeah," Chloe said. She really didn't want to talk about the dead girl. "Say, can I ask you about something? Do you know Stig Fjelstul?"

"Sure."

Of course she did. "He was telling me earlier today about conflicts between commercial fishermen and the DNR."

Brenda picked up a pebble and tossed it down the slope. "Yeah. It's sad, but nothing new. I live in Michigan, and the commercial fishermen up there really got screwed."

"So I heard."

"Was it right to completely ban gillnets?" Brenda spread her hands. "I honestly don't know. But people were fighting about fishing regulations back in Berglind's day. I don't suppose that will ever change."

"Do you think things could get violent? The situation is obviously weighing on Garrett's mind. He brought it up the day I arrived. And Stig really seemed torqued up." Chloe hesitated. "And isolated."

"I suppose so."

Chloe wasn't sure what else to say. Leave the problems for the people born and raised here, she told herself. She had all she could handle with the furnishings report.

Brenda wiped her hands on her jeans and stood. "Well, my boat's docked over at the main landing, and my dad's expecting me for dinner on Washington. He's still milking, bless his heart, and I like to help with chores."

"Have a good evening," Chloe called, and watched the archaeologist walk back to the trail. She was glad she'd run into Brenda, who'd seemed more friendly—less prickly—than on their first meeting. Maybe I *should* have asked Brenda about that letter from Juliana, she thought. Well, next time.

Chloe got to her feet—she needed to get going too. She did want to see the beach before hiking north, though. She skirted a shrubby grove of trees at the south edge of the meadow, looking for a path to the water, and was surprised to emerge suddenly into one of the remote campsites—a familiar one. The last time she'd been here, she'd been weak-kneed with relief to find kayakers Tim and Natalie. Now the site was empty.

Well, almost. A bouquet of asters and goldenrod, tied with a piece of twine, had been left behind to shrivel. You're not supposed to pick flowers in a state park, Chloe thought, but her mental rebuke was only mild. As she imagined Tim picking flowers for Natalie, Chloe felt a pinch of loneliness. It had been a long time since anyone had surprised her with a bouquet of wildflowers.

Get over it, she told herself. She was happy to be right here, right now. She really was.

After descending to the beach, Chloe picked her way along the cobbled crescent, imagining life as it had once been. She wasn't naïve enough to think of the past as "the good old days." The fishing families had lived daily with hard work and danger, and yet... if they felt mostly contented with their lot, she understood that too.

The idea of a murder seemed incongruous here. "Who died?" she whispered. "When? Why?"

Waves lapped gently against the beach. The breeze sighed among the nearby trees. There was no one to answer—

Except there *was*. A slight movement in her peripheral vision intruded into her reverie. Someone was walking along the beach south of her, right along the treeline.

Chloe waved. "Hello?" she called.

The figure, no more than a shadow in the fading light, slipped into the woods.

O-kay. Whoever was out for a twilight stroll didn't feel like chatting. Intellectually, Chloe—so protective of her own solitude—completely understood. And maybe I even imagined it, she thought. Shadows were stretching long. She'd been picturing people here. Maybe the figure was a manifestation created in her mind.

She rubbed her arms briskly as she turned back toward the trail. She still had a bit of a hike back to the lighthouse. And imaginary or not, something about the furtive movement she'd seen made her uneasy.

———

By the time Chloe arrived back at the clearing, the lighthouse stood black against a cobalt sky. She paused, savoring a delicious sense of arriving *home*. I bet Emily Betts felt this way, Chloe thought. She was viewing a scene that had been viewed for well over a century...

Except for the aluminum ladder standing against one wall, and the pile of tarps and tools, and row of modern paint cans left beside the summer kitchen steps.

Chloe sighed. Obviously Herb's painter had been at work while she was away. "Didya have to leave these right by the door?" she grumbled. She dropped her daypack and dragged all the equipment to a more discreet location. Visitors who trekked up here to see the lighthouse wanted to take photos without a bunch of maintenance junk marring the scene.

Before settling in she walked down the exterior steps and unlocked the cellar door. She needed to check out the space so she could answer questions for lighthouse junkies like Mr. Dix.

The cellar was dim and smelled musty. A large room along the east wall likely served as the schoolroom. Windows provided light, and the chimney showed evidence of a stovepipe hole. Chloe imagined children hurrying up the very trails she'd walked, scampering down here, settling down to recite spelling words and do sums.

Unfortunately, some modern junk had been tossed down here as well—two battered coolers, a piece of frayed rope, two large black plastic trash bags closed off with twisty ties. Chloe considered hauling those to the garbage can in the modern outhouse, but decided against imposing their stench on hikers. Why hadn't Maintenance Mel carted this crap away? With an aggrieved sigh she pulled the modern detritus around the corner, out of sight from anyone peeking in the windows.

The north and west rooms were more pedestrian, with some coal in an old bin and rows of dusty canning jars on a shelf. Newer bits and pieces from the restoration process had been stored here as well—packages of sandpaper, stray bits of new lumber, brooms and dustpans, a metal toolbox, and a bottle of sulfuric acid. "Mel better be using that to clean modern tools," Chloe said. She'd have to check with Herb to be sure that none of the restoration workers were using harsh chemicals.

With visual integrity restored to Pottawatomie Lighthouse, Chloe went outside and watched bats swoop through the clearing while she made tea in her Sierra cup and ate cheese and crackers. Then she went inside and sat down with one of the reference files. The original logbooks kept by the keepers were in the National Archives, but some wonderful RISC soul had photocopied them.

"I will read them all," Chloe promised, as she flipped pages to—ah, yes. The Betts era.

William Betts started his log sporadically, sometimes skipping several days, then writing at length when he had something to tell.

Since the 21st of this month there has been the worst weather that I can remember seeing. Not much wind but fog and rain.

A steamer on her way to Green Bay lay for 30 hours within
hearing of this lighthouse and could not make it through. A
brig got on the reef off SouthEast point of St. Martin's light,
got off without damage.

As Chloe read, William conjured vivid pictures of winter storms, fishermen frozen in their boat, a schooner wrecked on a nearby shoal. What he did not conjure was a picture of Emily.

"What was *happening* in your lives?" Chloe demanded, thumping the page with a frustrated fist. She had hoped that Emily herself, as assistant keeper, might have made some entries. Not the case, though. If Chloe hadn't known better, she'd have assumed that William managed the station alone.

The last lengthy entry came on July 26, 1877, when the supply steamer *Dahlia* arrived. An inspector toured the lighthouse, and brought with him a lampist to level the light pedestal. William seemed pleased with the results of the inspection, but evidently the inspector had been critical of his newsy log entries. From then on, William daily wrote a single terse line, citing wind direction and ships sighted. Period.

Chloe mourned the loss of anecdotes. "You should never stifle a storyteller!" she scolded the long-dead inspector. "Didn't you know that historians would be interested?"

Bleary eyed, she closed the file. She was too tired to creep through the rest of William's entries. She rested her face in her palms, elbows on the table. Emily felt as elusive as ever.

But she lived right *here*, Chloe thought. She tried to send a mental message: I want to tell your story, Emily. But so far, I haven't found it.

Emily didn't answer. Instead, the faint sound of children's laughter drifted into the room.

Chloe jerked upright. The lantern cast a yellow pool of light on the table. The kitchen was shadowed and, now, silent. But I did hear laughter, Chloe insisted to herself. She had not dozed off. She had not dreamed it. But... if that laughter had something to do with whatever story Emily wanted her to tell, the clues were too obscure.

"Shit," Chloe muttered. Why was she trying so hard? Flinging open the door to her bourgeoning perceptive abilities might well slam the door on a normal life—settling down, having a family. Did she want to lose the chance of a relationship with Roelke in order to pursue some bizarre sense of obligation to a woman who'd been dead for decades?

On the other hand... it seemed she'd been given the chance to set something right. Something so profoundly wrong that a vestige of it persisted for a century. Was it acceptable to walk away?

"All right," Chloe announced to whomever might be listening, "time for bed." She checked her watch and groaned: almost 2 AM.

She was heading for her sleeping bag when she remembered the barge she'd seen, and Brenda's reaction to it. She might as well check again. She grabbed her binoculars and climbed to the lantern room.

As soon as she emerged through the hatch she saw a cluster of lights in the distance. With her field glasses she got a better look—definitely a boat of some kind, but that was about all she could say. She remembered Brenda's harsh reaction to the news that a boat had anchored in the north channel in the wee hours. Brenda had also complained about colleagues who got funds to search "for

Viking ships and rune stones." Was someone searching the waters between Rock Island and the Michigan shore for wrecked Viking ships? Did Brenda think that someone was a competitor? Maybe Brenda's work on Rock Island was a cover for her own real interests. She did have a boat of her own, and spent a lot of time cruising back and forth... and *something* about the idea of a nocturnal ship had pissed Brenda off.

On the other hand, Brenda's interest in Rock Island's history seemed sincere. And she couldn't have faked that story about finding the netting needle. No way. The expression on her face had been passionate; the details specific...

Chloe was so focused on the distant boat lights that she didn't notice the *other* light for some time. A single light, faint as a firefly, twinkling from the water below the lighthouse. The field glasses magnified the light without illuminating its source. Chloe frowned. What the heck was that?

OK, she thought. Maybe someone on a small sailboat was anchored in the channel for the night. There was nothing wrong with that. Still, visions of someone creeping ashore, climbing the steps to the lighthouse clearing, gave her pause. It would be easy to—

"Stop it!" she snapped. She picked up her lantern and checked her watch. Two-thirty in the morning.

Chloe ground her molars. Time to leave the light tower. If she didn't she'd A., be comatose in the morning and B., completely spook herself out with wild imaginings. She'd report the barge to Garrett next time she saw him. Right now, she needed some sleep.

TWENTY: MAY, 1875

"WHAT DO YOU THINK?" Anders asked. He held out the netting needle he was whittling for Ragna. "Will this suit the best net maker on the island?"

Ragna put down her cup of morning coffee to accept the offering. "It's lovely," she said. Only Anders would take time to make sure it fit her hand perfectly, and to carve decorative flourishes in the wood.

"I'll finish it today," he said. He took the shuttle back and slipped it into his pocket before reaching for his warmest wool scarf. Their brief taste of spring had disappeared.

Ragna hoped she'd just passed her last winter on Rock Island. "Anders, we can surely buy a little place on Washington Island now. When the weather is fine you can still fish for us."

Anders patted her belly. "I've a growing family to provide for. I made more money selling trout last winter than I could make in two years of farming. Let's see how we do with the whitefish this season."

"But—"

"Enough!" he said sharply. Paul looked up from his oatmeal, his face puckering.

Ragna rose and walked away, arms crossed over her chest. She and Anders hadn't quarreled so since she'd pressed him to leave Denmark. She leaned against the windowsill, watching snow drift past the pane. "At least stay home today." Carl and Jens had gone to Washington Island for supplies the day before, and hadn't yet returned.

Anders joined her, gently turned her to face him, and gave her that lopsided smile she loved so much. "I've fish waiting in the nets."

"As soon as Carl and Jens come back, go talk to someone about whatever evidence you have about Dugan," Ragna said. "Don't put it off."

"I promise." Anders kissed her forehead. "Don't fret, love. I'll be home and wanting supper before you know it."

———

A misty cloud enveloped Ragna as she stood on the beach that afternoon, clutching Paul's hand. They were both cold and damp and tired. She knew she should take her little boy home, put him to bed, wait for Anders there. It would be best for her unborn babe as well. Ragna put a protective hand over her belly, but shook her head. Somewhere in the gray mist and cloud, her Anders was trying to make it home.

"Just a little longer," she whispered. "Your papa is still out on the lake." She couldn't bring herself to turn her back on the water.

Ragna paced back and forth past upturned boats. Most of the men had stayed home that day. Even Anton Jacobson, who'd been known to shake his fist and dare the lake to take him on, hadn't left shore.

She felt a tiny kick. The baby she carried was restless, often making her or his presence known with tiny fist or foot. "There now," Ragna crooned softly, shifting her weight back and forth.

Paul pulled his hand free and squatted down. "I want Papa home now," he complained.

"I do as well." She clenched her teeth, imagining just how tired her husband would be. The breeze that had filled his sail that morning had turned wild at mid-day, then died. Snow showers had given way to this silent creeping fog—disorienting for a weary fisherman rowing home.

Thank God he'd set his nets north of the island. He'd have Pottawatomie's powerful beacon to guide him back toward shore. Ragna imagined Emily or her husband tending the light, making sure that local men—not just the captains of trading vessels—would find safe harbor. Once reaching Rock, Anders would row around the island until he made the beach here by the village.

How many times had she walked this crescent of shoreline, waiting, worrying, wondering? I can't do this any longer, she thought. Can't watch Anders leave each dawn, not knowing when or even if she'd see him again.

"This is the last time," she told both of her children. "I think…"

Her voice trailed away. She'd heard the splash of an oar. Hadn't she? She stood erect, listening. Everything seemed unfamiliar in fog like this, the everyday sounds muffled and distorted, but—*yes*. There it was again. A boat was coming in.

Ragna grabbed Paul with one hand and held the lantern high. "Anders!" she cried. "Anders, here we are!"

The quiet splash of oars paused for a moment, then resumed. Finally a Mackinaw boat slid ghost-like from the mist.

"Anders!" Ragna called again, almost weak with joy. "I was so worried! I…" Her voice trailed away. She watched with dismay as Carrick Dugan stowed his oars, jumped over the side of his boat, grabbed the gunnel, and heaved his craft up on the beach.

Had it been any other man Ragna would have splashed out to join him, helping to tug the boat above the waterline. Not Dugan, though. And not *now*.

"Have you seen Anders?" She prayed that for once, just this once, he would understand, offer a word of comfort instead of threaten and snarl.

For a long moment she thought Dugan wasn't going to answer at all. Finally he turned his head and looked at her. Ragna raised the lantern again. His eyes looked wild, like a fanatical preacher she'd once heard exhorting his parishioners back in Denmark. Ragna's heart begin to skitter in her chest. Her skin prickled. The clamminess left her bones, replaced with a scorching heat.

"Your man must be gone," Dugan said at last. He drew a deep shuddering breath. "He must be gone." Then he walked away.

A roaring grew in Ragna's ears. She didn't know she was screaming until Paul jerked his hand from hers, staring at her with terrified eyes.

TWENTY-ONE

THE FOGHORN BLAST THAT seemed to come from an inch away brought Chloe upright in bed. "Geez Louise," she gasped, pressing one hand over her thumping heart. Half-hearted gray light filled the room. A drizzle of rain sulked down the windowpanes. Chloe groaned, rubbing her eyes. Only a second blast from the unseen ship passing through the channel, and the knowledge that some perky campers might hike up at first light, shoved her out of bed. Yawning, she pulled on jeans, sweatshirt, and a hooded jacket.

As she started making breakfast on the picnic table, the gray mist gave her a delicious sense of isolation. Then she remembered the figure near the fishing village site who'd ducked into the trees when she'd called. Someone else was on the island yesterday evening. She really wished that whoever it was had at least waved hello.

Well, Chloe told herself, your primary job is here, at the lighthouse. Maybe you should just stay away from the village site. While waiting for water to boil, she tried to understand what she found so compelling there. There was nothing to see, really. She had an abundance of stunning scenery and solitude and serenity here at Pottawatomie. And though she did enjoy indulging in her oh-so-active imagination, she could do that here as well.

But she was trying to understand Emily Betts, and the village had been part of Emily's community here on Rock. Understanding Emily's life was part of the consultant gig. Right?

The water simmered. Chloe tore the top from a packet of oatmeal, poured it into the pot, and stirred absently. Honestly, she couldn't claim that her fascination with the village site was all about Emily. There was something about the meadow that called to her. Something that went beyond the scope of her consultant job. She leaned against the table, eating oatmeal, watching the fog swirl past, thinking. Maybe there was a story she needed to tell at the village site too.

"Like I don't have enough problems?" she mumbled. Still, there was a certain freaky logic to that theory. At Pottawatomie, she had Emily Betts' photograph as a talisman. She walked the floorboards Emily had walked, she washed dishes in Emily's sink, she slept in the room where Emily had made love and given birth and watched the beacon shine over the midnight cliff and channel below. But at the meadow she had no talismans or tangibles. If there was something there for her, she'd have to work harder to find it. Maybe she was the only person who could.

Maybe she needed to think of her developing perceptive abilities as a gift instead of a nuisance.

Chloe was pondering that when a mechanical grumble announced the arrival of Maintenance Mel. She folded her arms, keeping her face neutral as he emerged from the park truck.

"Morning," he said, gruff as ever. He hefted an Igloo cooler from the truck and set it on the top step. "Here's drinking water. Got your buckets? I'll go down to the lake and fetch wash water for you."

"You don't have to—"

"Fetch 'em out," he said. "I'll save you a trip. Besides, you could break an ankle going down those steps in weather like this."

Chloe decided to do as instructed, and watched him disappear into the mist. Maintenance Mel, doing her a favor? Maybe that was his way of acknowledging that he'd been out of line the day before. She sighed, remembering what Stig had said about Mel getting forced out of the commercial fishing business. At least she had a better understanding of why Mel was grumpy.

"Thanks," she said when Mel returned with the water. "Say, I was down in the cellar yesterday and noticed some garbage and junk down there. Want to take that with you?"

"Too busy today." He got in the truck and spoke through the window. "All kinds of junk blows across from Michigan and washes up below the lighthouse. If you find trash on the beach, just dump it in the oil house. When I got a full load I'll haul it out."

Chloe was glad when the truck noise faded back to silence. She appreciated Mel's goodwill gesture of hauling water, but honestly? She *wanted* to see the beach shrouded in fog.

Ferns glistened with moisture along the woodland trail toward the staircase. Chloe imagined Emily Betts walking this same path, empty buckets in hand, as autumn began its inexorable descent on Rock Island.

Halfway down the old stone steps, Chloe noticed again the small cave near the path. The mist made it easier than ever to imagine the long-ago. Might the lighthouse families have used that cave for cool storage? Had Emily carried crocks of butter and strawberries to shelves beneath the limestone overhang?

Chloe left the trail and wandered to the opening. Although only a few feet deep, the cave was still dark on this sunless day. The walls near the opening showed evidence of wood smoke, but much as she enjoyed picturing long-dead traders smoking their pipes and roasting fish while waiting out a storm, she was pretty sure modern campers or kayakers had left the black stains.

Her fingers trailed along the wall as she moved inside. If she could find a nail—square and old, preferably—protruding from the stone she'd have evidence that someone had used the overhang for something other than campfires…

One more step and her left foot met air instead of rugged stone. She stumbled against the rough limestone wall. "Ow!" she whimpered. She took stock gingerly, flexing ankles, rubbing a scrape on her elbow. If she'd managed to incapacitate herself here, how long would it take someone to notice her absence and come looking?

Roelke's voice echoed accusingly in her head: *This trip is a very bad idea!*

"Yeah, yeah," she muttered. She pushed herself erect, wincing, and surveyed the booby-trap. Someone had dug a hole against the wall. No… several holes. She hadn't noticed at first because the stones had been tossed toward the back of the cave, in the deepest shadows.

Who the heck? And why? Somebody looking for the lost gold coins Brenda Noakes had mentioned? Chloe shook her head. Could someone really think that gold coins supposedly lost a hundred and thirty years ago might be calmly waiting in a cave that sat just a few yards from a trail the lighthouse families had used daily? Yes, no doubt someone really could.

"You could have at least cleaned up after yourself," Chloe grumbled. She kicked rubble back into the holes as best she could, hoping to keep the next inquisitive and hapless hiker from breaking an ankle.

When she descended the wooden stairs to the beach, she passed craggy limestone walls lining the north end of the island. There was no telling how many crannies and crawl-spaces might beckon thieves and treasure-seekers—long ago, here and now.

Despite Mel's dire prediction, Chloe managed to reach the beach safely. Which was good, since she'd already banged herself up once this morning. That was her quota.

She turned east and picked her way to the memorial cairn, hoping to find new evidence of mourning. Maybe even a whole first name, spelled in tiny pebbles. But the N remained as solitary epitaph, its maker evidently long gone. "I hope the officers can figure out who you are," Chloe told the dead young woman. She half-expected the dead girl herself to answer, but the girl stayed stubbornly silent.

Then Chloe noticed a bit of broken glass by her feet. Bits, actually, now that she looked more closely. She sighed, mentally scolding whichever picnicker had been too lazy and/or selfish to clean up after whatever mishap had left these shards. She wadded them into a tissue and carefully stuffed it in her pocket.

Then she stood, taking in the lake's new mood. The mist was cold on her face. She felt all alone, enveloped in drifting wet wisps of cloud. A loon, cloaked in fog, called nearby. The mist only intensified the sense of timelessness. She thought about all the souls who'd once walked this beach—the first landing for southern travelers after crossing from Michigan. And for a century keepers had walked here, too. She'd read that the lighthouse service had tried to maintain a dock on this northern shore, but every structure was destroyed by storms. Those keepers' families were pretty isolated. They must have so looked forward to the infrequent supply ship visits!

Part-way back to the stairs Chloe found a large flat rock a short way down the beach, perfect for sitting, as if planted by God for those compelled to linger. Or, she thought, for a mother who wanted to watch her children while they splashed on the beach? Had Emily sat on this very stone a century ago? Chloe blew out a long, deep breath as she settled down. She was suddenly sure of it. How often had Emily perched here, watching her children play, watching sleek schooners sail the passage? Chloe smiled. Emily's Rock. With no modern intrusions, it was *so* easy to imagine the scene...

TWENTY-TWO: MAY, 1876

EMILY LOVED THE DAWN hour, when the birds were waking, the light soft and pink, the day full of possibilities. She often watched morning come from the light tower. Today she'd descended to the beach. The cisterns were leaking, and she'd brought buckets to fill so she could start morning chores.

But instead of filling them and climbing back up the bluff, she picked her way to a large flat rock a short way down the beach, perfect for sitting, as if planted by God for those compelled to linger. Emily had come to think of it as *her* rock—a place to enjoy quiet moments among the constant commotion at the lighthouse. She'd bring Jane down to play when she was a little older.

Emily scanned the horizon, searching for the supply ship *Dahlia*. With luck, a new library box would be delivered that day. What a joy to discover the new books tucked inside! And often notes, too. The other lighthouse wives in the area were good friends. They kept in touch through letters, sharing news and seed packets and recipes. Emily smiled, watching three cormorants fly over the water at top speed. Her life was very full, very good. She was thankful that—

"Mrs. Betts!"

Emily scrambled to her feet. A woman was thumping down the steps, holding her skirt high so she wouldn't trip. Mette Friis, wasn't it? Yes. Emily made her way across the cobbles to meet her. "What is it? What's wrong?"

Mette struggled to catch her breath, and swiped tears from her eyes. "Please come."

Emily felt a hand grab her heart, squeeze. "Tell me, quickly!"

"It's Ragna." The older woman's eyes were dark with sorrow. "Oh, Mrs. Betts. She's in a bad way."

TWENTY-THREE

When Chloe emerged into the clearing, she was surprised to see someone wearing stained yellow rain pants and coat sitting at the picnic table. Sylvie Torgrimsson waved, grinning as Chloe joined her. "Good morning! I didn't know if you were still in bed, so I figured I'd wait here for you to show yourself."

"In bed?" Chloe scoffed, very glad she'd forced herself to rise and—well, if not actually shine, at least faintly glow. "Just finishing some chores. How did you get here?" The first *Karfi* run was still a couple of hours away.

"I've got my own boat," Sylvie said. "A fishing tug. My husband was a commercial fisherman. He's been dead for six years."

"I'm sorry."

"Me too. But he died on the water, and I was with him when he went. A heart attack. I thank God every day that he didn't waste away by inches, away from the lake."

Chloe nodded. She understood that thought completely.

"Anyway." Sylvie hoisted a weather-beaten canvas sack. "I brought coffee and homemade doughnuts."

"You," Chloe said fervently, "are my new best friend."

They went inside and settled down at the kitchen table. Sylvie poured coffee from a thermos and set out a sack of sugared doughnuts. "How's it going? Any questions?"

Lots of them, Chloe thought. She mentally shuffled through them, looking for something that was actually germane to the job the good RISC folks had brought her here to do. "Here's number one. Has the committee given any thought to a period to focus on in terms of furnishing the lighthouse?"

"A little," Sylvie said, "but we wanted to hear your recommendation."

Chloe considered, happily sipping coffee that was much better than the instant dreck she'd brought with her. She was sorely tempted to recommend interpreting the lighthouse during the Betts era, but professionally, that was not the best call. "I suggest the 1900–1910 range." Well after the Betts were gone. Chloe was proud of herself.

"Why then?"

"That's about mid-way through the period the lighthouse was inhabited," Chloe explained. "It will be easy to find documentation—Sears and Roebucks catalogs from the period will give a general sense of styles for everything from sofas to picture frames. And it shouldn't be too difficult to find original pieces from that era. The earlier you go, the harder and more expensive it will be to furnish the rooms."

"Good thinking. I'm sure everyone on the committee will agree."

Chloe smiled. She was so used to hearing complaints and criticism from her own boss, the infamous Ralph Petty, that even calm approval felt like a tidal wave of praise. This consultant project *was* doing good things for her mental health. It was pleasant to linger here in the lighthouse kitchen, chatting. The foggy weather made the rest of the world—even the campground and park office—feel a million miles away.

"We'll have some flexibility in terms of room use," Chloe added. "Obviously the second story rooms were allotted different functions depending on whether a single man or one family or two families were living in the lighthouse at a particular time."

"We'll need to keep the needs of the docents in mind," Sylvie said. "We can keep modern functions—a small refrigerator and stove, and a little space to sell souvenirs—in the summer kitchen."

"Perfect!" Chloe exclaimed. "That will provide a nice gathering space where the docents can provide a bit of orientation. A map of the islands would be helpful to make sure visitors understand why the lighthouse was needed here in the first place. Then, in the main building, visitors will find a period-appropriate presentation."

Sylvie cradled her mug in hands, and surveyed the nearly empty kitchen with satisfaction. "It does me good to see this old place coming back to life. We hope to have the docent program up and running by next season. I've got my name on the list."

"You're going to volunteer?" Chloe wouldn't have guessed Sylvie would enjoy handling guests all day.

"Don't look so surprised! I have a costume from that era that I wear to events at the Farm Museum on Washington, so I'm already set to give tours in style. After watching this lighthouse crumble for years, all boarded up, I want to help make visitors feel welcome."

"Once I get the furnishing plan written, we can start collecting," Chloe said. "I would expect that by spring we'll have enough pieces in place to start the docent program."

"Speaking of furnishings, I brought that list of potential donations I promised." Sylvie fished a folded piece of notebook paper from a pocket and handed it over.

"Thanks." Chloe skimmed the list, pleased to see that about half of the people who'd offered items lived on Washington Island. "I'll visit as many of the locals as I can. When I get home I'll write to the people who are farther away, asking them to provide a photograph and whatever information they have. I'll document as much as I can and send my recommendations to you."

"Sounds good." Sylvie leaned back in her chair, extended her legs, and crossed them at the ankles. "So, Chloe. How are you making on? I don't mean the project. I mean *you*."

"I'm doing fine," Chloe said cautiously.

"Not spooked staying here all alone?"

Chloe eyed the other woman. Did Sylvie know of a reason she *should* be spooked? "Well, the first time I went to the outhouse after dark my flashlight beam hit a pair of yellow eyes in the clearing. It was a fox, but for half a second I was a bit … startled."

Sylvie laughed. "Glad it was nothing more serious. How's Garrett been treating you? Got everything you need?"

"Yes." Chloe nodded emphatically. "He's been great."

"Have you met Brenda Noakes yet?"

"I have, yes."

"Has she … well." Sylvie paused, looking—for once—hesitant.

Chloe pulled a bag of dried apricots from her stash. What the heck was up? "I understand that there haven't been funds for archaeological work here or at the village site," she said, offering the fruit. "That's too bad, but I don't think it will affect our project too much. I can work from oral tradition and written sources."

Sylvie's face cleared, and she seemed to bury whatever she'd been about to say. "Have you been to the archives?"

"Yesterday. I'm heading back to Washington today. When I'm here during the day, it's too easy to get caught up in giving lighthouse tours. Don't get me wrong, I love showing people around! But it's not the best use of my time. My first priority is giving RISC as much as I can to help keep this restoration project moving forward."

"Then I best let you get to it."

Chloe's cheeks grew warm. "No—that's not what I meant!"

"Not to worry." Sylvie laughed. "Listen, before I head out, I want to ask you a personal favor."

"You've already bought my goodwill with breakfast," Chloe said. "What can I do for you?"

"I'd like you to write a nomination to get Pottawatomie Lighthouse on the National Register of Historic Places."

"Oh." Chloe took that in, turned it over in her mind. "It's a great idea, but—"

"It's *essential*. Right now the lighthouse has some protection because it's on state property. But what happens if some yahoo governor twenty or thirty years from now decides to fill his coffers by selling off parklands?"

Chloe winced. Wisconsin had a strong and proud tradition of preservation, but... it could happen.

"Pottawatomie deserves every ounce of protection we can provide." Sylvie's tone brooked no argument.

"I agree," Chloe said, "but I'm not the best person to write the nomination. Someone at the Historic Preservation office in Madison can point you to an architectural historian. Someone who knows all the lingo, and has been through the process before."

"I want someone who knows this place. Who *understands* this place."

Chloe thought about all the work left to do on the furnishings plan—work that would have to be concluded on her own time, once she got back to Old World Wisconsin's floodtide of curatorial needs. "What about the consultant who did the original structural report for you?"

Sylvie frowned, flapping one hand irritably. "He made mistakes. Told us we needed a specific type of paint for the lantern room and then ordered the wrong thing. He lost his work log and had to reproduce it from memory. I thought we'd hired a decent consultant, but—what an airhead!"

Chloe felt torn. She wanted Pottawatomie to receive federal protection as much as Sylvie did. But she truly believed an experienced architectural historian would be a better choice.

Then she glanced again at Sylvie's implacable face. "Well… maybe," Chloe hedged. "Let me give it some thought."

"Good." Sylvie shoved her chair back and got to her feet with an *Everything is decided* air. "I'm eager to get out on the lake."

"In this fog?" Chloe glanced out the kitchen window. Visibility seemed to be getting worse, not better.

"Oh, I love the lake in all its moods. This one best of all, perhaps."

Chloe had the sudden sense that she was talking with a kindred spirit. "I think I know what you mean."

Sylvie turned to go, but paused by the photo of Emily Betts that Chloe had propped beside some reference books. "I always liked that one," Sylvie said.

"I've been looking for more information about Emily Betts, but haven't unearthed much."

"Keep digging," Sylvie said. "Emily Betts was highly respected around here. Surely something will turn up."

I hope so, Chloe thought. For half a second she considered confiding in Sylvie, telling her that she felt inexplicably compelled to learn more about Emily Betts and her time at Pottawatomie. Then she imagined Sylvie reporting back to the RISC committee: "I thought we'd hired a decent consultant, but—what an airhead!"

"I'll keep digging," Chloe promised. "Thanks for coming by."

TWENTY-FOUR: MAY, 1875

Dawn found Ragna staring at the ceiling, eyes gritty from lack of sleep, heart scraped raw. She'd given birth to a premature daughter the day before—Christine, who'd lived less than an hour. Christine's tiny body had been washed and dressed in the gown Ragna had sewn and decorated with *hedebosøm*. Ragna's friends tenderly laid the dead infant in the tiny coffin Mette's husband had built. She would be buried that evening.

Emily had fallen asleep in the chair near the bed with her hands folded in her lap and her head resting against the wall. The women shouldn't have fetched Emily, Ragna thought. Emily had plenty of her own work. Besides, the good fishwives of Rock Island knew how to tend their own. One brought broth, another wine. Mette even made *rødgrød med fløde* with dried cherries and strawberries. Ragna's mother used to make *rødgrød* too, in full summer when ripe red fruit made a juicy and sweet pudding.

Only Emily had tried to give Ragna hope. "Anders may yet be drifting, waiting for the sun to come up and burn away the fog," she'd said. "Come, now. Don't despair yet." And such things did happen. More than once a fisherman had not come home, been mourned as lost, then turned up hours or days or even a week later.

But Ragna knew that all hope was gone. She understood that Anders was dead—and by Dugan's hand. She'd told Mette and she, bless her wise heart, had not argued.

Moving slowly, silently, Ragna sat up in bed. The cottage was no longer *hygge*, no longer a home. Anders was simply ... *gone*. His absence sucked the air from the room. I told him not to go out alone, Ragna thought, balling the sheet in her fists.

How had it happened? It was only too easy to imagine. Two men out on the big lake, each alone in a boat better tended by two. Anders had believed he'd found something to bring the law down on Dugan. Had Anders been so foolish as to confront Dugan with—with *whatever* that knowledge was? Had Dugan seen opportunity in the dense fog, silently rowed close to Anders' nets, simply waited for the right moment? Had Dugan shot Anders? Hit him over the head? Out on the lake Dugan could easily dump a body, sink the Mackinaw boat, come home with nothing to show for what he'd done ... except the look in his eyes.

Ragna winced as pain stabbed through her pelvis. At least the bleeding had stopped. *You can't be weak now,* she thought. Anders was dead, and Christine too. Paul was still hers, though. Paul needed a mother.

And Ragna needed to deal with Dugan. If only Anders had confided in her! Then she might be able to take the tale to the sheriff, or at least to William Betts. In trying to protect her, Anders had withheld what she needed to protect herself.

Gritting her teeth, Ragna pushed to her feet and slowly fastened a cloak over her nightdress. Paul slept on, and Emily too.

The village was stirring. Men shouted from the beach as they loaded nets boxes, shoved their boats into the water. Somewhere a dog barked. The scent of wood smoke drifted through the dawn as women fried eggs and cooked oatmeal. Ragna kept to the trees as she crept south, weaving past the village. Many homes were empty now, and the fog had lingered, so it was easy to stay hidden.

She came upon Dugan's cabin from behind. It leaned a bit, and the tiny garden patch grew as many weeds as potatoes and carrots. No smoke trailed from the chimney. The place looked deserted. Perhaps even Dugan knew he'd gone too far, and that he'd be wise to leave Rock Island. Perhaps, Ragna thought wearily, that is the best I can hope for.

Still, something compelled her to creep toward the cabin. When she was better rested and thinking more clearly, when the sun burned through the fog, she would not be so foolish. If I'm going to search Dugan's cabin, Ragna thought, it must be *now*.

TWENTY-FIVE

After Sylvie left, Chloe washed up and organized her research notes. Coming and going by ferry limited her time on Washington Island. She needed to make the most of it.

She enjoyed walking the forest trail to the dock while fog swirled through the trees, and she reached the boathouse with time to spare. A fishing tug with *Sylvie* painted in red on the bow was moored at the dock. Hadn't Sylvie said she was heading out on the water?

The tug was a clunky-looking wooden boat with a long cabin— probably where the fish were stored and processed—and a pilot-house at the stern. As Chloe wandered down the dock, idly curious, she heard voices coming from within the tug. A man's and a woman's. Suddenly the man spoke more harshly, and louder too: "I swear to God, Sylvie, if you don't stop—"

"You do *not* have permission to mind my business." Sylvie's voice rose, too.

Chloe turned silently and retreated to a bench on solid ground. A few minutes later a man emerged from the tug and strode up the dock—Garrett Smith. What on earth had Garrett been arguing with Sylvie about? Chloe hoped it had nothing to do with the lighthouse project. There was already tension between Sylvie and Herb Whitby, the RISC guy who'd come along on the first visit. It was disconcerting to think that Sylvie also had a troubled relationship with Garrett.

The park manager was almost upon Chloe before he noticed her sitting silently in the mist. He stopped, blinking. Chloe watched his clenched fists relax, as if he was making a conscious effort to switch into public servant mode.

"Good morning!" she said brightly. "I'm just waiting for the ferry. Heading over to Washington to do some more research."

"Sounds good." The *Sylvie*'s motor chugged to life. Garrett glanced over his shoulder, then gave Chloe a perfunctory smile. "Have a good day."

He'd walked on before Chloe remembered that she'd meant to tell him about the brightly lit barge she'd seen. Well, now was clearly not a good time.

Chloe was the sole passenger on the *Karfi*'s first run back to Washington. She collected her car from the lot near the dock and headed across the island. Once at Jackson Harbor, she found a pay phone and called Old World Wisconsin. She wanted to talk with her intern, but Nika didn't happen to be by her desk. "No, no message," Chloe told the receptionist. "I'll try again later."

Thwarted, Chloe stood by the phone, hesitating. Then she fished all the change she had from her wallet and stacked it on the ledge beneath the phone. This time she got lucky. "Ethan? It's me."

"Hey!" he sounded startled. "Why are you calling so early?"

"I'm not at home," she began. She quickly told her best friend about her trip to the tip of Door County. "There's no phone line on Rock, so since I'm here on Washington Island for the day, I—I just thought I'd call and say hi. See how you're doing."

"I'm doing fine. Things are pretty quiet at the moment." Ethan was a fire-jumper in Idaho. "I'm glad you called, though. I'm about to go backpacking for a few days."

"Chris going with you?"

"Nope. He's gotta work. That's OK, though. The last fire we got called out on—that one in Colorado—it was a bitch. I'm ready for some solitude."

"I was too!" Chloe exclaimed. "Why do so many people think you're weird if you need to be by yourself sometimes?"

"I don't know."

"Roelke's not real happy about me staying at the lighthouse. And I'm in a state park, for God's sake." She didn't mention finding the body on the beach. Ethan wouldn't be any happier about that little factoid than Roelke.

"Is this trip causing problems between you two? That doesn't bode well."

"Ethan..." Chloe watched a pickup truck circa 1950 putter by. "I care about Roelke. I really do. But sometimes I wonder if..."

"If what?"

"I'm pretty good with people when I'm working. You know, talking to visitors, training interpreters, that kind of thing." Not when dealing with her boss, but Petty was an ass, so that didn't count. "But I don't know if I'm meant to be in a long-term relationship."

"You and Markus were together for several years," Ethan observed.

Five. "Yeah, and look how that turned out."

His laugh was low and familiar. "If Roelke cares about you, he'll figure out that he needs to give you space from time to time."

"Yeah." Chloe felt her shoulders ease. "Listen, I'm about out of change. Have a good trip, OK? I'll be home next week, so call me when you get back."

She hung up the phone feeling immeasurably cheered. During their college days she and Ethan had often gone backpacking—sometimes the two of them, sometimes with a larger group of friends. When Chloe needed to escape on some mountain trail alone, all Ethan ever said was, "Have a good time. Call me when you get back."

Satisfied that she was not being completely unreasonable, Chloe considered the day. She had Sylvie's list of potential donors in hand, and it would be wise to try contacting them now. Time in the archives and local museums could happen around the visits.

She met first with an elderly couple who lived near Jackson Harbor. They'd offered a Hoosier cupboard that dated to 1905. "You've obviously taken excellent care of it," Chloe told them. "It's in superb condition."

The woman beamed. "My parents bought it the year they got married. I'd love to see it on display at the lighthouse."

"It's a great candidate," Chloe added carefully, "but I can't give you a final decision today. I'll make recommendations to the RISC committee, and then someone will be in touch."

The second visit involved a basement full of furniture from the 1950s. Chloe made careful notes, and repeated her words of curatorial caution. "No final decisions have been made about the period that will be represented at the lighthouse," she told the owners. "When that happens, someone will be in touch. We sure appreciate your generous offer, though."

The third stop took her to the east side of the island to examine a library box. Chloe had no idea what a library box was, but she was eager to find out.

Mrs. Gunderson, the donor, was a thin woman with short white hair and a warm demeanor. "Please call me Ruth," she said as she led Chloe to a back room in her ranch house. Standing on a card table was a battered wooden case, about two feet by two feet and eight inches deep. The front was a double door with brass fittings. "My grandparents were keepers at several lights in this area," she explained. "Starting in the 1870s."

The Betts era, Chloe thought, feeling a tiny tingle of anticipation. "What can you tell me about this box?"

Ruth turned on a lamp. "Can you see the lettering on the front? It's pretty faded now, but still legible."

Chloe squinted. "U.S.L.H. Library, Number 467."

"The U.S. Lighthouse Service had librarians fill these boxes, which circled from lighthouse to lighthouse." Ruth opened the box to reveal two shelves which, amazingly enough, still held books. Old books. Very old books.

Chloe's eyebrows lifted. "Wow!"

"My grandma used to say that getting a new library box was like Christmas. The librarians took great care to include a variety of books. Look at these—children's books, poetry, history... a little bit of everything." Ruth's eyes filled with pride. "The lighthouse families were well educated, you know. They had lots of long quiet evenings, and read everything they could get their hands on."

Chloe eased a volume from one of the shelves. *Around the World in Eighty Days* by Jules Verne, copyright 1873. "This trunk is like a snapshot in time."

"The box was damaged." Ruth pointed at one of the corners, which was split. "It must have been taken out of circulation right about the time my grandparents retired. That's why it's come down in my family." She rubbed at an invisible spot on the trunk. "I became a librarian, and I suspect it had a lot to do with me hearing how much these boxes meant to the lighthouse families."

"How very special." Chloe shook her head with awe. She opened another book—poetry, this time—and a folded slip of paper fell to the floor. "Oh, I'm sorry!" She gently retrieved it and squinted at the faded handwriting. On one side someone had scrawled *For Jeanette G.* On the other side, in the same handwriting, were directions for making a Danish apple cake.

"Jeanette was my grandma," Ruth explained. "The lighthouse families sometimes tucked in little notes for the next families on the circuit. My parents left everything in this box just as it was."

Treasure-treasure-*treasure!* "It's wonderful to have a cake recipe documented to two different women who lived in local lighthouses," Chloe exclaimed.

"And there's a letter in this geography book." Ruth extracted two pages of brittle stationary, covered with the same tight, slanting writing.

"Do you have a transcript of this?" Chloe asked. The ink was badly faded.

Ruth shook her head contritely. "No. I should have made a copy years ago, I guess."

"No problem. You kept this collection intact, which is *incredibly* wonderful."

The older woman looked relieved. "I'm glad you think so." She touched the library trunk with a gentle hand. "My parents and I cherished this. Do you think it should go to Pottawatomie? I do want to support the lighthouse restoration project." Her words were both sincere and hesitant. She gazed affectionately at the box.

"I can't provide a definitive answer today," Chloe began. "But I'm going to recommend to the RISC committee that they reproduce your trunk, instead of acquiring it. That way we can put a new-looking trunk on display in the lighthouse, and you can keep the original."

Ruth's face glowed. "That sounds perfect!"

Sometimes, Chloe thought, my work lets me do very good things. "With your permission, I'll borrow these pages." Ideally she would have examined them in greater detail there at Ruth's home, but with a ferry-imposed deadline, she didn't have that luxury. "I'll copy the recipe, and see if I can make something of this faded letter as well."

"Be my guest."

"Thank you." Chloe turned to the last page of the letter. The ink here was just as faded. Her gaze skimmed down the page.

Then her heart gave a little hitch. The signature, written larger than the text, was legible: *Emily B., Pottawatomie Station.*

"Was this written by Emily Betts?" Chloe leaned toward the window, squinting at handwriting faint and fine as a spider's web.

"It was." Ruth pinched her lips together thoughtfully, gazing blindly across the room. "My mother read the letter to me more than once when I was a child. I know Emily talked about two men who froze to death while trying to cross Death's Door during the winter of… well, I don't recall."

"Eighteen seventy-six," Chloe supplied helpfully. "I just read about that last night."

"The story gave me nightmares as a child," Ruth told her. "And let's see… I believe Emily wrote of being worried about a Danish friend who lived in the fishing village. That recipe likely came from her."

I *knew* there was a connection to the village! Chloe thought triumphantly. "Do you recall why she was worried?"

Ruth spread her hands. "I'm afraid not."

"No problem," Chloe said again. "With some time and sunshine, I think I can make it out."

TWENTY-SIX: MAY, 1876

EMILY WAS DUSTING THE portrait of President Grant in the parlor when movement caught her eye, and she glanced out the window. Horrified, she dropped the rag and ran to wrench open the west door. "Ragna!" she cried, hurrying to meet her friend. "What were you *thinking*? You shouldn't be out of bed, much less trekking up here!" The two-mile trail to the lighthouse was rough and sometimes steep. Only three days had passed since she'd stood in the little village cemetery with her arm around Ragna. Emily had tried to buoy her friend, holding her upright as Christine was laid in a tiny grave and a final prayer was said for Anders.

Now Ragna was walking slowly, hunched over, one arm pressed against her belly and the other cradling a small tin box. Dark smudges shadowed her eyes, and her cheeks were hollow. She let Emily help her inside.

After settling Ragna on the parlor sofa, Emily fetched a quilt from the bedroom to tuck around her shoulders. "Rest," she ordered. "I made a custard for you this morning—I'll fetch some.

And I'm going to make you some tea." She hurried into the kitchen, considering her supplies of medicinal herbs. She'd made a tincture of shepherd's purse leaves to help stop Ragna's bleeding on the night Christine was born. Chamomile and raspberry leaf tea today, she decided.

When everything was ready Emily carried a tray into the parlor. "Please, eat," she implored. "You need to rebuild your strength." She waited until Ragna reached for the spoon before retreating to her rocking chair. "Oh, Ragna. Why did you come? I was going to visit you this afternoon. And where's Paul?"

"Mette is watching Paul. I need to talk to your husband."

Emily blinked. "Why on earth…?"

"I found out," Ragna said.

"Found out what?"

"I found out why Anders thought he could summon the law about Dugan."

"And… what did you discover?"

Ragna told her. Emily listened with growing dismay.

"So I need to talk to your husband." Ragna said again. "He'll know what to do."

Emily looked away, trying to collect her thoughts. She loved this room, and had tried to make it welcoming—lace curtains at the windows, a warm wool carpet underfoot. In happier times she and Ragna had whiled away pleasant afternoons here, Emily with her knitting and Ragna with her *hedebosøm*. But the lighthouse wasn't just her home. It was a federal building, always open to the public, a tangible representation of law and government in this remote spot. This wasn't the first time someone had come seeking William's counsel.

"Is he here?" Ragna asked. She sipped some tea, using both hands to steady the cup.

Well, maybe William *would* know what to do. "He's in the watchroom," Emily said. "I'll fetch him."

Once summoned, William pulled a chair close to Ragna. "I am most sorry for your losses, Mrs. Anderson," he said. "Now please, tell me how I can be of service." He listened without change of expression. No one except his wife would have noticed the almost imperceptible stiffening in his shoulders, the tiny twitch by his mouth. As Ragna spoke, she showed William the contents of her box. He made no move to study what was inside.

"So please," Ragna said. "Can you summon the sheriff? This is proof that Dugan was breaking a law. He must be fined."

"What you have proves nothing," William told her gently. "You have no proof that it even belongs to him."

"It does!" Ragna cried. "This scrap is white. Carrick Dugan is the only fisherman on Rock too lazy to dye his nets."

"That may be. But this will not be enough to convince a sheriff to make the trip to Rock Island."

Emily saw something change in Ragna's eyes, as if a faint light had been snuffed and replaced with something dark and hard. Emily didn't know what Carrick Dugan had or hadn't done that foggy night. But Ragna believed that *she* knew. Emily was suddenly afraid of where that belief might take her friend.

"I'm truly sorry," William was saying. "I will leave you to my wife's tender care."

When William was gone Emily sat down beside Ragna. "Oh, my dear friend. I know you're disappointed, but William knows best about such things."

159

"I thought you would help me."

"I am *trying* to help you," Emily insisted, a little stung.

"An arrest and fine wouldn't be enough, of course," Ragna said, almost as if she were speaking to herself. "But Dugan cannot be permitted to flout the law. Anders... Anders believed..." Ragna's voice trailed away. Finally she murmured, "I think Anders was foolish enough to tell Dugan what he planned to do."

"*I* think we'll never know for sure what happened that day," Emily said briskly. She believed in hoping for the best, but as the days passed she'd reluctantly accepted what Ragna had known from the start: Anders Anderson had drowned in Lake Michigan.

"They had fought, you know. Dugan was furious."

Emily's heart ached. "Ragna," she said gently, "I'm sure your brothers will provide for you and Paul, but what do you want to do?"

Ragna, who'd been fiddling with her spoon, looked up. "I want to avenge my husband." Ragna's eyes were dry, her voice flat and calm. "And my daughter."

Emily felt a sliver of ice slide down her backbone. God save us, she thought. "You don't mean that."

"I do. Just like Miriam in that book you once read—"

"*Listen* to me," Emily hissed. "You mustn't say such things. It's wicked!"

Ragna flinched. For a moment she regarded her friend with eyes that showed hurt and pain. Then her gaze went iron again. She rose slowly and walked to the window.

Emily knew she'd said too much. "I am worried for you," she said, trying to find better words this time. "You would face a terrible punishment! You must think of Paul."

Ragna didn't answer.

An ache was growing beneath Emily's ribs. "Please promise me," she whispered. "Promise me you will put aside your thoughts of doing Dugan harm. That won't solve anything."

"I will not abandon my son," Ragna said at last. "Paul is all I have left."

Which did not, Emily thought, get to the heart of the matter at all.

TWENTY-SEVEN

Fog still overpowered the sun when Chloe left Ruth's house with the precious letter sandwiched safely between two pieces of cardboard. She bought a soda at Mann's grocery, which gave her more change, and was heading out when she almost collided with someone who'd paused to look at the notices on a community bulletin board.

"Excuse me—oh, hey!" Chloe blinked at Tim Brown, the kayaker, with surprise. "I thought you and Natalie were long gone from these parts."

"We paddled over to St. Martin's Island, but decided to swing back south. I just hitched a ride into town so I could pick up some supplies."

Chloe glanced at the notice he'd been reading, an advertisement for a fishing tug. "You thinking of taking up commercial fishing?"

Her words were light, so she was surprised when he shrugged. "Maybe. It's not easy to break in, though."

"I imagine that getting set up is expensive."

"Yeah." He looked again at the hand-lettered "For Sale" sign.

"Well, good luck," she said, and watched him disappear into the store. She remembered Tim whittling a stick to use for roasting marshmallows the evening she'd met him and Natalie. Now he was dreaming about buying a fishing rig.

So, what's wrong with that, she asked herself. But the real question was this: how long had it been since she'd made s'mores and dreamed of some new venture, however unlikely it might be? She sighed. Something about Tim made her feel old.

She circled back to a pay phone to try her intern again. "Tanika Austin," Nika said crisply.

Yahoo. "It's me," Chloe said. "How's it going?"

"Well, Petty convened a big meeting this morning. As lowly intern I wasn't invited, but I got the scoop. The audit report came in."

Chloe braced herself. "What did it say about collections?"

"Long story short? The site needs more resources to adequately care for the collection."

Chloe rolled her eyes. "Well, duh. What was the bottom line? Did the report provide more ammunition for the idiots who want to privatize historic sites?"

"I'm sure the people in favor of that will be able to use the report that way. 'A private enterprise focused on entertainment could do a better job of making money,' blah blah blah."

"What is *wrong* with these people?" Chloe demanded. Places like Rock Island State Park and Old World Wisconsin were state treasures, to be preserved and interpreted with integrity. She swatted irritably at a fly. "Anything else?"

"Not about the audit. A feature reporter from the *Milwaukee Journal* came out yesterday. Petty donned historic garb and took the woman and her photographer around himself. Wouldn't let them talk to anyone else. Guess whose picture ended up in the paper? The interpreters were pretty pissed."

"Another Petty atrocity," Chloe muttered. Suddenly she remembered she was on a pay phone, with limited silver on hand. "So, any luck finding information about archaeology projects in this area? I know I just talked with you yesterday, but—"

"I found quite a bit, actually."

No surprise there. Chloe wedged the phone between ear and shoulder, slapped her notebook open, and waited with pen poised. "OK. Let me have it."

"Well, there are two big archaeological grails up your way," Nika began. "First, how much do you know about *Le Griffon*?"

"Um, not a whole lot." As in, nothing.

"The *Griffon* was the first full-sized sailing vessel on the upper great lakes. It was built by La Salle—you know, the famous French explorer?"

"Sure." This was firmer ground for anyone who'd gone through twelve years of Wisconsin public school.

"In 1679, *Le Griffon* disappeared somewhere up your way. As you might imagine, people involved in underwater salvage drool with lust about the prospect of discovering it."

Chloe could imagine, all too well. "I have seen a barge or something, north of Rock Island, all lit up at midnight. Maybe some crew is searching for the *Griffon*." They'd want to keep something like that a secret, right? So every other salvage diver in the area didn't show up? They might want to hide from academics, too— historians more interested in documenting the past than profiting

164

from it. Chloe sucked in her lower lip, thinking. Did Brenda Noakes fit into one of those categories?

"There's more to the story," Nika told her. "According to the legend, an Iroquois prophet placed a curse on the *Griffon*. Some people say the ship's disappearance fulfilled that curse by sailing through a crack in the ice."

"That does not sound pleasant."

"And some say the *Griffon* still sails on foggy nights," Nika added cheerfully. "Maybe that's what you saw."

"I don't think so. I—hold on." An operator had cut in, telling Chloe to deposit more quarters. "OK. What was the second grail you mentioned?"

"Proof that Vikings traveled through the Great Lakes. A couple of rune stones have been found, but some historians believe they're fakes."

"Some, but not all." A raindrop hit Chloe's cheek. She wrestled to pull up her hood without dropping the phone.

"Right. Oral tradition among one of the Native American groups in the area does include reference to a group of whites that was defeated in battle near present day Oshkosh, centuries before La Salle showed up. No physical evidence of that has been found, so obviously most historians don't give that story much credence."

"Obviously," Chloe said dryly.

"That hasn't stopped a few people from risking their careers by searching for evidence of Viking travel. If someone could turn up something definitive—a Viking ship or something—it would be huge."

Chloe nodded. It would indeed.

"A friend of mine put me in touch with a friend of *hers* who works at one of the colleges up north." Nika paused. "Ms. Noakes was on the faculty at U-Michigan for a while, but she left after some clash with a tenured colleague."

Chloe leaned over, protecting her notebook from the drizzle. "It may be that her illustrious colleague got funding for a project and she didn't. She's a tad sensitive on that score."

"Or it could be she's on to something big, and the middle-aged white guys who run the world won't like it."

"That is also certainly possible."

"She ended up at Escanaba College, a tiny school in the Upper Peninsula. About two years ago she published an article about Rock Island."

"Yeah?" This sounded more interesting.

"In this article, Ms. Noakes talks about a murder," Nika said. "Some guy got killed for a stash of gold coins, and she talks about the treasure-hunters still salivating over the missing stash."

So much for new information. "Oh. Yeah, she told me about that."

"Then she goes on to say that this well-publicized tale shouldn't overshadow the other murder that took place on Rock Island."

The other murder? Chloe thought. So Brenda *did* know about the murder that had been hinted at in the Thordarson letter. "What did she say? Do you have a copy of the article?"

"Of course," Nika said calmly. "I had a copy faxed to my bank and I picked it up there. Just a sec." A pause, a rustle of distant paper. "OK, here's the bit: 'The fate of James McNeil, and the fate of his gold coins, has long been discussed and debated by local historians. It is distressing to observe, however, that rumors of a second murder on Rock Island have been ignored. Could it be because the source was a woman? Even worse, a woman who'd gained her information from a young girl? The community of traditional historians must begin to—'"

"Please deposit more coins," came a disembodied voice in Chloe's ear.

Chloe didn't have any more coins. "Nika?" she shouted, as if volume might prevail over the phone company's meter. "I gotta go, but I'll—"

Click.

"Call you back soon," Chloe told the dial tone. She replaced the phone and checked her watch. Three-fifteen. She still had some time before the last ferry of the day headed for Rock. The maritime museum Sylvie had told her about was in Jackson Harbor, very close to the *Karfi* dock. Why not take a quick peek at that? Munching a peanut butter sandwich that she'd made that morning, Chloe headed back across the island.

The museum had been established in two old fish sheds. A couple of tugs that looked almost identical to Sylvie's boat were moored at the dock. One, the *Seahawk*, had a small rowboat tied behind it. Hand-painted letters noted that another, the *Welcome*, had been built in Jackson Harbor in 1926. History everywhere I look, Chloe thought.

The museum itself seemed deserted, and she paused to study some photographs on the wall: men grinning from their tugs, men mending nets, men cleaning fish. She was squinting at one when an elderly black man came through a side door and greeted her with a surprised smile. "Hello! I didn't hear you come in."

"I just got here," Chloe assured him. Then she pointed at the image of a fair-haired, weather-coarsened man in overalls, standing on a dock with a wooden net box in his hands. "Who is that? For some reason he looks familiar."

The docent pulled off wire-rimmed glasses and leaned close. "Paul Anderson. He drowned in 1939—probably not too long after that photograph was taken. He was rowing from Rock Island to Washington and capsized." The man shook his head sadly. "People on shore launched a rescue boat when they spotted him clinging to a pound net stake, but it was rough waters and he couldn't hang on long enough."

"I read about that!" Chloe said. It had been one of the stories she'd found in Chester Thordarson's Viking Hall. "It's terrible to imagine an experienced fisherman drowning within sight of both islands."

"Bad years, the thirties, and not just because of the Depression. Smelt were making their way into the Great Lakes, which hit the herring and whitefish populations hard. Then there were all the rules the state kept laying down. Always tinkering with the mesh size." The docent tapped the glass over Paul Anderson's photograph with one gnarled finger. "Paul and a few of the men, they had a place on the island where they made illegal gillnets. Just trying to feed their families, you understand?"

"I do."

"Paul got himself arrested a few times, and finally gave up fishing. He went to work for Chester Thordarson." The man looked pensive for a moment. Then he put what difficult memories he had aside. "Well, now. If you'll sign our guest book, I'll be glad to show you around."

Chloe signed the book and stuffed a five dollar bill in the donation can. "I don't have much time," she said contritely. "I thought I'd get an idea of what was here, and then come back another day."

"Sure. I'll be glad to answer any questions." He gestured at the nearby displays with a big and calloused hand. The exhibits had obviously been put together with pride.

Chloe loved little museums like this, which said so much about local history and the people who worked to preserve it. "I can't imagine being a commercial fisherman," she said. "Being out in all kinds of weather…"

"Lord knows it gets bad out there." The docent looked toward the lake. "It's tough work, but I'll tell you this: the men are tougher." He grinned. "My father didn't get past seventh grade in school, but he was the smartest, most capable man I ever knew. All the old fishermen are like that. They can read the weather, fix a diesel engine, handle wiring, repair woodwork… anything. And nobody understands the lake better than we do. DNR men in the cities talk about 'lake ecology' like it's some new thing, but it's all bookwork to them."

"So you started fishing with your dad?"

"Went out with him when I was ten," he said proudly. "I fished commercial for almost seventy years. I'm still game, but my wife needs me home more. I just volunteer out here a couple of afternoons a week."

"Well, thank you for that," Chloe said, with deep sincerity. "Volunteers make the museum world go 'round. And perhaps you left the business at a good time. With all the problems…"

He sobered. "It's gotten nasty," he agreed. "I hate to see it. I wanted my grandson to take my rig, but in the end, I advised him against it. He loves being on the water, but he's also got a wife and baby now. He's a paralegal down in Green Bay."

The man's tone was a poignant mix of pride and regret. Chloe touched his arm. "I'm sorry," she said, "but it sounds like he's doing well for his family."

"He is." The old man studied a scar on his left thumb, rubbing it absently. "I tried to fish right. You know, make a living and protect the fish populations too. I switched to gillnets with a bigger mesh or a smaller mesh, whatever the DNR said. In the end, though, it wasn't enough to keep my rig in the family." Suddenly he blinked. "Sorry! I didn't mean to spout off like that. You go on and look around."

Chloe could easily imagine how hard it had been for this man to advise his grandson *against* picking up the family business. At least the elderly fisherman had the museum, she thought as she wandered around the room. Volunteering here would let him tell his stories to guests who loved fish boils but never thought twice about where the whitefish came from.

She stopped in front of a display of nets. One looked distressingly familiar. She touched it, picturing the dead fingers she'd seen poking through a net just like this.

"That's an old gillnet," the docent said.

"How old, do you suppose?"

He shrugged. "Hard to say, but most people switched to monofilament twenty years ago. See?" He pointed to an ephemeral net hanging nearby.

I am such an idiot, Chloe thought. When Garrett mentioned that the dead young woman had gotten tangled in an old net, it had never occurred to her that he meant an *old* net. As in, decades old.

Garrett had also told her that nets got left in the lake all the time. The woman who drowned happened to get caught in a very old one, that's all. It probably didn't mean anything. Did it?

When Chloe left the museum, the sound of angry voices drove the question from her mind. A car with DNR insignia was parked near the *Seahawk*. Melvin Jenks stood on the dock, arms folded, glowering at a man Chloe didn't recognize. Game warden, she figured.

"You got no right!" Jenks stood bare-headed in the rain, his thatch of white hair damp against his skull. "Next time, get a warrant."

"We don't need a warrant," the warden barked. He was probably twenty years younger than Jenks, but Chloe wouldn't have bet on him in a fight.

A second warden poked his head from the tug. "Everything's clean," he told his colleague. "No infractions."

Jenks' expression held both contempt and satisfaction. "I *told* you that. Now get the hell off my boat!" The wardens got in their car and drove away.

And I am outta here, Chloe thought. She headed to the *Karfi* dock, wishing she hadn't chanced upon that little encounter. Time to get back to the nineteenth century.

TWENTY-EIGHT:
NOVEMBER, 1880

"Paul," Ragna called. "Help me unreel this last net." Rock Island fishermen had not used the big outdoor reels in the early days. Now that the village was almost deserted, space didn't matter.

Her son emerged from the cottage munching an open-faced sandwich of smoked whitefish on buttered rye bread. Once he'd licked his fingers, they quickly got the net boxed and ready.

"We've got potatoes ready to dig," Ragna said. "Are you sure you want to go out with Uncle Jens and Uncle Carl today?"

"They need my help," Paul said quickly.

"Remember, your papa was a farmer."

He scowled. "My papa was a fisherman."

"He was a farmer first. We were going to buy a farm on Washington Island."

Paul shrugged.

Ragna sighed. Paul was eight years old now, and big for his age. Since Anders died he'd spent more and more time with her brothers. He made nets from scraps of old nets they gave him, and spent hours trying to catch suckers or perch from the dock. He helped Jens and Carl clean and pack fish. He pestered them for tales of their days on the lake.

And finally, this spring, he'd begged Ragna for permission to go out with them. That first time she'd watched Jens rowing the Mackinaw away with her boy in the bow she'd hardly been able to breathe. Perhaps he will be seasick, she'd thought. Perhaps he'll be bored. Perhaps he'll never want to go out again.

She'd known as soon as she saw his tired grin that evening that Paul was indeed his father's son.

"Do you remember what happened to your papa?" she asked now. It was important that he didn't forget.

Paul nodded, studying his toes.

"All right. Go find Jens and Carl." She forced a hug on the squirming boy before he raced off. Then she stood in the sun, facing another long and empty day.

She didn't make many nets now. One by one the men who'd been loyal even after moving away had come by, shame-faced. "Now that store-bought nets are available…" they'd say, not meeting her eye. "It doesn't matter," she told them, over and over. "It truly doesn't matter." The sack of coins and bills she'd planned to use to buy a farm still sat beneath her mattress.

Ragna glanced north. Maybe Emily would visit today. No, likely not. They didn't see each other as often as they did during those early years. Emily had three children now, besides her lighthouse duties. But honestly? Everything changed the night Anders didn't come home. Carrick Dugan killed Anders... and Christine... and Ragna's friendship with Emily Betts, too.

So be it. Dugan didn't spend much time on Rock anymore but he always came back, fishing from his old Mackinaw or through the ice for a few weeks at a time before disappearing again. Ragna liked to walk the beach, watching him as he'd once watched her. He didn't taunt her anymore. He never met her eye. But he knew she was waiting.

Ragna went back inside and checked Anders' pistol and the tin box, both hidden beneath the loose floorboard. Once assured that all was still safe, she settled in for a day of digging potatoes.

She had three bushels in the root cellar and soup bubbling on the stove by the time Paul burst through the door that evening. "Mama!" he cried. "We found this place where a ship must have split wide open!"

Ragna threw a sharp glance at her brothers as they followed Paul into the cottage. "This is true?"

Carl shrugged. "So it seemed. There was a lot of lumber afloat about eight miles out."

"Sit down, and I'll dish up supper." Ragna didn't like to think about any ship going down.

Paul took his place at the table. "There were lots and lots of logs, Mama. So many we got out of the boat and walked around on them!"

Ragna dropped the ladle and stared at her brothers. "You let him do this?"

Jens slid into a chair, avoiding her gaze. Carl shifted his weight from one foot to the other. "I kept an eye on the boy."

"You kept an eye on him? You kept an *eye* on him?"

"Now, Ragna—"

"What if he had fallen? What if he had gone under, and couldn't surface?" Ragna slapped Carl across the cheek.

"*Mama!*" Paul stared at her with wide eyes.

"You," Ragna said fiercely, "will not go out on the boat again. And *you* two—" she pointed from Carl to Jens—"will stay away from my son!"

TWENTY-NINE

THE RANGER WAS MOORED by the dock when the *Karfi* reached Rock Island, but the compound appeared deserted. Chloe considered her options. She wanted to run all the way to the lighthouse, lock the door, and settle down to decipher Emily Betts' letter. But *I'd go blind if I tried right now,* she concluded reluctantly, watching a cloud of water vapor mist by. She needed a dry day and good light for that project.

Thwarted, she decided to take the long way home so she could stop by the meadow. Perhaps Brenda Noakes was still at her lonesome work, digging test pits, a one-woman seeker of lives long gone. *If so,* Chloe thought, *maybe I can wiggle the second murder into the conversation.* She didn't want to show Brenda Emily's letter until she had a better sense of what Brenda was all about.

It was lovely to walk the trail in the fog. Chloe imagined Emily Betts striding through just such a cloud on this island a century earlier—perhaps visiting her Danish friend, perhaps going to deliver a child. She would have passed dead snags riddled with pileated woodpecker holes too, and seen Jack-in-the-Pulpit plants' clustered berries.

When Chloe reached the meadow she wandered slowly toward the shrouded lake, admiring how tiny droplets swirled through the air and clung to each blade of dead grass, each brown stalk of mullein. The fog was thicker here. Chloe zipped her jacket up to her chin, smiling idiotically. The evocative mist only intensified the lingering vibes. She almost heard the fishermen telling tales as they tended their boats and waited for the weather to clear ... almost smelled Danish apple cake baking in a tiny cookstove ... almost saw the women mending nets.

Chloe had reached the top of the rise above the beach when she heard a muffled scraping noise off to her right. Spade on earth, maybe. "Brenda?" Chloe called. No answer.

Paralleling the waterline, Chloe walked south toward the sound. When the meadow ended in a shrubby grove of deciduous trees, she kept going. Moisture dampened tree trunks, and mist clung to the seedpods and the burgundy leaves of columbine plants. "Brenda?"

Silence. Chloe felt a sudden need for caution. She took another step. One more.

Something new pricked her inner sensors. Something dark and angry. She froze, wide-eyed. Energy seemed to swirl past her, gaining strength, fading again. "Shit," she whispered, feeling the trembling malevolence now mingling with the fog. She took a few steps, then retraced them, like someone pacing with a Geiger counter. She didn't know how to get away.

The quickest route of escape led east. She scrambled through the underbrush, barely feeling branches that clawed at her jacket. She plunged from the trees and down the steep slope to the beach.

She didn't stop moving until she'd stumbled across the stones and reached the lake itself.

The shallow water lapped gently against the shore as if mocking her panic. Chloe put hands on knees and leaned over, willing her heart to return to normal cadence. "Note to self," she muttered. "Stay out of the south woods bordering the meadow." Something in that grove wanted… *what*? She had no idea.

Well, maybe you need to find out, she told herself. Maybe you're the only one who can.

"But I don't *want* to," she protested. She folded her arms. Then she sighed, adding, "This totally sucks."

OK. She wasn't a quitter. If she needed to face whatever was lingering in the grove, she would. Still, there was no reason she had to do so right this minute, was there? Brenda Noakes obviously wasn't here, and false twilight would come soon on such a gray day. Besides, Chloe was feeling hollow. A hot meal and a nice cup of chamomile tea at her cozy lighthouse would do her good. She'd tackle the black energy tomorrow.

Relieved with the self-determined postponement Chloe walked north along the water, looking for a decent path that led from the beach up to the meadow. From there, she could cut back to the main trail while staying well away from the spot where she'd felt such bad vibes.

Then she saw the fishnet, and the body.

Because of the mist, she was almost upon the dead woman before seeing her. Chloe's knees hit stones. No mistaking human for fish this time. Instead of being tangled in the old fishnet the woman was covered from toes to chest with it, tidy and snug as if tucked into bed beneath a blanket. Under the net she wore the long black skirt and white puffed-sleeve blouse of a long-gone era. The soaked clothing clung rudely to every curve of muscle and protrusion of bone. Above the woman's head, as if standing in for proper gravestone, a thick wooden stake had been pounded into the earth.

For one terrifying moment Chloe thought she'd truly slipped through time and conjured up a dead fishwife. Then she recognized the long gray braids, dark with lake water but still familiar. Sightless eyes stared from a weather-lined face—also familiar. Sylvie Torgrimsson lay in polite repose, hands crossed over her chest as if gently laid out by a grieving friend.

———

Chloe almost wept with relief when she reached the Viking Hall and saw the *Ranger* still tied at the dock. Thank *God*. As she pounded towards the boathouse Garrett emerged from the contact station and locked the door behind him.

"Garrett!" she squawked, breath coming in heaves. "*Garrett!*"

He looked up and frowned, bracing for whatever had catapulted her shrieking and breathless in his direction. "What's wrong?"

"I—I found another body," she gasped.

"Where?"

"On the—beach below—the fishing village meadow." She struggled to speak calmly. "It—it's Sylvie. Sylvie Torgrimsson."

Garrett took a step backward, as if taking a physical punch.

Chloe waited for something more. It didn't come. "Garrett, we have to call for help."

"She's … she's on the beach?" he echoed. "At the village site?"

179

"Yes." Chloe nodded. "But—"

He began to run.

"Garret, *wait!*" She forced her legs to chase him. She managed to catch up, grab his arm, drag him to a halt.

The park manager wrenched from her grasp. "I have to get to her."

Chloe grabbed the radio holstered on his belt. "Fine! Just give me the radio so I can try to raise someone on Washington."

Garrett didn't argue. As soon as she'd pulled the radio free, he took off again.

———

An hour later, Chloe watched a tableau both eerily familiar and rawly new. She and Garrett had jounced across the island in the DNR pickup truck driven much too fast. Once there Garrett had sent Chloe back with the truck to pick up the rescue crew, which had once again sped across the channel from Washington Island in motorboats.

Now the responders waited in a silent clump watching Stig Fjelstul document the scene. He peered, studied, frowned for an eternity before rising to his feet.

"No visible sign of struggle, or injury," he muttered. "She might have drowned, but it's too soon to say."

Chloe had assumed that Sylvie had drowned. But he's right, she thought. It was impossible to know if lake water or raindrops had soaked Sylvie's hair and clothing.

"Garrett, you saw the body before I did," Stig was saying. "Is that your take? Did you touch or move anything?"

Garrett crouched stone-like, staring at Sylvie.

Stig sharpened his voice. "Smith!"

"What?" The park manager blinked, turned his head, seemed to notice the deputy for the first time. "Oh. Fjelstul."

Chloe cringed from the contempt in his voice. She remembered Maintenance Melvin's scorn, the fish guts draped over Stig's truck.

Stig simplified his question. "Did you touch the body?"

"I—yes. Just on the shoulder." Garrett looked at his hand.

"Did you disturb anything else? Move anything?"

"No."

Stig turned to Chloe. "Does the scene look as it did when you left the beach after finding the body?"

Chloe swallowed hard. "Yes. She was just—just laid out like that. As if she was in some funeral home, already in her coffin. Draped in that fishnet. I didn't notice anything else except that." She pointed to the piece of wood pounded like a gravestone into the beach. "What *is* that?"

Stig was scribbling in his little notebook. One of the other men muttered, "It looks like a pound net marker."

"A pound net marker…?" Chloe had heard of pound nets, but she didn't know how they worked.

The deputy sighed impatiently. "Pound net sites are close to shore, and they're registered. Traditionally, men fishing with pound nets filed a claim with the closest justice of the peace, and then carved their names on markers and left them on the beach near their setups to mark their claim."

"Did Sylvie encroach on some other fisherman's place, do you think?" she asked.

"No," Garret said. "Sylvie didn't have a pound-net rig."

Chloe took her first good look at the wooden marker. It was about two feet tall, formed from rough wood, and carved with slashes and angles—like a capital A with a stem coming down from the horizontal line. She started to make an observation, realized how ludicrous it would sound, and went instead with a question: "But—but why would someone leave a marker near Sylvie's body?" She wanted answers, clear and precise, right *now*.

Garrett drew a deep, shuddering breath. "Sylvie did fish commercially, when she was in the mood. After her husband died she sometimes worked his rig."

"It's too early to speculate," Stig said curtly. He looked back at Chloe. "Was there any sign of her tug? Drifting off-shore, maybe?"

Chloe thought back, then shook her head. "I didn't see it. It was still foggy, though. And once I saw Sylvie…" She lifted both hands, palms up. "I just ran for help."

"OK. I'll get the Coasties looking for it. You two—" Stig included Garret in the order—"stay right here. There's no way to get the ME here before dark. I need to document the scene."

Chloe tipped her face skyward. The fog, perversely, was finally dissipating. The sun seemed determined to atone for its day-long sulk. The sky was pink.

"Surely this was an accident," she said finally. "I saw Sylvie just this morning! How could something like this happen?"

Garrett clenched and unclenched his fists convulsively. "Sylvie knew her way around a boat, but she could be… brash. Foolhardy, even."

"I thought of her as direct," Chloe said. "Although of course I didn't know her well." I liked her though, she added, silently and sadly. I liked her very much.

"Once, Sylvie found someone pulling up her nets," Garrett said. "Instead of calling for help, she confronted the guy. That was … I don't know, a year or so ago. After the quota system was implemented."

Stig didn't speak until he'd finished snapping photographs, nodded at the waiting rescue team, and walked back to Garrett and Chloe. "If you know the name of the man she confronted," he told Garrett, "write it down."

"I don't know the name. Someone from Michigan, I think. But we both know that's not the only problem." Garret raised his chin. "Sylvie uses—used—gillnets. I don't imagine that she would feel compelled to follow a law she didn't agree with. Maybe—"

"The fishing problems are not just political," Stig snapped. "As *you* well know. We've got pollution destroying the plankton, we've got lampreys, we've got—"

"Stop it!" Chloe cried. "What the hell is the *matter* with you two? How can you stand here and bicker at a moment like this?"

Both men actually looked chagrined. After a moment Stig said, "You're right." He exhaled slowly, and looked at Garrett. "Why don't you go along with them." He jerked his head toward the men now busy with the body. "We can talk again in the morning."

"Thank you," Garrett said, with formal courtesy. Then he looked at Chloe. "What about you? We now have two unexplained deaths on the island. The first looked accidental, but this one…"

Chloe looked at Sylvie's carefully folded hands, the odd marker pounded into the ground nearby. And the damn fishnet.

"There's no one in the campground tonight," Garrett added. "Chloe, I am not comfortable with the idea of you staying on the island alone."

Chloe hugged her arms over her chest. She had so longed to have at least one solitary night on Rock! All pleasure from that notion was gone now. "Well, I guess I'm not comfortable with that idea either," she admitted. "I'd like to get my things from the lighthouse, though."

"I'll go with you," Stig said. "Then we'll take my boat back to Washington."

Chloe blinked back tears. She didn't want Stig to order her around. She didn't want to leave the lighthouse. Most of all, she didn't want Sylvie to be dead.

THIRTY:
SEPTEMBER, 1882

"WILL YOU STAY TO dinner, Anton?" Emily asked. "We'd be de-lighted."

"Only if you're sure it's no trouble," Anton Jacobson said. "I heard the *Dahlia* came by yesterday. I wanted to see if Captain Betts got any newspapers."

"I'll fetch them," William said. "Please, sit down."

Emily set Amy, who'd recently turned seven, to watch the two little boys, William Jr. and DeElbert. "Jane," she added quietly, "please set the table."

Then Emily checked the potatoes—good, already tender—and put the trout filet in the skillet. She liked Anton, and knew William enjoyed his company. She'd had very little sleep in the past two days, though. DeElbert was cutting a tooth, and she'd delivered the twins of a young Norwegian bride who'd walked up from the village while in labor so Emily could "do" for her.

Thank heavens we're using kerosene in the lamp now, she thought. The supply ship had brought barrels of it. She and William didn't like having huge quantities of flammables inside their home, but tending the light had just gotten easier. No more kettles of lard simmering on the second-story stove day and night. No more scrubbing a patina of fat from glass and brass and woodwork. No more incessant smell of pork drifting through the house.

William and Anton leafed through the pages. "Any more on those new restrictions on gillnets?" Anton asked. Although heavily accented, his English was good. "Some of our boys fish in both Wisconsin and Michigan waters, you know, and we've got a problem each time the rules about mesh size changes."

"Here." William tapped a column with one finger. "Michigan law will now allow no smaller mesh than four and three-quarter inches."

Anton leaned close and read the fine print for himself. "Now, that's bad. Our nets are four and one-half inch mesh."

Nets. Mesh. I really must make an effort to see Ragna more often, Emily thought. If only—

"Mama?" Jane called. "The cisterns must be leaking again." She stood by the sink, hand on the pump. "All I can get's a trickle."

"Try to at least fill the pitcher." Emily stifled a sigh. The cisterns had only recently been replastered.

"I've heard men say all fishing with nets should be prohibited for two or three years," William was saying.

And what will Ragna and her brothers do then? Emily thought. "All right, gentlemen," she announced. "Clear the table, because the food is ready."

Anton smiled. "Say, I heard you did real good with those twins. Born so small, their mother said, that her wedding ring slipped over their hands like a bracelet."

"My biggest worry was keeping them warm," Emily said. A gale wind had blown drafts through every room that night. She'd wrapped the twins warmly, nestled them into a basket, and slipped them into the warming oven above the range. They'd come through the night just fine. Unlike Ragna's daughter. Christine Anderson was the only baby Emily hadn't been able to save.

"Someone's coming," William said. "Sit, Em. I'll get it."

Emily threw her husband a grateful glance. As she dished peas onto her plate she heard the murmur of male voices at the west door. A few moments later William returned to the kitchen, looking perplexed.

"Who was it?" Emily asked. "Didn't you invite them in?"

"A friend from Washington Island," William said. "He said he had to get back—he just wanted to deliver this." He held up an envelope. "It's from the lighthouse service, Emily. And it's addressed to you."

THIRTY-ONE

STIG TOOK THE LEAD as he and Chloe hiked north to the lighthouse. His duty belt reminded her of Roelke, who seemed very far away. Rays of late-day sun slanted through the trees. A spider's web sparkled with moisture. A warbler began its evening song. The beauty collided with the images in Chloe's head.

Finally they emerged into the lighthouse clearing—so lovely, so peaceful. "Give me your key," Stig said. "I'll check the building before you go inside. Stay right here and shout if you see anyone."

Chloe felt an abrupt and welcome boil of anger as he went inside the lighthouse. *Her* lighthouse. He didn't have to order her around like a child! Would Stig and Garrett even let her return in the morning? Was her time in Pottawatomie Lighthouse over for good?

He emerged five minutes later. "OK," he said. "Go grab your…" He turned his head as the noise of an approaching powerboat drifted through the evening. The engine slowed below the lighthouse, then stopped. Stig jogged to the edge of the bluff. "Can't see it from here," he said. "I'm going to take a look."

"I'm coming too."

Chloe felt a physical ache in her chest as they walked down the trail. Sylvie, irascible and supportive, brimming with life—dead! Chloe mourned the loss of such a fierce advocate for the lighthouse project. Someone who might have become a friend. Oh… and Emily! Chloe swiped at another tear. How could she discover Emily's story, if her project was shut down so abruptly?

I need to stay in the lighthouse, Chloe thought. She needed to be *here*, in this very place where Emily had once tended the light and her family. She needed to be on Rock Island, free to visit the village site.

She cursed whoever was behind Sylvie's death—or whoever had, at the very least, arranged her body so carefully before leaving her on the beach. Stig better find you, she told the guilty party grimly. And find you quick so—

Dire thoughts flew from Chloe's head as they reached the staircase leading to the beach. A small motorboat revved again, and zoomed north. But a man wearing denim cut-offs and a shapeless T-shirt was wading in the lake. Chloe's heart skittered into overtime before she reminded herself that someone knee-deep 150 feet below her could not constitute an immediate threat.

"Who the hell is that?" Stig asked.

Chloe had no idea. No one was camping on Rock. The last ferry had come and gone. Why was someone wading on her beach? She felt Stig tense, poised to shout or to run down the steps. She caught his eye, shook her head, and put a finger over her mouth. After several seconds he nodded.

Chloe squinted. The guy stood still as a heron waiting for fish. She wished she had her binoculars. Something about him seemed familiar. His back was toward her, but she could see longish dark hair, a slim build… Was it Camera Guy? It sure looked like Camera Guy—the young man who wanted to become a professional photographer. Perhaps he'd walked into Lake Michigan for his art, needing to study the play of fading light on the water.

The wader turned, looking back toward the beach. It *was* Camera Guy. Except… there was no dark shape against his light shirt. Camera Guy's camera was conspicuously missing.

Well, he'd probably left it on the beach, not wanting to risk ruining it if he stumbled. Or…? Another possibility wiggled into Chloe's beleaguered brain. She pressed one hand over her mouth, examining stray bits of information that flickered from her memory. Stories Stig had told her about fervent environmentalists, blessedly full of convictions and foolishly naïve about the natural world's indifference. A single small light in the Rock Island channel at night. A missing camera and shards of glass on the beach. An N made of pebbles, the lines crisp and sharp as Zorro's mark…

Shit. Chloe bit her lip, realizing she'd made a stupid assumption. Garrett and Stig had as well. Still.

Camera Guy pivoted again, once more facing north. Chloe cocked her head at Stig: *Come away.* They crept slowly back until she was sure they couldn't be seen from the water.

Stig glared. "Who is that?" he hissed. "I need to question him—"

"Just listen for a minute."

Stig tapped his thumb on his thigh, just the way Roelke did, while she told him what she was thinking. "So I want to talk to him," Chloe whispered. "To Camera Guy."

"*I* will talk to him."

"He'd be more likely to open up to me." She didn't know why she thought that, but she did.

"But—"

Chloe forced down her impatience. "Please. Just let me try. You can watch from the top of the steps."

For a long moment Stig didn't speak. A chickadee darted past. Finally the deputy said, "All right. You can give it a try."

Chloe didn't try to muffle her footsteps as she descended the stairs. The young man turned his head, looked at her, looked back to the lake. Once on the beach she saw his kayak, hauled dry and left against the limestone wall. It was a tandem.

He can't stay out there forever, Chloe thought. His feet must be numb. She made her way to Emily's Rock and sat down.

Camera Guy ignored her for a long time. Chloe expected an impatient Stig Fjelstul to pound down the steps any moment, but he stayed hidden. And finally, the young man turned and waded back to shore. He seemed to know that Chloe was waiting for him, for he came to stand before her, hands in pockets, head hung low.

Chloe drew in a careful breath. After talking Stig into this plan, she needed to handle things right. "What's your name?"

"Spencer Brant," he told the cobbles. He sounded weary.

"You don't have your camera today."

"I will *never* take another picture." He lifted his head and looked east, toward the cairn. His eyes filled with tears.

Chloe spoke gently. "Who was the young woman who drowned, Spencer? Did her name start with an N, or with a Z?" Z, like Zorro.

He didn't speak, didn't move.

Chloe circled her hand in a *You know* gesture. "I saw the initial made by the cairn. It's a lovely tribute, by the way. You made it, right?"

Finally he nodded. "It—I made it for Zana." He began to cry. "Oh, *God*."

Chloe refrained from smacking herself in the forehead. If we hadn't assumed that pebble zigzag formed an N, she thought, the poor girl might have been identified sooner.

Spencer Brant began weeping. "Why don't you sit down," she said, patting the stone beside her. When he didn't move she took his hand and tugged gently. "Please, Spencer. Sit down." She waited until he'd settled before saying, "You need to tell me what happened."

He hiccupped and sniffled and wiped his nose on his sleeve. "Zana and I c-came up here to—to protest fishing. *All* fishing. Fishermen are raping the Great Lakes, you know."

Chloe didn't respond. She needed to listen now, not educate.

"Zana had this great idea. She wanted me to photograph her in the water, wrapped in an old fishing net. We planned to use the photos to help people understand that for over a century, helpless creatures have been trapped like that."

Chloe imagined a passionate young woman—sure of herself, comfortable with her body, hopelessly naïve.

"So, we paddled out to the channel one evening. We got some good shots, but—but some wind did kick up. I wanted to go back, but Zana wasn't ready to leave."

"Why not?"

"The sun was setting, and the sky was really dramatic, you know? And Zana kept wanting to try one more shot, just one more shot. She'd hold onto the kayak, and tell me what she wanted, and then position herself in the net."

"What went wrong?"

"I don't know!" Spencer cried. "She had rolled herself in the net and was floating nearby. I had to turn the kayak so I could get her with the twilight sky as backdrop. Twilight, get it?"

Chloe's heart hurt. "I get it." Twilight for the fish populations. Twilight for the fishing industry.

"I didn't know Zana was in trouble. She didn't call for help or anything! I took a few last shots—the clouds really were awesome—and then..." His voice cracked. "She said, 'I need to get out.' I waited for her to unwind herself from the net, but she didn't. I—I put the camera down, and held out the paddle—she could have grabbed it even through the net—but she didn't! Why didn't she grab it?"

"Zana was probably getting hypothermia," Chloe said. "Water in the Great Lakes is *cold*, Spencer. Even at this time of year, people can get in trouble very quickly. Zana probably couldn't make her hands reach out and grab the paddle." She tried to keep her voice calm, even though the picture painted in her mind made her want to weep right along with him.

"I—I put the camera in a dry-bag before I tried to get her." Spencer's hands clawed convulsively at his thighs. "I put the damn camera away! My father gave it to me, and it was really expensive, and—and..."

"I doubt that extra moment made any difference." Chloe prayed that was true. "That's why you smashed the camera later, right? I cleaned up the glass this morning."

"I tried to smash it, but all I did was break the lens. So I pitched the camera into the lake." Spencer turned to her. "I tried to get Zana back in the kayak! I *really* tried."

"Were you wearing a life jacket?"

"No. I always wear a life jacket when I'm running a river. You know, in whitewater. But we didn't even bring them along. I mean, it's just a lake!"

Just a lake, Chloe thought. You foolish, *foolish* kid.

"Zana just… she just got away from me." Spencer stared over the water. "I freaked out and went in after her. But I couldn't find her in the water, and it was getting dark, and—and I did get really, *really* cold, and I—I just panicked. I was afraid I'd get lost myself if I didn't get back in the kayak and head to shore."

Chloe closed her eyes for a moment. "Why didn't you report what happened?"

"I just—just couldn't even think straight. My father—God, when my father hears about this, he'll…" He spread his hands, evidently unable to articulate that eventuality. "And Zana's parents! How can I tell them?"

"It was an accident, Spencer. A tragic accident. Zana played her own role in what happened."

"I guess I hoped that I'd find her. That maybe she somehow ended up on shore or something. That she was OK. I put on dry clothes and got a lantern from my car and went back out, searching for her. But I couldn't find her."

Chloe refrained from pointing out that kayaking alone, in the dark, when no one knew where he was, was just as dangerous as Zana's photo shoot.

"All I could do was imagine…" He shuddered so violently that Chloe put an arm around his thin shoulders. "Two days later I heard people talking in the general store, saying that her body had washed up on shore beneath the lighthouse."

Chloe nodded. "So you took the *Karfi* over and built the memorial cairn on the beach."

"Yeah." He stared at a black spider scuttling over the stones. "I needed to come here, to the beach. But I keep going back out on the water, too. Sometimes I go late at night and just sit out there in the kayak. I still can't believe she's really gone."

"Was Zana her real name?"

Brant shook his head. "Zana's real name is—was—Mary Pat. Everyone in our group chose a warrior name. Zana means 'God's Gift' in Hebrew." He planted his elbows on his knees, and his face in his palms.

"It's a lovely name," Chloe agreed. She sat for a moment, watching a herring gull bobbing offshore. Shadows were stretching long, now; the peaceful pink glow fading. Time to go.

"One more thing," she said. "Another body was found on Rock Island today, over a mile from here. An older woman, draped in a fishnet. Do you know anything about that?"

"What?" He stared at her, clearly bewildered. "No!"

"OK." Chloe believed him. She hoped Stig would as well.

The young man lifted his face, staring over the passage. "I don't know what to do."

"Zana needs to go home. Her body needs to be officially identified. She needs to be laid to rest with dignity."

"I don't even know who to talk to," Spencer mumbled. "They said there aren't any cops on Washington Island."

"No, but there's a sheriff's deputy." Chloe stood up. "Come on. I'll introduce you."

THIRTY-TWO:
NOVEMBER, 1882

RAGNA SAT BY HER stove, trying to remember what Anders looked like. She remembered his energy, his joy, his bubbling laughter; even the feel of his hands on cold nights. But after six years, it was getting harder and harder to recall his face. Too many dreams, she thought. She often dreamed of him sinking into the lake, tangled in one of her fishnets, the stones she'd hand-tied along one edge pulling him down…

She jumped when the door opened. Carl came inside and slammed it quickly to keep the icy wind from following him. "Where's Paul?" she cried. Oh dear God—

"He's fine," Carl said. "He and Jens are down at the shed." He frowned. "Did you let your fire go out?"

Paul's fine, Ragna told herself. Paul's *fine*. Then she checked the firebox. "It's not all the way out," she said. She blew on the glowing embers, added some kindling.

"Jesus, Ragna." Carl sounded disgusted.

"I made pea soup and dumplings. Go help Paul and Jens with the catch, and supper will be hot by the time you're done."

Carl didn't speak. He touched Anders' pipe, still hanging on the wall where he'd left it the day he disappeared. He walked to the window, scratched a hole in the frost, peered out. Finally he pulled out a chair by the table and sat.

Ragna knew something bad was coming. She just didn't know what. "Say what you have to say, Carl."

"Jens and I are leaving Rock Island."

"I see." Ragna stood, stirred the soup pot, fussed with the damper.

"We would have left long ago if you'd been willing to come with us. We need a bigger boat, and a deeper harbor."

Ragna reached for the bowls kept on a shelf.

"Come with us," Carl said. "We'll find a bigger place where all of us can live. You can keep house, and—"

Ragna wished she had the netting needle Anders had been carving for her. It had disappeared into the lake with him, but it would be nice to hold his last gift in her hand—especially when arguing with her brothers. "I will not leave Rock Island."

Carl stood again, looming over her. "Why *not*? There's nothing for you here!"

"Have you forgotten that my baby girl's grave is here? And that Anders is…" She waved an arm toward the lake, blinking back tears.

"How could we forget?" Carl shot back. "I understand your grief, Ragna—"

"You do not."

"—but Anders would not want this for you." He gestured vaguely around the room.

Oh, Ragna thought, but this *is* what Anders wanted. He wanted to stay right here.

Carl sighed. "Please, sister. Winter is coming down fast. Jens and I don't want to leave you here alone."

"Anton Jacobson is still here with his sister and his boy. And a few others as well." Not Mette Friis, though—her family had left two years earlier. Berglind Fridleifsdottir's family had packed up the year before that.

"Ragna—"

"Go. You have my blessing." Ragna folded her arms. "Paul and I will be fine."

"Paul wants to come with us."

Ragna's knees went soft. "You have discussed this with him? How could you? It was bad enough that you took him back out in the boat after I *forbade* you to, but—"

"You can't hold smoke in your hands." Carl shoved his hands in his pockets. He was muscled and brawny like all the fishermen. Like Anders had been. "That boy lives to be on the water. You can't stop him. Neither could Jens and I, even if we wanted to."

"You are taking my boy." Ragna pressed one hand over her heart, which seemed to be skittering very fast.

"I have to," Carl said grimly. "You are poisoning him, Ragna. He lost his father young, which is harsh. But he needs to have a life of his own! He needs to remember Anders as he lived, not as he died. Yet all you do is fill him with bitter tales."

They were taking her son. They were taking her boy. "At least wait until spring," Ragna begged. "You can fish through the ice here as well as anywhere."

Carl shook his head. "We've been offered work on Washington Island, trimming bark off cedar logs for telegraph poles. We start next week."

Ragna felt a wave of nausea. It reminded her of morning sickness.

"Well, I've said my piece. I'll go get the others." Carl walked to the door and paused, hand on the latch. "Dugan's gone, Ragna. He hasn't been seen in six months."

"He'll be back." He always came back.

"Are you staying to be near Christine and Anders?" Carl asked. "Or are you staying because of Dugan? Don't think I haven't seen you. You should be staying far away from the man, and instead..." He spread his hands. Fisherman's hands, strong and scarred. "You're taunting a boar, Ragna. There isn't a sheriff on the islands. If you—"

"Go," Ragna managed. "Just go."

"Poison," Carl muttered, and left.

THIRTY-THREE

STIG INSISTED THAT CHLOE leave Rock Island with him and Spencer Brant. She agreed only because she didn't want to argue in front of Spencer. The three of them walked in silence to the landing, guided by flashlight.

Stig made a radio call before they motored around Washington Island and on to the mainland. Another deputy was waiting at the dock.

"Good luck, Spencer," Chloe said. She took one of his hands, squeezed.

"Thank you," he whispered. "Thank you very much."

"What will happen to Spencer?" she asked, when Stig rejoined her on the deck.

"He'll get charged with failure to report an accident in a timely fashion, but it seems clear that the girl's death was an accident. A stupid, senseless accident, but an accident nonetheless." He sucked in a long breath, blew it out again. "Your instincts were good, Chloe. Thank you."

"You're welcome," she said, savoring his words. She hadn't felt particularly good about her people skills lately, but she'd somehow done an OK job with Spencer Brant.

"If you're not too tired," Stig began, "We still need to talk about Sylvie."

Chloe's bubble of satisfaction popped. *Sylvie.* "I'm not too tired," she told him. "Is the actual sheriff coming up too?" She flushed. "I mean, don't take that the wrong way, but—"

"Door County doesn't have a sheriff at the moment. We're waiting for Governor Dreyfus to appoint a new one. I'm afraid you're stuck with me."

Chloe sighed. "Sorry. I'm just tired."

"Where do you want to spend the night?"

"At the lighthouse."

"No."

"Excuse me?" Chloe gave him a pointed look. "Listen, Stig, I'm not a child, and I'm not stupid. I was ready to leave the lighthouse when we thought a serial killer might be on the loose. But there's not some maniac drowning women in Rock Island passage. We know how Zana died."

"That still leaves one unexplained death on Rock Island," he said grimly.

"But Sylvie's body was found over a mile away from Pottawatomie." She kept her voice firm, rational. "Look, I was only given a week to tackle this project. I'm making great progress, but time is running out."

"What difference does it make where you stay? The archives and museums are on Washington anyway."

"I need to be at Pottawatomie." If he didn't understand that, she couldn't explain it. "Is the park going to be closed tomorrow, do you think?"

He shrugged. "I doubt it. The death will be in the news. Any potential visitors can make their own decision."

That's one more point in my favor, Chloe thought.

Stig stared over the water, purple-black in the starlight. After a long moment he said, "Do you have any coffee at the lighthouse?"

Victory. "I do."

"Here's the deal, then. We go back to Pottawatomie, you make coffee, I get your statement. If you insist on staying at the lighthouse, I at least want to make sure you're locked up tight for the night."

————

An hour later Stig and Chloe were settled at the kitchen table in Pottawatomie Lighthouse. A lantern dispelled some of the shadows. Stig wrapped his hands around his Sierra cup of instant coffee, straight-up. Chloe had added cocoa powder and a peppermint to hers, and a dollop of honey too.

"So," Stig said. "Give me the sequence of events that led to you finding Sylvie's body."

Chloe told him about the conversation she'd had with Sylvie that morning—Geez, had it just been that morning?—before she headed to the dock. Suddenly she paused, reluctant to mention the argument she'd overheard between Garret and Sylvie.

"What?" Stig asked, eyes narrowing. "Why are you hesitating?"

No choice but to tell the tale. She did.

"But you didn't hear what Garrett and Sylvie were arguing about?"

"No. But Garrett…"

Stig frowned impatiently. "*What?*"

"He seemed really upset about Sylvie."

"They used to be married."

"They did?" Chloe leaned back in her chair. "OK, I did not see that coming. When? For how long?"

"Decades ago, and not for long. Maybe four or five years." Stig took off his glasses, rubbed his nose, replaced them. "They got divorced. A few years later, Sylvie remarried. She and her second husband were together a long time."

Geez Louise. No wonder Garrett had been shaken.

"Back to your story," Stig said. "What happened after you overheard Garrett and Sylvie arguing?"

Chloe summarized her day on Washington, taking the late *Karfi* to Rock, and deciding to circle past the meadow on the way home. "And then I wandered down to the beach, and was walking along the water, and—and there she was."

He cracked his knuckles, gaze never leaving Chloe. "How did you get to the beach? Were you walking south, or north?"

Chloe picked up her cup, took a slow sip, wiped her mouth with a napkin. She imagined trying to explain that swirl of dark energy she'd felt in the grove to this jaded officer. Imagined his skepticism—maybe ridicule. No, some details she'd keep to herself. Her sensors were tuned to times long past. She had no reason to believe that the malevolence that had sent her fleeing to the beach had anything to do with Sylvie.

"Well actually, I was just wandering around," she said at last. "Brenda Noakes described the village to me, and I was trying to picture it."

He studied her over his mug.

"It's important for my work," she added, hoping she didn't sound defensive. "So anyway, I sort of meandered into the grove south of the meadow, then ambled down to the beach." "Amble" was quite the euphemism for her headlong plunge, and she realized belatedly that Stig would likely find evidence of her crashing flight through the underbrush. "So I was walking north along the water," she concluded doggedly. "It was still foggy. I got pretty close to the body before I knew it was there."

"Describe what you saw."

She did. Then she wrote it down for him on a piece of paper torn from her notebook.

He folded it, tucked it into a pocket, and sat in brooding silence for several moments. "Do you have any idea why Sylvie would be wearing old-timey clothes? I can't figure the costume."

"She did tell me that she had a period outfit all ready," Chloe said. "She wanted to wear it when she gave lighthouse tours. I can't imagine why she'd be wearing it on her boat, though."

"Me either."

Chloe leaned back in her chair. "Stig, do you think it's possible that someone would actually kill a fisherman—fisherwoman— because of the new laws?"

He was silent again. Chloe watched a moth flitter around the lantern and imagined Emily Betts, sitting right here on countless dark and silent nights of her own, thinking through problems, perhaps watching ancestors of this very moth flit around *her* oil lamp. Finally Stig wiped a hand over his mouth. "Absolutely not."

"But—"

"Absolutely—*not*. Look, I know these people. I grew up with these people. Sure, tempers are flaring. But it's a mighty long leap from fish guts left on a car to murder."

"But you said her body showed no obvious sign of struggle. Doesn't that suggest that someone she knew was involved?"

"I can't speculate." He shoved to his feet and prowled the kitchen. "Her death might have been accidental. That long skirt might have played some role. Anyway, what we *do* know is that someone tampered with her body, laying it out that way on the beach."

"And pounding in the marker."

"Right. That too." He dropped back into his chair. "But we have no idea what that's supposed to signify."

"Did the carving on the stake mean anything?"

"Not to me."

She fiddled with her spoon. "The marks reminded me of the Appalachian Trail logo."

"The … *what*?"

"It's a backpacking trail that runs from Georgia to—"

"I know what the Appalachian Trail is," he growled. "What I don't know is why you're yammering about it."

Chloe frowned. "There's no need to get pissy. All I'm saying is that it looks like the same initials. An A over a T."

"Thank you, Ms. Ellefson. I'll keep that in mind."

OK, dead-end there. Chloe reached for the pot, and refilled her mug. "Sylvie said she liked going out in foggy weather. I can un-

derstand that—it does make it easier to imagine historical events."
She flushed again. It was impossible to imagine Stig Fjelstul evoking his ancestors on misty afternoons.

"Hmmn."

O-*kay*, no sale on that theory either. Chloe reached for the plastic bag of cocoa powder, spooned some into the coffee. "Is it possible that after Sylvie drowned—"

"You're *assuming* she drowned. Only the ME can ascertain that."

"My point is, do you think someone might have dressed her like that for a reason? Making some kind of a statement?"

"Can you imagine changing the clothes on a woman who just drowned?"

"No. But I can't imagine arranging a body on a public beach, either." Chloe grimaced. "What Sylvie was wearing seems key, though. Maybe her death had something to do with historic events."

He crossed his arms. "Like what?"

"Maybe she ran into someone looking for those lost gold coins."

Stig snorted. "Rock Island has been searched from shore to shore. Only an idiot would think they could find them now, a century and more later."

"I'm a curator," Chloe reminded him, "and believe me, I've known such people." She paused. "I've seen a large boat north of here a couple of times, very late at night, not moving but lit up."

"A freighter."

She shook her head. "I know the difference. I've heard about the *Griffon*. I'd imagine everyone from French nationals to college professors to treasure hunters would like to find that wreck. If someone did find it, they'd want to keep the location a secret, right? Maybe Sylvie went out in her tug and—and—I don't know, saw something she shouldn't have."

Stig regarded her, not even wasting energy on a snort this time. "And that would lead to a wooden marker being left by her body… how, exactly?"

"I don't know. It just seems to me that the person involved was trying to send some kind of message—hey, wait! Do you suppose the marks on the stake are runes?"

"Runes?"

"You know, letters in ancient Scandinavian alphabets. Some people would like to prove that Vikings once traveled through this area, and—"

"What in Hades are you talking about?"

"Oh, never mind." She waved a hand. Clearly Stig was not in the mood to think outside his little law enforcement box.

He sighed. "Look, tomorrow I'll interview people, follow up on some leads. If we get lucky, the Coast Guard will locate the tug." He got up and put his mug in the sink. "I'm going to head out. You sure you're OK here?"

"*Quite* sure. Let me just make a run to the privy, and then I'll be in for the night."

Ten minutes later Chloe was alone in the lighthouse. Alone on the island. And I'm OK with that, she thought. She'd stay inside until daylight, but yes, she still felt safe here.

Chloe washed the two mugs, using as little water as possible. Emily, she thought, how on earth did you manage? Emily and William had a large family, a large home, a large garden, a cow, horses, and a Fresnel lens to keep spotless. It boggled the mind.

Chloe checked her watch. Only 9:30? The evening's events had drained her, but the coffee was kicking in. She should have stuck with herbal tea. Once, months earlier, Roelke had made her herbal tea on a day that had sucked as badly as this one did. She smiled at the memory. He really could be a sweetie.

Then her smile disappeared. If Roelke learned that a murdered body had been found on Rock Island—by her, no less—he would freak out. If he knew she'd decided to stay alone in the lighthouse, against all advice, he'd probably get in his truck and start driving north.

Now that Stig was gone, and she wasn't on the defensive, she tried to parse out her own reasons for staying—reasons that, unlike her wish to learn more about Emily Betts, she could use to defend her decision. First and foremost, she wanted to do a good job for the RISC members. A good furnishings plan, well researched and supportive of key interpretive themes, would lay the groundwork for future fundraising and programming efforts. Chloe relished the special magic of quiet times at Pottawatomie— just as she loved wandering Old World Wisconsin after hours. But quiet times didn't impress auditors or legislators, and they didn't pay the bills. Some office-bound bureaucrats wanted to privatize Wisconsin's historic sites, and the same idiots might be hungry to build roads on Rock Island.

I made a commitment, Chloe thought, and I will do my damnedest to see it through. Once the lighthouse was open for tours and attracting more visitors to the park, even the urban boo-hoos might be convinced to leave the island alone.

But an unsolved murder on Rock wouldn't do anybody any good.

Grabbing her notebook, Chloe sat back down at the table. Stig had dismissed the idea that past events had any connection to Sylvie's death. OK, fine; he'd investigate all the obvious possibilities. But there wasn't any harm in her considering other possibilities, right?

She turned to a fresh page in her notebook. Who might have wished Sylvie ill?

1. Wreck divers searching for Le Griffon.

According to Nika, that quest was a high-stakes gambit. Sylvie might have motored close to the mystery ship in the fog, and challenged someone pirating an underwater site of such significance. But if so, how had her body ended up back on Rock?

2. Some academic seeking evidence of Viking travel through the area.

Maybe Sylvie had challenged wreck divers who were after evidence of a Viking ship at the bottom of Lake Michigan. Same problem as #1, though—why bring the body back to the beach for formal presentation?

Well, Chloe mused, finding a ship wasn't the only way to prove the Viking theory. If Sylvie had surprised some unethical academic in the act of defacing her beloved Rock Island by chiseling ancient runic markings from a somehow-overlooked limestone cliff, things could have turned nasty. But again—Sylvie had been lakebound.

Well... maybe that wasn't an issue. Stig hadn't speculated about time of death. Maybe Sylvie had gone out on the lake and then returned to the island before she died.

3. Treasure hunters looking for the lost "Yellow Boys" coins.

Sylvie would have confronted anyone she suspected of illegal digging. But Sylvie hadn't been found by newly dug holes or a limestone cliff. She'd been found on the village site beach. The site where Brenda Noakes worked. Chloe thought about that for a while, but couldn't come up with a way to connect the two women. Although it *had* seemed this morning as if Sylvie wanted to say something about Brenda... and then thought better of it. Chloe hoped that Sylvie's moment of reticence hadn't meant that a key piece of information had died with her.

Then there was that bizarre marker pounded into the beach by Sylvie's body. Might the odd carved marks really be runes? Chloe drew the marks in her notebook. One capital **A**, with a vertical line extending from the A's cross-stroke to form a **T**. Appalachian Trail. Or...? She sighed. Who knew? The initials hadn't meant anything to Stig, and he was a local. Besides, maybe her familiarity with the hiking trail symbol had skewed her thinking. Maybe the letters should be read T. A. The phrase "teaching assistant" came to mind, but the initials otherwise had no meaning.

Remembering the mistake she'd made with the N/Z pebble tribute Spencer Brant had made, Chloe turned her page sideways. Viewed that way, the marks could be runes. Or, the A's point became the tip of an arrow. On the stake, that tip had been pointing skyward. She couldn't fathom why a murderer might leave such a sign.

"This is ridiculous!" she exclaimed. Stig was right; she should leave such contemplation to him. She slapped the notebook closed, pushed back her chair, and climbed to the second-story landing. She planned to recommend putting a rocking chair in this spot. It was easy to imagine a keeper sitting here to reflect on the day.

Chloe leaned against the window frame. To the west, a quarter moon cast a milky trail on the water. The scene was so beautiful that Chloe's heart ached, actually ached in her chest. Tim's girlfriend, Natalie, had spoken of tragedies on the lake. So had Brenda Noakes. Poor Zana had come to grief. Now Sylvie was dead too.

I shouldn't be surprised, Chloe thought. She'd read many grim tales. William Betts had noted shipwrecks in his logbook, and included the horrid tale of the men who'd frozen to death in their boat. And … *yes*. When one of Chester Thordarson's employees capsized while rowing from Rock Island to Washington, he'd clung to a pound net stake in the water before getting washed away. The docent at the Maritime Museum had told her the victim's name: Paul Anderson.

Chloe stared at the marks she'd been trying to decipher. No way could she find a P, but the A was clear.

That might be important. Or it might have absolutely nothing to do with anything.

Chloe looked back out at the night, tired of mental debate, feeling inexpressibly sad. Finally she turned away from the window. Caffeine or no, it was time for bed.

In the bedroom she kicked off her shoes, pulled on her sweatshirt, and burrowed into her sleeping bag. Once cocooned in its warmth, she was asleep in moments…

Only to be jolted awake again by the sound of childish laughter.

This is insane, Chloe thought. A young woman has drowned, an old woman evidently has drowned, and what do I hear? Children at play in the middle of the night. She sat up in bed. Perhaps the coffee had been a good idea after all. Her brain seemed sharp and clear, as if she'd never been asleep. She tipped her head, waiting. A few seconds later she heard the laughter again—a girl's pealing laugh, a boy's chortle. Previously, she had imagined the laughter to be coming from inside the lighthouse. This time, the sounds came from the lawn outside her window.

Chloe unzipped her sleeping bag and got to her knees on the mattress. The bed stood less than a foot from the window, and she rested her palms on the sill and peered through the pane. Nothing to see but darkness.

The laughter came again. Definitely from outside. And she seemed to be hearing the same laughter over and over again. As in, the *exact* same laughter—one high peal, one joyful chortle.

Chloe sucked in her lower lip. If she was hearing two of the Betts children tonight, only a few moments were echoing through time. On the previous occasions it had seemed that a slightly longer exchange between the children was resonating into the present from... well, let's see, a century ago. More or less, anyway. She'd seen the Betts family tree, and if she was remembering correctly, William and Emily had four children by 1882. All very interesting, Chloe thought, but she had no idea what to make of it.

What she *did* know? Whether she liked it or not, she was hearing an auditory echo from times long gone. Besides the Betts children, she'd heard that scraping noise in the grove by the fishing village site. No one had been in the grove... except whomever was responsible for that sickening vortex of black energy.

Oh, Roelke, she thought, as if he might hear her. She'd been trying to decide if she was meant to be in a relationship. Maybe she was meant to connect only with history-junkies and elderly folks and yes, sometimes even the dead people whose lives she worked so hard to understand. What if she and Roelke were together and she started hearing things? What if he'd been with her when she sensed that whirlpool of evil energy in the grove south of the village site? Could she hide her feelings?

But that's not the right question, Chloe told herself. She couldn't deny who she was. Couldn't change her gift of perception. Besides, every once in awhile that perception let her do something good that needed doing. It had happened once at Old World Wisconsin, and it seemed to be happening here on Rock Island as well.

She blinked back sudden tears. It would not be fair to date Roelke without telling him what was going on. But how could she explain the unexplainable? At best he'd want to protect her. At worst he'd think she was whacko.

She got out of bed, grabbed her flashlight, and padded into the kitchen. She picked up the photo of Emily Betts and squinted at it in the yellow beam. The two children posed with Emily in the lighthouse doorway were so tiny and blurred Chloe couldn't even tell if they were girls or boys.

Tell our story. Put things right.

I'm trying, Chloe thought a bit testily. What *was* the story? Did Emily want to be sure that the Herb Whitbys of the world, so focused on regulations and male keepers and the mechanical workings of a Fresnel lens, did not squeeze family stories from lighthouse tours? Or did Emily—like Brenda Noakes—want Chloe to remember that the long-gone fisherfolk and native people, without a structure to serve as stage, could easily be lost? Or had something even more important been buried in time?

Chloe took the photo back to the bedroom and propped it on the windowsill. The sounds of childish glee drifted through the old glass several more times before silence reclaimed the night. Chloe curled back into her nylon nest, still listening, thoughts swirling from Emily to Roelke and back again, waiting for daylight.

THIRTY-FOUR: JULY, 1884

IN DAYLIGHT, WHEN EMILY could watch her children at play, she felt as she had when she'd come to Pottawatomie as a new bride— that the Lighthouse Establishment offered a wonderful life, that being industrious and surrounding herself with family and friends would always bring contentment in greater measure than worries or sorrow. But thirteen years had passed since her wedding day. She was twenty-nine years old with five children and worries aplenty.

It was nighttime now, and Emily sat in the rocking chair she'd placed by the window on the second-floor landing. Her family was asleep and she was on duty, helping William as she always did... even though she was no longer assistant keeper. Her joy in the switch from lard to kerosene had been short-lived, for the U.S. Lighthouse Service had used that change to justify abolishing her position. "Now that the work is significantly lessened," the letter had read, "we believe Pottawatomie Lighthouse can be adequately maintained by a single Keeper..." Emily didn't believe it for a moment. The inspectors knew that as William's wife, she'd of course continue to help him. No one man could tend Pottawatomie's light at night and tend to chores and visitors by day. The service wanted to save some money, and her growing family's annual income dropped from nine hundred and sixty dollars to five hundred and sixty. It was difficult not to be bitter.

And William was growing bitter too. Emily had seen his latest logbook entry: *If the men who pretend to keep up repairs at the light station do not provide for a water supply before long, I shall quit this business. They make wells at other stations where water is handy without wells but neglect this place almost entirely.*

She picked up her pen and continued the letter she'd started to her friend Jeanette, keeper's wife at a nearby lighthouse.

The cisterns have failed entirely and the Service has declared they will no longer attempt repairs. With this drought our rainbarrels are empty too. We sometimes smell the smoke from forest fires. I haul water up the steps from the lake until my shoulders burn and my palms are raw. My sweet Jane used to help, but the cliff steps are in such disrepair that William and I have forbidden the children to use them. I sometimes despair...

Emily abruptly tore the paper into bits. She'd have to start over. No letter from her hand would speak of despair.

She sighed. Perhaps she should visit Ragna again. She sorely missed the time when they'd been able to talk about anything.

But those days were past as well. Ragna's brothers and son visited her, brought her supplies, and helped chop firewood. Still, she'd had little but her own company in the past two years, and the change had not served her well. Last week Emily had walked to the cottage with a new library book and a crock of strawberry preserves. She'd found Ragna sitting at the table with a pistol in front of her.

"What are you doing?" Emily had gasped.

Ragna slipped the gun into her lap. "I need to clean it from time to time." But there had been no cloth or other cleaning supplies in evidence.

Now Emily stood and stepped to the open window, gazing out at the strong steady beam cast by the Fresnel lens. The Rock Island passage was as safe as she could make it. The smell of smoke drifted through the night, though, as if signaling worse times to come.

THIRTY-FIVE

AT 6:30 THE SUN rose over Pottawatomie Lighthouse, pouring through the windows, dispelling shadows and echoes and nocturnal musings. Chloe's first thoughts were of Sylvie. I'll do everything I can to help bring Pottawatomie Lighthouse back to life, Chloe promised silently, and—I'll try to get federal protection, too. She imagined Sylvie's impatient nod: *Of course you will.*

Chloe thought next of Roelke. Did she have the courage to tell him what was really going on with her? About the Betts children's lingering laughter; about the evil she'd sensed in the grove? No matter how hard she tried, she couldn't imagine that conversation going well. So ... should she tell him they needed to stay friends? She didn't like that idea any better. "Lovely," she muttered.

Finally she forced away lingering sadness, striving to be resolute. She didn't have to face Roelke today. Tackling the letter from Emily she'd borrowed from Ruth Gunderson was number one on her day's agenda. It was Saturday already. On Monday she had to catch the first *Karfi* run back to Washington Island, cross back over Death's Door, and head home. No amount of scholarly research at the state historical society could compensate for being here, in this place.

Outside, Chloe dragged the picnic table into the sun. She placed the letter on a clean T-shirt, and put the photo of Emily beside it before settling down with her coffee, notebook, and pencil. Between the faded ink and Emily's tight, slanting script, transcription was going to be a bitch.

Chloe didn't care. Squinting, mumbling words out loud as she deciphered them, she got to work.

July 1, 1884
Dear Jeanette,
I trust this finds you and family well. Was your station struck during the storm last week? From the tower, I watched the clouds boil black over the channel. How we hoped for rain! Since we have been unable to convince the U.S.L.S. to dig a well, rain is most agreeable.

Yes! Chloe thought. Finally, a personal glimpse of Emily Betts.

We expect to spend what William calls "the glorious fourth" quietly here at Pottawatomie. Often we can hear cannons from Escanaba. The children never tire of hearing their father's stories from the war years. I...

"Good morning," a man called.
Chloe allowed herself one frustrated sigh before looking up. Garrett lifted a hand in greeting as he crossed the clearing.

OK, Chloe told herself. This is Garrett. Park manager. The man who saw his ex-wife's body laid out on the beach yesterday. If he wanted to visit the lighthouse in the dawn's early light, he was allowed.

His expression was haggard, and he wore civvies. "I figured you'd be up," he said.

"Hey." She carefully anchored the letter with her notebook. "Want some coffee?"

"Coffee would be good. Black." He settled on the other side of the table. "I wanted to see how you were doing this morning. After the ... the shock."

She fired up her stove to heat more water. Gas escaping from the canister made a hissing sound before igniting. "I'm sorry too," she told him fervently. "But I'm OK. How about you?"

"Not good," he admitted. "I expect you know that Sylvie and I were once married."

"I heard." Chloe spooned coffee crystals into her spare Sierra cup.

"Obviously we had difficulties, or we wouldn't have gotten divorced." Garrett looked over the clearing. "But we made our peace long ago."

You didn't sound at peace when you were arguing with Sylvie, Chloe thought. She said, "I didn't know Sylvie well, but I liked her."

"People either liked Sylvie, or they didn't. No middle ground." He gave her the ghost of a smile. "She was honest and direct to a fault, always championing some cause. She was a big advocate for turning Rock into a roadless state park, for one thing. I don't know how many trips she made to Madison, haranguing politicians. She helped get the farm museum going, and she was involved in

221

developing the maritime museum as well. Where some people saw obstacles, she saw opportunity. And if somebody didn't agree with her, look out for squalls! She never backed away from an argument."

The water started to boil, so Chloe turned off the flame. "She was certainly a wonderful advocate for the lighthouse restoration project."

"That she was," Garrett agreed. "When we started talking about the lighthouse project, the potential price tag was a bit... daunting. Some people felt RISC should focus exclusively on the Thordarson story and buildings. Ah, thanks." He accepted the cup.

"She didn't strike me as someone who'd restore the Viking Hall and ignore the lighthouse."

"Sylvie?" Garrett snorted. "No, she loved this place. Last summer Herb hired a guy to do tuck-pointing between the stone blocks. The man did shoddy work—the plaster started crumbling within a month. Herb was defending the guy, hemming and hawing, and Sylvie finally said 'Oh for God's sake, Herb, if you're not willing to grow a pair, I'll hold the guy accountable myself.' She did, too."

Chloe watched a Buckeye butterfly flitting along the edge of the trees. Sylvie and Herb had been bickering the day she met them, too. *I'll have to mention that to Stig,* Chloe thought. *Geez, she hated this.*

Time to switch tack. "Garrett, do you have any idea why Sylvie might have been wearing period clothes when she was found?"

He planted his elbows on the table. "Sylvie had... well, if she hadn't been so ornery, I'd call it a romantic streak. Her people fished these waters for over a century. It's not safe to fish alone, but

222

once her husband died she went out by herself anyway. She set nets every now and again, and sold what she caught to a restaurant on the peninsula. She liked being on the water, carrying on the tradition. I can just picture her, heading out into the fog, dressed like one of her ancestors. That would be just her style."

"It's a nice image."

"Fjelstul asked me to meet him at 8:30 in my office, so we'll see if he's come up with anything new." Garrett held her eye. "Listen, Chloe, I wanted to ask again if you'd like to move over to Washington. There's no need to stay here on Rock if you're nervous or uncomfortable."

Chloe imagined saying, *Well, I am hearing children playing when I'm alone here at night, but I'm not sure what it means—any thoughts on that?* Instead she said, "Is the park open today?"

"We can't really close even if we wanted to, not when people can get here by kayak or boat anyway."

That's what she'd figured. "I really think it's OK for me to stay. I'll be careful, make sure the lighthouse is locked up tight at night. It just seems right to be here at the lighthouse while I finish up my survey."

"Are you managing to make progress, despite everything that's happened?" Garrett cocked his head at the photo of Emily Betts, and the letter.

"I am. I've started visiting potential donors. A lady named Ruth Gunderson has a lighthouse service traveling library box that I think we should replicate. And we found this letter inside. It was written by Emily Betts!"

"Really?" His eyebrows shot skyward. "I knew about the library box, but not the letter. What does it say?"

"I haven't gotten too far with the transcription yet." She gestured at the letter, her notebook. "It's really hard to read."

"Don't let me keep you." Garrett rose to his feet. "Thanks for the coffee."

Chloe got back to work. It would be really, *really* good if she could get through Emily's letter before heading to Washington Island. Chloe leaned over, nose inches above the page, and picked up where she'd left off.

The children never tire of hearing their father's stories from the war years. I shall bake a cherry pie, and whip cream.

Oh, Jeannette, I wish you were sitting in my kitchen right now. I'd serve <u>you</u> cherry pie and coffee and ask your advice. Do you recall the friend I told you about when last we met? The Danish woman in the fishing village? Since the tragedy, I grow more worried about her with each passing year.

Tragedy? Chloe thought. What tragedy?

I fear that—

A mechanical roar slid into the clearing, coming closer. The park's small pickup truck jounced from the main trail with Herb Whitby at the wheel. A man Chloe hadn't met was riding shotgun. The truck bed was filled with paint cans, tarps, tools. Herb parked right in front of the entrance to the summer kitchen.

"Um, Herb?" Chloe began. Then she paused. His face looked drawn, his eyes shadowed. Even if he and Sylvie hadn't gotten along well, her death was no doubt a terrible shock. She put one hand on his arm. "I'm so sorry about Sylvie."

"Work must continue." Herb nodded toward the man in stained work clothes emerging from the far side of the cab. "Painting the lantern room exterior needs to get underway. Oh, and Garrett asked me to bring out some drinking water for you." He reached for one of the Igloos loaded in the back.

O-kay, Herb did not want to talk about Sylvie. Chloe turned and gave Mr. Painter her brightest smile. "I'm Chloe Ellefson. Could you—"

"Ellefson?" He looked up from the paint cans he was unloading. "Any relation to—"

"Possibly. Listen, the other day I found a ladder and stuff right by the summer kitchen door. If you'll be leaving any equipment overnight, could you put it off to the side? I'd really appreciate it!" She used her best we-are-in-this-together voice. "People who hike up here want to photograph the lighthouse."

The painter gave a *yeah, whatever* shrug.

"A visitor could climb to the roof and get hurt if you leave a ladder standing against the building," Chloe added. "Or the ladder could get blown over and cause structural damage."

That pulled Herb into the conversation. "We can't have that."

"I'm glad we're all in agreement." She left the men to their task and returned to Emily's letter.

Do you recall the friend I told you about when last we met? The Danish woman in the fishing village? Since the tragedy, I grow more worried about her with each passing year. I fear that she will do something beyond redemption.

Chloe straightened, eyebrows raised, lips pursed. What the heck…?

Well, I try not to dwell on such things. Whenever I feel sad or worried I simply sit and watch my children play.

Just this once, Chloe thought, it would have been nice if you *had* dwelled on such things, since I have absolutely no idea what you were talking about. Pinching her lips in frustration, she worked through the rest of the letter. Emily wrote only of William's latest colt, delivering a baby, potato beetles.

Chloe straightened, stretching a kink from her back. These details of Emily Betts' daily life were all very interesting, and could be used to flesh out both the furnishings plan and suggestions for interpretive themes—but all that paled beside the tantalizing hints of tragedy and hidden secrets.

The painter, who had ascended to the platform outside the lantern room, turned on a boom box. The volume suggested that he wanted the entire county to know that Joan Jett and the Blackhearts loved rock and roll.

"Did I give you two cans of that black, or three?" Herb bellowed. He was still on the ground.

Chloe made a sound that was half-rude, half-frustrated. She wasn't going to accomplish anything else at Pottawatomie this morning. After loading her daypack, she set off for the landing. Halfway down the trail she remembered that she'd meant to ask Herb about the container of sulfuric acid she'd found in the cellar, but she didn't have the heart to turn around. She'd catch him next time.

She was coming down the hill toward the Viking Hall and dock when Stig appeared in the doorway of the stone cottage used for the ranger's office. "Got a minute?"

"More than a minute." She followed the deputy inside. Stig sat at the desk and waved Chloe into a chair. There was no sign of Garrett. She hoped his interview with Stig had gone OK, although that seemed unlikely.

"I'd wanted to catch you, actually," she said. She told him about the tension she'd observed between Herb and Sylvie during the RISC committee's orientation visit on Wednesday. Avoiding Stig's gaze, Chloe found herself staring at the horrid developers' vision for Rock Island. That did nothing to ease her nerves, so she looked out the window instead. "And when I saw Sylvie yesterday morning, we had a nice relaxed conversation until Brenda's name came up. Then Sylvie seemed sort of... I don't know... hesitant."

"Hesitant?"

Chloe spread her hands. "I felt as if Sylvie was about to say something about Brenda, and then decided not to."

Stig scribbled something in a small spiral notebook. Chloe flashed on Roelke doing the same thing. Some company must make a lot of money selling little notebooks to cops.

"Has any new information come to light?" she asked. Through the window she saw a fishing tug in the distance. It left Jackson Harbor and headed toward Rock Island.

"Melvin Jenks said Sylvie's tug headed passed the southeast end of the island at about 11:30 AM, heading east. He was over there clearing a downed tree. We don't know what Sylvie was wearing at the time, though. The fog was so thick that he couldn't see the boat, much less catch a glimpse of her inside."

"If he couldn't see the boat, how could he know it was her?"

"I don't doubt that a fisherman can recognize the local tugs by engine sound alone. It's good to establish Sylvie's departure time, and the direction she was heading. It might help the Coast Guard narrow the search for her tug."

I suppose it helps, Chloe thought dubiously. But Lake Michigan was mighty big. Sylvie could have gone in any direction after passing the point.

She rubbed her hands on her jeans. "Did you learn anything helpful from Garrett?"

"I wish." His mouth got tight. "Hard to get a straight answer from Smith."

"What is *up* with you two?" Honestly! Could Stig conduct a fair investigation if he couldn't even refer to Garrett without a grimace?

After a moment the deputy said, "Thank you for your help."

———

When Jack Cornell maneuvered the *Karfi* to another picture-perfect docking on his 10 AM run, Chloe was surprised to see six or eight passengers on the ferry. But it's a pretty Saturday, she reminded herself. She hoped that the visitors were coming to enjoy a late-summer hike, and not to gawk. Maybe Stig had been able to keep the details from the press, and all anyone knew was that a second woman had evidently drowned near Rock Island. Maybe these people were vacationers who didn't even know that a body had been found on the beach.

Her thoughts were interrupted when she saw a familiar face. "Mr. Dix!" she said, as the lighthouse fan from Massachusetts disembarked, burdened with camera slung on one shoulder, a notebook in hand, and a loaded knapsack on his back. "What are you doing here? I thought you were headed for the Upper Peninsula."

"I was." He rubbed his forehead. "But I had my film developed in Sturgeon Bay. Sixteen rolls, all streaked red and yellow! I must have purchased a bad batch." He sighed mournfully. "Now I'm retracing my steps."

"Bummer," Chloe said sympathetically. She'd had her share of film heartbreaks over the years. "I'm heading off-island, and there's a painter at the lighthouse today, so you'll have to stick to exterior shots."

"Fine," Mr. Dix said. "That's just fine." Chloe wished him better luck and boarded the *Karfi* as he began trudging toward Pottawatomie.

Chloe decided she was glad that visitors had come to Rock Island that day. Sylvie surely wouldn't have wanted the park to lock its metaphorical gates on her behalf. Life goes on, Chloe thought, as they headed south over the channel. But life would go on a whole lot better when the truth about Sylvie Torgrimsson's mysterious death came to light.

THIRTY-SIX:
MAY, 1886

EMILY WAS KNEELING IN her garden when she lifted her face and saw hundreds of migrating hawks high overhead, swirling and climbing until one by one they turned and flew north over the lake. It was a perfect spring day. The woods were carpeted with trillium. Monarch and Tiger Swallowtail butterflies were feasting on the lilacs. Her new baby, Merrit, was asleep on a blanket in the shade. Jane and Amy were trying to teach the younger children how to play croquet on the lawn. The sound of their laughter rang through the clearing.

Tears blurred Emily's vision. She fished a handkerchief from her pocket and wiped her eyes. Stop this, she ordered herself. All you can do is look forward. She picked up her trowel resolutely, determined to reclaim a few of her bulbs.

Then she saw Ragna emerging from the path, and scrambled to meet her. "What's wrong?" she cried. Ragna hadn't come to the lighthouse in eleven years. Not since the tragedy.

"I heard you're leaving," Ragna said. "I wanted to say good-bye."

Emily felt a flood of relief. And just what, she asked herself, did you fear Ragna was going to say? "Yes," she managed. "A new keeper has been assigned to take William's post. We're going to farm on Washington Island." She gestured to the blanket nearby. "Will you sit? I have something for you. I'll just fetch it from the house."

When Emily returned moments later she found Ragna settled down, watching the baby sleep. Emily handed her a book, its red cover embossed with gold leaf.

Ragna accepted it with a small smile. "*Around the World in Eighty Days*, by Jules Verne. Thank you."

"It's an adventure story," Emily told her. "A copy came in our library box, and William and I enjoyed it so much that I asked him to order one for you." She'd hoped it might spark some interest, maybe even prompt Ragna to leave Rock Island.

"I have something for you as well." Ragna pulled a piece of folded linen from her basket.

"A piece of your *hedebosøm!*" Emily spread the table runner across her lap, admiring the intricate needlework. "I can't imagine how long you must have worked on this."

"I have plenty of time. These pieces have been piling up. I'm taking pleasure in giving them away. Berglind Fridleifsdottir came to see me last week, and I gave her one as well."

"I'm sure she will treasure her piece, as I will mine," Emily said. "It will grace my new home." She reached for Ragna's hand. "Won't you consider leaving Rock? It's not safe for you to live alone, with no one but Anton and his sister left on the south end of the island."

"I can't leave."

"I worry for you. I... I worry that you'll do something you shouldn't." Emily couldn't bring herself to be more specific. "Something terrible."

Ragna turned her head, watching the children. Amy helped DeElbert knock the ball through a wicket, and he squealed triumphantly. Finally Ragna said, "That, perhaps, is the only thing that could make me leave Rock Island. If I did something like... *that*, I would have to go far away. Perhaps even back to Denmark. Did you know that Anders didn't want to leave the old country? It was my idea to come here. I pushed him to agree."

Emily felt as if a fisherman's heavy fist had clamped around her heart.

"I have something else to give you." Ragna reached into her basket again and withdrew a familiar tin box. Emily flinched.

"Will you take this with you? If something should happen to me—"

"Ragna, no."

"If something should happen to me," she repeated, "you must give it to Paul. I want him to have it."

Emily considered refusing. She considered snatching the box and hurling it off the cliff. But somehow it found its way into her hands.

THIRTY-SEVEN

CHLOE MET THAT MORNING with three more potential donors and examined their offerings. Strong candidates for acceptance included a quilt made in 1910, a blue and white china cup with lighthouse service motif, and a wooden potty chair. That original outhouse might be an historical treasure, but it seemed safe to assume that keepers and their families were less than charmed on sleety December nights.

When she stopped back at Ruth Gunderson's house to return the borrowed documents, the door swung open before Chloe even knocked. "Please come in," Ruth said. "I got so excited by your visit yesterday that I went rummaging in the attic. I found a shoebox of old letters that my grandmother had kept. A few are from other lighthouse women. Would you like to see them?"

"Yes!"

The earliest letter was dated 1871; the latest, 1919. There was no way Chloe could read them all in the limited time she had left, much less transcribe them. "These are fantastic," she said, as she began skimming through the fragile pages now spread across Ruth's kitchen table. "With your permission, I'll have one of the RISC committee people contact you about making copies."

As she gently turned over page after page of brittle notepaper, she searched for a familiar signature. Two-thirds of the way through the box she found it: *Emily*. This letter was dated 1886, two years after the letter she'd found tucked into the library trunk. This one was in better condition, and Chloe was able to read the entire note:

Dear Jeannette,
The sad day has come. William feels only relief, but it is not so easy for me. Despite the hardships—the failed cisterns, the drunken carpenter sent to repair our stairs, the winter storms that destroyed our dock—I have been happy here. However, one must confront the changes life inevitably bestows upon us. I believe we will be happier still on Washington Island.

Chloe paused. William must have retired. The Betts family's term of employment at Pottawatomie Lighthouse on Rock Island had ended that year.

I am choosing to leave any regrets here, at the station. I have begged Ragna to leave Rock as well, but she will not. Hers is such a familiar tale. Anders went out in his boat, alone, and did not return. But she has never been able to accept the tragedy.

Chloe felt chilled with yet another reminder of how unforgiving Lake Michigan could be. Emily's friend was named Ragna, and

Anders was presumably her husband. By 1886, the fishing village had all but been abandoned. So ... why did this Ragna want to stay?

When we said our good-byes Ragna gave me that dreadful box! I did not say so, but I have decided to leave it here on Rock. She wants me to save it for her son, but I can see no good purpose in the request. I have hidden it away and don't expect to set eyes on it again.

Chloe straightened, eyebrows raised. What the heck?

"Isn't that intriguing?" Ruth asked. "I read it last night."

"Intriguing is an understatement," Chloe murmured. "Do you have any idea what Emily was talking about?"

"Not really." Ruth tipped her head to one side. "I was trying to remember. I seem to recall my grandmother whispering about a woman named Ragna to one of her friends once, but they stopped right away when they realized I was listening."

"Hmm," Chloe said. She bent back over the letter.

And so, my friend, I will no longer be tethered to a lighthouse. That being so, I look forward to visiting you at your station as soon as conditions permit.

> *Yours most sincerely,*
> *Emily*

Chloe copied the letter into her notebook. "Is there something particularly helpful in that one, dear?" Ruth asked.

"I'm not sure," Chloe said honestly. "But overall, I can't even tell you how valuable these documents are for the lighthouse project."

Ruth twined her fingers together. "I heard about Sylvie Torgrimsson this morning. I know she was on the lighthouse restoration committee, and I thought that perhaps I'd volunteer to take her place. I grew up seeing that beautiful lighthouse all boarded up and abandoned. I'd like to help bring it back to life."

"Talk to Lorna Whitby," Chloe suggested. "I'm sure she'd be delighted with the offer." And so, she thought, would Sylvie.

———

When Chloe caught the four o'clock *Karfi* back to Rock Island, she found Stig Fjelstul talking with two couples who were in a small motorboat moored by the boathouse. "Those two big trophy trout are not fit for consumption," Stig was saying. He gestured toward an open beer-lined cooler where several fish were piled on ice. "Trout that big contain high levels of toxins."

"That's bogus," one of the men scoffed. He had a sunburned nose and a preppy haircut. "We had trout filets last night at a restaurant that were at least this big."

"Really? What was the name of the restaurant? Where's it located?"

Everyone got silent.

"Yeah," Stig said. "Listen, I don't care what consenting adults choose to do to themselves. But consuming too many trout can lead to cancer. And pregnant women are putting their babies at risk if they eat *any* trout from Lake Michigan, period, end of story."

When the group's boat had puttered away from the dock Chloe said, "I thought you weren't a game warden anymore. Wouldn't your life be easier if you stayed out of stuff like that?"

Stig hitched his shoulders in a weary shrug. "I probably should have kept my mouth shut. It looked like one woman might be expecting, though."

"I happened to see two game wardens searching Melvin Jenks' fishing tug yesterday."

"They find anything?"

"Nope."

"Good." Stig rubbed his jaw. "I never did either. I used to wonder if Jenks used that rowboat he tows to slip into places where he shouldn't be fishing, but if so, I never saw any sign of it. He told me once he likes to make short side trips without the motor chugging."

Really? Maintenance Mel? Chloe would not have guessed he'd care about quiet one way or another. Of course, she wouldn't have guessed that Sylvie would want to be a docent, or fish wearing nineteenth-century garb. Or that a modern kid like Tim Brown might want to trade his kayak for a tug. Commercial fishermen might have a difficult and dangerous job, and they might be immersed in ugly turmoil, but still... the life hadn't lost its allure, either.

"I'm about to head home," Stig said. "You OK here?"

"Of course," Chloe said firmly. "I'm heading straight to the lighthouse."

At Pottawatomie, after a supper of dehydrated veggie soup and a chocolate bar, Chloe took stock. She had a good sense of how the lighthouse rooms were used and the artifacts needed to represent a busy light station. There were only a few RISC files she hadn't scanned yet. She could read those this evening.

"But I don't want to read RISC files," she muttered. She didn't want to read Sue Grafton, either. What she *wanted* to do was look for the mysterious hidden box. Some instinct told her that she needed to see this box's contents in order to understand something important.

"So, Emily," Chloe said, "is the box still hidden? Does it have anything to do with the story you want me to get right? If so, can you maybe point me in the right direction?" She waited, trying to be open, trying to be receptive.

Zip. Chloe really wished that her "gift" had come with an instruction manual. She blew out a long, slow sigh. Well, all she could do was look.

Once her bowl was clean Chloe went outside, walked around to the cellar stairs, and worked the key in the padlock. She'd start the search here, even though Maintenance Mel and Herb Whitby had discouraged her from entering these nether regions.

Her hands stilled as she remembered just how strenuously Herb had objected to her exploring the cellar. Did he have a reason to keep her out? It seemed absurd, and yet… he had been emphatic. Well, she thought, I'll just have another look-see.

Skipping over the trash pile and the tools left by the restoration crew, Chloe used her flashlight to search the cellar carefully, trying to discern any century-old irregularity that might mark a forgotten niche. She found cobwebs and dead flies and mouse droppings, a shard of pottery and several square-head nails, but nothing more tantalizing.

Finally she gave up. If Herb had some secret in the cellar, she'd missed it. "And no snakes today, either," she muttered, tugging the padlock to make sure it was secure.

OK. She'd have to widen the search zone. Aside from the stone outhouse and the brick oil house where Mel stored toilet paper, the only original lighthouse structures were an old smokehouse and a stable's foundation stones. Chloe examined them both, crawling and tugging stones in search of long-lost hidey-holes. She found a snakeskin and deer poop and poison ivy, and "L loves P, 1978" carved into a tree, but—again—nothing more tantalizing.

Then she spent an hour or so wandering through the woods in increasing concentric circles, looking for long-dead trees, piles of stones, or anything else that might offer possibilities. She found owl pellets, a stand of raspberry bushes, and half a dozen crushed Miller cans in a trampled area near the precipice. That last was particularly discouraging. "You've got enough energy to haul full cans up here," she scolded the absent partiers, "but not enough to carry the empties back with you?" Jerks.

When Chloe crouched to pick them up she spotted a small orange plastic vial, the kind used to dispense prescription medication, which lay behind a fallen tree branch. It contained not pills, but three cigarette butts. Brenda Noakes' sardonic voice echoed in her memory: *Don't worry, I'm planning to quit.*

What had Brenda Noakes been doing here? Brenda's work and family story were confined to the fishing village site over a mile away. Chloe sat back on her heels and reminded herself—once again—that she was in a state park. Anyone, including Brenda, had a perfect right to wander wherever they wished on the island. Still, it seemed ... odd.

Chloe dumped the cans and vial in the outhouse trash can. Don't get distracted, she instructed herself, gnawing at a torn fingernail. Where next?

Might the box Ragna gave Emily have been hidden in the cave? It seemed impossible that anything secreted a century ago might still be hidden in the tiny room, but—but someone *had* been digging in the vicinity recently. She'd assumed the digger was looking for the long-lost gold pieces, but perhaps she'd been wrong.

The shallow cave looked no more hospitable than it had on her first visit. Chloe stepped carefully on the rubble. Her flashlight's strong beam didn't reveal anything hidden in any of the limestone walls' nooks and crevices. Outside, to the left, a man-made stone wall shored up the steps that led from the lighthouse clearing to the beach stairway. This wall had been constructed less carefully than the building foundations. Stones leaned this way and that, with occasional holes between them. Chloe poked into each fissure with a stick, tugged on each stone. Most of them were gray-green with age and lodged firmly in place, but—holy cow! One was lighter than the others, not yet covered with moss or lichen. It slid easily from its spot.

Emily could not have placed this new stone, Chloe reminded herself, squelching excitement. Her flashlight showed something indefinable shoved in the gap. Anticipation turned to disgust when she pulled free a dirty plastic sandwich bag. Chloe fished out a piece of paper tucked inside and read the inked scrawl: *Susan and Jeremy got engaged right here, August 14, 1982.*

"Well, jolly good for you," Chloe muttered sourly. She shoved the baggie in her pocket. Susan and Jeremy might be a great couple, but she wasn't going to put plastic back into the historic wall.

Then she made her way east through the trees, moving farther from the path. The terrain was steep. A slip here could lead to a tumble down the slope—the slope that ended abruptly at the top of the precipice below the lighthouse.

Since she stepped with extra care, she managed to spot the hole before she fell into it.

"Shit," she muttered, crouching for a closer look. Someone had shoveled soil from the ground beside a wedge of limestone, creating a depression perhaps a foot deep. And… there, and over there… as her eyes adjusted to the subtle coloration of the shady ground, she spotted half a dozen similar holes. Chloe looked at each without learning a thing about who'd been digging, or why.

"You better not have been after Emily's mysterious box," she muttered, as she made her way back to the trail. Surely that concern was ridiculous, right? Emily's letters had been tucked away in Ruth Gunderson's home for years. And the notion of sweet, elderly Ruth Gunderson showing them to Chloe while plotting a clandestine trip to Rock Island in order to dig holes beneath the lighthouse was absurd. *Beyond* absurd.

When Chloe returned to the trail she walked to the wooden staircase and settled on the top step. It was a wonderful spot for contemplation—peaceful and cool, with the beach and the lake spreading in all their cobbled and blue-green glory below. But for once, the scene didn't work its magic. Even though she'd known that any search for something hidden in 1886 was unlikely at best, she felt frustrated.

"I'm being dumb," Chloe told three cormorants, black avian missiles speeding over the water below. Their apparent hurry only reminded her that precious time was passing. She wanted to find that box, dammit!

"A clue would be good right now," she said, aiming her words and her thoughts back to Emily. "How big is the box? Did you hide it near the lighthouse? In the woods? Along the beach?"

Still nothing.

Chloe nibbled her lower lip, studying the limestone walls along the steps. If Emily had secured the box in the cliffs, it was at least *possible* that the hiding place still existed. The limestone was rugged, irregular, full of pockets.

OK. She'd take one last stab.

———

Roelke stalked into the EPD, jerked out the desk drawer where he kept in-progress reports, and settled down at the typewriter. He cranked a piece of paper around the platen, stared at it, got back to his feet, and prowled the room. Finally he turned on the clerk's radio and tuned it to a sports channel. Everyone was saying that the Milwaukee Brewers could take the American League Championship this year.

"—as we head into the eighth," the announcer was saying, "the Yankees are on top of the Brewers, twelve-two."

Roelke threw the radio a disgusted look. Maybe 1982 would not be a championship year after all.

Skeet walked in, clearly startled to see Roelke. "Hey!" Skeet said. "I didn't think you were on this afternoon."

"I'm not. I came in to catch up. And to talk to you."

"Yeah?" Skeet reached into his plastic mailbox on the wall and pulled out the accumulation. "Something going on I need to know about?"

"As a matter of fact there is," Roelke said. "Mrs. Saddler came by on Thursday. Remember her?"

A copy of *Police Product News* slipped to the floor. Skeet crouched to pick it up, and flipped to the centerfold—a blonde policewoman in hot pants, leaning seductively against a squad car. "Sure."

"Mrs. Saddler said one of the EMTs stole two pills from her husband's prescription container of Demerol." Roelke folded his arms and leaned against the counter.

For a long moment Skeet didn't move. Then he straightened. "That's bad."

"That's *bad*?" Roelke exploded. "That's not what happened! *You* were the one who went back in the house to get the container."

"Yeah, and I gave it to Denise Miller before the ambulance took off. Maybe she took the pills."

"I asked Denise. And I asked the other guys on the call too. None of them had any idea what I was talking about, so cut the bullshit. Man up and—"

"Man up? Man *up*?" Skeet flushed. "What the hell do you know about it?"

"I know you committed a crime. And I know I'll wonder if you've got my back next time we're out on a call and something goes sour. Is this the first time, or just the first time you got caught?"

"I didn't—"

"*Damn* it, Skeet! You can get addicted to Demerol! Is it just painkillers, or do you balance those with speed? Is that why you've been out sick? You were too messed up to come in?"

Skeet clenched fists. Stared at the floor.

"Look, Skeet, if you've got a problem, you need to deal with it. I know what it's like to go through a rough patch—"

"You don't know shit. Do you have kids? A mortgage? Assignments for your night school classes stacking up like cordwood? A wife who asks every damn day why you got passed over for promotion last month? If that's what you went home to every night, you might pocket some Demerol yourself." Skeet glared at him. "Have you forgotten how you got your permanent position, Roelke?"

"Do *not* throw that in my face." Roelke thrust his finger toward the other man's nose. "I never asked you to lie for me."

"Maybe not. But you sure didn't speak up, either."

Roelke shook his head. Before the village Police Committee members made their decision about the permanent hire, Roelke had assaulted a murder suspect. He'd fully expected to lose the position, if not his badge. But Skeet reported in first. Skeet had been the one to lie. Things got complicated after that... and Roelke got the full-time job.

The kicker now was that Roelke *had* tried to rectify the situation. His own initial report had described the incident truthfully. But there was no point trying to explain that to Skeet now.

"So," Skeet said, sounding for all the world like a sulky sixth-grader, "you gonna turn me in?"

"You should turn yourself in."

"That's not going to happen." Skeet lifted his chin. The challenge in his eyes was clear: *I lied for you. You owe me.*

Roelke'd had two days to think this mess through. He'd hoped that Skeet wouldn't put him in this position. Stealing the pills was bad enough. But this... Roelke shook his head in disgust.

"Here's how it's going to be," he said finally. "I am not going to tell the chief about this—"

Skeet sagged against his locker, all bravado gone. "Thank you."

"But I will not lie for you. Fix things with Mrs. Saddler."

Skeet nodded earnestly. "I can do that. I'll just tell her that—"

"I don't want to hear it!" Roelke barked. "And let me be very clear: you and I are square now. You will never mention that job thing again. And if I ever so much as suspect that you're doing drugs, I will bust your ass. No second chances."

"Nope, we're cool." Skeet buckled on his duty belt and reached for the car keys. "It will never happen again. I..." He was still making promises as he backed out the door.

"And the New York Yankees beat the Milwaukee Brewers fourteen-two," the announcer said.

Roelke turned off the radio. Then he closed his eyes, pressing one knuckle against his forehead. Skeet's right about one thing, he thought. I have no idea what it feels like to support a wife and kids on a part-time cop's salary. Just the thought made him nervous.

Well, he evidently didn't have to worry about that with Chloe.

He sighed, opening his eyes. He wished Chloe wasn't up on that dumb island—instead of here talking about what she wanted. And he especially wished she wasn't up on that dumb island all by her lonesome. He understood that she liked being independent. But once she got all revved up about something, she sometimes did stupid things.

THIRTY-EIGHT

CHLOE TRIED TO CONVINCE herself that she wasn't doing something stupid as she descended the stairs to the narrow beach. *You won't think so if you find the secret box Ragna gave Emily,* she reminded herself. She trudged along the cliff walls, first in one direction as far as seemed reasonable, then the other. She examined the limestone carefully, sometimes climbing a precarious foot or two to investigate a promising space above her head. No luck.

She had given up, and was making her way back to the wooden steps, when a pileated woodpecker shrilled above her head. Glancing up, she noticed an opening in the cliff. She hadn't seen it on her first pass because the opening angled away. The cavity was about the size of a breadbox, and maybe twelve feet above the beach. It seemed extremely unlikely that Emily Betts, wearing the feminine garb of the day, had climbed up the cliff to hide Ragna's box.

Then again... maybe not. Beaches were impermanent entities, shifting with every storm. Waves pounded, walls eroded, stones landed and fell. Maybe the hidey-hole had been more accessible in Emily's time.

"All right," Chloe announced. "This is my last try."

She eyed the wall carefully. She'd done some climbing in her days in the Outings Club at West Virginia University. While she wasn't a natural—some of her more spider-like friends could climb brick walls—she did have a little experience creeping up rock faces with only fingertips and toes to help her along.

Of course, she'd done so while roped and harnessed for safety, wearing a helmet, guided by pals above and below.

Just start climbing, she ordered herself. She eyeballed the first few steps and went at it.

The ascent wasn't too bad. She moved carefully, always keeping three points anchored while searching for the next fingertip- or toe-hold. Other than fretting about tiny plants (if they were hardy enough to live in these exposed crevices, it seemed quite unfair to crush them), she made it up the wall without difficulty.

The recess was shadowed, dark. Her flashlight was on the beach below. Chloe made sure that her left hand and both feet were firmly wedged on solid rock. Did badgers live in stone walls? No, she reminded herself, those particular chomping creatures lived underground. Hoping like anything that some other defensive creature was not in residence, she slid her right arm into the space.

Her groping fingers met only stone.

Chloe fought another wave of disappointment. Had she really thought that Emily had somehow guided her to notice this particular spot? Evidently so.

"Idiot," she reproached herself. Well, she'd tried. She'd failed. And she was now done. Shadows were growing long. She had some reading to finish tonight. Time to head back to the light-house.

As Chloe began to descend, she belatedly remembered something important: it was, for her at least, much harder to climb down a rock face than to climb up.

For a long moment she clung limpet-like to the wall, frozen, trying to decide if she needed to move a hand or a foot first. When this had happened in college, her buddy Ethan had always been on hand to help. "There's a great little ledge six inches to the right of your foot," he'd call, or "You can do it. Just make sure your hand-hold is stable before putting any weight on it."

No Ethan here. Evidently no Emily either. She was on her own.

Slowly, slowly, Chloe crept down the wall. The old rhythm finally kicked in: grope with right foot, then right hand; then left foot, left hand; repeat. She wedged her toes onto tiny outcrops, grasped more tiny outcrops with her fingertips, and made progress... until she reached a flat expanse.

Shit. How could this be? She'd climbed up this way. There *had* to be protrusions. But try as she might, she couldn't find any.

Chloe forced herself to look down over her shoulder. She was only about three feet above the beach, but those loose cobbles below were discouraging. If she landed wrong she might break something she'd rather not break.

On the other hand, her fingertips were starting to ache and her knees were developing an uncontrollable telltale quiver. OK. She'd try one more time to move her right foot down. If that didn't work, she'd have to jump.

That plan was abandoned as soon as she lifted her right toes from the wall. Her fingertips revolted against the extra weight. Chloe fell.

She landed hard and lay stunned on the rocky ground. Pain screamed through her right hip and arm—oh *geez*, had she broken her arm? Was it too late to get off the island? Shit, it was. She'd have to get through the night, and 'fess up to her stupid climb in the morning. How humiliating.

Eventually she forced herself to move again, gingerly taking stock. Her right arm exhibited not bone protruding through skin, but blood seeping from a bad scrape. Perhaps she'd cracked a bone, but that was it. That was good news, although how an arm could hurt this badly and not be snapped she didn't know.

The hip still functioned, too. Chloe staggered to her feet, limped to the steps, and plodded back toward the lighthouse.

Twilight was in full descent by the time she reached the clearing. She washed and bandaged the scrapes. Then she made a stop at the pit toilet and got out her stove. She wanted nothing more than to make a cup of tea, lock herself inside Pottawatomie, and retreat to her sleeping bag with a lantern to finish reading the final RISC files.

At the last minute she remembered the repeated bits of childish laughter she'd heard the night before, over and over. She nibbled her lower lip, thinking. Then she nodded. There was one more thing she wanted to do.

Chloe had done lots of backpacking in the southern Appalachians, often in the summer's worst heat, sometimes in dry spells where drinking water was scarce and wash water only a memory. Her trick for combating discomfort was to tuck a small container of baby powder into her pack. Her friends scoffed, but she found the indulgence worthwhile. When settling into a dry campsite, sticky-wet with sweat, it felt good to dry off with a dusting of powder.

She still had some powder in her necessaries bag, and she fetched it. Outside, she sprinkled the powder on the ground in an ephemeral ring around the lighthouse. Inside, she sprinkled more on the second floor, the steps, and the first floor.

All right, she thought, as she settled in to bed. At first daylight she'd quickly clean the powder away, before anyone could stop by and gain more evidence that the guest curator was a wee bit batty. But first, she'd look for child-sized footprints.

———

Chloe slept poorly, waking several times to the sound of the Betts children having fun. Or were *dreams* of the Betts children waking her? She couldn't be sure. Some of the giggles and chortles seemed random. Others repeated themselves.

She was up at first light on Sunday morning, feeling stiff and achy. Bruises the size of Rhode Island had blossomed in vivid color on her arms and legs, courtesy of the previous day's rapid descent from limestone wall to cobbled beach. Lovely.

Fortunately the morning was cool and drizzly. Chloe pulled on a pair of jeans, and a warm sweater over the T-shirt. She was anxious to clean up the baby powder she'd sprinkled before someone asked what for.

The dusting inside was undisturbed. Feeling ridiculous, she wiped up evidence of her folly. Then she went outside to kick the powder ring into oblivion. But on the lawn outside her bedroom, she *did* find footprints.

Chloe's skin abruptly felt one size too small. She extended one leg, holding her shoe above one of the clear tracks. Her foot was only slightly smaller than the footprint. "Shit," she whispered. Someone had walked outside her east window while she'd been sleeping. And whether corporeal or not, the trespasser had been an adult.

She squatted for a better look. It was difficult to discern much. Several prints were smudged, as if the person had come, turned around, and walked away again.

Narrowing her eyes, she tried to understand what she was seeing. The footsteps were clear enough, but... there. Something was different. A bit of baby powder had been marked with the corner of something square. A box? Or *what*? There were no shrubs around the lighthouse, no flower beds, no place to hide anything. Whatever had been placed on the ground was gone.

Chloe rose and walked around the building. The powder ring was intact on the north, west, and south sides of the lighthouse. Hugging her arms across her chest she turned, scanning the clearing, the woods beyond. Was someone watching her, right this minute?

Unease prickled the back of her neck. She abruptly ran to the summer kitchen door, scrambled up the steps, plunged inside, and locked the door behind her.

Then she paced, palms clutching elbows, trying to think. Maybe she was overreacting. Maybe the footprints belonged to a visitor. Dix had certainly crawled all around the lighthouse. Another lighthouse fanatic might have done the same, wanting to examine every construction detail. Or perhaps one of Herb Whitby's workmen had arrived early.

"Nice try," she mumbled, "but no cigar." She'd sprinkled the powder at dusk, and found the prints at dawn.

Should she report the footsteps? If so, to whom? How would she explain why she'd sprinkled baby powder around the lighthouse in the first place? "I was sorta looking for some ghost children," she imagined saying to Stig or Garrett, "but evidence of a grown person walking beneath my window at midnight was more than I bargained for." Maybe she should just keep this information to herself.

But ... no, she had to let Stig know. She'd tell him that she'd powdered the ground as defense against intruders. She'd sound neurotic, since she'd insisted on staying, but given all that had happened on the island lately it was at least plausible.

One little problem: the first *Karfi* run was hours away. Stig or Garrett might, or might not, be on the island. There was no way to know for sure if they'd boated over without hiking down to the park's main compound.

She marched into the bedroom and sank onto the bed, considering. Her backpack leaned against one wall. Her daypack sat beside it. She needed to ready one of them. She wasn't sure which.

Whoever left those prints *could* have harmed me and didn't, argued one side of her brain. If someone wanted to hurt her, there'd been ample opportunity. Maybe the footprints truly were a coincidence of some kind. Maybe the person who made them wanted only to scare her into leaving the island.

But that didn't make sense either. Unless Midnight Walker had watched from the woods while she sprinkled the powder, he would have had no idea he was actually leaving footprints behind. That brought her reasoning full-circle. What possible reason would someone have for being there?

Chloe thought again of that right-angle print she'd noticed. A possibility niggled at the back of her brain—a possibility that would explain the repeated sounds of childish glee she'd heard over and over. Had someone planted a cassette player after dark, and retrieved it again sometime before dawn?

She considered her options. Even now, the thought of being on the island during the *day* didn't make alarm bells ring. But this was the last day of her trip, and she hoped to track down the last potential donor on Washington Island.

She had planned to enjoy one final night in the lighthouse. And maybe I still should, she argued with herself. She'd wanted to stay on Rock Island after finding a body on the beach below the lighthouse. She'd even wanted to stay after finding Sylvie's body in much more troubling circumstances.

For the first time, though, the thought of spending the night here, even locked inside, was disturbing. Those man-sized footprints made her uneasy. Too uneasy to sleep alone on the island.

She muttered a Norwegian curse, grabbed her backpack, threw it on the bed, and started shoving belongings inside. When her down-filled cocoon billowed in all the wrong directions, she punched it into its sack with furious vehemence.

"You win, you SOB," she told Midnight Walker. "Deputy Fjelstul better arrest your sorry ass because my pacifist heart has had enough. If I find you before the law does, you will find yourself in a world of hurt." The boast was empty, though. Leaving a day early pissed Chloe off royally, but she harbored no illusions about her ability to actually kick anyone's butt.

Once her gear was subdued she selected a few of the reference materials the RISC committee had left, including the photo of Emily Betts, and tucked them into her backpack. Then she went out the summer kitchen door and locked it behind her.

Swiping at an angry tear, she took one last look around the clearing. Even on such a gray day, it looked peaceful. She didn't plan to go far; she would simply move over to Washington Island, find a cheap and sterile motel room, and spend her final twenty-four hours working there. But she hated leaving the lighthouse, this ground. There was more for her to do here, she was sure of it! Her heart ached as she shrugged into the backpack and clicked the hip strap in place.

It wasn't fair. She'd made a commitment to this project, and to exploring the tangible records and the impressions emanating from past lives on this island. She'd opened herself to her growing perceptive abilities—even though that made the likelihood of a romantic relationship with Roelke McKenna drift out of reach like an autumn leaf on the lake.

Now she was running away. I'm sorry, she told Emily. I tried to figure your story out, but I failed.

———

Chloe didn't see a soul as she hiked to the landing. When she descended the final hill she found Garrett Smith's office locked and dark. The Viking Hall and the contact station were as well. No boats bobbed beside the dock. As far as she could tell, she was alone on Rock Island.

She selected a couple of fist-sized stones from the beach before settling down at a picnic table to wait for the ferry. She had a pretty good pitching arm, and the cobbles gave her a whisper of security. After fishing a bag of Oreos from her pack, she pulled out one of the unread files and settled down to wait.

Reading staved away that sense of failure that had stalked her from the lighthouse. The file contained odds and ends: a dense Door County history written in 1910, a compilation of shipwrecks near Rock Island, a collection of poems about lighthouses. Chloe flipped through most of it, pausing frequently to scan the compound.

Then she found "An Informal History of Rock Island," handwritten in the 1930s by the wife of an assistant keeper stationed at Pottawatomie. She skimmed the script, looking for "Betts." Instead the name "Ragna" caught her eye.

Most accounts of this wind-blown island say Anton Jacobson, his sister, and his son were the last residents of the fishing village to reside here. But it appears that the true last resident was Ragna Anderson, widow of Anders Anderson, presumed drowned while fishing in 1876. The Andersons immigrated from Denmark sometime during the 1860s.

Anderson again, Chloe thought. Ragna's husband, Anders, drowned in 1876. Was Paul Anderson, who'd drowned in 1939, related? Hard to say... Anderson was a common name in Scandinavian communities.

I've spoken to two elderly women, now residents of Washington Island, who remember the lonely widow walking the beach as if waiting for her husband to rise from his watery grave. At some point she finally moved away. I found the tale romantic and tragic. Why, I asked, is the story of Ragna Anderson excluded from the history books? My informants—one a wrinkled old Dane herself, another born of Iceland—only shrugged.

Chloe turned that tidbit over in her mind, comparing it to the tidbits she'd gleaned from Emily's letters. There's more to the story, she thought, remembering Emily's fear that Ragna would do "something beyond redemption." Was Emily afraid Ragna might take her own life? Many people viewed suicide as a mortal sin.

She took a quick look around the compound—still deserted—before turning her attention back to Ragna Anderson. Maybe there was something else. Anders was "presumed drowned." Did Ragna believe something more sinister had happened to her husband? Was his death the second murder Emily Betts had spoken of? And if so … had Ragna finally moved from Rock Island because she'd somehow managed to—to *whatever*, and was running from the law?

If so, the old village women weren't saying. Chloe imagined them hushing the rumors, protecting one of their own.

You're probably getting carried away here, Chloe told herself. Indulging in a bit too much melodrama. She'd likely never know. But after the past few days on Rock Island, anything seemed possible.

In the distance the *Karfi* left Jackson Harbor, headed toward Rock Island. Chloe packed the file away. Fifteen minutes later, as the ferry approached the dock, she waved at Jack Cornell. "I'm glad you came over anyway," she called, gesturing to the empty benches—no day hikers this morning.

"I thought you might want to go to the service this morning," Jack said. His son, Jeff, jumped to the dock and secured a line.

"The service…?"

"There's going to be a memorial for Sylvie at eleven at the Lutheran church. Some of her friends didn't want to wait for… you know."

Chloe nodded. For the coroner to release the body. "Thanks for letting me know."

Jack grabbed her backpack and swung it aboard as if it were weightless. "You going home today? I had you down for tomorrow."

"I'm not going home," she said. "Just to Washington."

He shrugged and disappeared into the pilothouse. Chloe sat in the front-most seat. As they motored south she felt a visceral ache beneath her ribs, as if her heart was trying to tug her back to Rock Island.

The *Ranger* left Jackson Harbor as the *Karfi* approached, but Chloe couldn't see who was piloting. She wanted to tell Garrett she was leaving Pottawatomie. She also wanted to ask if he'd ever heard tales of Emily Betts hiding something at the light station. Chloe didn't know the Whitbys well enough to ask about that, and she didn't trust Brenda Noakes enough to raise the question with her.

Well, she'd surely see Garrett at the memorial. And if Stig were around, she'd tell him about her change in plans too. The last thing she wanted to do was panic anyone with an unexplained absence.

Once at the parking lot she tossed her backpack into the Pinto's hatch and glanced at her watch. The archives and library would be closed on a Sunday morning, and she had some time to fill before the service. She hesitated for just a moment before striding across the parking lot.

THIRTY-NINE

ROELKE WAS BREAKING EGGS into a bowl in his tiny kitchen—his cousin and her kids were coming over for brunch—when the phone rang on Sunday morning. He grabbed a towel and wiped his fingers as he jogged to the living room. That better not be Skeet calling in sick again, he thought.

Roelke managed to snatch the phone on its sixth ring. "McKenna here." He dropped onto his sofa.

Silence.

He frowned. "This is Roelke McKenna."

"Um, Roelke?"

"Chloe?" He sat up straight. "Where are you? What's wrong?"

"Nothing's wrong!" she protested. "I ... I'm going to attend a church service on Washington Island this morning, and I got over here early, and I ... I thought I'd call, and ... you know. Just say hi. So, hi! How are you doing?"

"Fine," he said cautiously, as every antenna in his psyche crackled. "How are you?"

"I'm good," she said. "Rock Island is beautiful, and the lighthouse is spectacular. I'm really glad I came."

"OK," Roelke said, even more cautiously. "So—"

"Look, I'm at a pay phone, and I'm out of change. I'll call you when I get home tomorrow, all right? Bye!"

Roelke replaced the receiver to its cradle. He sat for a few moments, thinking, right knee jiggling up and down.

Then he grabbed the phone again and dialed a familiar number. "Hey, Libby?" he said, when his cousin answered. "I'm really sorry, but I gotta bail on brunch today."

"Did you get called in to work again?"

"Yeah," he said, because he didn't have time to explain. "Tell the kids I'm sorry."

After hanging up he reached for the phone book he kept in an end table drawer and began flipping pages. A voice in his head said *Hold on, buddy. Don't be too hasty. You may be screwing the pooch here.*

Yeah, well, maybe, Roelke thought. He'd take that chance.

When he found the first number he wanted, he underlined it in ink. Sunday morning or not, he had a few calls to make.

———

Chloe hung up the phone with an inward wince. A quick call to Roelke, just to say hey, hadn't seemed out of order. Bad idea, though. What had she been thinking? With a sigh, she headed back to her car.

Trinity Evangelical Lutheran Church was just a short drive away. As Chloe settled into a back pew, wishing she'd worn something nicer than jeans, she realized she'd misinterpreted Jack Cornell's information. Regular Sunday service was starting, with the memorial to take place afterwards.

Chloe hadn't attended church lately, but she found the familiar cadences comforting. As she listened to Pastor Reiff her gaze fixed on a graceful model ship suspended from the ceiling. She'd seen them in churches before, placed so by generations of Scandinavians asking that grace be granted to those daring souls who ventured out in fragile vessels. Like Anders Anderson and Paul Anderson. Like Zana. Like Sylvie.

The memorial for Sylvie Torgrimsson was brief, but lovely. After the final prayer everyone in attendance moved to the fellowship hall. Women wearing aprons bustled about as they did at every church—pouring coffee, counting forks, setting out vases filled with flowers. Others arranged plates of Danish apple cake and *aebleskivers*, Norwegian *krumkakke* and *rosettes*, on long tables covered with plastic cloths.

Chloe filled a plate, accepted a cup of punch, and retreated to a corner. She said hello to a few people she recognized—the archivist, the docent she'd met at the Jackson Harbor Maritime Museum, two of the potential donors she'd visited. Melvin Jenks was there as well, looking uncomfortable in a time-worn navy suit. Chloe gave him a polite nod. He could be a jerk, but she was glad he'd come to honor Sylvie. Stig was not present—no doubt he was doing investigative stuff. Garrett Smith was absent too. Well, his situation was awkward. Maybe he'd decided to grieve in private.

Someone had put together tribute posters featuring snapshots taped in place above typewritten captions. One poster showed Sylvie over the years with a man who must have been her second husband; a few had been taken aboard their tug. Another poster featured pictures of Sylvie helping at various museums on Washington Island.

A third showcased Sylvie's work for Rock Island State Park. A faded newspaper article included a shot of Sylvie at a podium. The text read, "Mrs. Sylvie Torgrimsson was one of the Washington Island residents who spoke in favor of ignoring the state's fifty million dollar Outdoor Resource Priority List, and acting immediately to make Rock Island a state park. 'It would be a disgrace to let nine hundred acres of almost untouched wilderness fall into the hands of commercial developers,' Mrs. Torgrimsson said, adding, 'shame on you money-mongers who think otherwise.'"

Sylvie, Chloe thought, you were amazing.

The photograph had captured a scowling, dark-haired woman sitting in the front row of the audience. Chloe leaned closer. That wasn't all that long ago, she thought. Nineteen sixty-five. Had someone nursed a grudge for seventeen years? The woman in the photograph looked vaguely familiar. Might Ms. Sourpuss actually be in attendance today? Chloe tried surreptitiously to study the crowd, but couldn't find the scowler in the face of any of the kindly looking older women in the hall.

That clipping was surrounded by snapshots of happier times: Sylvie washing windows in the Viking Hall, scraping paint at Pottawatomie Lighthouse, grinning from the newly replaced lantern room just a few months earlier. Chloe felt a lump rise in her throat. Pottawatomie Lighthouse had lost a true friend.

"She was a busy lady."

Chloe jumped, almost spilling her punch. Lorna Whitby stood beside her. "Obviously," Chloe agreed. "Lorna, I'm so sorry about Sylvie. I expect you've known her for a long time."

"I have, yes." Lorna looked at the memorial posters.

"Is Herb here today?"

"He wasn't feeling well."

Yeah, maybe, Chloe thought. Or maybe after squabbling with Sylvie he's too uncomfortable to show up. "I hope he feels better soon."

Lorna gave a tired smile. "I'm sure Sylvie would be glad to know you're here, though."

"I liked her," Chloe said. "And... Lorna? Sylvie asked me to prepare a nomination so we can try to get Pottawatomie Lighthouse placed on the National Register of Historic Places. I'd like to talk to the RISC board about that."

Someone jostled Lorna, and she made a valiant and successful effort to keep a sugar-dusted *rosette* on her plate. "I'm sure everyone will be delighted by that idea."

"Good."

Lorna nibbled daintily. "So," she said, wiping the corners of her mouth with a paper napkin, "your time with us is almost over. How is the research coming along?"

"Quite well," Chloe assured her. "I've even found some new primary source materials—a couple of letters written by Emily Betts."

"An interesting family," Lorna said mildly. "William Betts seemed to take such pride in the lighthouse... it's a shame that the family was forced out of the service."

Chloe's eyebrows rose. Forced out? That was news to her. "What happened? I've read most of William's log entries, and I got the impression that he was considered an exemplary keeper." She had no doubt that Emily would have been hailed as an exemplary keeper too—if the reports hadn't ignored her service altogether.

"Well, Emily lost her job, you know," Lorna said. "Local people believed the lighthouse service abolished her position just to save money at the family's expense. Check the logbook when you get back to Pottawatomie. William wasn't a happy camper by the end."

"But—"

"Lorna!" A woman Chloe didn't recognize struck a determined course through the crowd. "Milly is insisting that it doesn't matter what dish towels she uses to dry the punch cups. We're going to have lint all over everything if someone doesn't..." The woman towed Lorna out of earshot.

Alone again, Chloe remembered Emily's comments in the letter to her friend Jeannette: *The sad day has come. William feels only relief, but it is not so easy for me. I have been happy here, despite the hardships. However, one must confront the changes life inevitably bestows upon us. I believe we will be happier still on Washington Island.*

Chloe tried to remember the year the Betts family had left Rock Island. Eighteen eighty-six, wasn't it? That was nine years after William's log entries had changed from newsy accounts to terse recitations of the weather, a change evidently dictated by the visiting inspector. Chloe gave herself a mental scolding. She should have steamed through to the end of the journal. What kind of a researcher was she, anyway? A piss-poor one. She'd formed an intense interest in Emily Betts, and yet she'd stopped reading William's log entries just because they got boring.

Even worse, she'd left that particular file back at the lighthouse.

Chloe checked her watch. If she left now she could catch the one o'clock *Karfi* run back to Rock. She'd fetch the file and have ample time to get back to the landing before catching the four o'clock ferry back to Washington. She'd be back off Rock hours before twilight set in. No problem. She could call that last donor tonight, or tomorrow before heading home.

Fifteen minutes later Chloe parked the Pinto back at the ferry lot. She got halfway to the dock before turning around, jogging back to the car, and grabbing her backpack. The photo of Emily was inside, and she wanted that with her when she returned to the lighthouse. Besides, she had a few Oreos left in there.

"Back so soon?" Jack asked, when she boarded again.

She gave him her best *Everything is cool* smile. "Yep. No day visitors? The rain's stopped."

"A few sprinkles in the morning is all it takes to keep most people away." He shrugged, clearly used to tourists' whims and foibles.

"Quick question," Chloe said. "I'm trying to get a handle on a local family. Do you happen to know if the Paul Anderson who drowned in 1939 was related to Anders Anderson who died back in the 1870s?"

"Sure," he said. "Paul was Anders' son. My grandfather always said those two had a reputation for being able to sweet-talk fish into their nets."

Good Lord, Chloe thought. After her husband drowned, Ragna Anderson had to watch her son take to the lake. No wonder Emily had worried about her friend.

FORTY: APRIL, 1890

RAGNA WAS WALKING ALONG the shoreline, watching one of the new excursion steamboats filled with tourists bound for Washington Island, when Anton Jacobson came storming down the beach. "We are packed!" he hollered. "Me and my son and my sister. We are ready to go."

"Safe travels," Ragna said.

Anton muttered a Norwegian curse. "You are a foolish woman, Ragna Anderson. For years I have watched you walk this shore." Anton gestured toward the lake. "He is not coming back, you know. Your Anders. You wait, and you watch, but you can't change the past."

But I'm not trying to change the past, Ragna thought. She wasn't watching for Anders to come home. She was watching for Carrick Dugan.

"... and now I am taking my family away. You will be the only soul left in the village."

"Good-bye, Anton," Ragna said. "Thank you for all you have done for me." Anton had often left fish or venison on her doorstep. His sister sometimes stopped by as well.

Anton shook his head.

"If you see my son over on Washington, give him my love." Paul was eighteen now, a grown man with a fisherman's big calloused hands and muscular arms. He hadn't come to see her for months. He still fished with his uncles, and they often went twenty, thirty miles out these days to set their nets.

Ragna thought about sending a greeting to Emily as well, but decided against it. Emily hadn't visited in over a year. She had a big family—nine children, now.

"Ragna…"

Anton looked so anguished that she flapped her hands in a shooing gesture. Still muttering, he turned and went back the way he'd come.

The most substantial house on southern Rock Island would now be empty. Ragna scanned the more humble dwellings where most of her neighbors had lived—cabins and cottages, many caving in. It was a good place for ghosts. There had been times during the past years when she'd longed to join Christine and Anders, to become a ghost herself.

But I waited them all out, she thought with a prick of triumph. Men came and went as keepers at Pottawatomie Lighthouse, but they paid no attention to the crumbling village or the last soul to inhabit it. Now—except for Dugan, whenever he returned—she was truly alone.

FORTY-ONE

THE HIKE UP THE familiar trail was as peaceful as ever, and arriving at the lighthouse gave Chloe a sense of coming home. An Igloo of drinking water was waiting on the step. "Remember to tell someone you've moved out," she reminded herself. And ... she'd forgotten to pack her towels, which she'd left hanging on the clothesline. She dumped her pack in the summer kitchen, hauled the cooler inside, and detoured to the side yard. She rounded the wall of lilac bushes—and froze.

The towels she'd left out to dry had disappeared. A diaphanous cloud of opaque monofilament hung in their place, tidily draped over the line. Chloe swallowed hard. A fishnet. Modern, but still a freaking fishnet. She scanned the clearing quickly—empty.

Then she darted inside the lighthouse and locked the door behind her. OK, she thought, willing her heart to slow back to a cadence at least within spitting distance of normal. Melvin or Garrett had been here to leave the Igloo, but anyone who didn't look behind the lilac hedge wouldn't have seen the net. So, who would have left this here? And *why*? Why was someone trying to frighten her?

Because this net *had* been left here to frighten her, she was sure of that. She'd found two dead bodies on this island in the past five days, and each had been shrouded with a fishnet. No one could think that the sight of a fishnet, *any* fishnet, would do anything except creep her out. And replacing her towels with a net seemed to send the same signal as the pound net stake hammered into the ground near Sylvie's body: *This ground has been claimed.*

"What the hell is going on?" Chloe exclaimed, pacing. Why was some SOB trying to scare her away from the lighthouse? What was he—or she—trying to find?

Chloe rubbed her forehead. It didn't make sense to search for anything on the island's northern tip. If Vikings had traveled through, they'd presumably anchored off the peaceful beaches on the other end of the island before carving runes in stone or losing some scrap of material culture for some enthusiastic archaeologist to find centuries later. Presumably James McNeil—he of the missing gold coins—had lived on Rock's southern end as well. The legend said he liked to show off his "Yellow Boys," so his hiding place must have been far away from the lighthouse.

But something was going on *here,* around Pottawatomie. Someone, perhaps several someones, had been drinking beer in the woods near the bluff's edge. Based on the prescription bottle/ashtray left behind, Brenda Noakes had been one of them. All that might point to nothing more than sloppy hikers or campers, but someone had been digging holes in the cave, and on the steep slope below the lighthouse, too.

She paused to look out a window. The yard was empty, but was someone watching from the woods beyond? "What are you *after?*" Chloe demanded. If her own quest for Emily's box had anything to do with the unseen intruder, she couldn't fathom it. And there was nothing else here. Aside from Pottawatomie Lighthouse, this northern tip of Rock Island was remote and undeveloped—

She bit her lip. *Remote and undeveloped* … Maybe she'd been looking at the situation sideways, as she had with Zana's memorial. Maybe she shouldn't be thinking about what an intruder might be searching for. Maybe she should be thinking about why an intruder wanted to keep even short-term visitors like her from settling in too comfortably at Pottawatomie Lighthouse.

Clasping her elbows, she tried sorting various scraps of information in her mind, trying them this way and that, searching for a pattern. She couldn't find a clear image, but a couple of possibilities did emerge. First and foremost: the island held hundreds of acres of forest and limestone cliffs, and only a few trails. If *whatever* was hidden in the woods, no one would care that Chloe was living and working in the lighthouse. But it seemed that someone *did* care. That meant there was something about this old magnificent building itself that she should be paying more attention to.

But I've crawled through every closet and cranny, she thought. There wasn't anything inside the lighthouse except a few pieces of furniture and lots of memories. Well, except for the cellar. She'd looked around down there, but maybe she'd missed something.

Chloe peeped out a window again. The clearing was still empty, but she didn't want to go outside—which going to the cellar required—until it was time to beat feet back down to the ferry dock. Shit, she thought. She *hated* feeling trapped.

Suddenly she remembered something Sylvie had told her the day the RISC committee had provided orientation. There were *two* ways to access the cellar.

Chloe hurried to one corner of the kitchen and kicked aside one of the beautiful woven rag rugs the RISC committee had put down, bless their protective hearts, to shield the floor from dirty shoes. She found a square trap door hidden beneath the pretty rugs. A heavy iron ring, resting in an indentation to keep the hatch flush with the floor, provided access. The ring wasn't designed for human fingers, and the door was heavy. She had to brace her feet and make several tries before finally wrestling the door up. It slammed over on the floor with a crash that made her wince. If she'd marred the floor she'd have Herb Whitby to answer to.

A wooden staircase disappeared into darkness. Now she was doubly glad she'd brought her pack with her. She grabbed her flashlight and began a cautious descent, flinching when cobwebs hit her face. Sylvie didn't say these stairs were dangerous, Chloe told herself, just that they hadn't been rebuilt. She held her breath, testing each riser before putting her weight on it, and managed to reach the bottom without collapse of wood or breakage of bone.

Chloe paused, playing the beam around the space, once again mindful of Herb's warnings. No sign of reptilian residents. But someone had been in the cellar since she'd last visited. One of the old coolers she'd dragged to the back room had been hauled back out and left near the door.

Chloe licked her dry lips. Before examining the cooler more closely she made a hasty check of all nooks and crannies in the cellar. Whoever had been here was gone.

OK, she thought, standing in front of the cooler. It looked so innocuous! Scuff marks suggested nothing more nefarious than picnics or tailgate parties. Maybe it was simply trash, gone overboard during a family sail and washed ashore.

Or maybe there was something hidden in that cooler that someone did not want her to see.

She reached for the cooler, jerked her hand back, and finally stood on one foot so she could nudge the lid up with the other. A few truly horrid images flashed through her brain. When the lid flipped open, though, she did not find a severed hand or pirated artifacts or a cache of weapons. The cooler held dead fish. A lot of fish, very *big* fish, but just... fish.

Chloe exhaled a long breath. Somebody had gone to the trouble of hiding these fish here. Were they too big? The wrong species? She had no idea, but what she'd read that morning about Ragna Anderson flickered into her brain. Ragna evidently believed that someone had harmed her fisherman-husband Anders. Stig had said that people had argued about fishing regulations for over a century.

Something else poked at her brain, and after a moment she captured the thought. She'd never asked Herb about the sulfuric acid in the cellar. He could be pompous, but he seemed to be overseeing the restoration with care; it was hard to imagine that *he'd* left the bottle there. She'd originally assumed that Melvin was using the corrosive to clean rust from tools or something, but he'd told her that he kept his tools locked in the oil house. She couldn't imagine why he'd store that one dangerous chemical in the lighthouse cellar.

Chloe couldn't imagine why anyone else would either, or how a bottle of acid could have anything to do with dead fish. But she was pretty sure that whoever was responsible would not take kindly to her discovery. And *that* person had a key to the lighthouse.

She closed the cooler again, retreated back upstairs, closed the trap door and replaced the rug. Right, she chided herself. As if hiding the door negated what she'd discovered.

Who'd been sneaking in and out of the cellar? Mel? Garrett? Brenda Noakes probably had access to the ranger station and spare keys. The RISC committee members had keys. And in a remote community... well, it wasn't hard to imagine a key being borrowed, maybe going missing. *Anyone* could be behind the trouble. Anyone at all.

Chloe checked the time—still over two hours to fill before Jack Cornell returned to Rock. Should she stay here until 4:00, or wait down at the landing? She considered only briefly. She might as well stay here and try to distract herself with the work she'd come to do. Then she'd scamper straight down to the landing and board the *Karfi*.

She grabbed the file containing William's log and settled down at the kitchen table. With her watch placed prominently nearby and Emily's picture at her elbow, she dug in.

Chloe had read William's notes through July, 1877, when the inspector had instructed William to be less chatty. The next few pages were filled with a single phrase per day noting passing ships and weather conditions. It was hard to shake off her spooks and settle in, but Chloe forced herself to read carefully. She got through two years of such entries—over seven hundred of them—before William expressed frustration in 1879.

The stairs up the bluff are in very dangerous condition and have been for some years.

Leaning on her forearms, Chloe pushed on. For five more years William was circumspect. Then, in July 1884, he exploded.

If the men who pretend to keep up repairs at the light station do not provide for a water supply here before long, I shall quit this business. They make wells at other stations where water is handy without wells, but neglect this place almost entirely.

Finally, on May 11, 1886, William made a final declaration.

I am glad to get away from here for I am as tired of this business as I can be.

Chloe stretched kinked muscles. Eighteen eighty-six—that matched the letter Emily had written about leaving Pottawatomie. It was sad to think that William and Emily had left the lighthouse on a bad note.

She picked up the photograph. "Well," she told the tiny figure captured posed in the west doorway, "you certainly had good cause to feel bitter." Emily losing her assistant keeper's salary had no doubt put a financial strain on the growing family. William clearly maintained the station as best he could, but when major repairs were needed, repeated requests for supplies and workers were ignored. Hauling water up steep steps was bad enough. Chloe could easily imagine how troubled Emily and William must have been if their stairs were unsafe.

"Especially once the cisterns dried up for good," Chloe told Emily. "If it was me, that would have been the last straw. Once you learned those cisterns had failed..."

Chloe jerked erect. The *cisterns*. She'd overlooked the obvious when searching for Emily's mystery box. The cisterns had officially been deemed irreparable long before the Betts family left Pottawatomie. And the useless cisterns weren't accessible through the main cellar, or from the outside of the lighthouse. Emily could have reasonably assumed that no one would ever approach them again.

Until now.

This time Chloe ran into the summer kitchen to uncover a trap door. She grabbed the ring and pulled. Nothing happened. She pulled harder, trying to ignore the protests from tender skin assaulted the day before during her futile climb up the limestone wall. Nothing happened. Dammit! This hatch door was wedged tighter than the first had been.

But no way was she giving up. No freakin' way. She squeezed the fingers of both hands through the ring and tried again, using every pound on her five-ten frame for assistance. When the door finally groaned loose from its casing, Chloe landed on her butt. She didn't care.

A flood of musty air emerged from the hole. Chloe grabbed her flashlight again. Holding her breath—as if that might make a difference—she inched down the steps.

As she reached solid earth she splashed her beam around, getting a sense of the space. The light caught a flicker that might have been a teensy ring-neck fleeing from the intrusion, but that was all. There was nothing else to see except the massive cisterns, which were at least six feet deep. Chloe leaned over one stone edge, then pulled back. If she fell in there she'd need a ladder to get out.

Now that she was here, Chloe had no idea where to begin. Would Emily have tried to bury the box Ragna had given her? Probably not. Emily knew that the mortar holding the cisterns' stone walls together was crumbling. The cisterns themselves seemed the most logical place to look for a hidey-hole.

Chloe began searching at the point where one cistern met the exterior wall. She switched the flashlight back and forth from one hand to the other, scrabbling at each stone with her fingers. When she could find purchase, she tugged. If the mortar was loose, she scraped it away. "But it shouldn't be too hard," she murmured. Emily had no reason to think that the next light keeper would do more than satisfy his curiosity with a quick peek down here.

Part way around the first cistern Chloe found a stone that projected several inches farther into the room than the others. She put the light down and grabbed the stone with both hands. It scraped free, sending a tiny shower of mortar dust and grit to the floor. Tossing it aside, Chloe snatched up the light and eagerly peered inside.

A small tin box, perhaps six inches square and blackened with age and moisture, had been shoved behind the loose stone. Chloe pulled it free. "Ragna's box," she whispered with awe. She had actually found the box Ragna gave Emily! The box with contents so troubling that Emily had chosen to hide it away when she left Rock Island for good.

Chloe tugged at the lid, but it didn't move. No surprise there. And this grubby space was not the place to examine the contents anyway. Clutching the box against her chest, she stumbled back up the stairs.

"I found the box!" she exulted as she put the find on the kitchen table beside Emily's photograph. She scrabbled in her backpack until she found her Swiss army knife. "*So* glad I brought the pack," she muttered. She was able to wedge the blade between lid and box. Working back and forth in a sawing motion, she cleared away a century's worth of dirt and rust. She tossed the knife aside and tugged the tin lid again. With a final wrench, it popped free. Holding her breath, Chloe peered inside.

A square of wood sat nestled on a fragment of old gillnet.

Chloe sat back in her chair, staring, trying to make sense of the find. She hadn't known what to expect, but another damn fishnet—even a scrap—wasn't it. Finally she picked up the block of wood. It was perhaps a half-inch thick and perfectly square, about four inches per side. In the center someone had carved the letter **R**. "Ragna," Chloe whispered. That much made sense, but she had no idea why the wood block had been carved in the first place, or why Ragna had chosen to secure it in the tin box, or why it had so upset Emily Betts.

She gently put the block aside and pulled out the cotton netting. It was cream-colored, just a few inches across. One edge was black, and felt slightly crusty. Perhaps this scrap was all that had escaped a fire.

Did something threading through the years connect Emily and Ragna with Sylvie? Chloe felt her jubilation over finding the box leaking away and she rubbed her temples, feeling stupid. OK, think. Why would a fisherman's widow choose to preserve a scrap of burned fishnet? And what possible connection could this little square of wood have? Someone had taken the time to carve it, and Ragna had chosen to include it in her precious box. Finally, frustrated, Chloe put the net on the table and the square on top of it.

And then she *got* it. The net was a mesh, made of individual squares, each perfectly uniform. The wooden piece was a perfect square as well—a perfect measure for the net maker. The wooden square, though, was slightly larger than the net's mesh. Maybe Anders Anderson had found out that someone was using an illegal gillnet. Maybe he'd threatened to call the law, and gotten killed for it.

Chloe checked her watch, pushed back her chair, and headed up one flight of stairs. At the second floor landing she leaned against the window frame, looking down at the Rock Island passage sparkling below. People had traveled that channel for centuries—ancient peoples, Pottawatomie families, French explorers, maybe even Vikings. People had fished these waters for centuries as well, and a few still did. People had been shipwrecked and drowned in the channel. Commercial captains continued to steer their crafts through its choppy waters. Zana had died there, and Spencer Brant had grieved there. Somewhere out there a nighttime crew might, or might not, be searching for the long-lost *Griffon*. Perhaps they'd even found it.

And through almost all that time, people had argued about who had the right to fish where, who could harvest what species, whether people should be fishing—for sport, for food, for money—at all. Ragna's shred of net reflected an old conflict... and the pound net marker by Sylvie's body likely reflected the current and bitter one. Had the person who left dead fish in the lighthouse carved that horrid marker? Was he trying to make the point that Sylvie was infringing on claimed ground? Or had Sylvie found somebody using an illegal net?

Chloe was so deep in thought that the faint click almost—almost—didn't penetrate her consciousness. But seconds later, a slightly louder metallic *snick* reached her ears. Someone was turning a key in the summer kitchen door's lock. Slowly. Stealthily.

Chloe tiptoed down several steps, straining her ears. A long, slow *cre-eak* echoed faintly from the summer kitchen as the intruder pushed the door open. "Hello?" she called sharply. "Who's there?"

For two seconds, maybe three, silence rang from the lighthouse walls. Then Chloe heard more footsteps. Heavy, now. Fast.

Something bitter and metallic pooled on her tongue. The footsteps rang from the kitchen. Into the parlor. Shit, was there more than one intruder? It sure sounded like it. And no way could she make it down the stairs and get out before *whoever* was upon her.

Chloe whirled, raced back up the stairs, swung around the corner on the landing. Then she scrambled up the steeper steps to the tiny watchroom landing.

"Might as well come down, bitch," a man growled.

Any hope that the intruders meant no harm disappeared. There was nowhere to go but up.

The final steps were ladder-like. Chloe managed to ascend without whacking her head as she emerged into the lantern room. That tiny victory was hollow, though. As she paused on the narrow walkway that circled the light, panting, she felt tears sting her eyes. She'd climbed three stories. The ground looked very far away. And now—except for the men chasing her, whoever they were—she was truly alone.

FORTY-TWO

ROELKE EXHALED A LONG breath of relief when he saw the northern tip of Door County appear through the cockpit window. Almost there, he thought. So far, so good.

Of course, he *was* crossing Death's Door. A more superstitious man might have dwelled on that. Roelke was trying very hard not to.

Roelke had earned his private pilot's license a year earlier. He'd logged eighty-seven hours of total flight time, most of that as pilot in command. He was qualified for VFR—visual flight rules. Still, the plane he'd rented that morning was a four-seater Cessna Skyhawk, bigger than he was used to flying. The little Cessna 152 he'd learned to fly in had also been available, but it was a slower ride. Not acceptable.

After calling Palmyra's municipal airport that morning, he'd phoned a DNR warden who worked in the Kettle Moraine State Forest nearby. "I'm thinking of flying up to Door County for a little getaway," Roelke had said. "Anything going on up there?"

The answer had been succinct. Had Roelke heard about the apparent murder on Rock Island?

When Roelke could breathe again he called Skeet. "I need you to take my shifts for the next couple of days," he'd said without preamble. Skeet launched into enthusiastic assurances. Roelke had slammed the receiver down mid-stream.

Now he began to descend to the traffic pattern altitude he'd need at the Washington Island Airport strip. Beneath the cloudy sky, the water below had an ominous gray-green cast. Passing beyond Death's Door did little to ease his nerves. The same thoughts continued to bounce through his brain like rubber balls. Apparent murder... Rock Island... Chloe... murder...

"Stop it," he muttered. He set his radio to the common traffic advisory frequency, listened for other aircraft announcing themselves, and keyed his own mic. "Washington Island traffic, this is Cessna November-Three-Four-Seven-Seven-Echo, five miles southwest, inbound for landing on runway Two-Two."

Roelke pulled back on the throttle to slow the descent, and lowered the wing flaps. He was tempted to come straight in, but he'd never seen the field before, and he was way too wired to risk making a stupid mistake. "Washington Island traffic, Seven-Seven-Echo is left downwind for Two-Two."

As he entered the pattern, paralleling runway Two-Two so he could assess the approach and eyeball the terrain, he glimpsed Rock Island in the distance—mostly covered with dense forest, more bleak and isolated than he'd even imagined. Roelke's jaw began to ache. Although Chloe had called from Washington Island that morning, he was very much afraid that for some ridiculous reason she had blithely returned to Rock to spend one last night in the old lighthouse.

"Focus," he muttered. The strip was clear but the distraction had made him late making the necessary turn, which screwed up his descent. He'd have to speed up a little for a longer approach.

He made two left turns, which brought him in line with the runway. Airspeed and descent looked good. "Washington Island traffic, Seven-Seven-Echo on final for Two-Two." There were trees near the approach end of the grass strip, so he set the flaps full down.

He was clearing the woods when the deer bounded from the cover. Three of them, all does, running straight toward Two-Two.

Dammit. Roelke pulled back on the yoke and shoved the throttle forward, trying to get the Cessna to climb. Instead of ramping up the engine hesitated.

What the hell was wrong? A few eternal seconds later, the engine recovered with a roar, but airspeed was still dropping. The stall warning began to wail.

I'm screwed, Roelke thought. He was seconds away from a crash.

———

Before Chloe could catch her breath from her ascent to the lantern room, she heard her pursuers thundering up the stairs to the watchroom just below. Then footsteps started clomping up the ladder. Could she kick the lead guy as he emerged through the hatch? Maybe shove him back down? Not likely.

Chloe cast wildly about. *There*—two cans of paint. She grabbed one. The first man banged his head against the edge of the hatch with a resounding thud, buying her a few seconds. As she spun around, lifting the can above her head, she caught a glimpse of a man wearing a dark balaclava. She heaved the can down through the hatch with all her strength. Cursing, Balaclava Man crashed down the steps. Chloe hurled the second can after the first.

"Oh, *fuck*," he groaned. A second male voice muttered something inaudible.

Chloe didn't waste time on a glance through the hatch. She'd slowed Balaclava Man down. Maybe even disabled him. Guy Two could be after her any moment, though. The instinct to *run-run-run* buzzed through her brain.

She couldn't go down. She couldn't go up. Only option: going out.

Chloe dropped to her knees beside a low wooden door, wrenched it open, and scrambled onto the narrow walkway outside the lantern room. "Oh God," she whimpered, clutching the paint-sticky railing, fighting a wave of vertigo. The trees and picnic table and outhouse below looked dollhouse-sized.

The roof's peak stretched south from the lantern room. The roof itself fell steeply on either side. Chloe's stomach twisted again as she imagined trying to creep down to the gutters without falling.

Wait. A heavy cord of braided copper ran from the lightning rod on top of the tower down the west side of the roof before disappearing over the edge of the gutters.

Chloe bit her lip hard. Would the cable support her weight? And even if she did make the gutters without somersaulting into thin air, what then? The gutters were placed along a narrow ledge at the roof's edge that might, if she were very lucky, support her. Could she crawl along until she came to a downspout? And if so, was she acrobatic enough to go over the ledge and shimmy down two stories? Would a downspout support her weight? Not likely, and oh *shit*, those downspouts were original fixtures, and if she damaged one and broke her neck anyway—

With considerable effort Chloe wrenched her mind from inevitable failure. There were no signs of fresh pursuit—*yet*. The men probably assumed she was trapped. Bottom line, she could stay where she was until someone did come after her. Or she could try to keep putting distance between them.

Chloe crawled under the walkway railing to the roof. After rubbing sweat from her palms she grabbed the copper cable.

The roof was too steep, and her muscles too trembly, for a controlled descent. With one terrified hitch she felt herself skidding. She clung desperately to the cable as she slid, clenching her teeth against pain as slivers of copper dug into her palms. The narrow gutter raced to meet her. Too fast, too fast!

At the last possible moment she managed to twist onto her right hip. Her right foot hit the gutter with shockwave force. Her knee buckled and her hands were on fire and she knew to her marrow that she was about to fly over the gutter.

But somehow, *somehow*, she managed to stop her freefall. She closed her eyes, dizzy with fear and relief. She was one story closer to the ground than she had been.

Keep going, shrilled the voice in her brain. *Run-run-run*.

Chloe opened her eyes. The only possible route from roof to ground lay along an antique downspout. OK, she told herself.

Don't think. Just get your bearings. Still clinging to the grounding wire, she forced herself to look over the edge of the gutter.

A burst of hysterical laughter bubbled inside. A ladder leaned against the wall. Herb's lazy no-good painter had, despite her specific requests, left a ladder leaning against the wall just a few feet away. She might actually be able to reach the ground without killing herself.

Chloe thought that the hardest part would be letting go of the cable. It took raw willpower to unclench her death-grip on the copper cord. Then she realized that the hardest part would be scuttling along the gutter, leaning against the roof, praying the ledge would continue to hold her weight. But then she discovered that by far the hardest part would be easing herself from gutter ledge to ladder.

It took several attempts. She couldn't actually see the top of the ladder. It was frightening to leave even the flimsy security of solid roof, narrow gutter. In the end she knelt on the gutter with one hand clutching the ledge and the other pressed against the roof for support, and extended one leg out behind her. Hours seemed to pass as she inched it back and forth through empty air, terrified that she might kick the ladder over by mistake. Finally she felt the side of the ladder, and then the horizontal safety of a rung beneath her sole. Holding her breath, she managed to slide eel-like over the gutter and plant her other shoe on the next rung.

Moments later she was on the ground. She took off, racing for the trail to the park's main compound. She might have reached terra firma, but she was far from safe.

———

The stall warning shrieked again. Roelke's hand quivered on the yoke, wanting desperately to personally muscle the plane up. He didn't want to kill the deer. He didn't want to kill himself. He needed lift. Now.

But training took command: *No*. A Cessna needed at least two hundred feet to recover from a stall. He didn't have that kind of altitude. He had to wait, to let the plane gain enough speed to begin climbing.

A few more heartbeats passed. RPMs were rising, the prop spinning faster, but the plane pulled up so sluggishly that Roelke imagined the wheels grazing the animals. Did he still have full flaps? He did. He should have reduced his flaps from thirty degrees to twenty on the go-around.

When he was finally truly airborne, and risked a glance back, he was astonished to see the deer unharmed, loping gracefully across the grass.

Roelke's breath escaped in a rush. He climbed and headed away from the airport. He needed a breather. And he needed to figure out why the engine had hesitated in the first place. He ran through a mental list: carburetor icing, sparkplug fouling, low oil pressure. Nope, nope, nope.

Then he walked himself through his landing checklist, and... *damn*. He'd been so eager to land that he hadn't adjusted the fuel mixture from the lean cruise setting to full rich. The engine had choked when he'd shoved the throttle. On top of that, he'd let the sight of Rock Island distract him when he should have been studying not just the designated grass runway, but the entire field. The strip had been clear, but he might have been able to see the deer near the trees if he'd actually looked.

Roelke circled back to try the landing again. This time he managed it.

When he'd taxied to a tie-down he cut the plane's engine and sat, nerves buzzing, flexing aching fingers. Finally he glanced at the small parking lot. Empty, thank God. At least no one had seen him screw up. He hadn't stalled. And he hadn't hit the deer. A collision would have damaged the plane. And if Chloe heard that he'd mowed down three whitetails…

The thought of Chloe got him moving again. He went through his checklist for shutting down the aircraft with scrupulous care. By the time Jim's Island Taxi turned into the parking lot, Roelke had closed his flight plan, secured the plane, placed the tie-down fee in an envelope, and shoved it through the slot provided on the box. His knees still felt a little wobbly, but he was ready to pull it together.

Roelke strode across the gravel to meet the driver, glad he'd thought to make arrangements for a ride before leaving Palmyra. "I'm Officer Roelke McKenna, Eagle PD," he said. "I need to see Deputy Fjelstul."

"Then you've got a problem," the driver said. "Nobody knows where he is."

———

Chloe knew that if one of the intruders had climbed to the light tower or looked out a window, he'd have seen her hit the trail. Maybe they're not coming after me, she thought. Maybe they gave up.

More likely they didn't.

Who the hell *were* these guys? Chloe had seen through the hatchway a black splash as one of the paint can lids came off. She grieved about that oil-based pigment staining walls and stairs and woodwork—but it surely had splashed on Balaclava Man too. If she could escape the island and get help, that paint might help identify the SOB. Black drops would have hit his hands, and might have splashed through the eye- and mouth-holes in his balaclava too. At the very least, it should be all over his clothes—

His *clothes*.

Chloe's foot hit a rut. She fell. For a few seconds she was too stunned to move. That damned balaclava wasn't the only thing sinister about the man's attire. It hadn't registered at the time, but she'd seen too much of the Department of Natural Resources' muted gray-green uniforms lately to mistake them.

A stick snapped somewhere behind her. She scrambled to her feet and began to run again, mind racing too. Melvin Jenks had been surly, gruffly polite, and indifferent by turns. She could imagine him in the role of attacker. Maybe he'd been scamming DNR wardens, hiding illegal fish in the isolated lighthouse so he could cruise into dock for inspections with confidence. It would be easy enough for him to meet someone else—maybe an unscrupulous restaurant owner in a pleasure boat—and sell the fish without anyone being the wiser.

The only other park employee she'd met was Garrett Smith. Had Garrett actually crept into the lighthouse intending to harm her? Had he killed Sylvie, too? Even if some thread of a tangled relationship with his ex-wife had snapped and he'd killed Sylvie, Chloe thought, why come after *me*?

Jagged memories flickered through her brain as she ran, trying not to trip, trying not to fall. Garrett tense with worry, Garret professional and friendly. He'd been calm and collected when she'd found Zana's body, and he'd been solicitous and concerned afterwards… Afterwards, like when she'd told him about hearing children laughing in the night. Several days later, it seemed, someone had placed a cassette player beneath her bedroom window set to play a loop of recorded laughter. Maybe Garrett is coming after me, Chloe thought, because he hadn't been able to scare me away from the lighthouse. Maybe Garrett and Mel are working together.

Run-run-run.

She stumbled more often, breaking stride, once or twice going down on hands and knees. By the time she started down the final slope her lungs were burning. Anyone following would have no trouble hearing her gasping for breath.

Chloe was clinging to a single strand of hope. Aside from the men she was fleeing, only one person knew she was on Rock Island: Jack Cornell, captain of the *Karfi*. She had no idea what time it was. Maybe he'd already made his four o'clock run. And unless some campers had shown up, Jack might not make the trip anyway. Since she'd brought her backpack on her return to Rock that afternoon, he might reasonably assume she was settling in for her final night at the lighthouse. She hadn't thought to tell him she'd need a ride back to Washington.

But maybe I'll get lucky, Chloe thought. Maybe the timing will be perfect. Maybe I can get away on the *Karfi* and Jack will help me find Stig—

The memory of meeting Deputy Stig Fjelstul that first night on Rock slapped Chloe like a physical blow. Stig had been wearing his old DNR jacket. Garrett Smith and Melvin Jenks were not the only two local men who owned DNR uniforms.

Chloe burst from the trees and scanned the channel. She spotted the *Karfi*—not anchoring at Rock, but instead motoring back into Jackson Harbor a mile away. Captain Jack *had* come to make sure Chloe wanted to spend the night on Rock Island. But she'd reached the dock too late.

She stumbled to a halt and leaned over, hands on quivering knees. The last ferry of the day had come and gone. The main park compound was empty, and the campground too. And she was still alone on the island with two men who seemed to want her dead.

FORTY-THREE: AUGUST, 1891

RAGNA WAS HAULING WATER up from the beach when she saw smoke pluming from Carrick Dugan's chimney. She put the bucket down. So. He had come. She stood for a long moment, listening to the waves gently slapping the stones, hearing gulls squabbling down the shore, feeling sunshine warm as a blanket on her shoulders.

Then she walked to her cottage and fetched the pistol. It was clean, oiled, loaded. She paused here as well, touching Anders' pipe, the wooden animals he'd carved for Paul, the baby blanket she'd made for Christine. Then she left the cottage.

When she reached Dugan's cabin she opened the door and stepped inside. He sat at his table with half a loaf of bread and some dried fish on a plate. He looks old, Ragna thought. While she'd lived with her own changing body, her aches and pains, she hadn't been so close to Dugan for fifteen years, and he'd lived in memory as she'd known him then. Now gray dulled his red hair.

His cheeks were hollow. Deep lines had etched patterns into the skin.

Dugan slowly rose to his feet. His gaze flicked from her face to the pistol in her hand.

"I know you killed Anders," Ragna said. "And I know Anders saw you using an illegal gillnet. The day after you killed him I came to this place and found the ashes where you'd burned it. But I also found a scrap that survived, and measured the mesh."

A muscle twitched in Dugan's cheek.

"You would have been fined, nothing more." Ragna was pleased with how even her voice was—no trembles. "But you hated Anders. Learning what he intended to do was more than you could abide. Did you shoot him from a distance, like a coward? Did you knock him senseless and wrap him in a weighted net before tossing him overboard to drown?"

Dugan took one small step sideways, clearing himself from the table. His trousers were stained, threadbare.

She took one step as well, matching him. "Did you hate us so much?"

"It was him."

"*Why*? Why did you hate Anders so much?"

"No man tells me how or where to fish." Dugan's eyes never left her face. "Besides … he was just so damn cheerful."

He lunged as Ragna raised the pistol, but she'd expected that; sidestepped. In the seconds before the explosion she wondered if whitefish were confused when nets caught their gills, or if they knew they were about to die.

FORTY-FOUR

CHLOE WAS UNABLE TO find a drop of hope in the *Karfi's* wake. Flooded instead with a profound loneliness, she watched the ferry dock a mile away. From the hill she could see the deserted compound, the wooded campground beyond the Viking Hall, the narrow spit of land that curved from Rock Island's southern tip. Nothing offered solace.

Run-run-run.

Blinking back tears, Chloe jogged on down the hill. The *Ranger* now bobbed at the dock, and she made a quick detour to see if the pilot—Mel? Garrett?—had conveniently left the keys in the ignition. No such luck.

She pushed on past the Viking Hall. Her knees felt like jelly. Her lungs felt Lilliputian. Panting, she paused and glanced over her shoulder just as a figure emerged in the distance from the lighthouse trail. If she could see him, he could see her. Chloe willed herself back into motion.

The trail entered the woods and wound past dim, deserted campsites. Should she try to hide? No. Her pursuer knew the island much better than she did. She couldn't trust anyone wearing a DNR uniform. Melvin, Garrett, even Stig. Was Stig a murderer? Had his concern been a ruse? If so, why come after her now? She'd been at the lighthouse for almost a week; alone with each of these men during that time. Someone had tried to scare her, but no one had tried to harm her. Something had changed.

Run-run-run.

The trail forked. No point in circling back toward the lighthouse. Chloe took a smaller side path that continued south.

Soon the trees gave way to scrubby shrubs, the skeleton of a dead birch, a few stunted cedars, clumps of jewelweed and asters. Then earth surrendered to loose cobbles. Rocks shifted underfoot, grating like thunder in Chloe's ears. She stopped, listening for the scrape of rock on rock behind her. All she heard was the gentle lap of tiny waves reaching shore off to her right.

Finally Chloe passed the last shrubby cover. A stony, barren spit stretched in front of her, pointing south. She felt horribly exposed, but it was too late for second thoughts. She exhaled one shuddering breath and picked her way forward. Now water whispered against stone on each side as the spit shrank to just a few yards in width. Then she hit water in front, too. She'd reached the beginning of the reef that zigzagged from Rock Island to Washington Island. Clouds filled the sky, gray as gunmetal. The water looked cold and unwelcoming.

Lake Michigan is a single ecosystem, Brenda had said. *A thunderstorm in Escanaba affects conditions here. You can get current going one way over the reef, and wind going the other—the water just boils.* Chloe had no idea if it was storming in Escanaba, but the water did not appear to be boiling between here and the Washington shore.

Besides, what choice did she have? OK. She was going for it.

Chloe waded into Lake Michigan. It's not so cold, she told herself, fending off the shock of soaked shoes, socks, jeans. Brenda had said the water was between knee- and waist-high on the reef. She could handle that.

The skin between Chloe's shoulder blades twitched in sick anticipation—what if Guy Two had a gun?—but it was impossible to hurry. The reef was formed of stones which moved with each step. At first she could see them clearly. As the lake rose to her knees the stones appeared to waver beneath the moving water, distorting her view. Once she felt the stones beneath her right foot give way. She lunged toward the reef's solid center, landing with a splash.

"Terrific," she muttered, staggering back to her feet. Her whole left side was wet now. She began to shiver.

Chloe clenched her jaw and got moving again. Step carefully. Don't look back. Step carefully. Keep going. Don't look at the gravel bar over there; it's not part of the reef. Stay on the reef.

The water that had looked so placid from shore grew animated, tugging at her legs. Chloe walked with arms out, fighting for balance. If only the cobbles weren't so treacherous. If only the water weren't so cold. If only she weren't so tired. If only the current didn't seem to be gaining strength. Her vision of stones and water wavered into different images—Zana, drowned, lying on one stone beach; Sylvie, drowned, lying on another stone beach; even the carved face of Aegir in the Viking Hall, whose wife, Ran, pulled drowning travelers into the depths of the sea with her net.

One more wobbly step. Another. Chloe felt her forward motion slowing, slowing. She was shaking convulsively. Her numb legs became harder to control. The water rose inch by inch, pulling at her, wanting her. By the time it reached her hips it was hard to stand erect, much less make progress.

I don't think I can do it, she thought. But—she would not give up. Lake Michigan might win in the end, but she'd fight it all the way.

OK, she told herself. Don't look up. Take one step more. Then one step more. She forced one leg forward, probing for a secure spot before shifting her weight. One more step…

Chloe almost lost her balance when a burst of fluid motion pierced her peripheral vision. By the time she steadied herself the kayak was approaching quickly. The woman paddling looked determined, capable. Chloe blinked in bewilderment. What was Natalie doing here?

Then a flood of gratitude washed away confusion. Natalie had come to the rescue after Chloe found Zana's body. Chloe was happy to let Natalie come to the rescue again.

Natalie didn't speak, clearly saving her energy as she angled the kayak toward the reef. But—*dammit!*—the current flowing over the reef must be stronger than she'd realized. She's miscalculated, Chloe thought. The kayak slid over the reef a foot or so away. Natalie dug her paddle vertically into the reef, trying to stop forward momentum. The paddle served as a pivot instead. Chloe saw a blur of green plastic slamming toward her. She threw up both arms, palms out, trying to stave off collision. The kayak hit her hands with hurricane force.

Pain shuddered through her arms as she tumbled backward. Her butt hit cobbles and she plunged underwater. She tried to hold her breath but sucked in lake water instead, disoriented by the frigid shock and odd echoes of sound. Panic forced another dash of adrenaline through her veins. When her feet hit rocks she scrabbled for purchase. For an agony of time the cobbles gave way. Then one sole found firm stones.

Chloe pushed up hard and surfaced, coughing, choking, her vision blurred by icy streams of water. She shoved hair from her forehead, looking frantically about for Natalie. There she was—not too far away. Chloe croaked, "Try again!"

Natalie positioned herself for another approach. "Throw me your life vest!" Chloe called as the green kayak came near. An actual rescue would prove impossible on this spit of shifting stones and racing water.

Instead of unbuckling her vest as the kayak drew close, Natalie lifted her paddle from the water. *Yes*—that would be quicker. Chloe stretched one arm forward, fighting the current, struggling to remain upright. "Go ahead!" she gasped. "I can reach it!"

Natalie raised the paddle over her head. Then the blade sliced down.

Chloe threw herself sideways. The blow landed on her shoulder instead of her skull. She went under again, Lake Michigan numbing the explosion of pain.

This time she landed more solidly on the reef. She got her feet beneath her, broke the surface, and launched herself toward the kayak, landing on the paddle before Natalie could wrestle it aloft again. Chloe's weight anchored one blade on the reef.

Natalie still clung to the paddle with two black-gloved hands. "Let *go!*"

Chloe wrapped legs and arms around the narrow blade and clung, leech-like. Natalie, her mouth an ugly scrawl, fought to free her weapon. Chloe had no idea how to get away from her. Hang on, she told herself, as the paddle twitched beneath her. Just hang on.

Natalie gave one more mighty heave. The paddle jerked Chloe inches closer to the kayak. The boat was slowly swinging east toward the open lake, pivoting around the paddle, surrendering to the water surging over the reef. With another yank Natalie managed to wrench Chloe closer still.

Chloe was shuddering with cold and trembling with exhaustion. The younger woman looked fresh, determined. Natalie's going to win, Chloe thought. Her brain felt numb. The next pull loosened Chloe's grip and she slid sideways, now clinging to the paddle with only her left elbow and knee. Natalie's eyes blazed with triumph. She repositioned her grip and heaved again. Chloe's left knuckles scraped the kayak.

But her right hand flew from the water clutching a heavy cobble. The stone hit the side of Natalie's forehead with a sickening thump. For an instant Natalie looked shocked. Then she slumped forward. The kayak pitched away.

Momentum rolled Chloe into the lake. The current tumbled her on over the reef to deep water. She managed to surface, gasping, and glimpsed the green kayak drifting out toward Lake Michigan's expanse. A yellow kayak streaked past, heading toward the other boat. Tim.

No time to think about Tim and Natalie. Treading water, Chloe looked toward Washington Island. It seemed *so* close! What, maybe half a mile? But she didn't have the strength to swim that far. She had to get back to the reef.

Chloe faced into the current and tried to swim. *Stroke! Kick!* Her arms and legs did not obey. The flow was dragging her ever farther from the reef. She had no reserves left. With a flash of clarity she understood that Lake Michigan was stronger than she was. The struggle was over. I'm sorry, she thought, as the current swept her away.

———

"She wouldn't have gone this way," the woman said.

Roelke ignored her. They stood at the tip of a narrow spit of cobbles extending south from Rock Island. He scanned the reef, the gravel bars, the marshy shoreline on the far side of the channel. Nothing.

"Officer McKenna." She put a hand on his arm. "Chloe and I talked about how dangerous this crossing can be. She *must* be hiding somewhere on Rock."

Roelke couldn't remember the woman's name. He'd met a handful of people in the last hour or so, and he couldn't remember any of their names—even the volunteers helping him search. Ever since they'd found that SOB with the broken leg in the lighthouse, Roelke's brain had shed the extraneous and funneled down to the essential: Chloe was missing.

"We've got nine hundred acres to search," the woman added. "Let's head inland."

Roelke looked back across the channel. He couldn't shake the feeling that Chloe *had* tried to get off the island on her own. "No," he said. "I need to search the Washington shore."

"Well … all right," she said. The look in her eyes said what she did not: *This will be on you.* "Let's head back to the boathouse."

Once they met the others, the return trip to Washington took an eternity. No one spoke. When the boat docked Roelke leapt to the pier. "Which way?" he barked.

One of the men pointed east. "Current would have taken her that way." Roelke took off.

The shoreline meandered, sometimes sandy, more often rocky. The first stretch was wild and undisturbed. Then they moved onto private property. Some of the secluded homes built along Washington Island's northeastern shore had lawns; some wooded shores. Roelke kept moving, searching among marshy edges, scanning manicured yards. Nothing. *Nothing*, Goddammit, and Chloe was missing.

He whirled when a flash of motion caught his eye. Just a dog on a patio, lifting his head to survey the trespassers. The local man who'd kept up with Roelke said, "It's OK, boy." The dog didn't bother to bark.

Roelke clenched his jaw. Cop mode, he needed to stay in cop mode. Just keep moving, keep looking. Chloe was missing …

They'd gone a mile, maybe two, before Roelke looked ahead through some trees and saw something moving on the ground. He pointed, unable to find words. Chloe was creeping toward a house on hands and knees—soaked, shuddering violently.

"*Jesus,*" the other man said.

They plunged through some juniper trees and into the yard. Chloe didn't seem to notice. Roelke sucked in a deep breath, needing a second to steady his knees. The other man ran past, taking the lead.

They were almost upon Chloe before she turned her head. Her eyes went wide with a look of fear that tore into Roelke's heart like a blade. *"Chloe!"*

Her gaze shifted from the other man to Roelke. "Oh, thank God," she whispered. Her eyes closed, and she slumped to the ground.

FORTY-FIVE

"Hey, you awake?" Brenda asked softly.

Struggling up from sleep, Chloe tried to make sense of the question ... *right*. After the miracle of making shore, Roelke—Roelke!—and Stig had found her. Paramedics warmed her up and monitored her vitals until they were sure she was OK. They'd also picked slivers of copper from palms burned raw from the lightning cord during her roof-slide descent, and bandaged them. She'd given Stig a condensed version of the afternoon's events. Then Brenda Noakes had appeared and announced she was taking Chloe to her dad's house.

Now Chloe was nestled on a couch in the living room, cocooned in blankets. "How long was I asleep?" she mumbled. Window shades were drawn against the night.

"A couple of hours. You feeling ready to talk to the boys? They're in the kitchen, and one or another's about to tear the door down."

"Yeah," Chloe said. She struggled to sit up, wincing. "I'm ready."

304

Once summoned, the three men seemed to fill the room: Roelke, Stig, Garrett. Roelke's mouth was tight, his gaze intense.

"I'm OK," she told him. "Honestly." He squeezed her shoulder, letting his fingers convey what he left unsaid. Then he sat down beside her.

Stig and Garrett settled into easy chairs. Brenda took a rocking chair by the fireplace. "My dad is fixing a tray," she said. "He'll be along in a minute."

Chloe fixed her gaze on Stig. Her clearest memory of the rescue was the absolute sense of defeat she'd felt when she'd looked up from her crawl and seen Stig looming over her.

"We told you about Melvin Jenks, remember?" he asked, as if reading her mind. "By the time we found you, Jenks was already in custody. We found him up on the watchroom landing with a broken leg, lying in a pool of black paint."

"I told you about the fish in the cellar, right?" Chloe asked. "And the net on the clothesline? I think he was breaking fishing laws, leaving the evidence at the lighthouse, and cruising on to Jackson Harbor for inspection."

"We're recovering the evidence," Stig assured her. "Trout, which is illegal for a commercial fisherman to harvest, including some too large for consumption. I didn't see a net, though."

"But… oh!" she exclaimed. "There was a bottle of sulfuric acid in the cellar. Is it possible that—"

"It's an old trick," Stig said. "If you get caught with a gillnet that doesn't conform to regulations, a few splashes of sulfuric acid can destroy the net—and the evidence. I think we'll have enough to nail him."

"I wonder if that's why Jenks was rude to me one day and offered to haul water for me the next," Chloe said. "Maybe there was something on the beach he didn't want me to see. He definitely tried to scare me into staying away from the cellar."

"It's probably been going on for a long time," Brenda muttered. "The north end of the island is so damn deserted."

Chloe felt Roelke's *I told you so* stare. She carefully avoided eye contact.

"That explains his rowboat, too," Garrett mused. "He could anchor his tug off the north end of Rock, row ashore with whatever he didn't want the wardens to see, and stash it at the lighthouse until it was time to make the next hand-off to whoever was buying from him."

"But who was the other guy who came after me in the lighthouse?" Chloe asked. This time she saw Roelke's hand clench convulsively. "Was it Tim? Did someone find him and Natalie?"

"The Coast Guard picked them up about the same time we found you," Stig said. "She's on her way to the Sturgeon Bay hospital with a bad concussion. Her brother's in jail."

Chloe closed her eyes with relief. She didn't want to be responsible for anyone's death—even someone who'd tried to kill her. Then she opened them again. "Wait. Tim is Natalie's brother?" She looked at Garrett. "You told me they were a couple."

"They registered for the campsite using the same last name, Brown. I made an assumption."

And so did I, Chloe thought, even though I didn't see a hint of anything romantic between them. Well, except for the bouquet of flowers she'd found in their campsite—but she'd made assumptions about that too.

"I talked to Tim earlier," Stig said. "After I pointed out the splashes of black paint on his skin, he admitted that he went to Pottawatomie Lighthouse with Jenks this afternoon."

To kill me, Chloe thought. She tugged the blanket up to her chin with her fingertips and made a mental note to send champagne to Herb's most wonderful painter. Between the paint cans and the ladder, she had a lot to feel grateful about.

"After you escaped the lighthouse, Tim chased you down to the landing, saw you struggling with Natalie on the reef, and jumped in his own kayak. When you brained Natalie, he let you go in favor of helping her. They'd hidden both kayaks in the boathouse."

Of *course*. It would have been easy for Natalie and Tim to paddle unseen into the watery cavern beneath the Viking Hall. Maybe Natalie had been waiting there to rendezvous with Tim after his trip to Pottawatomie. Or maybe, Chloe thought, she'd been waiting to make sure that I didn't do something stupid like try to escape on the reef.

"It's a relief to see you looking better," Garrett said hoarsely. "Hypothermia can … well, I'm just glad they found you in time. But to learn that Melvin Jenks—my own employee—"

"Actually," Chloe said, "we should have guessed that Melvin was making trouble."

Stig's eyebrows rose. "And why is that?"

"From everything I've heard, fishermen are pretty darn handy," she said. "Jenks was maintenance man for the park, but all kinds of things have gone wrong lately. The phone cable was cut, circuits blew in the Viking Hall, the park service boat had engine trouble—and that's just since I've been here! There've been problems at the lighthouse, too. A missing repair log, the wrong paint showing up, crumbling plaster. See? The common denominator was Jenks. He had access to everything. Maybe Herb's consultants did everything right, and Jenks tampered with their stuff."

Stig rubbed his chin, looking from Roelke to Garrett. "She may be on to something."

"I try not to underestimate her," Roelke said.

Chloe smiled, grateful that he'd managed a mild tone. Then she hesitated, trying to decide how much to say. "There's something else, too. The first night I was at the lighthouse I dreamed of hearing children's laughter. The next morning I mentioned that to you, Garrett. Well, one night I heard laughter again—but it was repetitive. I found a mark beneath my window, like the corner of a box or something had been put down. I think it was a cassette player. I think somebody was trying to scare me." She felt another of Roelke's accusatory stares. "I was going to tell someone about the recording," she added defensively. "I never got the chance."

Garrett looked appalled. "Did you think *I* left it?"

Her cheeks grew warm. "Well, it did cross my mind after I realized that one of the men in the lighthouse this afternoon was wearing a DNR uniform. Tim and Natalie were with us that morning, though. They must have told Jenks." She struggled to sit up a little straighter, a difficult task with two bandaged hands. "But please—can someone start at the beginning? I'm still confused."

"We don't know everything yet," Stig admitted, "but here goes. This morning Brenda called and asked me to go over to Rock with her to—"

"Hot chocolate, anyone?" an elderly man asked as he entered the room. He set a laden tray on a coffee table and smiled at Chloe. "I don't know if you remember me, but I'm—"

"The archivist!"

"That's right. I volunteer there." He put a steaming mug on an end table beside her, thoughtfully armed with a bendy straw.

Chloe sipped some of the hot chocolate and nearly swooned. Definitely homemade, with rich chocolate, whole milk, and a hint of cinnamon. "This is heavenly, Mr. Noakes."

He beamed. "I'll be back with sandwiches."

"Thanks, Dad," Brenda called after him. Then she picked up the story. "I'd been planning to call Stig because I'd been finding evidence of fresh digging all over the island. Including up by the lighthouse."

Ah, Chloe thought. That explained why Brenda had been wandering through the north woods. "I saw signs of digging below the lighthouse, too. And in the little cave. Was that Jenks?"

"If so, we don't know why," Brenda said. "When Sylvie died, I figured I should give Stig time to work on that before bugging him about some holes. But this morning, just after dawn, I saw Jenks' fishing tug and a motorboat anchored below the lighthouse. Several big coolers got passed from the tug to the second boat, which then took off toward Michigan. There have been reports of bad fish reaching Escanaba markets lately, so I thought someone official should know about the exchange." She looked at Garrett. "I didn't want to call you on the day of Sylvie's memorial."

Garrett blew out a long breath. "Sylvie and I argued yesterday morning. I didn't think she should take the tug out alone anymore. She told me to go stuff myself." He tried to smile, without success. "So anyway, I went out on the lake at dawn today myself. *That's* where I wanted to memorialize Sylvie."

The pain in his voice nipped at Chloe's heart. "I'm sorry, Garrett."

Stig cleared his throat. "So Brenda and I went over to Rock. After trekking around we ended up by the lighthouse. Then *this* guy comes out of the woods with Jack Cornell." Stig jerked his head toward Roelke.

Chloe looked expectantly at Roelke. He shrugged. "Your phone call made me nervous."

"How'd you get up here so fast?"

"Oh. I rented a plane."

He rented a *plane*? Yikes. He rented a plane.

"When Roelke said he was worried about you," Stig said, "we all went inside the lighthouse. We found your backpack, and Jenks. We just didn't find you. It was clear that you'd left the lighthouse in a hurry, so we split up to search."

"Roelke was sure you'd tried to get across the reef," Brenda said, "even though I'd *told* you it was too dangerous."

"I didn't have a whole lot of options," Chloe protested.

"What I don't know is how you survived," Brenda said flatly. "You said you got swept away...?"

Chloe tried to remember. "I tried to swim back to the reef, but... I was too tired and cold. I gave up and let the current take me."

Roelke's knee began to bounce. Brenda said, "giving up was good, actually. You'd never have reached the reef again."

"After awhile I saw Natalie's paddle. The current was easing up and I managed to grab it. It gave me something to lean on. I pointed myself toward shore and tried to kick." Everything beyond that was pretty fuzzy. Chloe stared at her bandaged hands. She knew she'd been very lucky. Unlike Zana ... and Sylvie. "Stig," she said quietly, "Did Melvin and the Browns murder Sylvie?"

"Yes." Stig pulled off his glasses, rubbed his nose, put them on again. "Tim claims he and Natalie didn't know what Jenks was planning for Sylvie, that Jenks just said he wanted to teach her a lesson—

"A lesson about *what*?" Brenda demanded.

"Sylvie was on to Jenks," Stig explained. "She saw him coming ashore below Pottawatomie with a cooler. She confronted him about it—"

"She would," Garrett muttered.

"—and told Jenks that if he didn't quit, she'd turn him in."

Brenda folded her arms. "No. I'm sorry, but some dispute about fish is *not* cause for murder."

Chloe struggled to adjust the blanket, and Roelke tucked it back over her knees. She was wearing an old sweat suit of Brenda's, but the extra warmth was still comforting. "It's happened before," she said. "A century ago. I've been picking up bits of evidence in my research." She paused. Should she explain the contents of Ragna's tin box? No. This was not the time, and telling these lawmen was not the action needed.

"I didn't want to believe it either," Stig said. "But it's pretty clear. Sylvie tried to give Jenks a break, knowing he'd had it tough lately, but that just enraged him. He put water in the fuel tank of Sylvie's tug, knowing that in time it would mix with the fuel and work its way to the engine. I imagine she was well out in the lake before the engine started running rough, and then quit altogether."

Chloe felt a twist of nausea. "Sylvie knew him, which would explain why there was no sign of struggle. Jenks has his own boat, and access to the *Ranger*. He easily could have gone after her tug in the fog."

Stig nodded. "Right. Then he showed up to offer assistance, and..." For the first time he hesitated.

"Go ahead," Chloe said quietly. "We all need to know."

"Jenks went aboard Sylvie's tug, knocked her senseless, and smothered her."

Chloe clenched her teeth, trying to stave away unwanted mental pictures. "But why all the ritual? Why bring her body back to Rock?"

"Maybe they got the idea after hearing about Zana being found wrapped in the fishnet," Brenda mused. "Jenks was angry about the new fishing laws."

"Tim claims that Jenks told him and Natalie that they would be tried as accomplices if they didn't keep quiet about Sylvie's death," Stig added. "They hated Sylvie, so I'm guessing they weren't that hard to convince."

"But why?" Brenda demanded. "Who *are* these kids? Why would Tim and Natalie Brown get involved with a low-life like Melvin Jenks?"

Her father walked back into the room with a second tray. "Tim and Natalie Brown?" he asked slowly. "You mean Gloria Brown's kids?"

"Who's Gloria Brown?" Roelke asked.

"Evert Anderson's ex-wife," Stig said.

Chloe gasped. "That means Tim and Natalie are descendants of Ragna and Anders Anderson!" She tried to absorb that, to make the connections.

"Who are Ragna and Anders Anderson?" Roelke asked.

312

"Danish immigrants who settled in the fishing village on Rock Island," Chloe said. "It's a long story. But that explains why the photograph of Paul Anderson I saw at the maritime museum reminded me of someone. Tim is his grandson."

Brenda reached for a cheese sandwich. "I was a little girl when Paul drowned in the channel between Washington and Rock. That was … let's see … "

"Nineteen thirty-nine," Chloe said, which earned her a startled look. "What? The docent at the Maritime Museum told me."

Roelke scrubbed his face with his palms. "OK, stop. I need someone to lay all of this out for me. Clearly."

"Paul Anderson, son of Ragna and Anders, was a fisherman," Mr. Noakes said. "One of the very best, but not a happy man. During one of the lean years, Paul went to work for Chester Thordarson."

"The guy from Iceland who bought up most of Rock Island," Brenda added for Roelke's benefit. "One day Paul was in a rowboat, coming home to Washington, and he capsized. He clung to a pound net stake for a while, but a wave knocked him under before help arrived. His body was found the next day. A lot of people, including Paul's son Evert, blamed Thordarson for that."

"But that's not fair," Chloe exclaimed, earning more startled looks. "What? I read about it in the Viking Hall. Chester Thordarson had been trying to get a phone cable put in, but without success. He was terribly upset when Paul drowned."

Mr. Noakes sighed. "The Anderson family seemed to live under a black cloud. Nobody could find fish the way Paul did, but he went through life with a chip on his shoulder." He shrugged. "I'm not sure why."

"I think I know," Chloe said. Heads swiveled in her direction. "Look, I've spent the last five days immersed in local history. Paul's mother, Ragna Anderson, believed someone killed her husband. And I saw a bouquet of flowers in the campsite where Tim and Natalie stayed—right by the fishing village site. Maybe they left it as a memorial to their ancestors. I saw someone walking there one evening, too. I bet it was one of them."

"Gloria wasn't a local girl," Mr. Noakes said. "She came to vacation one summer and ended up married to Evert. He was as sour as his father."

Garrett snapped his fingers. "I remember now. When the state was deciding whether to buy Rock Island, Gloria fought it hard. She was a real estate agent, and she hooked up with a developer who wanted to build luxury hotels, that kind of thing."

"And she had a site for her own condo already picked out," Chloe added, remembering the map she'd seen in Garrett's office—the one with a site marked "Brown" already laid out on the island's eastern shore. "Did she have dark hair? I saw an old newspaper photo at Sylvie's memorial. A woman in the front row looked furious."

Mr. Noakes nodded. "That probably was Gloria."

Another bulb flickered on in Chloe's memory. "T-A," she said. "That was carved on the wooden stake by Sylvie's body, remember? Tim—Anderson. He *was* making a statement. On top of the old Anderson family tragedies, his mother probably raised him and Natalie to believe that they'd been cheated out of reclaiming a lovely plot of land at the fishing village site on Rock." She remembered seeing Tim whittling a stick to roast marshmallows, how sweet and naive it had seemed.

"Gloria and Evert split about the time the state bought Rock for a park," Mr. Noakes said. "Gloria left the islands and took the kids with her. Settled in Michigan, I think. I hadn't thought about her in years, but a few months ago someone sent us her obituary for our files. She died of cancer."

Chloe sucked in her lower lip. "So... some fifteen-year-old argument between Gloria and Sylvie, and a recent argument between Melvin and Sylvie, led to murder. But why did they decide to come after *me*?" Her voice came out a little wobbly.

"I'd like to know that too," Roelke growled. His knee was jouncing so hard that the sofa was vibrating. "Chloe was alone at Pottawatomie for a week, and nobody bothered her until Sunday afternoon. *Something* must have changed."

"I found some stinky trash bags and a couple of those coolers in the cellar a few days ago," Chloe said. "I didn't open them, but I did mention them to Jenks, so maybe he thought I was close to figuring things out. I left this morning with my pack, though, and told Jack Cornell I was moving over to Washington. When I found that net hanging on the clothesline I assumed someone was still trying to frighten me. Maybe Jenks saw me return. If he looked through a window he could have even seen me go down to the cellar and check the cooler. He might have guessed I was about to ruin his scam."

"Maybe." Stig didn't sound convinced.

"The only other thing I did this morning was go to church and Sylvie's memorial," Chloe added. "Jenks was there, and I nodded hello, but we didn't speak. I didn't talk to anyone except Lorna Whitby." She looked at Roelke. "She's one of the RISC committee people."

"What did you talk to Lorna about?" Stig asked.

Chloe shrugged. "Nothing, really. I said how sorry I was about Sylvie, and ... well, I did tell Lorna that I wanted to nominate Pottawatomie to the National Register."

Roelke looked as if he was getting a headache. "The what?"

"The National Register of Historic Places," Chloe explained. "It provides federal protection for historic structures."

"Maybe once you mentioned going after federal protection, you went from being a temporary nuisance to someone actively making it harder for him to run his black-market business," Brenda said slowly. "Jenks wanted to discourage visitors to Rock Island, and to slow down or even halt the lighthouse restoration. Tim and Natalie Brown-Anderson grew up hearing their parents complain about old injustices and new injustices."

"Then here I come," Chloe said, "an outsider who wants to do everything possible to protect the park and encourage visitors to come visit the lighthouse." Was that enough to spin Jenks to violence? Evidently so.

"This ugliness has been festering for a long time." Brenda sighed. "And Jenks used to fish with Evert Anderson. It's not surprising that the Browns would remember him, and get back in touch."

"I ran into Tim at the market one day," Chloe said. "He said he wanted to become a commercial fisherman."

"Did Tim know that's gotten a whole lot harder lately?" Brenda asked.

"Evidently he learned that the hard way." Garrett worked his jaw. "Tim and Natalie might have decided to come back to the islands after Gloria died. Maybe her death kicked this whole thing into motion."

"No," Stig said.

Chloe realized it was the first time the deputy had spoken in quite some time. "No?"

"Gloria's death wasn't the trigger. Evert's was."

Roelke leaned close to Chloe. "Evert was Tim and Natalie's father, right?" he whispered.

"Right," Chloe whispered back, but her gaze was on Stig.

"The Brown-Anderson kids' mother died, so they decided to reconnect with their dad," Stig said. "But before they got here, their dad had a stroke and died. Right after I arrested him."

"*You* arrested him?" Chloe repeated. When telling her the story, he'd left out that teensy detail.

Brenda stared at the deputy with wide eyes. "Stig, you're the only person alive that Tim and Natalie could directly link to one of their family tragedies. And Mel Jenks hates you. If the three of them were so bitter that they went after Sylvie and Chloe, what did they have in mind for you?"

"Jesus," Roelke muttered.

Chloe felt another sick curl in her stomach as she realized the implications. "Stig, when you went to Rock Island with Brenda today, whose boat did you take?"

"Mine," Brenda said.

Stig got to his feet. "Thanks, everyone. I've got to go." He looked at Roelke. "Want to help me out?"

Roelke looked at Chloe. "You're OK?"

She knew he didn't want to leave. "I'm fine," she said firmly.

"You need to get more rest anyway," he said, obviously trying to convince himself of that. "But I'll be around. Do you want to head home tomorrow?"

"No," she told him. "I want to show you the lighthouse."

FORTY-SIX

"So," Stig said, as he and Roelke got into his truck. "Chloe's looking better."

Roelke didn't answer. Better? A livid bruise bloomed purple and green on her right cheek. Her hands were swaddled like infants. God only knew how traumatized she was. Jenks had almost killed her, and hypothermia could lead to coma, even death. When he thought about how close she'd come to—

"She's an interesting woman." Stig put the truck in gear and backed out of the driveway.

"She is."

Stig threw him a sideways look. "Are you two a couple?"

"Yeah," Roelke lied. "Why do you ask?"

"I've been thinking about asking her out."

"Don't."

"Got it." Stig flipped on his blinker and passed a blue sedan. "Thanks for the backup. I appreciate it."

I haven't done much, Roelke thought. He had no grasp of the tangled local history that evidently triggered the crimes committed. He hadn't even swooped in and saved Chloe. She'd been in bad shape when they found her—just thinking about it frosted his blood—but she was moving. If rescue hadn't arrived, she would have kept crawling across the lawn to the house and found help there.

Well, he told himself, give yourself a little credit. Everybody else was sure she was still on Rock. The house might have been empty.

Roelke beat a percussive rhythm on his thigh with one thumb. He appreciated Stig treating him like a colleague, but he hadn't had a moment alone with Chloe and he felt ready to explode. He didn't even know if she was pissed at him for flying up. He didn't intend to take any crap about that, but it would be nice to know what she was thinking. He hoped she wouldn't ask too many questions. No way he could explain why he'd felt so compelled to get to the islands, ASAP. Or why he'd been sure Chloe had tried to cross the reef. He remembered Mrs. Saddler's calm statement about her husband's heart attack: *Something made me turn off the coffeepot and go back to check on him. I just knew.*

Stig interrupted his thoughts. "Here we go." He wheeled into a parking space beside a small marina, parked, and grabbed a heavy flashlight. He was jogging down the dock before Roelke had his seatbelt unfastened. Roelke followed to a motorboat called *Escape* in the last slip.

Stig was examining the engine. "Son of a bitch," Stig muttered as Roelke stepped on board. "Take a look at this."

———

Chloe woke the next morning feeling as if someone had pummeled her. She managed to strip off the borrowed nightgown and survey her bruises. She looked as if someone had pummeled her, too.

Her own clothes had been dried and left folded on a chair. Once dressed she followed the sound of voices to a spacious kitchen. The stove and countertop were decades old, but the walls were a cheerful yellow. A colorful platter hanging on one wall was rosemaled in the Norwegian style.

Mr. Noakes and Brenda were alone in the room. Where had Roelke spent the night? Where was he now? Chloe started to ask, but realized just in time that she should start with something a bit more courteous. "Good morning."

"Hey, there you are!" Brenda turned from the stove, spatula in hand.

Mr. Noakes pulled out a chair for her. "Chloe, I think we've got a connection. Brenda's mother's cousin was an Ellefson, and—"

"Dad," Brenda said, "please give Chloe some time before launching into the genealogy stuff, all right?"

"It's OK," Chloe said. "My mom's a genealogist too. She said there was some distant connection of my dad's here on the island."

"Well, there you have it." Mr. Noakes gave his daughter an *I told you so* look.

Brenda ignored it. "I'm making Icelandic pancakes," she told Chloe. "Are you hungry?"

"I am," Chloe admitted. "And Icelandic pancakes sound heavenly."

"I've got cows to milk," Mr. Noakes said. "I'll let you two talk." He left through the back door.

"Stig called earlier," Brenda said. "Your friend stayed at his place last night. They were heading down to Sturgeon Bay, but Stig said they could meet us at the park dock later. That is, if you still want to go back to Rock...?"

"I do," Chloe said firmly. If she didn't stare the bad memories down, they'd follow her back home.

"All right, then. We can take my boat over."

Once Chloe figured out how to manipulate a fork without putting pressure on her bandaged palms, she tucked into thin vanilla-scented pancakes, which had been spread with strawberry jam, rolled, and dusted with powdered sugar. After three bites, a glass of OJ, and a few sips of strong coffee, she was beginning to feel a faint resemblance to something human.

Brenda put a platter with more pancakes on the table and slid into the chair across from Chloe. "Help yourself."

Chloe did. The good food, the simple normalcy of it, the memory of Roelke's grip on her shoulder last night... it all left her feeling ridiculously emotional.

Pull it together, she told herself. One or two questions remained to be answered. "Brenda," she said finally. "The last time I talked with Sylvie, she mentioned your name. She seemed about to tell me something. Then she changed her mind."

"We had an argument the day before she died. But it's not what you probably think."

"I don't know what to think."

"Sylvie and I both kept a sharp eye on Rock Island. Garret doesn't have the time or manpower to do it." Brenda helped herself to a pancake. "We'd been seeing more and more signs of activity up near the lighthouse. Sylvie thought we should tell you about

322

it. I didn't think that would be fair to you." Brenda's mouth twisted. "I'm sorry, Chloe. I should have handled things differently. Obviously we had no idea the situation would get deadly."

"No one could have predicted that," Chloe said. "Please don't beat yourself up about that. But there is one more thing. It's been a joy to uncover stories about the keepers and their families. I've been particularly intrigued by Emily Betts—"

"Interesting woman," Brenda agreed.

"But I've also been drawn to the village site." Chloe wiped up some powdered sugar with her last bit of pancake before popping it into her mouth. "I didn't know why, at first. Then a couple of letters written by Emily turned up. I thought about showing them to you, but that day I met you at the meadow, and we talked about your work, you were a bit…intense. And you said there'd been *one* murder on Rock Island, but I know you've seen that letter in the Viking Hall that refers to a second." Chloe was pretty sure there had been three murders in days of old, actually, but there would never be any way to prove whether someone helped Anders Anderson into his watery grave. "And when I mentioned seeing that barge or whatever in the channel at night…you got angry, but you also claimed you had no idea what it might be."

Brenda leaned back in her chair and sighed. "I taught at U-Michigan before going to Escanaba College. And while there I got…romantically involved with a colleague. We found ourselves competing for the same grant money, the same research gigs, all the little plums that can show up in academic life. Our relationship ended. Badly."

"You think it was your ex out in the channel?"

"I think it's very likely. He's devoted his career to proving that Vikings traveled through the area." Brenda shoved hair away from her face. "Look, I shouldn't have dumped on you that day, Chloe. In general, I really don't begrudge the people who end up in the spotlight. If they want to search for Viking rune stones or whatever, so be it."

"But...?"

"But my ex is a condescending jerk, and it still galls me to see him succeed when I can't get money to hire one or two undergrads for a proper dig on Rock Island. The stories of my ancestors who settled in the fishing village are getting lost." She leaned forward again, forearms on the table. "I don't have a Viking Hall or a Pottawatomie Lighthouse to attract attention to their lives."

"Which is too bad."

"At this point I'm not hankering for academic glory. I'll finish my career at a community college, and that's OK. But..." Brenda ran both hands through her hair, leaving ends sticking out in all directions. "Look, this may sound over-the-top, but I *know* there's something waiting at the village site. Something I need to discover."

"I think so too," Chloe said. "And if you'll take me out there, I think I can help you find it."

Brenda's eyebrows shot toward the ceiling. "Um... really? And just how, exactly, do you plan to do that?"

"Let's go over to Rock early, before meeting the guys," Chloe said. "It will be easier to show you than tell you."

Brenda eyed her dubiously. "Well, OK, I guess." Her tone said, *I better humor her.*

Chloe focused on a pancake, and was glad when the doorbell rang. A moment later Brenda ushered the Whitbys into the kitchen. "Sit down," she said. "Have you had breakfast? Want some coffee?"

"No thank you," Herb said stiffly.

Lorna sat down beside Chloe and put a hand on her arm. "When we heard what happened," Lorna said, "we wanted to make sure you were all right. I'm *so* sorry you got caught up in this! Here we thought we were offering a consultant a peaceful week…"

"I'm fine," Chloe assured her. "And I'm not sorry I came. The project will continue to move forward." Then she looked at Herb. "I can't help wondering, though. You were in and out of that cellar. Did you ever notice Jenks' coolers? Or see him drying nets, and wonder?"

Herb looked even more uncomfortable. "He said he was just storing garbage he picked up on the north end of the island. He showed me an empty cooler once, stuffed with trash. After that…"

"I understand," Chloe said. Herb had enough to regret without her adding any more guilt.

He cleared his throat. "So, we'll leave you to rest. As Lorna said, we felt duty-bound to express our regrets for these unfortunate incidents in person."

Suddenly Chloe thought of one little detail Herb might not have heard. "And I must express regrets for hurling the cans of black paint down the ladder from the lantern room," she said soberly. "I'm afraid it's now splashed all over the watchroom."

"*What?*" His eyes went wide. "Good God, that's oil-based paint! That will set us back—"

"Hush, Herb," Lorna said. "Just hush."

When the Whitbys had gone on their way, Brenda said, "Don't mind Herb."

Chloe smiled, remembering that Sylvie had once told her the very same thing. "I don't. I've become rather fond of Herb, actually. He works with good people."

"Listen, Chloe, I've been thinking about how horrid your time here has been. That's not what life on these islands is about."

"I know."

Brenda got up and fetched a folded piece of cream-colored linen from a counter. "I want you to have this."

The cloth felt soft in Chloe's hands. Definitely old, she thought. She opened the rectangle over her lap, revealing a table runner inlaid with needle lace. "Brenda! I can't accept this."

"Yes you can."

Chloe squinted at the handwork. "I don't recognize this type of lace." The stitch motifs favored rings and pyramids.

"It's hedebo. *Hedebosøm,* in Danish. Ragna Anderson gave it to Berglind, my great-grandmother from Iceland who lived in the fishing village."

"*Ragna* made this?" Chloe's sternum quivered.

"Yes. My mom passed it on to me, but I don't have any kids. It feels right to give it to you."

"Well… thank you. I'll treasure it." Chloe stroked the handwork with a gentle finger. "I haven't even thanked you for your hospitality. I'm very grateful."

Brenda got up and began stacking dirty plates. "The last thing you needed last night was a trip to the Sturgeon Bay hospital or a night in a hotel room." She grinned over her shoulder. "Besides, aren't we sixth cousins fourteen times removed or something? Definitely family."

Definitely family.

"See that?" Brenda pointed to a plaque hanging over the door, painted with Scandinavian flourishes.

"What does *Athabold* mean?"

"*Athabold* is an Icelandic word," Brenda said. "It means 'Everyone welcome.'"

FORTY-SEVEN:
MARCH, 1906

THAT DAWN, EMILY'S GREATEST wish had been to get through her daughter's funeral without weeping uncontrollably, even collapsing. Her daughter Lillian was dead of diphtheria at age eighteen. Emily didn't know how to compose herself in the face of that loss.

But instead of hysteria, a foggy numbness had seized her. When her friends offered condolences inside the church, she had a hard time parsing the words. During the graveside prayers she slipped further away, as if she were watching through the wrong end of a telescope.

Although Emily had spent decades nursing the sick—first on Rock Island, later on Washington—she hadn't been able to save her own child. She had eight other children. Jane, her oldest, was thirty-three; Eugenie, her youngest, was eleven. She knew William and the older children were worried about her, and that the younger ones needed her to be strong. But for the first time in her life, she didn't feel capable of staring trouble in the eye.

Now, the services complete, people stood in quiet clumps in the church graveyard. Emily walked away from the crowd. *Oh Ragna,* she thought, *I know now how it feels to bury a daughter. But when you heard that first dirt clod hit Christine's coffin I stood beside you, holding you up.*

Emily closed her eyes for a moment, confused. Where had *that* thought come from? Had she expected Ragna to appear now? Tragedies had darkened Ragna's heart. And when Carrick Dugan had been found shot to death on Rock Island four years earlier, Emily had not been surprised to learn that Ragna was nowhere to be found. She'd done a horrible thing and fled, just as she had said she would. And she'd never had the grace to send her old friend so much as a letter.

"Emily?" Her friend Jeannette approached, eyes damp and concerned. "Your friends will help you through these dark days."

"I wish Ragna were here," Emily said.

"Ragna Anderson?" Jeannette looked startled. "Gracious, dear, don't dwell on *her*. No one wants to say so out loud, but... well, you weren't surprised that she finally left Rock Island after that Irishman was killed. She's probably back in Denmark."

"I suppose so."

Jeannette kissed her cheek. "I must get back to the lighthouse. Please come for a long visit soon, all right? The change would do you good."

Emily blinked. "Yes, I will," she murmured. "A visit."

After Jeannette walked away another woman approached. Mette Friis, Emily thought. One of Ragna's friends.

"Mrs. Betts? I'm ever so sorry for your loss."

"Thank you." Emily hesitated. "Mette … have you ever heard from Ragna?"

"Heard from Ragna?" Mette glanced over her shoulder.

Emily drew her farther away from the clumps of people. "Didn't you help Ragna get away? Just as you once helped Carrick Dugan's wife get away from him?"

Mette's eyes widened. "You knew about that?"

"Of course." Emily waved a hand; she had no energy for polite niceties. "I doubt if there was a man on either island who knew, or a woman who didn't."

Mette adjusted her hat. "I just came to say how sorry I was to hear about your girl."

Emily caught Mette by the arm. "I don't need to know where Ragna's hiding. I just hope she's happier. That's all." Emily wasn't sure why it mattered now, but today, it did.

"Mrs. Betts, I didn't help Ragna get away." Mette hesitated before squaring her shoulders and leaning close. "I didn't help her because I didn't get there in time."

"You didn't get there in time …?"

"One day, fifteen years ago, Berglind Fridleifsdottir and I sailed over to Rock Island with our husbands. We docked on the west side because our men wanted to go to the lighthouse while we visited Ragna. Berglind and I were walking the path through the woods to the village when we heard a shot." Mette began twisting a lacey handkerchief in her fingers. "We went on real quiet, scared of what we'd find."

"What did you find?" Emily whispered.

"Carrick Dugan, shoveling earth into a new-made grave beside his cabin. There was a pistol sitting on the doorstep."

Emily shook her head slightly, trying to clear it, trying to understand.

"Berglind screamed, 'Did you kill Ragna? Did you kill Ragna too?' Dugan started after her. Berglind snatched a dead tree branch and swung it at him. It wouldn't have done more than slow the man down." Mette stopped twisting the handkerchief, and her blue eyes now held Emily's gaze. "I got to the pistol first. And I killed Carrick Dugan, Mrs. Betts. I shot him dead."

Emily pressed one hand over her chest. "Dear *God*..."

"Berglind and I dragged him down to the beach and left him. Then we washed our hands and walked back to the dock to wait for our husbands."

"Did... did you tell them what happened?"

"No ma'am," Mette said. "We figured the wolves could have Dugan and none would be the wiser. But Anton Jacobson took some friends over for a picnic at the old homeplace the next day, and found the body. They didn't send for the authorities because everyone disliked or feared Dugan. Anton didn't want Ragna to be accused of murder, so he buried Dugan quick and quiet. But of course word trickled out."

One of Mette's daughters approached. "Mama? Papa says we need to leave soon so he can get home in time to milk."

"Tell him that I'll be there in a moment." Mette waited until the young woman was out of earshot. "Mrs. Betts, I'm not sorry for what I did. And I didn't break my silence to burden you. You and Ragna were close once. I hope it helps you to know that Ragna wasn't the one who killed him."

Emily watched Mette walk away. "No one wants to say so out loud…" Jeannette had said, speaking of the whispers that had followed Ragna's disappearance. Heaven help me, Emily thought. Had she started the whispers by confiding her fears? One thing was clear: she could never—*would* never—betray Mette's confidence. That would only cause more pain, ruin more lives.

Pressing her fingers against her forehead, Emily tried to send Ragna a silent message: *Oh, my dear old friend, I've done you an injustice. And I see no earthly way to make things right.*

FORTY-EIGHT

"Oh, my." Chloe groaned as she slowly maneuvered herself out of the park's ancient pickup. Brenda had driven to the village site as slowly as possible, but it was impossible to avoid ruts and tree roots.

"Want to go back?" Brenda clearly considered this excursion a fool's errand.

"No." Chloe forced herself to present an impression of something at least a smidge better than death warmed on toast. "This is important." She led the way to the south end of the meadow.

When the grasses gave way to shrubby growth she paused, steeling herself. Then she walked into the grove. Something tingled along her backbone. That same malevolent energy she'd felt before quivered like a live thing, waiting to pounce. Keep going, she told herself. Find the center.

"Are you OK?" Brenda asked. "You don't look so good."

One more step. Another. And—Chloe couldn't move. She could hardly breathe. "Here," she managed. "Right here."

Brenda gave her a skeptical look. "What is it you expect me to find? And I can't just hack away, you know. There are proper procedures to follow. I have to—"

"Get your tools and do whatever you need to do," Chloe said through gritted teeth. "I don't think it will take long. I'll wait out in the sunshine."

She retreated to the meadow and sat on the rise above the beach, letting the evil leak away like water. A sense of peace flowed into its place. It was impossible to look at the beach below without thinking of Sylvie... but at least her killers would be brought to justice. And I helped with that too, Chloe thought. That felt good.

And soon, the black energy trapped in the grove would be gone. Soon, the sound of an archaeologist's tools would replace the lingering shovel-scrape of a killer digging a grave. Chloe was pretty sure she knew who'd been dumped in that obscure grave. And—like Zana, and Sylvie—she deserved to be buried with dignity and respect.

This is what I can do, Chloe thought. She sometimes wished she could reject her heightened sense of perception... but since she could not, it was comforting to know that every once in awhile she could use it to accomplish something good. She sat, mesmerized by the gentle waves. It was pleasant to be here again, peaceful. She felt herself drowsing...

Then Brenda crashed from the trees. "You were right!" she gasped. "I don't know how you knew, but oh my God, Chloe, you were *right*."

———

If Brenda hadn't made arrangements to meet Stig and Roelke at the Viking Hall, Chloe might never have dragged her away from the meadow. "But it's just as well," Brenda told Garrett, when she and Chloe went to his office to return the truck keys. "I'm going to call the UW archaeology department and see if they want to send somebody up. I mean—my God—a skeleton! A skeleton with what sure looks to me like a bullet hole in the skull. I've only uncovered the face, but ..."

Chloe leaned against the wall, watching Garrett and Brenda make plans. After a week of tragedies, it was wonderful to see them excited. Wonderful to hear Garrett vow that after a century of obscurity, the bones of the poor soul who'd received only rough burial would be recovered and ultimately interred in one of the island cemeteries.

Finally Brenda glanced out the window. "There's the *Karfi*," she told Garrett. "Looks like you've got some visitors. I'll fill you in later."

Garrett locked the office so he could walk down to the dock with them. "Say, there was a bit of a hullabaloo this morning," he said. "Remember that tourist from Massachusetts, Chloe? You gave him a tour."

"Mr. Dix? Sure. He came back one more time because his photos didn't turn out."

"Well, photos were not his prime concern," Garrett said dryly. "Mr. Dix has been trying to discover where lighthouse families dumped their garbage. After two visits he was afraid of attracting notice, so he's been paddling out to the island on his own."

"That jerk!" Chloe remembered how unbothered Dix had been when she told him he couldn't go back inside the lighthouse—

despite the fact that he'd taken dozens of interior photographs during his first visit. "He is a lighthouse fanatic, so he'd certainly know how valuable even a rusty old oil can would be to a collector. Was he digging?"

"Yep," Garrett confirmed. "He dug a bunch of test holes without uncovering anything. So this morning he decided to climb one of the limestone walls right below the lighthouse, trying to reach a ledge where something tossed over the precipice might have landed. He fell, of course. Broke his arm." He shook his head. "The idiot is lucky he's still here to tell the tale."

"Good grief," Brenda said with disgust. "Can you imagine being so stupid as to try climbing a rock wall without gear?"

"Dumb," Chloe agreed, avoiding eye contact. "Pretty darn dumb."

They reached the dock below the Viking Hall as Stig and Roelke stepped from the *Karfi*. Roelke wore jeans and hiking boots and a red wool shirt. Seeing him here in this special place made something beneath Chloe's ribs hitch tight.

"Anything new?" Garrett asked Stig.

The deputy nodded grimly. "Sylvie's tug was recovered this morning. Jenks tampered with the engine in my boat, too. Explosives. Evidence guys are crawling over both boats. I need to take some photos in the lighthouse, and to look for whatever remnants of Jenks' net might have survived an acid bath. I want this case to be rock-solid."

"I'll go with you," Garrett said, "and run you back to Washington whenever you're ready."

Stig and Garrett drove to the lighthouse; Chloe insisted on walking. "With any luck they'll be done by the time we get there," she told Roelke as they headed north. "Those two seemed downright amiable today, but they've been sniping at each other all week. I have no idea why."

"I do," he said. "It came up last night while we were waiting for you to wake up. A couple of years ago Stig found Garrett fishing outside of some zone or other. Garrett claimed he didn't realize he was in the wrong place, and thought he deserved a warning, but Stig gave him a citation." He held a branch aside so it wouldn't slap Chloe in the face. "I think they both realize that a citation was a silly thing to hold a grudge about. A murder—and attempted murders—tend to help people put things in perspective."

"What strikes me is that everybody wants the same thing," Chloe said sadly. "The commercial fishermen, the sport fishermen, the DNR wardens, the environmentalists…everyone wants to protect the lake. They just have different ideas sometimes about how to do that."

"*Most* everybody," Roelke growled. "Jenks and his young friends…"

"Yeah." Chloe blew out a long breath. "It's so weird. Natalie really helped me out that first night by going to get help. The next day, Tim gave me a granola bar. Melvin Jenks brought me drinking water. And then they killed Sylvie, and tried to kill me."

"And Stig," Roelke added. "If he'd taken his boat out yesterday morning, he'd probably be dead as well."

Chloe shuddered. "I'd like to take a little break from talking about the bad stuff."

They walked in silence for a while. Then Roelke said, "You know, I don't really get your job. I mean, I think studying history is a good thing. But—how much can you ever really know? Don't you worry about getting stuff wrong?"

"I do," Chloe admitted. "We can never really have more than just the barest hint of what some long-dead person's life was like... but it's important to make the attempt."

"Hunh," he said thoughtfully. "I can see that."

"There are legislators trying to turn Old World Wisconsin into a theme park," she added. "And some people fought hard to keep Rock Island from becoming a state park. Working as a curator, trying to dig out stories and protect the places and artifacts left behind...I guess I feel as if I'm doing something important."

"Yeah," Roelke said. "I feel like that about my job, too."

As they approached the lighthouse Chloe found her steps slowing. Her feet stopped altogether as they approached the final rise before reaching the clearing.

"You don't have to do this," Roelke said.

Chloe's heart was skittering in her chest. She swallowed, trying to hide sudden panic. "I think I do," she managed finally. "I love this place, Roelke. If I don't go back now, I'm afraid I never will. I will not let Jenks and the Brown-Andersons ruin this experience for me."

"OK, then," he said. "Take your time."

She did, trying to focus on this moment and let yesterday fade. The air was cool against her cheeks. A solomon's seal plant beside the trail had produced a cluster of purple berries, lovely against their still-green leaves. A warbler sang from a beech tree.

Roelke leaned over to pick up a single scarlet maple leaf from the trail. "Here," he said, and handed it to her.

"Oh, Roelke." Her voice trembled. "Thank you. I'll press it. And—and keep it as a reminder of all the *good* things that happened during my time on Rock Island."

"Isn't this amazing?" Chloe asked. She and Roelke were sitting on the front steps of the lighthouse, looking over the lake as the late-afternoon sun eased into the western sky. Stig and Garrett were gone, taking their cameras and evidence bags. She'd sent Ragna's box back with them, too. Like Emily, she wanted to banish the reminder of evil.

"It's pretty special," Roelke agreed. "Still, when I think about you isolated here…"

"Don't. Please. I'm fine."

"I told you it was not a good idea for you to be here by yourself."

She looked at the red maple leaf, now resting on her knee. "I needed to be alone. I do need that sometimes, Roelke."

"You live alone in a ten-room farmhouse."

"That's not what I mean."

He sighed, keeping his gaze on the lake. "I know. But sometimes you do stuff that…I just think you're too trusting sometimes. I worry, that's all."

"And you're a cop," Chloe reminded him. "If I let myself, I'd worry about you every time you went to work. I could try to talk you into doing something else, but that wouldn't be fair. Being a cop is who you are."

For a while neither spoke. Finally Roelke said, "I gotta admit, it's beautiful here."

It's magical, Chloe thought, but she was willing to accept "beautiful." She needed this clearing's magic to soak into all the scraped-raw places in her heart. "It was important for me to actually be here while working on the lighthouse project," she told him. "The stories I found … well, it's like I was saying before. I just try to gather all the scraps I can, and then stitch them into some kind of whole cloth. And sometimes …" She let her voice trail away. Sometimes extra bits reverberated through time, and gave her more to work with.

She thought about all the people who'd come to Rock and gone again over the centuries, people who lived through joy and grief and then disappeared without a trace. She'd heard just a few stories—James McNeil and his Yellow Boys, Viking travelers overpowered by native people, the ill-fated *Griffon*. Most of the strange things she'd encountered that week had been explained, but she still didn't know who was anchoring in the channel after dark. Maybe the legends were true, and the *Griffon* still sailed on foggy nights. Maybe Brenda's ex had found a Viking ship. Maybe they'd never know. And you know what? Chloe thought. That's OK.

A cardinal landed in a honeysuckle bush and started to sing. Then the sound of childish laughter drifted over the grass. "Did you hear that?" she asked.

"The engine, you mean?" Roelke shaded his eyes, scanning the channel. "It's just a powerboat. Pretty far away."

Chloe felt her throat thicken, and tears sting her eyes. She was more sure than ever that this was what she was meant to do—work as a curator, dig out lost stories, sometimes hone in on old vibes as she'd done in the lighthouse and at the fishing village site. Roelke wanted to be with her, but he had no idea what he was getting into.

So tell him, she ordered herself. This man has saved you from harm, saved you from despair, waited for months while you dither.

He deserves to know. She slid a sideways glance Roelke's way. He seemed to be lost in his own thoughts.

The laughter came again. Chloe shut her eyes, trying to open herself to whatever or whomever might be waiting. *Emily*, she thought, *I didn't find your story.*

What she perceived was a growing sense of contentment. *I was happy here. Not because of the beauty, although I treasured every sunrise. Not because I once was assistant keeper, although that gave me great satisfaction and pride. I was happy here because of time shared with my family, and with my friends.*

Chloe opened her eyes. She waited to hear the laughter again. It didn't come.

"Roelke," she said. "I … I wanted to have some time alone because I've been wrestling with a lot of stuff. I spent years in a screwed-up relationship, and I almost made the same mistake last month."

"Yeah. You did."

"Sometimes I think I do better with historical people than present-day ones. I don't know if I'm meant to be in a serious relationship." She hesitated, keeping her gaze north.

Roelke rubbed his face with his palms. "Chloe, I came up here because I thought you were in trouble."

"I *was* in trouble."

"If I hadn't shown up, you would have made it to that house and gotten help."

She considered. "I'd like to think so."

"We'll never know," Roelke said. "But I'm the one who discovered you were missing. I'm the one who wanted to search the Washington Island shore for you."

"I know," she said humbly. "Thank you. You'll never know how good it felt to see you."

"I'm not sorry I came," he added, as if feeling the need for emphasis.

Tell him, Chloe ordered herself again. Either tell him you just want to be friends or tell him about everything that's happened this week with Emily Betts and Ragna Anderson.

The words simply wouldn't come.

Finally she reached for one of his hands and twined her fingers through his. He put his arm around her and pulled her close. She leaned her head against his shoulder. He felt warm, solid.

"Roelke?"

"Yeah?"

"I'm glad you're here."

He blew out a long, slow sigh. Chloe watched five white pelicans soar serenely over the water, their prehistoric profiles both ungainly and impossibly graceful.

Roelke pulled away, shifted to face her, and cradled her face gently in his palms. The words "Tell him!" flashed through her brain one last time but he kissed her before she could speak. The sensation was delicious, somehow exciting and comforting at once.

When he finally released her she nestled her head back against his shoulder. "You know," she said softly, "there's a spare sleeping bag in the closet. We could spend the night here."

"Yeah?"

Her cheeks flamed. "I didn't mean—that is, I thought we might just— "

He kissed the top of her head. "I'd like to stay over."

Chloe picked up the crimson maple leaf and twirled its stem in her fingers. The day hung poised between summer and autumn, hinting of changes to come. For the moment, though, she chose to be content.

THE END

ACKNOWLEDGMENTS

The Betts family were real people and although I've imagined Emily's relationship with the fictional Ragna Anderson, the basic details of their experiences at Pottawatomie Lighthouse are presented accurately.

The only other real people mentioned in the book are members of the Cornell family, who have and continue to operate the *Karfi*, and Anton Jacobson, one of the last people to live in the fishing village, and the Thordarsons.

I've tried to present a reasonable overview of the long and complicated history of commercial fishing in Lake Michigan. Conflicting opinions about how to best protect the lake ecology have existed since the first Yankee and European fishermen arrived, and the early 1980s were a particularly troubled time. Although environmentalists, commercial fishermen, sport fishermen, game wardens, and biologists might approach conservation with different perspectives, everyone wants to see healthy lakes and fish populations.

Many wonderful published volumes can provide more information about the islands and their history. For details about commercial fishing, I'm particularly indebted to Trygvie Jensen's *Wooden Boats and Iron Men: History of Commercial Fishing in Northern Lake Michigan & Door County, 1850–2005,* Paisa (Alt) Publishing Co., De Pere, WI, 2007. The volume describing the beautiful carved furniture in the Viking Hall is *Valhalla in America: Norse Myths in Wood at Rock Island State Park*, by Dag Rossman, Sharon Rossman, and William Olson (photographer), Jackson Harbor

Press, Washington Island, WI, 1999. Any errors in the book are, of course, my own.

I'm deeply grateful to:
The Friends of Rock Island, for preserving and protecting Pottawatomie Lighthouse in the first place, and for allowing Scott and me to serve as docents; and to "Ranger Randy" Holm, former park manager Kirby Foss, and naturalist Paul King for their warm welcome and assistance.

Jake Ellefson and Ken Koyen, for answering a novice's questions about commercial fishing; and Jeff Cornell, for providing such lovely transportation.

Pamela Jean Young, of the Jackson Harbor Inn, and everyone at Findlay's Holiday Inn, for providing such lovely accommodations; and everyone at the Red Cup Coffee Shop, for your hospitality.

Janet Berggren and volunteers at the Washington Island Historical Archives, for their always-cheerful help.

The Village of Eagle Police Department, especially Officer Gwen Bruckner, for ongoing assistance.

Roger Buhr, for introducing me to the lovely art of *hedebosøm*.

Laurie Rosengren, for being all-around wonderful; and to my agent, Andrea Cascardi, and the entire Midnight Ink team, for everything.

Scott, my partner in crime, for sharing adventures; and Meg, for keeping the home fires burning, and to my family, for ever-present enthusiasm.

And finally, to the readers, for so enriching this journey.

ABOUT THE AUTHOR

Kathleen Ernst is a novelist, social historian, and educator. She moved to Wisconsin in 1982 to take an interpreter job at Old World Wisconsin, and later served as a Curator of Interpretation and Collections at the historic site.

The Light Keeper's Legacy is Kathleen's third Chloe Ellefson mystery. Her historical fiction for children and young adults includes eight historical mysteries. Honors for her fiction include Edgar and Agatha nominations.

Kathleen lives and writes in Middleton, Wisconsin, and still visits historic sites every chance she gets! She also blogs about the relationship between fiction and museums at www.sitesandstories .wordpress.com. Learn more about Kathleen and her work at www.kathleenernst.com.